I0784284

A Kingdom of Pleasure and Torment

ABIGAIL BARNETTE

Content Warnings

- Non-con/Dub-con/Consensual Non-con
- Violence/Gore
- Death
- Suicidal ideation
- Pairings and groups of multiple genders
- Piercing
- Sadism
- Foot torture
- Exhibitionism/Voyeurism
- Fluid play
- Humiliation
- Domination/Submission
- Sex with mythical creatures, including scenes with tentacles and vines

Please heed all content warnings before proceeding to make the best choice for your reading experience.

A Kingdom of Pleasure and Torment originally appeared as *The Princes of Pleasure and Torment* on the Radish Fiction app.

Chapter One

Mother is dead.

Dead and buried beneath the cenere tree where she first wished for me. The tree that inspired my name.

Mother's murderer is seated beside me in the carriage. He believes I don't suspect him. How could I not? Faeries are immortal, but my mother died. Someone had a hand in it. Why not the villain who stands to benefit most from her death?

Every bump and jostle makes my knees smash into those of Lord Cadwyn Thrace of Elegwyn Manor, very recently widowed. His mourning blacks are garish, his cravat too big, the tails of his coat slightly too long. He cut a dashing figure at his wife's funeral.

No doubt, he's already looking for someone new to warm his bed and line his pockets. It will be especially easy now that he's stolen my title, my lands, and my mother through his treachery. He plays the part of the wealthy, distinguished faery well, and wins hearts with his rakish charm. Mother fell so hard that even learning that his fortune was non-existent wasn't enough to shake her resolve to have him.

Now, only a year later, he has inherited what should be mine, and I return to the only home I've ever known as my stepfather's guest.

"You'll be all right." When he tries to force his pale face into a kind expression, it looks more like a smirk. "I'll give you a stipend, of course."

"I am tired," I say, and turn my attention to the raindrops pelting the window. "I don't wish to discuss this now."

"Unfortunately, we must. It may seem vulgar to speak of money so soon after your mother's internment—"

"It is vulgar for you to speak of my mother's money at all," I snap.

"Cenere..." he begins, the antennae at his hairline glowing softly with an insincere silver-white light. "I'm not throwing you out. You're in a unique predicament. It would be cruel of me to expect you to fend for yourself. You're leagues from the nearest human settlement—"

"I know where the human settlements are." I've often wondered if a faery lives there in my place. My mother never hid the fact that I was born of a wish, but she didn't let her human daughter believe in a fantasy of wishes without consequences. I came from somewhere. Certainly not from my fae mother.

"You'll need my guidance," Thrace goes on. I hear him, but I don't listen.

Outside, the forest grieves for its mistress. It robed itself in dense, ghostly fog the moment my mother's light faded. Since then, the sky has been dirty white and hazy. I wonder how long it will last. How will the buds know to bloom in the spring without mother to sing them softly awake? I can't do it. I will never be able to do it.

If I am a changeling, I was chosen well. My looks match my mother's; generous flesh of milky rose, hair that gleams like the copper rays of a setting sun. I look like a Spring Fae. I have all the powers of a human.

I will never know what it is to have wings. I will never wield magic or see all the splendor of a faery court. But perhaps most unfairly, I will never have the power to bring Cadwyn Thrace to justice for my mother's death.

* * * *

The flames in the parlor's hearth do nothing to warm me. If I change out of my sodden mourning dress, perhaps it will chase off the chill. I don't believe it matters; I will be cold to the marrow of my bones for the rest of my life.

I know that Thrace killed my mother. That truth freezes me. That truth, and the knowledge that he will never face justice, are slowly turning me to ice from the inside out. The proof I have is flimsy, a single empty glass with a trace of iron powder at its bottom. But my mother was in exile from her court when she died, and the fae prefer to handle their own grievances among themselves. With no power—magical, symbolic, or otherwise—I will only be able to watch as Thrace spends my fortune and seeks out his next victim.

"It's freezing in here." The floor creaks under Thrace's feet, but only because he wants it to. He has a gift of moving silently, like an insect. He chooses to let me hear his slow approach. "And you're still in those damp clothes."

"It makes no difference." I rise from my chair. "I

don't wish to disturb you with my presence in your parlor."

The speed with which he stands before me is frightening. So, too, is the smirk that grows across his cruelly beautiful mouth. "Come now. Do you think I would expel you from your home? Nothing has changed, Cenere. You're still a member of my family."

I've never been a part of anyone's family. It was Mother and I alone for twenty-five years, and we liked it that way.

At least, I thought we liked it that way, before Mother met Thrace. Then, she was all too eager for new company.

I tried not to take it personally. I still try.

"We are not family," I say, my hand curling into a limp fist at my side.

I can't get past him. He looms over me. "That is easily rectified."

His sneer tells me a truth I don't want to know: we have been playing a game, and I am unaware that I have been losing the entire time.

"Just as your mother neglected to declare you her inheritor, she also failed to declare you my ward." He reaches out and snags a long, copper ringlet that fell from my bun. "But there are other ways."

The backs of his fingers brush my cheekbone as he tucks the hair behind my ear.

I step back, shivering with rage and disgust. "I'm not interested in those other ways. This is my home. I don't care what anyone says. It's my house and I want you out!"

Where did that boldness come from? Not my mother, who never raised her voice above the playful stirring of rowdy leaves on the wind. Maybe this is my magic; this rage, this loss of control.

He shakes his head. "Oh, Cenere. Why must you

be so obstinate?"

I bolt for the door, but I am exhausted and trapped far too easily by Thrace. He grips me by the wrist and drags me through the parlor.

"We'll perform the binding oath tonight," he says, while I dig my heels futilely against the floor. Well, not so futilely; my shoes catch the lip of the foyer rug and I trip, momentarily twisting enough in his grasp to rip my arm away. He swipes out for me, but I dodge him. He catches a ruffle at my waist and it tears away. I hold up my skirts and throw myself out the door, into freezing rain that slashes against my face. Thrace will not pursue me. It's too much effort, and he is patient in his deviousness.

He will enjoy it all the more when I return, defeated. When I have no choice for survival but to submit to him.

I run, with no notion of where I'm going, through the mist-shrouded forest, through the rain that pricks like needles against my cheeks and turns my hair into a sopping pile atop my head. I don't even think of my destination until the hem of my torn dress is weighted with mud and my soaked slippers touch the cobblestone path through the graveyard. My aching lungs beg me to slow, and the sacred ground seems to pull the last of the strength from my legs, as if to assure me that I'm safe now. That I can rest.

It isn't true, but I let myself believe it enough to catch my breath and press my hand to my cramping side. Stumbling, I make my way to the ancient cenere tree in the middle of the graveyard.

My mother named me after this tree, this specific one. The one she now rots beneath. So often, she combed through my curls and told me the story of how she sat beside the cenere sapling and how her tears watered it and made it strong.

"It was the first time I felt the full strength of the fae magic in my blood," she said. *"And that blood runs in you."*

It's a nice thought, but ultimately untrue. I have no magic. I won't find it now, lying exhausted in the cradle of the tree's roots. The tree where my mother made a wish that brought her a thoroughly un-magical, human child.

"I wish," I whisper, sinking my hands into the soil. But there is too much to wish, and my tears will not make them come true, anyway.

"What do you wish?"

I push up on my arms, glancing around frantically. I was alone in the graveyard when I put down my head. Now, someone is with me. Not Thrace. The voice is too lilting and musical, but also deep and sonorous. Something moves at the edge of my vision, as if detaching from the shadows of the tree roots. A sleek black boot rests its toe delicately near my face, and I follow a lean leg painted in dragon-scale leather up to a muscular abdomen and broad chest revealed by a deep part in the fabric of his black shirt. The skin covering that expanse is as gray-blue as twilight and rises in a thick column of neck to a face with a wide jaw, strong chin, and cruelly slanted lips of deep silver. They match the gleam off the stranger's eyes, which flash like mirrors one moment, a fathomless, starry sky the next. The glaucus face doesn't seem to know where it should end, pulled back in points as if held by invisible pins. Long, gleaming hair of blue-black hangs unbound down the stranger's back, almost touching the ground.

"Who are you?" I whisper in wonder.

"Luthian of Mithrax," he says. He bows so deeply, our noses nearly touch. "Think of me as your faery guardian."

Chapter Two

I open my mouth to ask a million questions, but I can't settle on one.

Luthian offers me his hand. "Come on. You're soaked to the bone. Let's get you someplace dry."

Not knowing what else to do, I reach up for him. The moment my muddy fingertips touch his gloved hand, my vision goes white. I blink it away and find myself in a place I don't recognize.

The room is small, with deep cerulean walls and black furnishings. Even the fireplace is black, and the scorching blue flame from the hearth casts long, eerie shadows. I suspect that wherever I am, Thrace will not be able to find me, and I am warm and dry.

Warm and dry? I glance down at my hands in alarm. Just seconds before, I was lying in the crook of some tree roots, weighed down by my sopping funeral raiment. Now, silver satin brushes my comfortable skin, and over that, a luxurious robe of dark-blue velvet with a high collar and outrageously puffed sleeves.

There has been no time to change, and I don't own anything so fine. My usual nightdress is a simple linen shift.

"There."

I turn in my chair, peeking past the tall wing. Luthian stands framed by an enormous, round window, through which only a brilliant night sky shows. I'm not an expert in constellations, but intuition tells me that, should I study those stars, I will find they aren't the same ones that shine in the sky above Fablemere.

"Isn't that so much better?" he asks, striding to the chair opposite mine.

"Y-yes." I swallow thickly. "Thank you?"

"Refreshment?" He rolls his hand on the end of his wrist, and a goblet appears. Its contents glow like a sapphire lit from within, and glittering metal embellishments cup the glass.

I reach for it, mesmerized, then pull my hand back. "We're in Faeryland, are we not?"

He nods, the corners of his mouth curling up in mischievous acknowledgement.

"I know better than to eat or drink anything." But my mouth becomes more parched the longer I stare at the glass.

"You're here as my guest. I would not trick you into staying forever." He leans forward and presses the cup into my hand. "Not for lack of wanting. But I can't, even though you are..."

His eyes rake down my body.

The nightgown is thin. I grip the front of the robe closed with one hand. "Why couldn't you trick me into staying? Not that I'd prefer it. But why did you even appear to me, at all?"

"The deal I made with your mother." He waves his

fingers at the glass. "You can trust me. You must be thirsty, after your run."

"You saw me?" I wet my lips before I touch them to the rim of the glass. Whatever is inside smells fruity and sweet and cold, and my sandy throat can't resist it any longer. I take a huge gulp.

"I knew it would only be a matter of time until the cenere tree drew its namesake," he says, a lazy, predatory smile growing across his face. "Destiny is a force one cannot ignore."

"Destiny?" I wipe my mouth with the back of my hand, and I'm instantly mortified at my lack of manners. "I'm sorry—"

"It's nothing," he assures me. "Your mother told you about your conception, yes?"

"She wished at the cenere tree and was granted a child."

"She left out an important part of the tale." He plucks another glass from the air and swirls the liquid inside. "I offered her three wishes. She only used one. The rest pass on to the next in her line."

I can't think up any words. I point to my chest.

"Exactly." He sips from his glass. "As your faery guardian, it is my job to make your two wishes come true."

Two wishes? Even just one wish is unthinkable. Wishes are rarely granted, and certainly never to unimportant people like me.

"You don't have to use them today," he begins. "In fact, I have a proposal—"

I don't hesitate; I don't hope, either. Wishes and magic only go so far, and I know the moment I utter the words that my wish can never be. "I wish my mother was alive again."

Sadness flickers across his face like cold flame. We both know his answer before he speaks it. "Everyone knows that a wish cannot restore life once the spirit leaves this sphere."

"Then I wish Cadwyn Thrace dead!" I blurt.

"Death?" Luthian blinks at me. "Death, then? Not something more... satisfying?"

"I..." Now that he mentions it, maybe it is a little too simple. "Can I take it back?"

"I didn't hear a thing," Luthian says somberly. "But may I offer you an alternate deal?"

I nod, ashamed to have jumped in so quickly to wishing. I'm one of a very lucky few. Wishes don't happen every day. I need to think carefully, view my requests from every possible angle. Wishes do go wrong.

All it takes is a blink, and Luthian stands beside me, one long-fingered hand walking on its tips from my chin to my collar bones. "You could wish for his death, but I would personally find it too quick. It's a sentence, not revenge."

Revenge. The possibility lights a poisoned flame in my heart.

"You could wish for power. You could wish for riches," he goes on.

"Power comes with riches," I counter.

His beautiful mouth grins wide and he's close enough that I feel his breath against my cheek when he speaks. "You're clever. That cleverness means you won't choose incorrectly."

Luthian crouches in front of me with the long-limbed grace of a spider. "Wishes are powerful. And rare. Why would you waste them on something so petty as revenge? Or riches, which will only make you more attractive to your enemy?"

I get the distinct feeling that he's trying to pull some fae trickery. "Why should you be so set upon me retaining my wishes? So that you don't have to grant them?"

"My, but you are like your mother, aren't you?"

He holds my gaze for a long, silent moment, then rises and paces back to the window. "I know of a way that you could keep your wishes until you truly need them."

"And I know that a faery would never make such a deal without a reason." My mother taught me well. She was teasing, of course, when she would hold a daisy out to my chubby, child's hand and croon, *"Come and give me a kiss for it."* There were other lessons, later, but those first games laid a foundation for my distrust of her kind.

"My mother taught me that no deal with her kind comes without a price."

Luthian doesn't deny it. "Smart. But ultimately, not something you need worry about with this deal. I will still owe you two wishes when our venture is complete. But you're right; I'm not doing this out of sentimentality or altruism. I stand to gain quite a lot if you agree to my proposal. But so do you."

The way he stares into my eyes, as if he can push my acquiescence from some precipice and into the pit of his desires, unsettles me. I hear a voice quite like my mother's, urging me to reject him, to leave Faeryland and never be tempted back.

But I'm too curious. That's her fault, too. "What do you stand to gain?"

Perhaps it's a fae trick, but when he turns back to me, there is an earnestness in his expression that wasn't there before. "I have fallen out of favor with my court. I plan to use you to get back into favor."

"Be more specific." For all I know, he could plan to present me trussed and roasted at a banquet with an apple in my mouth. He would still owe me the wishes.

"The king has two sons. I loathe the eldest, but the second is a dear friend of mine. He will be my ticket to return to the heights I commanded previous to the… indiscretion that resulted in my banishment."

His hesitation sparks my curiosity. "And what indiscretion did you commit?"

He thinks for a moment. "The same indiscretion that resulted in the queen losing her head."

I'm unfamiliar with the faery courts and their kings and queens, but it isn't difficult to infer his meaning. "What have I to offer this prince?"

"What don't you have to offer him?" Luthian approaches me again. "Have you no looking glasses in your home? Have you never seen your smooth, milky skin? Your copper-kissed hair? Have you never noticed the stares when you pass people in the village?"

"So, I'm to seduce him?" I cut directly to the point; Mother also warned me about flattery. "I'm so sorry to disappoint you, but I haven't the skill for it."

"Does a sculptor choose stone that's already been chiseled into perfection? Or does he find the raw material that will help him accomplish his artistic vision?" Luthian counters.

"I'm to be your raw material? A stone you can sculpt into the perfect seductress, capable of altering the destiny of a kingdom?" I laugh, but it dies it in my throat when he doesn't laugh with me.

"That is exactly what I'm proposing." He offers me his hand. The goblet in mine vanishes. I slip my fingers into his and he draws me close, close, closer, until I feel the warmth of his skin through our clothes. "But you cannot be stone. If you accept what I'm offering, you must yield to me. Completely. Every request. Every command. You will acquiesce to me in all things and deny me nothing."

"You still haven't said, plainly, what you're proposing." I hope he doesn't think I haven't noticed.

"I want Prince Cassan to be king. He will be when all of my plans fall into place. And you will rule at his side, as his queen. And with that power—"

He doesn't need to finish. I know exactly what I will do with such power. "I can crush Cadwyn Thrace."

I can make him far more miserable as his queen than any one wish ever could. I am not inventively cruel enough to think of a wish that could inflict a satisfactory amount of pain upon him, but given time to slowly torture him, keep him alive, heal him and then break him over and over until my pain is satisfied...

The thought is delicious enough to make me shiver.

"And you'll still have your wishes. Should you need them." Luthian strokes the backs of his fingers down my throat. "All you must do is surrender to me, totally. Give me all of your trust, swear you will do exactly as I say, no matter the request, and most importantly, you must drop every inhibition in pursuit of this power. Can you do that?"

I imagine Cadwyn Thrace on his knees in chains. It's almost pleasurable enough to make me swoon.

Still, "That's an awful lot to ask. You're basically asking me to give up my free will."

"It's exactly what I'm asking," he agrees. "Until the crown is placed upon your head, you will be entirely mine to command."

I hold his stare for a long moment, the only sound the silver fire crackling in the hearth.

"Nothing without a price," he whispers, in a voice that could turn sunlight to ice. And he extends one graceful hand, waiting for me to clasp it in agreement.

A crown can't coax winter blossoms from beneath the snow or a heal a wounded sap-sparrow's wing. I'm not meant for that type of power. But I can see myself in a crown, see Thrace's blood running over my hands.

But I wonder, "I'm human. Why would Cassan deign to speak to me, let alone make me his queen?"

Luthian's hand remains open to me. "You needn't worry about the details. Of all the fae courts, his is the least concerned with such trivial matters."

I reach forward. Our fingers almost touch.

I snatch mine back. "You never told me which court."

Luthian sighs as if caught at some innocent mischief. "It makes a difference?"

"It does. My mother was cast out of the Court of Seasons. I won't dishonor her memory by groveling for their approval." I don't know why she was cast out, but I don't need to know. They didn't deserve her, and they don't deserve me.

"The Court of Pleasure and Torment." He flexes his hand, silently urging me to take it.

My heart stops between beats. It refuses to go further down this mad path with me. The Court of Pleasure and Torment. The infamous kingdom of sensuality and depravity, where the fae indulge their every perversion and sick desire.

"Give me all of your trust, swear you will do exactly as I say, and most importantly, you must drop every inhibition in pursuit of this power."

My tongue thick with fear, I ask, "Do you swear an oath upon every last drop of your fae magic that I will not be killed?"

His dark brows rise. "Killed? Is that how far you're willing to go for your revenge? The only line too far to cross is death?"

"Do you swear?" I repeat. Thrace murdered my mother. I would shove him from a cliff and fall with him if it were the only way to assure his death. I would drink from a poison cup just to induce him to do the same.

There is no line too far. But I can't let a faery know that.

"I swear it," Luthian answers in the space of a blink. "Surrender to me, and I will deliver a crown and two untouched wishes to you on a platter, with room to spare for your murdering stepfather's head. But be warned: if you enter into this endeavor with me and you do not see it through, I will find someone more deserving of your wishes. And you will be left with nothing but ash."

There will be consequences, my conscience screams. It sounds unnervingly like my mother. But even her voice can't drown out the exhilarating, laughing hatred in my heart at the thought of Thrace's future suffering.

Judging from his smile, I think Luthian can hear it, too.

Nothing without a price.

I place my hand in his.

"We have a deal."

Chapter Three

The moment our palms touch, a shock reverberates around the room, in rings of invisible intensity. It's as if someone's dropped a stone in a puddle of magic, rippling the environment around us.

Luthian releases my hand, and I wiggle my fingers. They buzz as though they're crawling with insects, and it's a long moment before the sensation passes.

"There. Our pact is sealed. Now, you remember what I asked of you?"

"All of my trust. I will do as you say. And I will drop every inhibition." On the other side of a magically sealed agreement, it seems so much bigger. Just words before. Now...

He can do anything to me.

Luthian's gaze holds mine. I don't dare to breathe, wondering what he plans behind the starry depths of his eyes. His mouth twists into a cruel grin.

This is not the charming faery with whom I bargained. The Luthian before me, in total control of me, is predatory and terrifying. He feels the fabric of the robe with haughty disinterest, flicking it away from his fingers.

"Take that off."

I hesitate only a breath before remembering my vow. What a waste, to make such a bargain, to give him my wishes as collateral, only to default immediately.

I agreed to let him mold me into a seductress fit for a prince. A king, really. Did I think that he would teach me from a book? That my inhibitions, which he so clearly mentioned in the terms, would not be tested?

The robe slips from my shoulders and to the floor, leaving me in the gown of sheerest silk. I don't cover myself.

"You're embarrassed," Luthian says, never taking his eyes off mine as he traces a line from my collar bones to one tight nipple poking at the silk. My knees wobble at his touch and a breathy cry forces its way up my throat when he pinches that dusky peak, silk and all.

"This is new to me," I explain softly. "I've never had someone pay such lustful attention to me before."

"You'll soon abandon your shyness. I hope you'll enjoy most of our lessons," he says, stroking delightful sensitivity into my flesh. "Some, you will not."

His nails bite into the silk, into the skin beneath, and I gasp at the shock of razor-sharp pain before he releases me.

"To survive the Court of Pleasure and Torment, you must learn that the two cannot exist without each other. Without pain, one can never know true

ecstasy. And I will give you pain, honey flower."
He falls to his knees and examines my breast, the blossom of blood on the silk. He covers it with his mouth and I'm weak, leaning forward to brace myself with my hands on his shoulders. The tiny crescent wounds throb beneath his tongue, while the surrounding flesh screams out in rapture.

All too quickly, he stops, standing and leaving me to sway on my feet, dangerously unsteady.

"No matter what I ask of you, remember what you stand to lose if you deny me." Luthian's tone is utterly cold. "Think of your sad little life as the sad little wife of that disgusting Cadwyn Thrace, and how you will spend every moment of every day wondering how things could have been different if you'd simply fulfilled your vow to me."

I can't stop my limbs trembling enough to wipe the tears from my lashes.

"Take off your nightgown."

My fingers are stiff, but so is my resolve. I would sooner die than accept the life he described. The silk falls around my feet on a whisper.

"How do you feel?" he asks, walking around me to examine me from all sides.

"Exposed."

"You'll need to get used to it," he warns. "There is no room for modesty at your future court, Your Majesty."

The words run like a shiver up my spine. I can almost feel the weight of the crown upon my head. That imaginary crown is my suit of armor as I stand naked before the most dangerous creature I've ever known.

"That's a lesson we can learn... now." Luthian snaps his fingers and I'm momentarily blinded by a flash of white. Though I can't see our surroundings change, I hear them, feel them: the shuffle of bodies, the murmur of excited conversation, the heavy feeling of warm, smoke-hazed air. And when the light clears, I stand on a stage, surrounded by luminescent crystals that offer me no shadow to conceal my nakedness.

There is an audience of faeries, seated in spindly chairs, watching me with bemused interest. They smoke pipes and peer through monocles and opera glasses at my defenseless body.

Luthian leans close to my ear. "Touch yourself for them."

I lift my hand. I know what he means. I'm not so innocent that I can pretend I've never given myself relief on a restless night.

But I'm not quick enough to obey, so he takes my hand and guides it for me, stepping behind me to slide our joined fingers down my stomach, to the apex of my thighs. I'm already hot and slick there, already longing despite everything in me crying out that this is shocking. This is wrong.

Perhaps that's why it's so arousing.

He spreads the petals of my sex to expose the tingling stamin inside and runs his fingers along either side of its slippery hood. I moan and lean into his touch.

An appreciative murmur passes through the audience.

He replaces his hand with mine and steps back. "Open your eyes, honey flower. Watch all of them watching you."

Slowly, I lift my face to the audience. My eyes lock with those of a faery in a gown of glittering chains. She wets her lips and pushes the chains aside to reveal her breast and thumb one rosy nipple. My free hand drifts to my own breast. The faery beside her has his cock out; I've only ever seen one in paintings, and I can't tear my gaze from the sight of it passing through his fist again and again. He's unaware of my attention because his is focused entirely on my hand working between my legs.

"Do you like that?" Luthian asks, pointing to the faery's long, stiff member.

"I'm not sure," I confess.

"No, you're not educated," he corrects me. "You're sure that you want all of that hard cock inside of you. Your cunt is crying at its emptiness right now."

How did he know? How could he possibly have known that every time I stroked myself beneath the covers, I clenched and ached and longed to be filled?

"Put a finger inside," he orders, and I comply with a groan of relief.

Someone in the audience groans, as well.

"If you like the feeling of your finger, why not the feeling of a cock?" Luthian asks. "I know you're untouched. It's not the prize humans make of it. We'll deal with that, in time."

We? I imagine him between my legs, crushing me down in a silken bed, holding my hands above my head as he drives into me again and again. His name is on my lips in my fantasy as I throw my head back, mouth open in a cry drowned to silence in a sea of pleasure.

"Keep your eyes open," Luthian says. I'm so lost in my reverie, I didn't realize I closed them.

Everyone in the audience is captivated by me now. They no longer speak amongst themselves, but their breathing is audible, as is the rustle of their clothing as they indulge themselves in their own self-pleasure.

I whimper. My toes curl and pop on the stage. My calves ache as if I'm physically climbing toward my peak, and I'm there, nearly there, fingers rubbing inside and out, picking up frantic speed, ready to break. I'm going to come. I'm going to come in front of everyone. They're going to hear my moans, see me shake, watch me in my most vulnerable moment. I'm going to... I'm...

"Stop."

The theater around us disappears. We're in Luthian's parlor again, and I am dressed in the fine robe and nightgown. Only the throbbing that screams through my denied body is proof that anything happened at all.

"That's enough practice for tonight." He waves a hand at me.

A cry sticks in my throat and emerges as an outraged croak.

"I know, I know. You were so close." He feigns pity to mock me.

"I don't understand." I ache, still teetering on the very precipice of release. Why have I been denied?

He turns away and flicks a hand at the hearth, instantly dousing the silver flame there. "You're not allowed to come tonight. Don't try. Even should you give into temptation, you won't be able to finish."

My mouth drops open.

"I told you, torment, as well." He shrugs elegantly. "Now, you've had a very difficult day, I presume, with your mother's funeral and your stepfather's lechery and your stunning performance a moment ago. You should sleep. Fortify yourself for the task ahead, honey flower."

"I—" I begin to protest, still wanting to plead for relief from the agonizing need burning at my core. But I stop. "Why do you keep calling me that? Honey flower?"

His smile is almost tender. He touches my cheek, takes my chin in his hand to tip my face up. "After the blossom of the honey flower bush, of course."

"That flower is poisonous."

"Indeed, it is. But so beautiful, no butterfly, nor

sprite, nor dragonfly, nor daisywing can resist its allure. They drink of its sweet nectar, but if they drink too deeply, the poison does its work." He brushes his thumb over my bottom lip. "That's you, Cenere. They'll taste you, and you'll be sweet, but beneath that sweetness runs the poison of your desire for revenge. And that... that makes you irresistible."

His words are a spell over me. He's been cruel and cold, but gentle at turns. And I think perhaps what makes me irresistible to him, what makes me his honey flower, is that he and I are the same. Cruelty lies in wait beneath my gentle exterior, and I long to loose it upon my enemies.

I think he might kiss me; his lips are so close to mine. "From now on, you are my ward. You'll call me Guardian or be punished. You'll be grateful for all I provide to you. Do you understand?"

"Yes," I whisper.

He bites my bottom lip hard, and I cry out. "Try again."

"Yes, Guardian." I taste blood on my lip.

He whispers, "Sleep," and passes a hand over my face.

Suddenly, it's morning. I can tell from the weak white light peeking around the edges of the drapes. I am rested, in the softest bed I've ever touched, warm and safe in the most beautiful room I've ever seen.

I am alone, and I have no idea where I am.

Chapter Four

"Wake up!"

I startle at the sight of a small, hunched figure waddling to the drapes in the muted gray dimness. When it throws the curtains open, the figure itself remains muted and gray, in a plain, slate dress buttoned all the way up to her chin and dull silver hair scraped back severely beneath a stiff-looking snood. "I said wake up!"

"You're a human," I breathe in wonder, not caring at all about her scowl or the way she keeps barking at me.

"And you've got a busy day," she snaps, bustling from the room and returning in a flash with a breakfast tray.

"Busy?" I hold my head and squint against the light. It seems only seconds since I stood in that strange parlor with Luthian. I'm disoriented, and I only vaguely remember the night before. "Busy with what?"

I made a deal.

I debased myself in front of strangers.

Luthian...

The human servant twists her face up even more if that's possible. "I'm sure that's none of my business. Now, eat!"

My face flames. Of course, the servant knows what I'm here for. Servants always know.

At least, the old woman removes her shadowy presence so that I can enjoy my breakfast in peace. There's a perfectly boiled egg perched atop a silver cup, the lavender shell already cracked for me, revealing the firm, golden glaire and runny purple yolk. Two pieces of fluffy orange toast, a slice of fellboar, and a flute of pomegranate juice complete the feast. My grief has suppressed my appetite since mother died, and I'm thankful that the servant isn't here to judge how desperately I scarf down every morsel on my tray.

Licking my fingers, I throw my legs over the edge of the tall bed. My feet don't touch the ground. I slide down carefully and pad over to one of the enormous windows to kneel on the cushioned seat.

The view is spectacular. A long, sculptured garden flows toward the horizon in a series of tiers, each with its own fountain throwing rainbows up in their spray. Trees and hedges stand as pruned sentries, some simple cones or spheres, some intricate, verdant statues.

And walking on the white stone path, heading toward wherever I now find myself, is Luthian. It startles me to see him in the daylight; he seems a creature of the night to me, even as he strolls in the sun. His long hair is tied back at the nape of his neck, and he's wearing plain black leather breeches and a white shirt with blousy sleeves. He's far too plain, too…normal looking.

At his side is another faery, this one dressed similarly, with gleaming black hair that reminds me of onyx and skin the color of a doe's fur. His wings are unfurled, painted in shades of turning leaves. He hops in playful circles around Luthian, who responds by swiping an arm out around his companion's shoulders and bringing him in for an embrace that is obscured by those green-and-gold-and-orange-flecked wings.

I turn away. Whatever I've witnessed is intimate, and not for me to spy on. But my stomach sours for reasons I can't name and don't wish to examine. Perhaps I feel an ownership over Luthian owing to our deal, an ownership that's inappropriate and illogical. Our arrangement will consume my life; is it unfair of me to wish it would consume his, as well?

"Merry morning!"

I turn sharply at the words and the sound of the doors opening. The voice is far too cheerful to belong to the old servant. It belongs to a faery who flutters in with the toes of her pastel blue slippers skimming the richly stained wood floor.

"Sorry to have startled you," the faery says, and I detect the elegant accent of the Springlands. "I thought you were expecting me."

I shake my head, too dumbstruck by her beauty to use my voice. She has wings of intricate lace and pale blue hair mixed with string and yarn and ribbons in a thick pouf. A fascinator styled like a tiny sewing basket sits cocked to the side of her head. Her gown, a wide, panniered mountain of pearlescent gossamer rising to a satin bodice with a scandalously low scooping neckline, matches her hair. I am overwhelmed by her beauty, her nearly-transparent skin that glows like the surface of a pearl, her broad smile showing even whiter teeth, the beauty mark in the shape of a heart at the corner of her lower lip.

She looks like a doll.

"Well, leave it to the old witch to not announce me." Lace wings whirring, the faery moves across the room and plucks the fascinator from her hair. She drops it to the floor, and it springs open, ejecting a dressmaker's mannequin, trifold mirror with gilt edges, bolts of fabric and spools of thread that scatter across the floor. "I'm Sarta. Luthian summoned me to...help him with your transformation."

"Oh." I glance down at my nightgown; the crimson stain from the night before is gone. "Well, I don't have any clothes. So, I'm glad to see you."

The faery laughs like wind chimes.

"I've never been to a dressmaker," I admit haltingly. "My mother made my dresses. She was a faery, like you. She used her magic and..."

My throat sticks shut as if to protect me from more words, more memory. Isn't my mother the reason I'm here? Why should remembrance of her be so difficult?

"Luthian told me all about her," Sarta says with a tinkling laugh. "That she was beautiful. Powerful. Very like her daughter."

I flush at the comparison. "I'm afraid he over-praised me. I am not so very much like my mother. She was a conduit for the springtime. I'm a human. I have no magic."

"Ah, but your magic..." She waves a finger in a circle in the air, about the height of my midsection. The circle grows smaller and she fixes her gaze on my thighs. "You humans have a different kind of magic."

I look down and understand with another furious blush. "You mean..."

"Human pussy, I'm told, feels incredible." Sarta lifts an eyebrow before turning toward her supplies.

"You need a full wardrobe, then?"

"This is all I have," I say, lifting my arms.

"Then we shall start with underthings and work our way out from there." Sarta pushes back the sleeves of her gown and shakes a terrifyingly long needle into her hand. It rests between her thumb and forefinger, perfectly balanced as she bobs it in the air, lost in thought. "We'll need measurements."

With a wave of her needle wand, my nightgown deftly unsews itself, falling into unfinished parts on the floor. I stand before her completely naked, my skin immediately puckering into goose flesh.

"You need stockings, of course." She waves the wand again. White silk stockings, tied just above my knees with garter ribbons, materialize on my legs. Kneeling before me, she places a hand on my calf and smooths her palm up, to where my bare skin meets the silk. "How do these feel?"

"Luxurious," I say, my gaze captivated by the sight of her long, slender fingers stroking my leg.

"Perhaps you'd like them better if they were tied a bit lower?" Before I can answer, she unties the ribbon and swiftly rolls the stocking down, her fingertips grazing my skin. She clucks her tongue. "No. Higher, I think."

I gasp as she pushes the silk up and smooths over the inside of my thigh. When she leans in to tie the garter, her cheek brushes my mound. And when she looks up at me, a coy glance from her sideways turned face, I know it's intentional.

"Ah," I say with a wry smile. "My 'transformation.' Not just my wardrobe."

"My attempt at tact. Though, I prefer a more direct..." She walks her fingers slowly up my inner thigh as she talks, her breath stirring the downy curls at my center. "Approach."

She parts my folds as she leans in to place a kiss

directly on my quivering bud. Her lips are silky as they close over the hood and linger, pulling back gently.

She leaves me barely able to stand and goes back to her sewing supplies. "You'll need, oh... three hundred pair, I think."

"Three hundred?" My desire instantly turns to astonishment. "Stockings?"

"Six hundred, if we're counting by the stocking. But yes. You don't want to go to court a pauper," she says.

I wonder how much she knows about my "transformation" and what it's intended to achieve. Surely, Luthian isn't telling everyone he plans to assassinate a king.

"Did Luthian tell you why he's taking me to court with him?" I ask.

"He plans to win the king's favor. By making you queen, you lucky girl." She shivers. "King Arcus is quite inventive, though I've never had the pleasure."

I play along, knowing it is the second prince whose attention I ultimately need to capture. "I just hope I please him."

"Then you should look the part. Panties." She waves the needle again and I find myself in thin lace that barely covers me, then in a wisp of silk that slides into the cleft of my buttocks as if I'm wearing nothing at all.

"You may need some without a crotch," she muses, and flicks her wand again.

The lace returns, this time with a notable difference. "Why wear any at all?" I ask.

"Style. Two hundred pair of each." She licks the tip of her needle-wand and writes with it in the air, taking an invisible note. "And of course, you'll need corsets."

The wind is crushed out of me before I can speak.

I'm encased from hips to bust in a tightly laced garment of ivory brocade. It cycles through an entire rainbow before Sarta is satisfied.

Looking to the door, she flashes a brilliant smile. "What do you think?"

I turn to see Luthian there, his night-sky eyes hooded, a slanted smile on his mouth. "You're a master at your work, Sarta."

She dips her head, but not before I see the blush on her cheeks. "We were just about to move onto gowns."

"No, I think she's dressed appropriately for our lesson." He vanishes the breakfast tray from the bed, leaving the covers smoothed and neatly tucked.

"Why do you keep that mean servant around if you can just do that?" I blurt.

He shrugs. "Style."

I see why he and Sarta are friends.

"Now," he says, patting the bed. "Come here and spread your legs for us."

Chapter Five

I obey him.

I wonder, as I slide onto the satin coverlet, if a time will come that I do as he says without question because I'm conditioned to, and not because of our deal. Because his tone of voice, the way he moves slowly toward me, enchant me. I could fall under his spell, like the foolish human I am, despite the warnings I heard all of my life.

Of course, my mother fell under such a spell. Thrace's spell. Luthian is just as dangerous, and I need to keep my wits about me.

But it's difficult, with the way he looks at me.

Sarta waves her wand and is instantly transformed. Her string and ribbon hair lays in an impossibly long curtain of ringlets against her pearl skin, every inch of which is exposed. Her lace wings are folded against her back, and the two small protrusions from her forehead glimmer with light so pure, it looks like diamonds sparkling in the air.

"I firmly believe that one learns best by doing. And, it helps if one learns from an expert. Wouldn't you agree, Sartas?"

I frown at the mispronunciation of the name, until the mattress dips and I find myself with my head between Sarta's thighs, her hands on my breasts, while she also stands beside Luthian.

"I-I don't understand."

"I'm very busy. I wouldn't be able to sustain my career as the foremost designer to the most glamorous court in Fablemere if I couldn't divide up my time," the Sarta beside Luthian explains. The Sarta at my head adds, "And while Luthian is extremely skilled at this particular activity, it truly takes someone who owns a cunt to teach the deepest possible understanding in this endeavor."

"Sarta will use her mouth on you," Luthian explains. "You will be called upon by many different types of faeries at court, and you'll need to know how to pleasure them all. You'll imitate what you feel on Sarta as she demonstrates."

The Sarta at my head carefully moves my hair to avoid kneeling on it as she straddles my face, and I am confronted with a delicate blue shell, complete with a violet pearl. I've been curious enough to peak at myself in the looking glass, so I'm familiar with the parts, but hers are different. Smoother, hairless, and without the frilled inner labia. Still, she's similar enough that I recognize her anatomy.

What I have never been confronted with is the sensation of a wet, pointed tongue swiping across my sex. I gasp and instinctively raise my hips to follow it.

"That's not what you're here for," Luthian reprimands me. "Which is why you won't reach climax during this exercise, no matter how close she will bring you. Now, Sarta, again. And Cenere? Remember to mirror her."

Sarta repeats the tongue swipe, and I mimic it, tasting the silky wetness on her double. She tastes the way I imagine the sea might.

But she sounds better, giving a little gasp of excitement. Knowing that I've caused it sends a pulse of desire to my singing flesh. I want to make her gasp again.

Sarta between my legs gives me another lick, this time downward, her tongue poking into my entrance. I dutifully repeat the action, and Sarta on my face squirms.

"Good," Luthian murmurs. I feel his weight as he settles beside us on the bed. His clothed body presses against me, his hands find my breasts. Lost in dizzying arousal, I almost forget that I must mimic the wide, up-and-down sweep of Sarta's tongue as she bathes my intimate flesh in her saliva.

"She should be getting very wet now," Luthian says, and I don't know if he's talking about me or Sarta. I am very wet; I feel the silken heaviness of it leaking from my opening.

Sarta continues the same lazy motion. I try to wriggle closer to her wicked tongue, my stiff, aching bud desperate for more attention. I know that she feels exactly what she's doing to me, because I'm copying her every stroke. How has she not gone mad from the anticipation yet?

She parts me with her fingers, and I reach up to do the same. Her pussy makes a slick sound. She runs her tongue up the frilled edge of one of my inner petals. Here, our anatomy diverges; instead of two folds of inner flesh, there are smooth ridges. When I test them with my tongue the way she's licking me, she moans loudly.

"Where your clitoris is a little, hooded pearl," Luthian begins, and his fingertip touches the named part, not moving, just applying maddening pressure. "Hers is more like... like the fork in a tree branch. When you touch a faery there, it feels quite like... well, show her, Sarta."

Sarta's tongue laves over my clit and I buck my hips.

I forget to repeat the action, and her mouth pulls away. She holds me open wide for Luthian to deliver a sharp slap to my most sensitive area.

Crying out, I rush to lick the Sarta on my face, and she coos and rocks her hips.

"Keep going like that," she moans, while the version of her between my legs shows me exactly how.

The pleasure is unbearable. Building, building, piling on top of what I felt the night before, but never breaking. I need release, badly. I would beg for it, if my mouth wasn't full of Sarta's clit, her juices. I bury my face in her, gasp for air, and go back for more.

Sarta between my legs is struggling to maintain focus; it's apparent from the erratic, stuttering movements of her tongue. I follow each one exactly, intoxicated by the knowledge that I'm making her come so undone that she can't concentrate, even though she's the one directing me. Still, it's not enough. Every one of her sucking kisses and rapid flicks should be the one that sends me screaming into an abyss of ecstasy, but it never happens. I'm suspended on the painful edge of a powerful climax, with nothing but Luthian's magic holding me back.

When she cries out with her release, I wail in disappointment.

"Well done," Luthian says, and gives Sarta on my face a little pat. "Now, another game."

"Please let me come," I beg him. "Please. I feel like I'm going to die."

"Get used to it," he says flatly. "There will be many times that you're forced to watch someone else have the pleasure you crave. Right now, for example."

Sarta climbs off my face and lies down beside me, her naked flesh warm and replete with satisfaction while I sweat and shake, poised on the brink.

The other Sarta slides to the end of the bed and bends over it, while Luthian goes to stand behind her, unlacing his breeches. I watch with fascination as he frees his cock and strokes the impressive length.

"Describe it for her, Sarta," he instructs. "And demonstrate with your fingers."

Sarta beside me places her hand between my legs and slowly eases a finger into me as he pushes into her counterpart's body.

Luthian groans and clucks his tongue. "Just one finger? I'm insulted."

She tips her head back and moans. She withdraws in time with him, cups her hand, and this time, pushes all four fingers into my tight opening. I curl up, clenching down on the fullness.

"Mmm, that's what it feels like," Sarta at the end of the bed tells me. Her hand speeds up as Luthian's hips do, and soon the room is filled with the slap of skin against skin, the obscene, thick, wet sound of her fingers plunging and twisting, and her breathless voice trying to describe it all.

"He's so big," she moans. "So hard."

My cunt aches to be filled deeper, to take Luthian inside of me. I can't tear my gaze away from the sheer bliss on their faces. Every one of her moans is echoed by her double at my side, who whispers torturous things like, "I'm so close. He's going to make me come. Are you close, Cenere?"

"Yes," I whisper, my eyes shining with tears. "Yes, I'm so close. Please, let me come!"

The three of them laugh and I sob in despair.

"He's close, too." Sarta's teeth close over my earlobe, sending a renewed shudder of sensation through me as her hand pummels my cunt. She writhes, stiffens, cries out in unison with Sarta at the end of the bed, while I throb, still suspended precariously close to the edge but unable to fall over.

"He's coming," she gasps, still in the throes of ecstasy. "I can feel it bursting inside of me."

When he withdraws, he thrusts his cock through his fist a few more times, releasing slashes of cum across her back with each stroke. Her fingers withdraw, too, and I whine in disappointment.

Luthian staggers to a chair and falls heavily into it, and Sarta enfolds her double into an embrace, becoming one body again.

"Come sit in my lap," Luthian tells me, still stroking himself after the shimmering white fluid has subsided. I think of the length of him, coated in it, how it would slide so easily into me.

But when I reach him, he spins me to sit with my back against his chest, his cock trapped between us, resting against the cleft of my ass. He grinds on me and traps one of my ankles then the other against the legs of the chair with his booted feet.

"Don't struggle," he warns, capturing my arms and twisting them behind my back. "Be a good girl and I promise you; you will be rewarded."

All I can think of is how much I want to come. How I've teetered on the edge, ready to spill over, for what feels like hours. Surely, he's saying that he'll let me, finally, if I obey him. Fighting would be futile, anyway; I've already agreed to let him utterly control me.

When Sarta approaches with her wand, my body writhes against my will. I want to sit still. I want to do everything he's asking me. But the wand grows smaller, smaller, until it's an actual needle, and she kneels between my legs.

"A little pain, that's all," Luthian croons in my ear.

I gasp. "What?"

Sarta holds up a delicate golden ring with a dangling pearl. "It's the fashion at court. And it will look very pretty on you."

"Wait..." My throat goes utterly dry with fear and I try to shift away from her.

"Hold still," Luthian growls. "Or I might never let you come."

I whimper and squeeze my eyes shut as Sarta's fingers probe my throbbing clit. The tip of what must be her pinkie finger glides beneath the hood, stretches it, and I bite my lip. My body trembles in fear.

When the needle pricks that most intimate flesh, I imagine a searing poker thrusting through Cadwyn Thrace's neck. Luthian's tongue curls around my ear. "Come."

I scream and curl up, not only from the agonizing punch of the needle sliding through, but the long-denied pleasure that entwines itself with that pain, exploding through me. I feel Luthian's cock, hot and sticky against my ass, and I want to lift myself up and impale myself on him, as I imagine impaling Thrace, as I see the needle violating my flesh in my mind's eye.

"Come," Luthian whispers again, and my body obeys him. My legs kick and wetness bursts from my core, bathing my thighs. "Come."

I lose all sense of where I am as I climax seemingly endlessly after hours of torturous denial. I forget Sarta between my legs, Luthian at my back. The pleasure is too much, the stinging of my punctured flesh is too much, and I'm lost, sobbing, my body snapping like a whip in the bonds of Luthian's hold on me.

"Come," he snarls, his teeth sinking into the skin below my ear.

"No!" I cry out. "Not again, please!" And it's all I can manage before I'm brutally shoved over the edge again, my sensitive flesh and worn out muscles screaming for mercy.

He grips my jaw painfully, pushing my cheeks into my teeth in his punishing grasp. "You are never to speak that word to me again. Do you understand?"

Tears stream down my face, over his fingers, as I try to nod.

He stands, dragging me to my feet, and jerks me across the floor to the bed. He shoves me onto the mattress without a care for how I land upon it, which is in a jumble of limbs.

"You'll stay here and rest," he orders coldly. "I expect to see you apply some of your new knowledge at dinner tonight. Dress appropriately."

"Yes, Guardian." I somehow manage to force my voice past the tears in my throat.

"In the meantime..." He tucks himself away and laces up his breeches with nimble fingers. "Come. Until you lose consciousness."

He flicks his fingers, dooming me, and leaves the room.

Chapter Six

When I rouse from my nap, Marie has left a book beside me on the bed. It's large, swathed in her signature light blue silk, and embellished with diamonds. I flinch at the soreness between my legs when I sit up. It isn't unbearable, but it does feel strange. Pushing the covers back, I get to my feet and make my way to the tall oval looking glass. There, nestled between my folds, a pale pink pearl dangles on the golden ring that passes through my intimate skin.

The sight of it sends a flush of blood to the affected part, tightens my nipples. *I endured that pain,* I think proudly. I remember Luthian's hold over me, how I couldn't struggle to free myself from the needle. In hindsight, perhaps I wouldn't have. He could have ordered me to sit still, and I would have obeyed. But being overpowered had been as arousing as Sarta's tongue on me, or watching Luthian pound into her.

This world is new and exciting and terrifying. It's pain that becomes pleasure and pleasure that turns into unbearable pain. Nothing in my life has ever prepared me for anything like it.

And the magic...

They use magic here as if it will never run out. Mother warned of temperance. Of not relying on magic. The dangers of overuse. Here, as in most things, there is no taboo. Only flagrant, joyous use of magic with wild abandon.

At that thought, my eyes fall upon the book. I go back to the bed and sit gingerly cross-legged, dragging it into my lap.

I open the cover and a scrap of parchment falls out.

C.

Please forgive me for leaving before you woke, but I do have other clients. Here is the wardrobe I have chosen for you. Use the pins to mark the pages and the garments will appear on the mannequin. I apologize that I can't dress you, but that requires magic I cannot work from afar. However, Luthian is an expert at handling women's clothing. I'm sure he'll help as needed.

S.

"Use the pins?" I wonder aloud. I open the cover fully and note a ribbon fixed inside, holding several long, diamond-topped pins. I turn the first page, decorated with a "C" constructed of loops and swirls, to find a table of contents listing types of clothing. I flip to the first page of gowns.

"I expect to see you apply some of your new knowledge at dinner tonight. Dress appropriately," Luthian said.

I examine the sketches, each of them accompanied by swatches of fabric, thinking about what my guardian considers "appropriate." Certainly not the riding habit with the full sleeves and jacket with tails. Perhaps the clinging, pearlescent white gown that hangs from tiny straps that tie behind the neck. I imagine Luthian slowly untying the bow. Or untying it myself, for him. I want to impress him with my boldness, to make him see that I am learning, that I understand what will be expected of me.

I choose instead a gown of black silk so sheer it feels fragile between my fingers. Black leather encircles the waist in a tight band, scooping up beneath the wearer's exposed breasts.

Luthian will certainly find this appropriate, I think to myself as I select a pin from the front of the book and slide it through the page. The dress appears on the mannequin as promised. The moment I touch it, the fabric flows down my arms and crawls over my body until it is perfectly tucked and fastened.

I check my reflection and know at once that my guardian will be pleased.

* * * *

It's only when I'm on my way to his chambers that I consider we might not be dining alone. The thought only excites me more when I imagine how pleased Luthian will be to see me, barely dressed, in front of guests.

Mother never instilled any sense of shame in me regarding my body, but she did teach me a sense of propriety. The court she came from—the one that had cruelly rejected her—doesn't behave as freely, as indulgently as the Court of Pleasure and Torment. Before Luthian, I never would have imagined a scenario when my nakedness would be put on display, or that I would so enjoy it. I'm crestfallen when I enter his parlor and find it is only him waiting for me.

His reaction quickly dispels my disappointment. He rises as if in a trance at the sight of me, silver lips parted. "Cenere. You look beautiful."

I've left my long hair down, but brushed the ringlets out into soft waves and two slender braids that cross each other in a band over the crown of my head. I toss my hair over my shoulders, revealing my bare breasts framed by the sheer black silk. "You did say to dress appropriately."

"You've succeeded. Please, come in." He gestures to the doors, and they shut behind me. There is a table with food, but only one plate, one goblet, one set of utensils—although there are many of those. "Sit."

He takes the only chair.

I go to him, not bothering to look for another seat. I know I won't find one. I arrange my slit skirts around my otherwise bare lower half and take my place on his knee.

"Good girl." His mouth slants in an approving smirk. "It's time for another lesson."

He leans around me, one long arm pouring wine from a crystal flagon into the goblet.

"You can't just make it appear by magic?" I ask.

Instantly, I know it is the wrong thing to have asked. He puts the flagon down and uses the same hand to grip the hair at my nape and jerk my head back roughly. "Who do you think you are to question the strength of my power?"

"I-I wasn't—"

"But you were," his grip tightens, tugging at my scalp. "Do you think the king will allow you to speak to him in that way? Do you think he would issue you such a kind warning?"

"No. I'm sorry, Guardian." I lower my head as

much as I can to display my obedience and remorse. "But may I ask you a question?"

He loosens his grip and nods.

"You talk about the king. I thought I was going to court to seduce a prince." It made sense to me that Sarta would say so; that he might not have given her the whole plan. But now, he speaks of the king as an inevitability, as well.

"Of course, you'll seduce the prince." Luthian combs his fingers through my locks, soothing my tender scalp. "But you'll be the talk of the court. The king will at least sample you. Perhaps, he'll take you as a mistress. But remember, his death is already arranged. You won't find yourself in his company for long."

"And the prince will still want me?"

"I dare say you'll inspire a rivalry between them," he says, and takes the goblet in his hand. "There is nothing Arcus loves more than displaying his power, especially over his sons.

"Food is an important component of court life," he changes the subject, his tone studious. "Refreshment is available in nearly every room. The meals are sumptuous banquets that last for hours, with dozens of courses. You'll dine upon fruits you've never seen before, creatures you've never heard of. But you will do it, as you will do all things, with sensuality. You will be provocative in your manner. For example..."

He dips two fingers into the wine glass and touches them to my bottom lip. I open and suck them in, gratified by the crease between his brow as he watches my lips slide closed, down to his middle knuckle. I swirl my tongue around them, sure that some of the skills I learned today would be effective on other parts. My instinct is correct, because he makes a noise low in his throat before he removes his hand.

"And how would you share the wine with me?" he

asks, still distracted by my mouth.

I reach for the cup, but he withholds it. "No. I don't ever wish to see you feeding yourself at my table. I wouldn't have you even touch a fork or glass. While you are with me, you are to be fed. It might amuse courtiers to do so, as well."

He presses the rim of the goblet against my bottom lip, and I take a sip. I hold it in and lean forward to kiss him. He drinks the wine from me and claims a dribble from the corner of my mouth with his tongue.

"Good girl."

The praise is effervescent in my veins. I'm doing well. I'm going to have the power he promised me, and the wishes, too. I'm going to see Thrace in chains, humiliated. I think of displaying him before my throne at court, leaving him there to be leered at the way he's leered at me ever since he married my mother.

"Cenere?" Luthian's voice brings me back to him. "You've wandered off."

"Please, pardon me, Guardian," I whisper, my cheeks flushing with shame. He needn't know the contents of my fantasies, though. "I was considering other ways I might serve you the wine."

I put two fingers into the goblet, withdrawing them to drip wine above the peak of one breast. I paint a wet circle around my rosy nipple and lift my chest toward him.

"You're better at this than I expected you to be," he says with a smirk.

Then he lowers his head and sucks my nipple into his mouth and it's as if lightning has struck directly to my core. My clit throbs and the new piercing stings. I squeeze my legs shut against both.

"Thank you, Guardian," I say in response to both the compliment and his tongue playing in delicious circles over my flesh.

He lifts his head and puts the goblet on the table. "You must be hungry. Here."

Luthian picks up a fork and spears a slice of a root vegetable. "There's no way to make an arousing display out of this, surely?"

I consider the challenge. I never would have considered eating an arousing activity, in the first place. But I assume, based on the way his chest rises and falls as he watches me wet my lips, that it's my mouth that's meant to tempt him.

And so, I lean toward the bite he offers me, chin lifted and chest tipped to give him a better view of my exposed breasts, and ever so slightly show my teeth before I take the bite, my lips lingering as I pull back.

The smile he gives me fills some long neglected well in my heart. I'm pleasing him. I want to please him.

I should want to please the prince, I realize. That's my goal, the entire reason I'm sitting in Luthian's lap right now. And not just the prince; I'll likely find myself in the king's bed.

"Perhaps while you feed me, you can tell me about the king," I suggest, walking my fingertips up Luthian's chest.

He considers me a moment, evaluating my performance. "Cut back the simpering. Not too much. But you come off as transparently wheedling."

"Oh. Thank you, Guardian." I wait for his next instruction.

To my surprise, he offers me another bite and begins, "Neither he nor the prince will be impressed by a breathy, obvious show. But with the king, you must be more careful. He embodies the court, and so takes pleasure to the limits of torment, derives great pleasure from that torment. He will likely hurt you, in body and spirit. He won't kill you or disfigure you.

That ruins the game for him. But he *will* hurt you."

I shiver, barely able to swallow the bite I've taken. I want to cling to Luthian, to demand why he'd hand me over to someone who would harm me. But I'm not supposed to question. "I trust you, Guardian."

He goes quite still, searching my face. And after a very long, silent moment during which the sound of my own heartbeat seems to triple in volume, he says, "Very good. I believed it, for a second."

"Thank you, Guardian," I say, but I must look down.

If he doesn't want to believe it, I can't stand for him to accidentally see that it's true.

"Guardian," I begin, while he selects the next morsel for me. "Forgive me, but you said that you would... that we..."

How do I broach the topic of my inexperience? I've never considered it at all, until he brought it up. I'm not sure I have the words to describe what I'm asking, because it seems so absurd.

"Find your voice, Cenere. I do so loathe indecision," he warns me.

"I thought you would couple with me. You seemed disappointed that I haven't been intimate with another, before."

The corners of his eyes crinkle with amusement. "Haven't you?"

"Well.." I don't remember it. Maybe he was with me while I was insensate with pleasure. But I remember keenly every moment of the agony he left me in that morning, twisting the pillows in my hands, arching my back, screaming under an onslaught of climaxes that I only escaped through unconsciousness. I would have known if he'd pinned me down with his body and pushed that massive cock into me.

"Do you think that what you did with Sarta wasn't physical intimacy? That it's not sex because you weren't penetrated by a cock?" he asks and selects a roasted glimmer fern stem. He taps the end against my lips and I open for it, flicking my tongue across it before taking a dainty bite.

After I swallow, I answer him. "It was intimate. And not. It was instructive and pleasurable, but it did lack the passion I've read about in books."

"It's passion you want." He isn't asking me.

I discern that this is a trick. "It doesn't matter what I want, Guardian. I know I'm learning the mechanics of it all. I shouldn't have questioned you."

"Some questions are useful," he tells me, giving me another bite. "You will need to learn passion, both earnestly and how to feign it. But you're correct. It's important now to become skilled at the mechanics, so those become second nature. I promise, I will take you soon. When you've proven yourself a worthy enough lover."

Worthy enough for him, or for the court, I wonder. I suspect that isn't one of his "useful" questions. "Then, I'll strive to earn your cock, Guardian."

The named part shifts beneath me. His breeches can't disguise it.

"You've become adept at manipulation rather quickly," he chides me. "Or, did you have it in you this whole time?"

"The rules of these games seem fairly simple, Guardian. I say the correct things, and I am rewarded, either with pleasure or with pain, which I am to learn as another type of pleasure. It isn't so complicated as you have made it out to be."

"It isn't?" He offers me another bite of the glimmer fern. "Your confidence may be your undoing."

"Shouldn't I present myself confidently at court?"

"Confident. Not cocky." He taps the end of my nose. "Now, continue with this lesson. Don't worry about the future."

"But Guardian, I thought this was about both of our futures." I blink innocently at him.

His expression darkens. He looks like the menacing faeries my mother warned me about. The ones that can't be trusted, no matter what a heart might say. And while I've agreed to so many things, come willingly to his palace of depravity, allowed him to violate my body, I can't lose sight of what he is. What he could be capable of.

Faster than a flash of lightning in the summer sky, he grips my chin cruelly. There is no friendliness, no pride or indulgence. Only fury at my disobedience. "You are not so skilled at manipulation that you should continue to try it on me. Unless you wish to be chained in my dungeon, under my spell, twisting and screaming from pleasure that will not stop, not even when you sleep. You know I can do it. I did it to you this morning. I can keep you suspended in such a state until the moment of your mortal death. Which I promise, you will plead for."

My body trembles at the threat.

"Now, do you wish to test me?" he asks, giving my jaw a painful shake.

Tears roll from the corners of my eyes. "No, Guardian," I manage.

At once, the Luthian I was growing fond of, growing trustful of, returns. He releases me and places a kiss on my cheek. "Good. Then let's continue with our lesson."

I suspect that I've just learned one far more important than table manners.

Chapter Seven

My second morning starts with a lesson.

A terrible lesson that is not as fun as the lessons of the day before.

"Ouch! Witch!" I hiss under my breath, nursing my reddened knuckles.

The housekeeper, Brujon, flips her stick up and paces behind me. I'm in the dining room for breakfast, learning each of the numerous and complicated arrangements of tableware.

"Pick up the fruit knife," the old ghoul commands me again.

"As I've already explained," I say through gritted teeth, "Luthian said he never wants to see me feeding myself here. I'm not supposed to touch any of these—"

She snatches my hand and strikes it with the stick again. I shout in pain and outrage. But I will not pick up the knife. I will obey Luthian. And I don't know which is the fruit knife, anyway.

"Brujon!" Luthian barks as he enters the dining room. "What are you doing to my ward?"

"Educating me on the proper utensils to use at a meal," I answer before she can.

He frowns at me. "And you will not cooperate?"

"You said I'm not to feed myself, that you wouldn't have me touch a single fork or glass at your table. I don't wish to do anything that breaks your rules." I blink at him, awaiting his reply.

His lips part, but whatever he meant to say stalls there. He waves a hand at the place setting. "You should know these things, even if you're not meant to utilize them. But Brujon, I didn't give you permission to punish her. Any punishments she receives will be of my own devising. And far more imaginative."

The old human huffs in disgust and shuffles off.

"You, come with me." He turns and walks without checking to see if I follow.

The skirts of my modest gown rustle against the floor as I hurry to catch up to him. The dress is deep blue velvet, sprinkled with blinding diamond stars, with buttons up the high collar and at the wrists of the tight sleeves.

"Why are you dressed like a Librarian of Avalon?" he asks, still not looking at me.

"I'm not familiar with the fashion customs of Avalon, Guardian. I thought I would look studious for my lessons today." And I didn't particularly want to dress the way I had for dinner last night for instruction with Brujon.

"What a happy coincidence; I've adopted a more professorial attitude." He takes me down a hallway and pushes open a door.

It's a library, with shelves so tall, ladders lead to balconies for access. I've never seen so many books, nor such beautiful ceilings. Faeries and sylphs wind through a twilight sky over our heads, wings and clouds and diaphanous garments fluttering in enchanted paint.

We walk toward a massive fireplace, flames crackling in its hearth. Before it, where I would have perhaps placed some chairs for reading and a cart for cozy tea, is a long, narrow table, upon which lies the faery I saw in the garden the day before. His arms are stretched above his head, bound to the corners of the table, as are his splayed legs.

He's completely nude.

"Yesterday, you learned about anatomy that is familiar to you. Today's lesson requires me to take a more hands-on approach." Luthian stands beside the table and glides one finger down the faery's perspiring chest, all the way to his thick cock, hard and straining for touch. Luthian stops just short of contact, though.

"This is Firo. Another of my students," Luthian says casually.

I didn't realize he had other students. I don't like it. I certainly don't like that I don't like it. I temper my expression as I examine the faery laid out before me.

Rather than succumb to petty jealousy, I use the moment to learn. With Sarta, it was easy enough. We have all the same components. While I saw Luthian pleasuring himself the day before, and the faery in the audience my first night, I've never had an opportunity to become so thoroughly acquainted with a body that's different from mine. Where I am all softness and curves, this faery is lean and tightly muscled. His skin gleams like warm flame through smokey quartz.

"Faeries don't seem to have body hair," I muse aloud.

"Good observation," Luthian says. To the panting, writhing Firo, he notes, "Cenere is a human. Today, you'll help her to learn exactly how to pleasure a body like yours."

"And what will I learn?" Firo asks.

He does not use a title to address Luthian, the way I must.

Luthian doesn't correct him, either. "You will learn endurance. I told you that this lesson would be long, and you would not enjoy it."

With a cruel sneer, Luthian leans down and places a gentle kiss on Firo's sweating brow. My guardian straightens and tells me, "I've gotten him started for you. We've been up since dawn, haven't we, Firo?"

Firo doesn't answer.

Luthian trails his fingertips down Firo's face, his neck, over his chest again, but this time he brushes over the tip of Firo's cock, too. It's as if Luthian has struck him. The poor, bound faery hisses and jerks up, but the bonds hold tightly and Firo gives up with a sob of defeat.

"You see? Only a few hours of this..." Luthian curls his hand around Firo's cock and gives it a few slow strokes. "And he's already mindless with need."

Luthian takes my hand and brings it to join his. Firo's flesh is burning hot and unyielding beneath my fingers, and the groan the faery makes stirs me at my very core.

"Firo, if I asked you for anything right now, you would grant it to me, would you not?" Luthian asks him.

The faery hesitates.

"If I asked you to trade your kingdom just to be allowed to come, you would give it to me?" Luthian clarifies.

"If I had a kingdom," Firo replies. "You know I have none. Please, just let me... ah!"

His hips jerk and Luthian pulls both our hands away.

"Too close," Luthian explains. "He's been nearly ready to spill for hours now. Pleading. Crying, sometimes."

I believe him, because Firo squeezes his eyes shut at the denial and bangs his head against the table. "Please! I'm almost there!"

"We'll give him a moment to cool down before we try that again." Luthian sighs. "I fear I may have kept him too long at the precipice. He's so sensitive now, he won't be able to withstand much more."

"You're too good a tutor," Firo says through gritted teeth.

I agree with him on that score, having been just as mindless and wild myself.

"Cenere is fully aware of my capabilities. Are you not?" Luthian asks, arching a brow.

I nod. "Yes, Guardian."

"And you plead more prettily," he says. "I believe you were actually in tears before I rewarded you."

I can't disguise my puzzled frown.

"When I allowed you to have all of the climaxes I held back from you," he reminds me, as if wounded that I forgot.

I did not forget. "I thought that was a punishment, Guardian."

It's the correct answer, I think, because he smiles at me. "Is torture a punishment? Or is it a gateway to greater pleasure?"

I don't have an answer.

"That is the lesson you'll learn today. Both of you. Firo, you're happy enough to inflict suffering, but you have yet to learn to accept it. Cenere is too gentle, too innocent to properly torment someone." He addresses me. "How would you make him suffer, Cenere? What, do you believe, would be the most unbearable pain in this moment?"

"I..." My imagination stalls. I don't want to hurt anyone, but as Luthian has reminded me, torment is as crucial as pleasure in the court. "I suppose one could use implements of torture. Pincers. Branding. Piercing, as you subjected me to." I cannot push a needle through Firo's flesh. I nearly gag at the thought.

"That is an idea. Wonderful job." Luthian's praise is as effective as a tongue against my clit and I squeeze my thighs together. "Those are excellent physical punishments. And his cock would look so pretty with a piece of jewelry. Perhaps one to match yours. Show him."

I obediently ruck up my skirts to display my bare lower half. Luthian uses two fingers to part me, to reveal the ring through my hood. Firo's eyes boggle at the sight.

"I think I will give you one," Luthian muses, touching the dripping slit at the tip of Firo's cock. "Through here, perhaps, and out the top."

Firo whimpers. I don't know if it's from fear or the desperation of his arousal.

"If I let you come, you'll allow me to do that to you?" Luthian asks him.

"Anything," Firo agrees with a sob. "Please, anything."

"Guardian, are you using your magic to stop him from climaxing?" I ask.

"No. What I'm teaching him is a bit more advanced. He must fight his body, resist everything in him that screams out for release. He knows there will be a punishment if he comes without permission," Luthian tells me. "You'll learn to do the same, in time."

I do not look forward to such a lesson.

"You've considered physical pain," he goes on.

"What about torment of the mind. When you were in such a state, what maddened you most?"

I think of Sarta's cunt bathing my mouth, my chin, hearing her wail as her thighs shuddered against my cheeks. "Seeing someone else granted such a release, Guardian."

"You're learning fast." Luthian begins to work the laces of his breeches. "Time for another lesson. Get on your knees."

I glance to Firo, who has resorted to staring at the ceiling.

"You're going to suck my cock," Luthian tells me. "And if he doesn't watch, he'll receive twenty lashes. Do you understand, Firo?"

The bound faery faces us, grim resolve written on his features.

I drop to my knees before Luthian.

A smile slowly spreads across his face as he gazes down at me and frees his cock. He's not quite erect, and he strokes himself as he looks down at me.

"Should I undress, Guardian?" I ask.

He shakes his head. "No. I rather enjoy the modesty, now. It will be a pleasant contrast when I come in your mouth."

I wet my lips, my chest rising and falling in anticipation as he readies himself for me.

"Are you watching, Firo?" Luthian asks.

"Yes," comes the strangled answer, but I can't tear my eyes away from Luthian to confirm it. For his part, Luthian doesn't look away, either.

"She's never done this before," he tells Firo. "I will be the first to penetrate that sweet mouth. To fuck that gorgeous face."

He talks about me like I'm an object. Like I'm not there, right in front of them both, hearing every word.

It's painfully arousing.

Luthian brushes his thumb over my bottom lip, then pushes the tip inside. "Remember how you teased Sarta yesterday with your tongue? Those light touches, initially?"

"Yes, Guardian."

"That's a good place to start." Fully hard now, he replaces his thumb with his cock. He holds himself for me, and I consider how best to demonstrate my skills. Teasing? I think I know a bit about that, by now. So, I move his hand aside and wrap my fingers around the thick column of flesh as much as I can.

Then, I do nothing. I hold him, barely touching him to my parted mouth. I let my breath cascade over him, brush him accidentally with my tongue as I wet my lips again. He takes a deep inhale, and I know I'm succeeding at my task. I slowly move my head side to side, catch the ridge of skin around him and hold it for the briefest of moments.

He shudders, but when he speaks, he maintains his unaffected tone. "She's a natural, really. Oh, Firo, if you could feel this, you wouldn't be able to hold back. You'd bathe her pretty face in your cum before she even took you into her mouth."

Firo makes a guttural noise of despair.

"Perhaps I'll have her finish you this way," Luthian muses, and Firo makes another pitiable sound.

I want Luthian's attention back. I don't know why I'm so disappointed to know that I'm not his only student, but now I want to be his favorite student, the best of all of them, however many our number may be. So, I lick my lips again and apply a sucking kiss to his pulsing tip. His hand falls to the back of my head, which I take as a sign of approval. I do it again and again, until his cock leaps to meet each one, until I hear his breath quicken.

Then, I open wide and take only the head of him past my lips, curling my tongue back so there is no contact. I have him in my mouth, where he so desperately wants to be, and I won't give him the satisfaction of sensation.

I hold his gaze with mine, gratified by his expression of pride.

Then, slowly, I uncurl my tongue and sweep it around him.

He groans, hips jerking forward as surprise widens his eyes.

"You've never done this before?" he asks, with a tone that suggests he doesn't believe me.

I give the smallest shake of my head, still twisting my tongue around his flesh. There is no flavor to him, none of the delicious saltiness of Sarta. That's a bit disappointing. I quite enjoyed the way her soft cunt spread open over my nose and mouth, the inviting scent of her. Sucking a cock isn't as interesting.

It could be the disinterest that I assume Luthian is feigning. "She does have a wickedly talented tongue, Firo. If only you could feel it. So warm and wet, and such instinct. Though, I do wonder how much she can take. Open wider, Cenere."

I do as he says and he pushes deeper to the back of my throat. I want to gag, but not wishing to humiliate myself by vomiting, I force myself to relax, to ignore the panic in my head at the realization that the further he goes, the less I can breathe, the harder it is to keep myself from choking. My eyes water, but still, I hold his gaze, hoping he sees how hard I'm trying, how I want to please him.

He withdraws slowly, and I do choke, a little, a stream of saliva pouring from the corner of my mouth. But he doesn't seem angered. If anything, the flesh in my hand throbs more ardently. He enters my mouth again, slowly, withdraws, picking up speed, his fingers twisting in my hair to hold me still. I try to use my tongue, and he rewards me with a groan.

"I'm in practically to the root," he tells Firo. "The back of her throat milks me as she chokes. It's truly extraordinary to watch her, isn't it? On her knees, taking my cock so obediently. Take notes, for I'll prevail upon you, as well."

"I'll do anything," Firo gasps. "Please, just let me—"

"Begging doesn't become you," Luthian admonishes him. "Close your lips around me, Cenere. You're doing such a good job. Use your tongue. That's it. Good girl."

My clit aches with need. My hand strays to my lap, but my skirts are in the way.

"Not without my permission," Luthian warns, and though a barrier prevents me from touching myself, I move my hand away.

I haven't forgotten his threat from last night.

"I'm not going to be gentle with you anymore, Cenere," he tells me. "There will be many times that your exquisite tongue will be put to use for languid hours, but you'll also be called upon to endure roughness. Like this."

His grip tightens on my head, and he forces me forward as he drives his cock in hard. There is no way to stop myself from gagging, no way to avoid choking mouthfuls of drool as he pummels the back of my throat again and again. I whimper, raise my hands to try to stop him, then catch myself. I want to be here. I asked to be here. I agreed to be here. My wishes, my goal, my revenge is on the line.

I will not disappoint myself.

I stare into his eyes. Not defiant. Not afraid. I stare into his eyes with gratitude and admiration, and they widen in shock. His lips part. He makes a noise that's almost despair, almost rapture. A burst of salt and wet heat strikes my throat, and he pulls out of my mouth to pump sticky slashes across my face.

He grabs me, hauls me to my feet, and for a moment, I'm terrified that I've done something very wrong. I feel the chains around my wrists in a cold dungeon cell. I know that I am condemned to die a screaming, agonizing, but not painful death.

But he's not angry. He laughs as he forces my head down, bringing my face close to Firo's. A glob of pearly white falls from my cheek and onto his.

"Now, Firo," Luthian says, breathless. "Clean her up."

Chapter Eight

"Clean her up," Luthian repeats, "and we'll let you come."

Firo's tongue is dry against my cheek. I wonder if he's had anything to drink at all during the hours he's been tied down, because he sucks Luthian's cum from my face as if it's lifegiving water in the desolation of the Sorrowlands.

"Don't forget her mouth," Luthian commands him. "it's quite talented. Perhaps I'll allow you to try it sometime."

Firo's lips claim mine with fierce passion that leaves my head spinning. I've always thought of kisses as something given out of love and affection, but all I feel from him is desperation to consume me, to be consumed by me. I give in, sweeping my tongue into his mouth as he does to mine, tasting him and Luthian and swooning for more when my Guardian lifts my head away.

"That's enough for now, Cenere." There's an amused note in Luthian's voice. "Lest we get caught up and ruin our lesson."

Still holding me by my nape, he pushes me toward the middle of the table, directly in front of Firo's helplessly bobbing cock.

"He's had some time to cool down, so it should be safe to touch him now. But if I tell you to stop, you must; he can't come yet," Luthian explains.

"Yes, Guardian, but... How will you know?" How will *I* know?

"There are telltale signs that release is imminent. For example, here," Luthian cups the fleshy sack beneath Firo's cock. "Not everyone displays the same signs, but a common one, one that you'll notice in Firo is that he'll draw up tightly here. Notice, too, how he drips?"

Luthian takes my hand, curling all but one of my fingers into my palm. He traces that fingertip across the slit in the head of Firo's cock. The bound faery hisses.

"Are you a bit sensitive?" Luthian mocks him. He straightens my fingers and moves my hand over Firo's shaft. "You may feel his pulse increase. He'll rock his hips up to meet you, trying to go faster to reach his climax. But you must always maintain control. Don't match his speed."

Luthian wraps our joined hands around Firo's flushed, straining cock. Instantly, the faery on the table bucks and moans with relief.

"We're going to practice that control, now," Luthian explains, gliding my hand slowly up Firo's length. "You may find yourself growing excited. You might wish to speed up. But we'll stay at this pace. Even when he's teetering on the brink. Even when he begs."

"Yes, Guardian." I let him take complete control

of my hand and commit everything to memory. The slight flick of my wrist to glide my palm over Firo's tip before beginning the journey down again. The pause at the base before another gentle rise. Firo writhes and groans, bites back pleas. A steady stream of clear fluid slicks my hand and pours freely onto his stomach. Just as Luthian described, Firo tries to lift his hips in his own rhythm.

"Haven't I warned you already?" Luthian chides him. He releases my hand. "But still, you disobey me. Cenere, keep up what you're doing. If he moves at all, stop. Take your hand away from him entirely."

"Yes, Guardian." I concentrate on keeping my pace steady, just as he showed me, but watch from the corner of my eye as Luthian moves to the end of the table. He produces a long, thin rod and gives it a few sharp swings, slicing the air.

"You know the punishment, this time," Luthian says, and without any further warning, snaps the reed across the bottoms of Firo's spread feet.

Firo screams, his body bucking.

"Does that count as moving, Guardian?" I ask.

"It does. Take your hand away."

"No!" Firo screams. "No, please, I was so close!"

"You won't be rewarded for disobedience." Luthian slashes the rod across Firo's feet again. Another strike, and another, while Firo screams for mercy. And yet, through the pain, his cock never flags. Not even when the strikes of the cane split his skin, arcing droplets of blue-black faery blood over Luthian's white tunic.

I want to beg for mercy for Firo. I don't. It has become clear that mercy will not be a part of my training.

Finally, after twenty brutal, cutting blows, Luthian stops. He's breathing hard, and I note that he's erect again. Inflicting that pain has aroused him.

How many of the faeries at the Court of Pleasure and Torment will be the same?

"*And he* will *hurt you,*" Luthian said of the King.

I only hope they take my human fragility into account; faeries, while immortal but not invulnerable, are made of stronger stuff than my mortal body.

Firo sobs, tears running down his face and into his dark hair.

"Resume, Cenere," Luthian says, wicking the blood from the cane. "And Firo, if you wish to finish, you will hold entirely still. If not, you won't come until sunset. In three days' time."

Firo whimpers. His hands fist with the effort of not moving while I resume his torment. Up, down, slowly, slowly. I don't speed up, don't increase the squeeze of my fingers around him. I keep pumping, watching his body for the signs Luthian has taught me, though Firo doesn't shift an inch. Luthian stands by, not speaking, not showing a flicker of emotion on his face. He observes silently, cane still in his hand, while Firo stares up at the ceiling. His lips part slightly. He gulps in air once, twice, and when it releases, it's on a scream of rapture as he erupts over my hand.

"Keep going. The same speed," Luthian instructs. "Firo, you may move, if you wish."

Long, viscous white strands fly from Firo's tip still. His shaft twitches and pulses with each one. He groans and shakes until finally, sweat and tears rolling down his face, he goes slack on the table.

"Keep going," Luthian commands me.

Firo's eyes fly open, wide. I see "No!" form on his lips, but his voice doesn't come out.

"I've silenced him," Luthian explains. "Some students find the screaming involved in the next part... disquieting. Same tempo, please."

I can't help but note the agony twisting Firo's

features. He's long since stopped coming, and he struggles against the bonds, bangs his head against the table. But I do as Luthian commands, watching Firo's feet flex, his hands grasp for something intangible.

I don't know what comes over me. "Guardian, if you don't mind... I would quite like to hear him."

A cruel smile passes over Luthian's lips. "Very well."

He lifts the spell with a wave of his hand and Firo's hoarse, painful screams echo through the cavernous library.

"Please! Stop!" he cries. "I'll give you anything!"

I don't know what's come over me. I imagine my smile is very much like Luthian's, mocking tenderness, pretend concern. And though my Guardian hasn't instructed me to, I coo sweetly, "Anything?"

"Anything! Please!" He sobs, squeezes his eyes shut.

And I laugh at him. I laugh at his torment.

And I understand.

There is pleasure in pain. Pleasure can become pain. They are inseparable. It doesn't matter if I'm giving the pain, as I am now, or receiving it, as I did spread wide for Sarta's needle. I revel in his agony.

Luthian tilts his head at my taunting. Is he proud? Is he angry? I can't tell. I can imagine the cane slicing into my feet and they tingle. So does my aching, stiff pearl.

"I'm... I'm..." This time, when Firo comes, his emission trickles.

And I laugh at him again. "That's not nearly so impressive, Guardian. Will the next one be?"

Luthian smiles indulgently. "I wasn't going to continue, but what an excellent question. Shall we test it out, Firo?"

"No, please, no more. No more!" he begs.

Luthian pretends to consider, then nods to me. "More."

I feel dizzy with the power I'm exerting over poor Firo, and guilty at the pain I'm causing. But it's exhilarating, too, to watch him fight his bonds uselessly, then give up, then struggle again with renewed vigor.

"Pay more attention to the head," Luthian advises. "If you wish to be truly cruel."

On the next upward slide, I twist my palm roughly over the bright red, sore-looking tip, and I'm rewarded with more pitiable sobbing and shrieking. I put my other hand to work on his shaft, still slow and steady.

When he comes a third time, he begs for it not to happen. A pathetic few drops escape him. He's entirely dry.

"That's enough," Luthian says finally. I take my hands away and, with no other way to clean them, wipe them on my skirt. They're sticky, the remnants of multiple releases pilled on my fingers and palms. Luthian leans over Firo, presses his hand on the faery's trembling, jerking chest. He places the softest kiss on the hollow of Firo's throat and runs a hand over the cum turned watery on his stomach.

"You've done so well," my Guardian murmurs. Then, he takes his dripping hand and smears it over Firo's face. With a snap of Luthian's fingers, the bindings are gone. He helps Firo sit up. "I'm very proud of you."

I feel the strangest flicker of jealousy at that. After all, I've done the work. It's my arm that aches. My body that throbs in desperate need of release.

"I haven't forgotten you," Luthian says with a crooked smile, and I wonder if he can read my thoughts. "Your lesson isn't done today. You have my permission to relieve your need. Then, you may join me in my study. Brujon knows the way."

"Thank you, Guardian," I say, and bow my head to him before I leave the library.

As I walk away, I hear him murmuring words of comfort to Firo.

Chapter Nine

As commanded, I go to Luthian's study, my core still wet and slick from my release. Since he found my choice of dress "studious," I'm still wearing it when I knock on the door.

"Enter," he calls from within, and I step inside.

At first sight, I realize that what Luthian "studies" is not a subject with which I am familiar.

The room is an octagon beneath a glass dome like a spiderweb. Daylight streams down on a dais in the center that's surrounded by polished wood railings, but somehow the illumination doesn't reach the dark outer perimeter. Candles light sixteen corners and the walls painted with murals.

Luthian himself stands in one of these shadowy places, browsing a shelf.

It doesn't hold books.

"I am here, Guardian," I say, shifting nervously on my feet.

He doesn't turn to me, but says, "Still dressed for the archives? Well, that won't do."

I gasp at my instant nakedness. My nipples pucker in the chill; there is no hearth to warm me.

"Step onto the dais," he orders. "I'm selecting the tools we'll need."

The shelf in front of him holds an assortment of impressive, very realistic phalluses. I hold my breath as I watch him decide. He takes down one, then another, hefting them both in his hands. They're huge, much bigger than Firo or Luthian, and they don't appear to be shaped for either human or faery. Though they're both intimidating, I'm glad he left the largest ones behind. I'm certain the cocks on the bottom shelf must be modeled after ogres and trolls.

"I was very impressed this morning," he says, waving a hand. A table like the one from the library appears just inches from me. "You took great pleasure in torturing Firo."

"I did." I bite my lip. "But Guardian... did I give him pleasure?"

Luthian chuckles. "Oh, you did. Most assuredly."

"In the moment, I enjoyed it, but after, I felt mean," I confess.

"That feeling will pass. Soon enough, you'll become utterly indifferent to the screams of the tormented." He means to reassure me, I think, but it's far from it.

Do I truly wish to inflict that kind of suffering? Do I want to become so callous to it?

"Guardian, forgive me, but if I am indifferent, how will I know if I'm truly hurting someone?"

"That's an excellent question."

My heart swells with pride, beating itself against my ribs.

He taps his lips with his forefinger. "These aren't skills you should employ outside of the Court. You might, of course. If you and your lover wished it. But the lovers you'll take at court will expect and revel in such behavior. Outside of the court, these activities should only be undertaken with trust and strict understanding of how to know when your partner has had enough. A word, for example, that only the two or three or eight, whatever you will, know, which always means to stop."

Eight? I boggle at the notion, but the idea of a magic word sparks my interest. "And we don't have those at the Court of Pleasure and Torment?"

"There is no mercy at the Court of Pleasure and Torment. Therefore, it needs no language." He goes to a cabinet and opens it. Inside stands a glittering array of bottles and phials. Some glow with their own light, gleaming emerald, fire-lit ruby, and blinding white. He takes down an ampoule of something purple. "But I don't believe it's a language you could master, anyway."

"I don't know what you mean." I rub my hands down my bare arms. The sunlight through the web of windows overhead is cool by the time it touches my skin. I wonder if this is a test of my patience, to see how long I'll endure the physical discomfort of freezing.

"You enjoyed watching me lash Firo's feet," Luthian says, depositing the potions on the table.

"I've never seen such a thing before," I confess. "I've never even seen a criminal whipped in the village square."

Luthian's nose wrinkles in distaste. "I forget that you're not just a human, but you've been raised among them. Imagine, reducing the elegance of pain down to such petty barbarism."

"I must admit to a morbid curiosity, Guardian." I'm as ashamed to reveal it to him now as I was the time I asked my mother for permission to watch punishments doled out in the square. She was gentle and kind in dissuading me, but I received the message all too effectively: it was wrong of me to desire another's pain. "Mother couldn't stand to think of it, though."

"Perhaps you're more faery than your mother was."

It's a joke, I know. But it pleases me that he's said it. Should it please me? After all, I've spent so much of my life wishing I could be fae, wondering if I'll ever fit in with the humans we lived among yet rarely encountered. But my mother also worried that she wasn't fae enough. She was shunned by her court, after all.

"I'm a human," I say, helpless to control the note of self-pity in my tone.

Luthian just waves a hand. "You're potential. Nothing more at this stage, and nothing less. But potential is mighty. You've been here for two days, and you've already learned important truths about yourself and your desires."

"I'm doing well, then?"

"I'm delighted with your progress," he confirms. "But don't congratulate yourself. There is still much for you to learn and experience, and we've not much time."

"There isn't?" I'm puzzled at that; he hasn't mentioned time before.

"For my plan to work, you need to have ensnared Cassan by the night of his birthday party," Luthian explains. "You needn't know every detail. Just trust that it will work."

"Yes, Guardian." I'll be more careful with my questions in the future.

"You enjoyed it when I inflicted pain upon Firo," Luthian says, bringing us back to the original subject of our conversation. "But you'll need to enjoy having pain inflicted upon you, as well."

"Enjoy it, or bear it, Guardian?" I ask for clarity.

He seems delighted at the distinction. "This is what makes you such a good student. Enjoy, not just bear. This comes naturally to some. There are those truly blessed with an understanding of pain. Or a lack of fear. Others need to work at appreciating pain. The layers of meaning to it. You, for example. I believe you are a rare jewel, Cenere. One who can receive pain with the appreciation of all of your senses, but who can also create that pain and revel in it. If I teach you well enough—I assure you, I can—and you apply yourself to your studies, I dare say that your humanity will never be a burden or failing in the eyes of the court. And it will be more than adequate proof that you deserve the throne."

"But only if I do exactly as you command, Guardian," I add, because I'm still so eager to please him. I want to be his grandest creation, fulfill the potential he's seen in me.

A smile tilts his lips. "Your skills at manipulation, however, need polishing."

I lower my head in profound shame. "My apologies, Guardian. It was meant in earnest."

"I know." He walks slowly to stand before me, takes my chin in his hand to tip my gaze up. "That's what requires polishing. There is no room for honesty at court if we are to achieve our goals."

I wonder if that includes honesty between the two of us, but he is a faery. *"Nothing without a price,"* rings in my head, one of few rational thoughts that still intrude in my quiet moments. Is there some spell over me, some magic that Luthian has worked to keep me infatuated with his lessons? These thoughts of safety annoy me. They pass quickly, and I assume they will come less frequently throughout our practice.

"You've just learned to inflict torment. You've made a brief acquaintanceship with it, yourself. Now, it's time to learn true erotic suffering." Luthian uncorks the ampule and sprinkles seven drops in a circle around me. Then he steps back and waits in silence.

A dire rumble shakes the room. The candles gutter and flare, their wicks drowning in their waxy seas. The bottoms of my feet absorb the dreadful vibration and I stagger. I look down to see the stone floor of the dais creak and split. A wriggling black vine bursts up in front of me, slimy and coated with short, hooked thorns. It swivels about as if seeking something out. Another rises beside me, more behind me, and soon I am caged in by countless dripping, prickly stems.

Finding its mark, the first slaps against my wrist and wraps around and around, forming a gauntlet on my forearm. I shriek and try to pull away, but the thorns pierce my skin, holding me fast. The more I struggle, the more I tear at my flesh, and there is no hope of escaping, anyway; my knees buckle as another vine catches my foot. It fixes itself with its cruel thorns up the back of my thigh as a twin does the same work. They grasp my buttocks and join at my spine, winding all the way to my shoulders in a harness of pain. My other arm is captured, and soon I'm bound, impaled on hundreds of the cruel thorns.

I sag against the vines at my back, though the very action makes me cry out as the spikes drive deeper. I know they're only as long as a fingernail, but to my mind, they're enormous, ripping me apart. So, I do not fight against them as they raise my feet off the ground, tip me back, spread me wide. I'm supported by a throne of pain, in a chamber gone so utterly silent that only my muffled weeping is louder than the sound of my blood dripping on the broken floor.

Luthian steps forward, standing between my legs. "You know that you cannot possibly escape, don't you?"

I want to nod, but any movement causes the vines to tighten.

"You know that I won't let them kill you," he says.

"Yes, Guardian," I whimper.

"Yet still you fear?"

I do. I fear that whatever comes next will be too much to endure. But I don't fear *him*. Foolish though it may be, I trust him when he promises that no real harm will come to me. So, I find my voice again to say, "I fear the pain, Guardian. I do not fear you."

His starry eyes light with cold flame. "That is the wrong answer, Cenere."

My stomach drops.

"You will find many at court who enjoy fear. Who employ it as another form of pleasure. You can, after all, sense that they are sisters, can you not?" He crooks a finger, beckoning, and something slithers where I cannot see. It's another vine, sliding into place between my spread legs. My eyes widen as Luthian pets it. "I could, if I wished, command this vine to enter you as a lover. To rake its thorns through your untried flesh, to burrow deeply, to coil itself around and around, until its thickest part stretches your opening past its limit. I could do that to you right now."

I watch in horror as the tip of the vine moves closer to my unguarded center. It touches me, at the bottom of my opening, and I clench, not just from fear, but another, more wretched instinct. I am exposed. Vulnerable. Terrified. And wet. Throbbing. His words have touched off a hunger in me that whispers perhaps it would not be so bad, if only my cunt could be filled. If only the emptiness that has plagued me since the moment Sarta withdrew her tongue from my aching channel could be banished.

Luthian grins cruelly down at me. "Do you feel it? Your body crying out for something you don't want? Something that will cause you untold agony?"

"Yes, Guardian." But I don't know if my answer will condemn me to that unimaginable pain. A tear rolls down my cheek and I tremble.

He leans over me, places a gentle kiss at the corner of my mouth. "Good girl."

The vine falls.

"Various implements can be used to cause pain. Not all of them magical." Luthian turns away, leaving me suspended in my cradle of thorns.

"You're acquainted with the cane." He moves from my limited vision, and I hear him shifting objects in the darkness. "But there are tools for bruising. Lashing. Inflicting pain in pinpoints and cuts or deep, bloodless injuries. A universe of exquisite agonies, with nary a potion or wand in sight. It's important that you know you aren't limited due to your lack of magic."

"Yes, Guardian." Cold sweat trickles down my spine. Or perhaps it's blood from the thorns.

"This will be your final lesson of the day." He strides onto the dais again, but I still cannot see him. He stands behind me and the vines shift, tilting me to stare at the floor, my knees wide, ass upturned. Where he stands, he can see all of me, every intimate part of me, on full display. And though I know he's seen every inch of me before, it feels more dangerous now. More vulnerable.

He says nothing, but I feel his presence, unmoving, behind me. I hear my own ragged breath, cast my gaze about for something other than the floor, to no avail. I wait. And I wait.

A resounding crack splits the air, startling me

enough to cry out before I even feel the pain.

Chapter Ten

He's struck me with something hard, across my buttocks, and with enough force that the vines rock. I squeeze my eyes shut, grit my teeth, but a pained gasp escapes, nevertheless.

"You'll count each one," he orders. "And you'll thank me for them. Try it now."

"Yes, Guardian." I sniff back tears. "One. Thank you, Guardian."

I'm barely finished when the object hits me again, igniting a fire in my already inflamed skin. I cry out and say, "Two. Thank you, Guardian."

"Can you guess what I'm using on you?" he asks, and scrapes a broad, rough edge over my screaming flesh, digging in as he drags it down.

It's wide, flat, and totally unyielding. "Is it a book, Guardian?"

He strikes me again, harder, and this time, he doesn't pause between blows.

"Three, thank you, Guardian! Four, thank you, Guardian!" I yelp as the fifth lands. "Five! Thank you, Guardian!"

My chest heaves. My stomach roils.

"Guess again."

It seems the punishment for a wrong answer will be more smacks. I should wish to avoid that, shouldn't I? But all I can think of is the shock of the pain and the way my body is responding to it. I'm growing slick between my thighs, and heavy there with growing need.

"Answer," he barks, and slaps me with the object again.

"Six! Thank you, Guardian!" But still, I have no clue, only guesses. "Is it a wooden plank, Guardian?"

The time, I receive five, all in a frenzy, alternating between cheeks. I can barely keep up with the counting, shrieking, "Seven! Eight! Nine! Ten! Thank you, Guardian! Eleven! Thank you! Thank you, Guardian!"

Tears stream freely from my eyes now, and drool from my slack mouth.

"Guess again, my honey flower," he whispers in my ear.

If I guess again, there will be more pain. If I don't guess, the pain will be much worse.

"A breadboard?" I try, and again, he strikes me with the implement. The vines tighten, driving their thorns deeper. There's a broken scream from somewhere. From me? I must be the source, but I have no control over my body. I'm alight with pain, yet I somehow crave more. The anticipation is delicious.

"Ah ah, you didn't count that one," he says.

I tremble all over. "I'm so sorry, Guardian! I won't disappoint you again, Guardian! Please, just—"

"Hmm? Are you making a request of me, now?" This time, when he strikes me, it's not with such force. He comes to stand before me and shows me the object of my torture. "A paddle. This one, you see, is studded with iron. That's something to keep in mind for faeries who wish to be dominated by you. Iron is deeply uncomfortable."

He passes his hand over the blunt, flat studs and a curl of white smoke comes up. Then, he flips over his palm to display a rime of frost across it. The skin bubbles black, then heals before my eyes. "But you must be cautious. Too much can be fatal."

I know this too well.

"Yes, Guardian. I'll remember. Thank you, Guardian." My throat is parched, and my body is weak. I must rely on the stinging vines for stability, but there is no shifting to make them more comfortable. They tilt me again, tipping me back and raising my knees, holding me wide open.

"You were worried that you haven't been penetrated by a cock before," he says, turning to the disturbingly fleshly ones he's left on the table. "I think you're correct; you do need the experience before we go to court, and frankly, before we continue our lessons here."

The one in his hand is huge, easily as wide as my own fist, and I silently beg him, *no, not that one. Not this.*

The corners of his mouth unfurl a grin and I know that he's seen my fear plainly. "I do have a centaur's, if this is too small."

He moves as if to retrieve it and I shriek, "No! No, please, Guardian!"

"You needn't fear this." He holds the appendage up. It looks even larger upright. "It will fit. And if it does not, I can always repair the damage. You'll be traumatized, of course—"

I sob aloud.

"Oh, my honey flower, I'm only teasing." He beckons the vines at my feet, and one rises up between my legs again. It wraps around the phallus and holds it tight while he sprinkles more of the potion from the ampoule onto it. I watch, eyes wide, as the thorns shed from the plant and it fuses to the cock. It waves menacingly close to my unguarded center. Luthian brushes it aside and touches his fingertips to my slit. "You're positively dripping."

Despite the pain I've endured, the fear and the helplessness I've experienced at his hands, the words make me wetter.

Perhaps because of the fear and pain. Is it possible that violence is, to me, as arousing as gentleness?

He goes to his potions and returns with an unguent in a pot. "This will help ease the way," he assures me, scooping out a large dollop on his fingers. He slaps it onto my parted flesh and spreads it about my folds as if his hand is a trowel. The matter-of-fact way he applies it makes it almost redundant, because my arousal grows more as he treats me like an object to be prepared for use.

Then, he scoops out more and his hand glides lower. I tense, but the thorny vines urge my cheeks apart and hold them open; Luthian smooths a liberal amount of the ointment there, too, and I shudder in embarrassment. I can't imagine what the purpose of it could be.

Then he pushes his fingertip forward, and I understand.

He goes to the table and picks up the other, smaller phallus.

I fight the vines, not caring how their thorns score my flesh. "No, no, you can't—"

"I can't?" He blinks at me.

At once, I understand that I've breached our contract, simply by denying him. I've allowed him to debase me, to violate me, to display me, to hurt me, and now with my words, I've wasted the opportunity he's offered.

I can't lose my revenge. I can't lose my wishes.

I swallow and clear my throat, "You can't mean to pleasure me with these, alone, Guardian. I wanted your cock in me. I've craved it since I tasted it this morning."

"That's what I thought you meant." He nods in approval. "But you haven't earned it. And I daresay, you wouldn't survive the pleasure I would give you. Not yet."

Not yet. The words tingle at the bottom of my feet, tease my tightened nipples. But I still recoil as I watch him grease the other phallus and walk behind me with the ampule.

"Do you know what creatures provided these?" He asks, walking around to lovingly stroke the monstrous vine between my legs.

"No, Guardian." I've never even seen creatures other than faeries or humans, aside from in stories.

"The one behind you is a werewolf." He crooks his fingers and the vine bearing the organ shifts over my shoulder. "You'll notice the large bulb at the base. It will swell further when it's inside of you."

The cock-vine slinks out of view again.

"And this happy fellow is a vampire," he says, patting the vine between my thighs. "See the bumps here?"

Nodules like pearls beneath the skin lie in a ridge from base to tip on the top and bottom of the shaft, ending at the bulbous head.

"You'll like how those will feel," he promises. He motions the vine forward, until the tip of the horrible thing touches me. I choke back my disgust. I've always assumed this moment would happen with *someone*, not *something*. And the vine, phallus and all, seems somehow aware of me and its purpose. It's alive, but not, a creature of magic, nothing I can reason with.

"Go slowly, pet," he croons to the appendage, and gently opens my petals to it. "This one is pretty. Let's not break it until we're ready."

I tremble in terrified anticipation as the head of the phallus stretches my opening.

"Tell me it's too big, Cenere," Luthian murmurs.

This requires no acting on my part. "It's too big, Guardian!"

It moves slowly forward, but steadily, and at the first sign of resistance, I try to twist away. The vines hold me firm, and Luthian snaps his fingers. Another lashes across the burning skin of my backside, the thorns gouging my skin. I cry out pitifully, and the cock never stops advancing. The head forces into me, opens me painfully, pushes my untried channel so wide I think I'll split in two.

"Beg me to stop. You have my permission, just this once," he growls.

"Please!" I cry. "Please, take it out!"

And it's barely inside.

"Tell me you're afraid, Cenere."

Another command that requires no pretending. I'm shaking, tears running down my face as the vine advances. "I'm afraid, Guardian!"

"Good. You're meant to fear this," he says with a note of satisfaction. "Fear is a torment of its own."

I can barely hear him over the instinct roaring in my head, urging me to fight, to struggle, to free myself. The phallus is deep now, but there is so much more of it go, and it doesn't seem intent on stopping.

"Sometimes, pain can be enjoyable because it's expected," Luthian goes on. "By the time I was finished paddling you, you craved the pain, did you not?"

"Yes, Guardian." But my entire being is focused on escaping the vine between my legs, which feeds more and more of the terrible instrument into me. I want to scream for Luthian to stop, then remember my bargain once more, how I surrendered my will to him.

I think of Cadwyn Thrace's wings ripped from his body, two trails of blood behind him as he crawls desperately across the floor like a half-squashed insect. I imagine the knife in my hand.

"I'm... I'm..." I gasp out, and I can't help my movements then. My body is alight with pleasure, spasming all around the invading cock, legs flailing in my bonds. The vines allow this, moving languidly with each spasm and contraction my muscles, rocking me almost tenderly through my release.

Luthian laughs. "Tell me how afraid you are, now."

"I'm not, Guardian." I can barely catch my breath, and now the phallus is withdrawing, dragging those ridges over my inner flesh with agonizing slowness, awakening my body's hunger once more.

My answer takes him aback. "You aren't afraid?"

I shake my head. "I am not afraid, Guardian."

I'm determined.

His gaze darkens. Saying nothing, he nods past me.

The pointed tip of the phallus behind me touches my greased ass. I clench, but the vines pry my cheeks apart again, and I can do nothing to escape the insistent pressure. Even with the unguent melting to oil on my flesh, the vine doesn't penetrate me easily. What begins as a pinprick of pain becomes a splitting, tearing, burning thing.

Luthian watches the horrible thing penetrate me, cruel amusement twisting his features. "It's barely inside of you. There's so much more to go."

I squeeze my eyes shut.

"Are you afraid, now?" he asks.

"Yes, Guardian!" Perhaps, now that my fear is renewed, he'll feel that he's made his point.

"As I was saying, the anticipation of the pain, the fear of it, makes the pleasure sweeter. As pleasure can become pain, pain can become pleasure. Fear can be an aphrodisiac." He points to the glass overhead. "Look up."

The window transforms into a mirror. I see myself displayed lewdly, see the cocks between my legs. Two more vines unfurl beneath me and rise to curl around my breasts, wrapping and wrapping until they're tight and flushing. Blood runs in thin streaks from every thorn embedded in my skin.

The image changes, showing me my own body from an angle I could never possibly view on my own; my cunt spread wide around the impossibly huge phallus, the terrible length barely inside my ass. The vampire cock hasn't stopped moving, but the werewolf vine has, and despite the agony of its intrusion, the nodules tickling the inside of my cunt send spikes of pleasure above the pain.

"Anticipation intensifies every sensation," Luthian goes on. "You know what this feels like—"

The cock in my ass gives a little wiggle, and I gasp.

"So, imagine how it will feel when, upon my command, it buries itself entirely, in one swift, brutal thrust."

My skin goes cold all over. I can't stop my limbs from trembling.

"You're going to watch, of course," He says. "If you close your eyes, if you look away, I'll make sure you can see. You don't want my pets to mark up your pretty face, do you?"

The thought of the deadly thorns anywhere near

my eyes is enough to make me widen them and stare dutifully up at the image above me.

"Beg me," he instructs again. "Let yourself believe you can convince me to stop, only if you plead desperately enough. Become frantic in your terror and helplessness."

The werewolf cock is long. The bulb at the base as round as a man's fist. I swallow and whimper, "Please, Guardian—"

"I'll count down, shall I?" He comes to stand close to my head, leans down to whisper in my ear. "Three..."

"Please!" I focus on my fear, let it drive my need higher. This is going to happen. I'm going to feel myself split apart, cruel inch by cruel inch, watch it with no way to stop it.

"Two."

I can imagine it now, the pain I already feel, amplified, and refreshed. I try one last, pathetic time, my throat raw with desperation that I hope pleases him. "I beg you, Guardian, don't do this—"

His tongue traces the shell of my ear.

"One."

Chapter Eleven

A haze of red washes over my vision as the vine thrusts the cock swiftly forward, spearing deep into my passage. I can't breathe, can't move, can't think about anything but the pain, but I cannot look away from the horrible sight of the length vanishing into my body. The bulbous knot at the base bumps me and I pray that it's simply too much, that it can't penetrate me, but the pressure increases for only a breath before the impossible strength of the vine forces it forward, splitting me while I scream my agony and keep my eyes open wide.

"There," Luthian croons, stroking back my sweat-damp hair and caressing my jaw with his elegant fingers. He wipes tears from my face that are instantly refreshed. Still, I stare up at the sight of my body opened by the monstrous vines. "The worst of it is finished."

I trust him not to inflict permanent harm on me.

I don't trust him not to inflict more pain. I clench my jaw, grind my teeth against the tearing and aching and throbbing that have coalesced into one and lie, "Thank you, Guardian."

The image above me changes, and I once again see myself bound and splayed. The vine at my cunt has almost completely withdrawn, the ridge at the tip of the phallus just visible between my folds. It pushes back in with the same terrible slowness.

"As I said, the worst of it," Luthian goes on, as I knew he would.

There is always a catch.

"It's still going to be terrible, of course."

My breasts are numb, swollen and purplish in the reflection. Luthian pinches one of my protruding nipples, but I barely feel it. Then, he pets the vines that hold my breasts bound, and the fall away, revealing a multitude of pinpricks that weep droplets of blood as my pulse rushes back into my denied flesh. A new ache, a new horrid throbbing, but his hand moves lower, to my clit, red and swollen and slick and straining. I watch warily as his fingers gently find me and work my hood back and forth over the delicate nerve, the smooth metal ring stimulating me with barely any pressure.

"Would you like to come, Cenere?" he asks, rubbing in slow, steady circles as the vampire cock pushes deeper.

Unbelievably, I do. After the horror and pain I've experienced, somehow, my body rouses at his attentions. "Oh, please, Guardian."

He kisses my cheek. "My pet is very good at fucking, Cenere. But I think it's sad."

I squeeze on the organ filling my cunt, my muscles tightening with impending release. The pace of Luthian's finger is maddening. If only he would speed up a bit...

"Why is it sad, Guardian?" I ask, breathless with need.

"Because it thinks you don't like it, of course." He sounds teasingly sympathetic to the monstrosity he's created. "You're not having any fun."

"I'm sorry, Guardian." It's becoming more difficult to concentrate on anything but his too-gentle touch on my clit.

"It's so good at fucking, and you don't appreciate it." He clucks his tongue. "It will have to work harder, I think, to win your affection."

The cock in my ass tugs backward, as if to withdraw its huge knot, and my eyes widen. To my relief, it does not. It does, however begin to pump in short, stabbing thrusts that take my breath away on a fresh wave of pain. But I'm so close to my climax, it can't distract me. My toes curl, joints popping. Almost there... almost...

The phallus in my cunt has completely buried itself once more. This time, when it begins to withdraw, it goes a bit faster, then strokes forward faster, as if it's building toward something.

I'm building, too, toward a release I desperately crave, hoping it will drive away my body's memory of all I've endured so far. Luthian's fingers circle and circle, until—

"Come," he commands, but pulls his fingers away before I do.

"No!" I scream in desperation, my climax bursting and fading without stimulation. It's gone, escaped me, stranded me in nothing but my stubbornly lingering pain.

His hand, which has just brought me so much pleasure, lashes out with a stinging slap across my face. "That is twice now. A third time, and I'll grant your wish."

And I'll lose all of mine, I realize. "I'm sorry,

Guardian!"

"What are you sorry for?" he demands.

"For…" It's becoming difficult to speak; the vine in my cunt is going faster now, the one in my ass is jerking forward and back rapidly. "I'm sorry for my greed, Guardian."

Another climax explodes through me in a shower of white-cold sparks that fizzle up my back and down my legs, making me shiver with the pleasure.

"What else?" he demands.

My mouth hangs slack, frozen in my wordless cry. I fight to continue, to find a reason I should need to apologize. "For denying you, Guardian!"

Another orgasm comes on the heels of the first, before it can fade away, and I realize that it's Luthian doing this, commanding my body to enjoy what's happening despite the violation and pain.

"What else?"

What else, indeed? I want to scream. The vines pummel in and out, and the reflection changes back to the angle I saw before. My thighs, the surface of the vines, and of course, the phalluses gleam with the sheen of the greasy unguent mingled with my own gushing juices.

"For insulting your pet with my ungratefulness, Guardian," I moan over the obscene squelching of my cunt.

"Very good, my honey flower. I think it's happy now. It's going to reward you."

The vines supporting my back fall away, peeling off in an agony of hooked barbs leaving my skin. I'm held aloft only by their grip on my wrists and ankles, and the weight of my body drives me more fully onto the invading appendages. My voice has long since lost its capacity for screaming. A ragged sob is all I can manage.

"When it does," Luthian goes on, "You'll be incapacitated for quite some time. You see, werewolves and vampires have their unusual physical attributes, which are useful. But did you know that ogres have an advantage that has nothing to do with their size?"

"No, I didn't, Guardian." How can I still speak, impaled on this disgusting monster? How can my body still find pleasure in this depravity? But as I watch the vines do their work, I revel in how disgusting they look, how filthy and slimy. I find myself longing for it to be worse, to have a cock in my mouth, in my hands, to be suspended in a net of foul vines and disembodied phalluses that take my body over and over again.

"You're about to discover it," Luthian promises. "For while I used the werewolf and the vampire, they're merely vessels for the ogre's particular advantage. And I see that my pet is about to spend. The first time, anyway."

The thought of the horrid creature filling me with its seed makes me gag in revulsion, but it's too late; the vine in my ass stills, stiffens, drives impossibly deeper and wrenching newfound pain as it fills spaces it hasn't yet touched. I feel a thick, hot squirt of something deep in me and shudder, vomit burning my throat in a warning. *Don't think about it, don't think about it.*

Don't think about being taken by a featureless monster, an abomination.

I sob in disgust.

The phallus in my cunt thrusts with dizzing speed that rocks me in my bindings, faster and faster while I kick my legs and howl. My mind screams for help, for pity, for anything but this, to no avail. The vampire cock thrusts so deep it fully disappears into my helpless body, and bathes my core with another foul burst. A defeated, disgusted sob wrenches from me.

And then, I'm seized in pleasure so impossible that I forget to breathe. The cocks continue to discharge their fluids, and with every lurching eruption, I come again. I'm trapped in a tide of ecstasy that never recedes. It crests and deposits me onto the breaking swell of another and another, as hot, sticky cum overflows from my cunt and bathes my thighs. The bulging cock in my ass holds everything inside, though, and that's even more intense; it's how I know that it's the plant's seed that's causing this reaction.

No, not the plant's seed. Luthian had said—

"Ogre cum is incredible. I don't know why more people don't try it." He scoops some off my thigh and rubs it between his hands before palming my breasts. The application of it causes another cycle of release, and it's as if those climaxes race directly from my nipples to my spasming clit. "I've been with an ogre before, you know. They lock together during mating. It lasts for hours. Days, sometimes. I didn't think I would survive."

The plant continues to thrust, its unoccupied vines thrashing about as if in its own passionate throes. The tip of a vine touches my face and, to the horror of the only rational part of my mind that's left, I open my mouth and tease it with my tongue. Its thorns drop away, and it pushes inside, darting touches on my tongue that are very like kissing. I suck it, tease it, rub my face against the length of it before it returns to my mouth. Another vine wraps my waist, this one without it thorns, as well; it holds me almost protectively, squeezes me like an embrace.

I can't watch myself in the reflection anymore. I'm too lost in the ecstasy, in the depravity. I lavish the vine at my mouth with kisses, arch my back in the bonds that no longer hurt me.

"Yes," I hiss against the stalk that caresses my

face. "Oh, yes, fuck me!"

And though it already is, it replies to my request with fervor. It stretches my arms and legs as wide as it can and pumps itself into me, the cocks moving in time with each other, the vines holding me steady for its punishing thrusts.

"Oh, harder," I moan, taking the vine at my mouth deeper, like I pleasured Luthian before. I break free and beg, "Don't stop!"

I'm drunk on the unrelenting orgasms, intoxicated by the obscenity I'm committing. I want this beast to hurt me, to tear me to bits, to burst me apart with every inhuman thrust. I scream and struggle against it, kiss it and urge it along, hump my hips against the force of its invasion. I never want it to stop.

I don't know how long it goes on. Perhaps days, as Luthian said. I know he's spoken to me, but I haven't been able to answer him. I don't want to answer him. Even if he threatened to break our deal, I would not stop. I crave the vines. Tears stream from my eyes like the never-ending gush of wetness between my legs, like the senseless, babbling pleas from my mouth.

Then, it all...stops. The pleasure fades away, but I don't mourn its loss. I'm replete, satiated beyond my wildest imaginings. The cocks soften and pull free, their sticky emissions splattering onto the base of the creature below me. I did not see it before, but the vines converge at a center point, a giant, rust-colored eye with a slit pupil.

It's been watching me the entire time. I look up to the ceiling. The glass overhead is clear now, showing a starry sky.

It *has* been hours.

The vines begin to lower me, but they do not release. The phalluses, disembodied once more, plop softly, almost comically onto the floor.

"My pet is pleased with you," Luthian says as one of the vines nuzzles against his face. The ones holding me tip me up, as if I'm standing with my arms and legs ridiculously spread in an anatomical illustration.

"I am pleased with it, Guardian." My voice is a razor-lined rasp. I need water and sleep and perhaps to never come again.

"Good," is the sum of Luthian's response. But the creature doesn't release me.

I look down at the eye. It blinks and rolls back, revealing what appears to be a kind of...mouth.

"Oh, is my precious hungry?" Luthian asks the vine that lies against his chest as if spent.

My heart hammers with reawaked fear. I know that Luthian won't feed me to the monster, but now its strange jaws terrify me. Circular row upon circular row of tall fangs begin to rotate and rise in tiers. The smallest approaches my swollen, weeping center, those thorny teeth whirring. It touches my thigh and I brace for the tearing of my skin. But these thorns are soft, more like leaves, tickling as they buzz closer to my cunt.

"Do you know what a creature like this eats?" Luthian asks.

I can't take anymore, I think, in a true panic. My muscles ache from straining. My cunt and ass are raw. I cannot, cannot climax again.

"They thrive on the essence of your orgasms." He strokes the vine languidly. "Unfortunately, he didn't get to taste any of yours. He must be starving."

"Guardian!" I begin to plead, but it's no use. I cry out in despair as the soft, wriggling worm of its mouth enters me.

Luthian gives me a cruel smile and says, "All right, my lovely pet. Feed."

* * * *

"Where do you go?"

It's a struggle to open my eyes. I'm so warm and content and relaxed in my bath. The fire crackles in the hearth and Luthian's fingers are delicious on my scalp as he washes my hair. "Hmm?"

His fingers still, and a smile crosses my mouth. "'Hmm,' Guardian?"

His chuckle flows like melted wax through my veins. How can I want more from him when I should be satisfied for days?

"You push through your fear, escape your pain somehow. All of my students do, but it's something some must be taught. You allow yourself to enter that place without instruction. I want to know..." He dips his fingers into the water and trails droplets up my arm before returning to my head. "Where do you go?"

I've been here, in this bathtub, in his arms, for what seems like hours, but my skin hasn't chilled, the water hasn't cooled, and he's taken his time and care washing every part of me with soap whose lather never seems to pollute the tub. It's the most relaxed I've ever been in my life, and he wishes me to think?

I choose not to think, and instead let the words come out as they will. "I picture my revenge, Guardian."

Luthian's fingers still again.

Though he doesn't solicit further, I continue. "I imagine all of my pain as the pain that will be inflicted on him. Breaking his bones. Slashing his flesh. I envision making him kneel before me. I feel myself cutting his wings off."

My guardian hisses, goes rigid behind me.

"Soap is getting into my eyes, Guardian." Have I stunned him? Frightened him? Let him be a little afraid of me. Now that I've learned the power of fear, it tastes delicious.

"Those are quite inventive thoughts," he murmurs. There's a scrape of glass as he lifts a decanter from the small table beside us. Warm water pours over my head, rinsing the suds and vanishing any trace of the dirt they carry away. "I do hope you'll never direct that ire toward me."

"I don't think I would ever be able to, Guardian." I let my head loll back onto his shoulder as rivulets flow down my neck and breasts.

"Cenere, I could almost believe that you like me." He traces one of those watery paths down my chest, beneath the surface, and cups my mound. "Or at the very least, you don't resent me."

I close my eyes and sigh. "Why wouldn't I like you, Guardian? You're upholding your end of our agreement. You're going to make me a queen. And I'll be able to fulfill every one of my revenge fantasies."

When he speaks again, his tone is different. Not teasing. Softer, almost pleading. "Don't let them consume you, Cenere. Your spirit is too bright a flame to be extinguished by hatred."

He can't possibly understand my hatred. There's no way anyone could. My rage is my own, a terrible thing locked away in my heart, a burning ember I will tend and feed until the blaze of it consumes my mother's killer.

"Yes, Guardian." I close my eyes and give myself over to his tender hands smoothing over my body.

It's the first promise I've made to him that I do not intend to keep.

Chapter Twelve

My day is free from lessons, but there's little for me to do at Luthian's home. Grand as it is, it offers little in the way of diversion. There are books, of course, but they're written in fae languages I can't understand. Even if I could read them, I would have to do so standing up; my backside is too sore for sitting. The ancient housekeeper offers to give me chores if it will prevent me from straying into her line of sight, so I opt instead to walk in the gardens.

I'm not certain where we are. I know I'm in Fablemere; the stars outside my windows at night are in their familiar constellations. Perhaps Luthian lives in the Springlands; the balmy weather and cheerful blooms on the hedges support that theory. I can rule out the Sorrowlands, where nothing grows and the sky is stained red. I suppose we could be near Lua, across The Divide. But we are far from my home in Grimm. Winter still held the land in its rainy grasp when I left there.

The garden is endless to my eye, tier after tier of fountains, hedges, and paths descending in slices toward an impossible horizon. I carefully note how far I walk, for I'll have to return. There is no chance I'll make it to the end, and even less that I would be able to make it all the way back.

So, I amuse myself by skipping stones in a basin of fish that leap with excitement at every ripple, their bodies painted in piebald spots of purple and green and creamy pearl. I smell the flowers, then pick some, winding stems and grass and blooms into a girlish crown for my hair. I'm lying on the grass, nearly napping in the warmth of the late afternoon sun, when a whisper of breeze and the tinkling of bells disturbs me.

Firo rides on a palanquin, his bandaged feet elevated before him. It appears his conveyance hovers in the air, but a shimmering, pale blue outlines the four sylphs that bear him; it's their language I heard floating on the air.

"Here," he commands them, and they sink to deposit the chair on the grass very near me before he waves his hand, dissipating them.

I'm unsure of what to do. I haven't been forbidden to speak to him, but I don't wish to. He's Luthian's student, as I am, but I feel no kinship toward him. It startles me to realize that I'm competitive; even when Cadwyn Thrace entered my mother's life and stole her attention from me, I felt my place in her heart was secure. But this situation, my deal with Luthian, the esteem with which he holds me, seems not only threatened by Firo's mere existence, but robbed of something I am innately entitled to.

Such emotions make humans ugly, I know. I try to banish them, but it's difficult. Firo is a faery. He has powers that I do not, allure that I cannot match.

I don't want him to be Luthian's pupil. I want to hold that position—and my Guardian's attention—alone.

"I thought faeries could heal themselves," I say with a sniff, covering my eyes with my forearm and lying back.

"We can. Luthian has forbidden it." Maddeningly, Firo seems unafflicted by the sickness of envy; his voice is cheerful and friendly.

I do not wish to be friends. "Why?"

"He says I won't learn obedience without consequence. That I should be more accepting of pain. Like you."

I push myself up. "Why are you speaking about me outside of my presence? I won't be the subject of gossip."

"You were the subject of praise, gentle lady." He smiles, and it is charming. Infuriatingly charming.

I sit up fully and arrange the skirts of my poofy white linen day dress around myself modestly. It's ridiculous, I know, considering what I've done to him and what he's seen me do with Luthian.

I chide myself for resorting to such posturing when it matters so little.

"You don't like me," Firo says, still smiling.

"I have no opinion of you. You're simply a student of Luthian's, as I am." I brush a small beetle from my sleeve.

"A student. Nothing more," Firo says pointedly. "There is nothing to fear from my presence."

My jaw drops. "You've mistaken my intent here."

"I beg ever so many pardons. I assumed you carried some romantic feeling for our teacher, and therefore disliked me out of a lover's jealousy." He fixes me with a teasing stare, challenging me to deny it.

And I can deny it because he's wrong. "If I perceive you as a threat, it is only because my purpose here is so great. I stand to lose much if I'm not successful."

"Do you believe I'm here out of curiosity, then? Nothing to gain from my presence?" he asks mildly.

"Your reason for being here is none of my concern." And yet, I'm curious. Greatly so. I do so desperately want to know what kind of deal Firo has made with Luthian, and if it has anything in common with mine. Instead, I ask him, "Why this ridiculous palanquin? Why not simply fly?"

"Because my wings are also healing," he says, spreading his hands. "And Luthian has told me that I lack in style. I thought he would approve of my choice of transport."

I can't help the smile that touches the corners of my mouth. "Style does seem to be a primary concern."

"I'm learning. Where I'm from, there isn't much use for it. Impractical, you see."

"And where are you from?" I ask.

"The Court of Time and Destiny." He holds up one hand and points to a signet I don't recognize. "I'm to be an ambassador to the Court of Pleasure and Torment."

"Ah. You need to learn the customs and ways." I nod in understanding. "I confess, I'm not familiar with the faery courts. Only the Court of Seasons, and the one we're training for."

"And why are you training for it?" he asks.

My tongue pauses at the roof of my mouth. I would have revealed the entire plan, anyway, but I recognize how very careful I must be in speaking to a future ambassador to the court. "My mother was a faery."

"Was?" he interjects with a frown.

Faeries, I know, often forget that immortality and invulnerability aren't interchangeable. While the ravages of time never touch them—thanks in part to the magic of the very court from whence Firo hails—they can still die. Yet, free from the curse of age, the possibility of their own mortality slips their minds.

"She was poisoned. By Cadwyn Thrace." I don't realize that I hoped for a flicker of recognition at the name until none comes. "He's a faery. He doesn't live at a court, but perhaps—"

Firo shakes his head. "I'm terribly sorry for your mother's death, but that name means nothing. Still, tell me why tragedy has brought you here."

"Luthian is my faery guardian. He granted the wish that resulted in my birth." That's safe enough to tell, I think.

"So, you're here out of obligation?" Firo is incredulous.

How much more can I reveal? "In a sense. I'm human but raised by faeries. I have no living family, having sprouted from a wish. I have none of the magical ability that made my mother an asset to the Court of Seasons, and no prospects among humans. But at the Court of Pleasure and Torment, I'll have value. I'll be desired and, hopefully, I'll earn a place there."

This answer seems to satisfy Firo. "Oh, they'll desire you. You were magnificent yesterday."

My face flushes hot and I look away. "I'm sorry. For the things I did to you. I know you didn't want them."

"I'm here of my free will," he says with a shrug. "And I learned from you."

It's not praise or flattery, but a statement of fact. And it makes jealousy's grip loosen a bit. I turn my face to the sky, relishing the sun, and ask, "Where are we? The Springlands?"

"Fellmoor," he says. "The south. About a day's ride from Siren's Call."

"I don't know where that is. I've had no formal lessons. My mother attempted to teach me, but she abhorred books. If it couldn't be learned from sinking my hands into the dirt, I didn't need to know it." I laugh fondly.

It's the first time her memory hasn't pricked at me like Luthian's diabolical thorn vines. I'm shocked into silence.

"It is like a faery, isn't it?" Firo muses to himself. "No matter. You won't be asked to draw any maps at court."

"No, I dare say my mind will not be what ensures my future." I snort derisively, a cold feeling settling into the pit of my stomach. I don't think of myself as particularly brilliant, and I'm certainly no conversationalist, having spent most of my life in the company of only my mother. It would be nice, though, to think that I could be valued for more than my beauty and Luthian's teachings.

It would be nice, I think, for someone like Firo to believe I have such value.

"May I tell you a secret?" I ask.

His eyes narrow. "Secrets are currency among the courts. Are you so sure you wish to spend one of yours on me?"

I don't see the harm, especially as he didn't recognize the name of my enemy. "Cadwyn Thrace, the faery that killed my mother... I'm going to the court to seek my revenge."

Firo tilts his head. "Go on."

"My hope is to make powerful connections." No need to tell him how powerful. "Then, when I have the means, I'll destroy him."

A smile widens Firo's mouth. "You're far more interesting now. Although, I wouldn't mention your plan to anyone. Faeries don't like to be manipulated. Especially by a human. And you never know what kind of allies a faery, even a solitary one, may have."

"I'll take that under advisement." And I'll wonder endlessly if I should have told this to Firo.

"Humans can have allies, too, of course," he says, lifting his face to the sun and blinking at the light.

"Are you suggesting that you might be mine?"

"That, lovely Cenere," he says, looking to me with a lop-sided grin, "is not impossible."

Chapter Thirteen

Time moved strangely through the next few weeks. It seemed to me, for a while, that I would be an ancient hag before we left for the Court of Pleasure and Torment. Now, though, I have the way of things. I rise in the morning and take my breakfast, usually with some wicked pleasure that Luthian has dreamed up. Then, it's to my lessons. The afternoon is almost always concentrated on pain and endurance, but dinner and after is a time for all manner of sensual delights. Then, when the moon is high, I bathe and slink exhausted between the covers to start all over again the next day.

"I have a surprise for you."

I'm seated on Luthian's lap, eating the most sumptuous little roasted mushrooms he feeds me by hand. His dressing gown cannot disguise the leap of his cock against me when he says the words.

I notice that more now, too; his arousal in the

early days always seemed perfunctory, a tool to be employed in teaching. Now, it is automatic; he genuinely wants me. I never mention it, as I don't think he'll like that I noticed.

I lift my brows as I swallow my last bite. "What have I done to earn a surprise?"

"You've been a very good student." He pauses. "And it's another lesson."

I want to scowl. I pout instead. Pouting, he's taught me, is playful and attractive, and often more effective than a frown.

He taps the end of my nose with his finger. "You'll enjoy it. And it's easy. Firo will do most of the work."

I squeeze my thighs together. "I do love watching you work with Firo."

"I knew you would. Are you still hungry?"

I shake my head.

He lifts his goblet of wine and presses it to my lips for a final drink. "Now, run along to your bedroom. Firo and I will be up soon."

As I walk to my room, my mind spins. Firo has never been in my bedroom. We've always had our lessons in the library or the study. Once, in the garden.

But never my room.

I enter as Brujon leaves. I still haven't discovered why she's there or what her purpose is, when Luthian can run the entire household on magic. Even the brooms here are enchanted to sweep on their own.

"Good evening, Brujon," I say with a courteous nod.

She mutters under her breath and bustles out.

My bathtub stands before the fire, as always. I almost call her back to tell her that my lessons aren't finished for the day. Then I realize that the white foam on the surface isn't a fluffy cloud of bubbles as it usually is.

Pearls.

The bathtub is filled with pearls.

I clap my hands in delight and drop to my knees beside the tub. The glimmering spheres are of a uniform, vibrant white, but not uniform in size; there are some so small, they could fit on the tiniest ring for the most diminutive pixie, and some so large, I dread the thought of the oyster they'd been harvested from. I dip my hand into them and relish the satiny feeling. I've become far more observant of sensation in my time with Luthian. We've had lessons to train me in that, too. I sat blindfolded in his study while he touched me with all manner of objects and quizzed me as to what they were made of and how they felt on—and inside of—my body.

I'm a different person now than the night I ran to the cenere tree and watered its roots with my tears. I was innocent then. My thoughts would not have turned, upon seeing a bathtub full of pearls, to how they might feel against my throat, my breasts, my thighs. But they do, and I assume that's the point. I quickly strip off my gown and drop it to the floor, where it vanishes, banished to the pages of the book once more.

My toes have only just touched the surface when the door opens and Luthian enters, followed by Firo. Luthian is still in his dressing gown, but Firo has been marched here nude and coated in shining oil.

Luthian grins at my nakedness, my foot poised to step into the tub. "I see you understood the purpose of my gift."

"I guessed at it, Guardian."

"Go on, then. Climb in."

My breath catches as my toes break the surface. It feels better than I imagined it would, the smooth, satiny spheres rolling over every inch of my exposed skin. I find the bottom of the tub, nudging pearls out of the way so I don't tumble, then step fully inside.

"While you were having your supper, Firo was being tended by some of my pets." Luthian strokes Firo's hair gently. "Tell her."

Firo swallows thickly, his eyes trained on my naked body as I lower myself into the pearls. I gasp when they touch my intimate flesh, and he looks almost pained. "A pile of writhing vines."

"Cenere knows all about my vines," Luthian sing-songs as he moves about the room extinguishing candles with two fingers. I've long ago stopped asking him why he does things physically that he could do with magic; the answer is always "style."

I squint, examining Firo's skin. "I see no blood, no pricks or scratches, Guardian."

"No thorns," Luthian says. "It was a different type of training."

My core floods with excitement at the scenarios that fill my mind.

"It was a rather intense session of denial." The words are tight leaving Firo's mouth. I know that of all the exercises, edging is the one he dislikes most.

It also means that he's desperate now, craving release.

Once, Luthian immobilized Firo and I with magic, barely a breath apart, so close we could feel the heat of each other's bodies, and tortured us with denial from dawn to nightfall, until we were both sobbing and begging and wild with lust. If Firo could have, he confessed later, he would have thrown me to the ground and fucked me so hard, we would have shattered the floor.

But after Luthian finished him off with mouth and deviously placed fingers, Firo was too exhausted to even remove himself from the study.

Luthian drops his dressing gown, revealing every inch of his blue-gray skin. His muscles ripple, feline and graceful, as he prowls a circle around my suffering companion. "We're celebrating tonight, Cenere. Firo has completed his training and in the morning, he'll leave for court."

My stomach drops. Firo and I don't know each other well; we are rarely in a position to speak alone and usually see each other only at lessons. But I hoped we could become allies, as he said in the garden. I expected that we would go to court at the same time, though I don't know where that expectation came from. Now, I will go alone, be alone, with no guarantee that our shared experience will unite us in purpose.

He can't be united in your purpose, I remind myself. *Your purpose requires the assassination of the king, the seduction of a prince.*

It's one thing for Firo to know my motivation. It's another entirely for an ambassador to the court to know the details of the plan.

I swallow down my disappointment and fix my expression to reveal none of it.

"Shall we give him the send-off he deserves, honey flower?" Luthian asks, stroking himself to hardness.

"Give me what I've waited for." Firo laughs breathlessly. "I'll be happy with that."

"I'll do better than that." Luthian gestures to me. "I'm going to give you Cenere."

My most intimate part clenches and I almost moan aloud. I've experienced the vines. Luthian has used all manner of wicked objects in me. But this is completely new, and I do desire Firo. Who would not? His skin like smoke-stained amber, the hard-etched lines of his lean body, the smoldering fire in his faery eyes.

"First, though, a treat for my lovely honey flower." Luthian points to the floor beside the tub. "Firo. On your knees."

When Firo steps closer, I see clearer that the sheen on his body is not oil, but drying sweat. I want to taste it. But I wasn't given permission to leave the tub, so I recline against the tall back and rest my arms on the sides. Even the slightest movement shifts the pearls all around me; a few slip between my folds to meet my own pearl, hard and insistent, nestled in its slick setting.

Luthian touches the head of his cock to Firo's lips. "Open."

Firo obeys. They're close enough that I miss no detail. The slippery shine of Firo's saliva on Luthian's blue-flushed skin. The pink of Firo's tongue darting out below Luthian's shaft in a movement that makes my Guardian's back go straight, his eyes pinch.

"He is exceptionally skilled," Luthian tells me when he finds himself again. "But you knew that."

"Yes, Guardian." I knew it well, for Luthian had once bound my legs open wide for Firo to feast between them until I screamed and begged for the pleasure to stop.

With a deep, shuddering inhale, Luthian tips his head back and surrenders to that singular talent, but moans, "Touch yourself, Cenere."

I scoop up a handful of the pearls and let them fall over my exposed breasts, shivering as they roll down. I take another and this time use the flat of my hand to rub them over my skin, as if soaping myself in a real bath. I do this again and again, while Luthian and Firo both steal glances. I smooth another handful over my throat, down again to play against my taut nipples. I writhe my hips beneath the surface, and the pearls at my center roll and gently pinch my labia and clit.

"Put them inside," Luthian commands, as if he sees what's happening beneath my legs.

I work my hand into the mass of spheres and

sweep a handful to my core, where I ache with emptiness. It's more unbearable now that I know I'll be filled by the long, hard length of Firo's cock. When I push the first of the pearls into my cunt, I clench down, thinking of how Firo's cum will feel leaking out of me as I lie, spent, in my bed. I shove in more, and more, until it seems impossible that another will fit. Then, I push my finger inside.

I gasp.

Luthian's mouth bends in an approving smile, but he doesn't open his eyes. "Make yourself come, honey flower."

My other hand joins its twin, stroking my clit while the pearls inside me roll with every pump of my finger, teasing my inner walls. Now and then, a few slip from me, coated in my juices, and I push more into their place. I rock my hips and the pearls all around me move, caressing me with phantom hands. I slide down, draw up my knees and let them fall wide apart. The pearls aren't enough; I crave Firo's cock, now that I know I'll have it. I push my finger deeper and another joins it, displacing more of the beads inside. My clit withdraws beneath my touch, my cunt clutches, body straining toward my impending release. I cry out at the pleasure, at the decadence of it all, and Luthian growls low his throat.

Pulling free from Firo's mouth, Luthian turns and finishes himself with a few swift strokes of his own fist, erupting over my upturned face, my heaving breasts, my open mouth. He scoops up some of the pearls and rubs them into the puddles on my skin as I swallow his seed with a grateful smile. With a flick of his hand, the pearls melt, leaving me coated in an impossible amount of cum. For a moment, I'm stunned into silence, until a laugh burbles up my throat.

Luthian reaches into the silky fluid and finds my

center. The pearls there have vanished, too, and he pushes his fingers in. I squeeze down on him, and the corner of his mouth lifts in amusement. "I think he's waited long enough, Cenere. It's time for Firo to have you."

Luthian takes my hand to help me up. He doesn't offer me a towel or to clean up any of the mess he's made; slippery footprints trail me all the way to my bed, which I don't care to lie on in this state.

I've done messier things in my time with them, I suppose, though I don't relish the idea of sleeping in stiff, dried sheets.

Luthian doesn't pull back the coverlet, which makes it a bit better. I slide across the silk with a giggle. The fluid on my skin hasn't dried at all. *Too bad it isn't the ogre cum,* I think. *I quite enjoyed that.*

I lie back and wait, watching the rise and jerking fall of Firo's chest.

"I apologize for the mess she's making," Luthian tells him. "I just couldn't bear to let you bathe her in yours without doing it first."

I doubt that Firo's raging, straining cock is too troubled by the thought. If anything, it flushes even darker.

"Come on, then." Luthian opens my legs for Firo. "Hop in."

Chapter Fourteen

As if unleashed, Firo is on me before I see him move. Faeries are fast, I've learned, when they wish to be. There is no art in his fucking. He merely wishes to spend. Having endured the talents of Luthian's "pet," I assume the denial was torturous. Firo plunges into me without hesitation, sobbing aloud in relief as he sinks in to the root.

"Wrap your legs around him," Luthian instructs me. "You won't hurt his wings. He'll move them."

I tentatively lift one knee back, and Firo's wings unfurl over us in an autumn-colored canopy nearly as wide as the one over the bed. Emboldened, I lift my other leg around his waist. It changes the fit of him against me, brings him tighter to me, and I gasp. It's so different, feeling another body atop mine, lying between my legs and inside of me. My skin prickles with anticipation everywhere it touches his. I find I must put my arms around his shoulders, too, and cling to him, pressing all of his flesh against mine.

Firo's hips move to withdraw, and he plunges in again before Luthian can stop him with a sternly barked, "I haven't given you permission to fuck her. Only to enter her!"

Sweat drips from Firo's brow with the agony of his restraint. "Please. I can't take anymore. I have to come."

It's unfair of me, but I intentionally ripple my muscles around him and giggle at his groan. Perhaps I can make him spend without him ever having to move. How disappointing that would be, I imagine.

"Poor Firo," Luthian says with a sly smile my way. "I fear you may be in some danger. She has a devious look about her."

"It's as good as they say," Firo gasps, sweat dripping from his forehead and onto mine, and I remember what Sarta said about faeries enjoying human pussy.

Luthian glances down at his nails. "I wouldn't know. All right, I suppose you may take your reward."

He wouldn't know?

Firo's fingers sink into my thigh, gripping me with bruising strength. My question over Luthian's words evaporates from my mind, consumed by the strength of Firo's body moving against mine, our skin sliding together, aided by the slippery fluid coating me.

"I can't hold out," Firo sobs, his hips lurching forward punishingly hard.

"I think you'll find that you can," Luthian says mildly.

Firo's eyes squeeze tightly shut. His movements lose their rhythm, and his mouth drops open to emit a groan.

He freezes. Luthian chuckles archly.

"Remove the spell!" Firo gasps.

"I will," Luthian says. Then, at Firo's sharp glance, Luthian holds his hands up innocently and adds, "I promise. But this is the first time Cenere has ever experienced this. I want it to be good for her. Don't you want to make it good for her?"

"I want to come!" Firo snarls, his desperation making him a wild thing. He pummels his cock into me and I squeak in surprise and pain, but his determination leaves him after a few futile thrusts.

Luthian clucks his tongue in pity. "You are free to come once Cenere has."

It shouldn't be difficult; the intimacy of our joining intensifies every sensation. But the thought of him spending inside me triggers a thought I've never had before. "Guardian... can a faery make a human pregnant?"

"Yes," Luthian answers, and at my wide-eyed panic he adds, "But only with intention. He will not release living essence into you."

"It won't matter because I will be dead," Firo seethes. "Please, Cenre. Please make yourself come."

I move a hand between us to relieve us both, my fingers playing a tune they know very well over my clit. I lock my ankles together behind his back, arch up from the bed, every muscle drawn tight with my impending release.

I should have known better than to take Luthian at his word, because the moment I reach the apex, the heartbeat that I'm about to tumble over...

I don't.

I gasp and blink up at Firo, and he knows. I'm trapped in the same state as he is, suspended on the very edge of release. It's always as terrible as the last time, and Firo has suffered this way for hours.

"Please," he whines, actual tears forming in his eyes. "Please, I can't take it. She feels so good."

"That's what I like to hear," Luthian says. "Tell me

how good she feels."

Firo swallows, closes his eyes, and strokes into me once, twice, enough to push me over the edge, if either of us could fall. "She's so hot and wet...and rough inside. There are ridges and... old gods, I can feel every one of them catching me."

"It is better than my pet?" Luthian asks.

"Yes!" Firo gasps without hesitation. "She's squeezing and... oh, fuck, I'm going to come!"

"You're not," Luthian says boredly. "I've heard that human cunts have the same effect on us as ogre cum."

"But not as violent. Not as overwhelming. I can feel everything. All of her. Not just on my cock but... oh fuck, it's like all of me is inside her, and every fiber of me is about to climax."

I laugh breathlessly at the description. I thought I learned all there was to know about the exciting sexual properties of the creatures of Fablemere. I never thought of myself as having those properties.

Luthian makes an interested noise, as if he's studying us and taking notes. "What would you give me, to be able to come inside her right now?"

"Anything," Firo answers. He doesn't even stop to think. "Gold. Jewels. Ships. Anything you ask of me, you can have."

"A tempting offer, but that isn't what I want," Luthian says. "What about information? Secrets?"

"I'll tell you anything!"

My eyes widen. Even caught as I am on the precipice of release, I recognize the danger of Firo's words.

I'm sure that's the point, as Luthian goes on, "Would you betray the secrets of your own court?"

"Yes!"

Anger flashes hot through me. That's not why he's been tormenting Firo, surely? To force him to give away information against his will?

"Would you murder the leader of your council?" Luthian paces around the bed. "If I put the blade in your hand and promised you this joy, would you sink a dagger into your Hierophant's heart?"

Firo grinds his teeth, taking a longer moment with this question. But his hips keep pumping between my thighs and he sobs, "Yes. Old gods, help me, I would. I would."

"And if I demanded a favor of you," Luthian asks. "You would agree, here and now, to perform that task, regardless of what it may entail?"

"Yes!"

"Then promise me. A binding vow, at this moment." Luthian's voice is low and serious, and I see on Firo's face that he knows it's no longer a game. "You will give me a favor."

Firo growls his helpless rage as he fights against himself. Finally, with a sob, he agrees. "Luthian of Mithrax, I grant you a favor! Now, let me come!"

Luthian snaps his fingers.

Firo's frantic thrusting ceases, but not before I'm tossed over the edge and into a churning sea of my own pleasure. I'm keenly aware of Firo's shout, a long, tortured cry that sounds like his very spirit has been torn out of him through his throat. I shake with the force of our mingled climax, wail with relief with each hot, strong burst of him. He empties all of his strength into me, it seems, for he slumps senseless over me, his head pinning my hair to the pillows while his cock still twitches and spurts.

"Congratulations, Cenere," Luthian says. "You've learned exactly how much that beautiful little cunt of yours is worth."

Ignoring him, Firo kisses my cheek. "It's wonderful, Cenere. You feel incredible."

"Thank you?" I'm not certain how I should respond to the compliment. I haven't done anything to cause it. The praise is entirely unearned.

Firo slides from my body with a groan. "If I stayed inside, I would never have left. Luthian, be serious. You've had her, haven't you?"

Luthian shakes his head. "No. You were the first to sample her."

"Then you've been with other humans like this one," Firo says.

Again, a shake of the head. "Never."

Firo climbs off the bed and strides to the bathtub, taking a towel to clean himself off. I lie frozen, stunned. Luthian has never been with a human? But he has knowledge of so many different creatures. Why are humans different?

Does he not want to lie with me?

Does he feel I am beneath him?

"Thank you, Luthian," Firo says, tossing the towel aside. He gestures to himself and is fully clothed at once, in fine satin breeches and a long coat with tails, in hues that match his broad, autumn wings. "Your teaching has been most enlightening."

"You've been a good student," Luthian tells him, dressing himself, as well. "You'll more than survive at court. I dare say you'll thrive there."

They clasp each other's forearms. It's as if I'm not there, as if there is no witness at all to this tender parting scene. They say their farewells, and Firo gives me a glance and a small nod as he strides from the room.

When the door is closed, Luthian finally deigns to look at me.

I push myself up and reach for the goblet of water on the side table.

"My honey flower, you should be very prou—"

I hurl the glass at him, and nearly hit him. He barely has time to wave the projectile out of existence before it smacks him. His brows draw together.

"Have I done something wrong?"

"Is that all I am to you? A means to an end?" I shout, trying pathetically to cover myself with my arms. I don't want to be naked in front of him. It's too vulnerable, even though he's seen every part of me already.

He tilts his head. "Yes. That cannot be news to you. I'm a means to an end for you, as well."

What a fool I am. Of course, I know all of this. But I'm angry and hurt, and I'm not sure why. "Why haven't you been with a human?"

"I've never had an interest," he says with maddening calm. "Cenere, I'm shocked at this outburst. We made an agreement."

"An agreement that you would train me," I spit back. "Not that you would use me to... That you would weaponize me and..."

But that was all part of what we discussed. Every bit of it.

"You entered this arrangement with the same goal I have. To make you a queen, ruling at Cassan's side. Human memories are short, but not that short." His eyes narrow. "Has something changed?"

Nothing has, but everything has, in ways I cannot begin to express in words, because I can't identify what I'm feeling. I'm angry, and that anger clouds every other thought in my mind. So, I ask again, "Why haven't you ever been with a human?"

"As I already told you, I'm not interested." He's annoyed with me; it radiates from him. "I'm going. You need time to calm yourself—"

"Is it because I'm ugly?" I demand, climbing from the bed to follow him toward the door. "Because I'm too innocent, even now? Am I beneath you because I'll never be as depraved as you are? As cruel and disaffected?"

He reaches for the handle and I make a swipe for

his arm, briefly catching his elbow before he wrenches away.

"Or am I beneath you because I'm human?" I demand.

One moment, I'm standing behind him. The next,
my back is against the door and his hand is around
my throat. He doesn't choke me, as he's done in our
games before. This is not a game. He's furious, his
starry gaze alight with a rain of silver fire.

"The reason I have not fucked you, Cenere, is not
because you're a human. It's because if I fucked you,
I would never stop. I would let my palace crumble, let
the world forget who I am, that I have ever existed. I
would abandon every scheme, forget every slight I've
yet to repay. Because if I were ever to be inside of
you, I would never leave."

"Then don't." I whisper.

My plea undoes something in him. The rage in
his eyes quells. The grip at my neck loosens. And
then his mouth is on mine, he's pressing me tighter against the door until the ornamental whorls in
the wood dig into my back. He fumbles between us
to unlace his breeches. My hands find their way beneath his shirt, roaming over his tightly muscled
chest, desperate to touch all of him. He jerks my
leg up to girdle his hip and I feel the tip of his cock
brush my center, the head of him barely pushing inside. I cry out in anticipation and—

He vanishes. I stand motionless, holding nothing,
my body aching and clenching, still longing to be
joined to him.

But he's gone.

Chapter Fifteen

The days following Firo's departure are not so dreary and lonely as I anticipated. His absence accelerates my training, likely because Luthian has more time now. He doesn't mention what happened after Firo left, and I don't either. It's an unspoken agreement: that moment never happened.

Not all of my lessons are pleasurable, tormented or not. I spend a full day in mind-numbing, knuckle-splitting tedium with the housekeeper, who I now suspect is kept around for more than simply style. She has a mental library of manners and protocol, and she doesn't want me to embarrass her.

In the evening, I'm fed by Luthian, teased, and tortured by him, but there is one boundary he never crosses. And at night, when my desire should be all but wrung out of me, I can't stop remembering how I was fucked by Firo in that very same bed, the incredible intimacy of being face-to-face, breath mingling, bodies straining together toward ecstasy.

Why, I wonder, would Luthian pass up the opportunity to have me in the same manner?

He's also stressed the importance of tenderness in the wake of our consensual violence. I worry that perhaps I don't fully understand how to turn my emotions so quickly from a desire to inflict suffering to nurturing. I suppose I'll simply mimic what I've experienced with my teacher, should the need arise. Luthian is a marvel, where such delicate care is concerned. I never leave an encounter feeling afraid or resentful, or as if I've done something reprehensible by enjoying myself.

Tonight, after a long session with a spurred whip, I lie across my bed while Luthian tends the wounds on my back. He passes his hand over the slashes he left behind, and my skin tingles as it knits back together.

"If anyone ever fails to heal you when they're finished with you, come to me," Luthian tells me. He doesn't sound as he usually does, cocky and in good humor.

"Guardian? Is anything the matter?" Asking him is better than imagining the harm that could come to me, harm that someone might not heal. That is a concern for later.

He sighs heavily and trails his fingertips down my now-smooth back before giving me a pat on my ass. "Let's get you into the bath."

Usually, he would join me in the tub, but tonight he simply carries me to it and lowers me into the steaming water. He doesn't remove his shirt, a black one with billowy sleeves and laces to draw it tight at his trim waist, or his black leather breeches.

I reach a hand out and touch his hip. "I like this, Guardian. You look very handsome."

"Thank you," he says benignly, but there is still

a sense that something isn't quite right. His smile is tight as he holds up two bottles of soap. "Stargrass or Sorrow Lily?"

"Sorrow Lily, please, Guardian," I say and watch silently as he adds the soap to my bath. With a snap of his fingers, the water in the tub begins to froth, stirring up a cloud of suds.

The movement and temperature of the water is exquisite on my exhausted body, and I close my eyes and recline my head with a soft moan of contentment.

Luthian inhales suddenly.

"Did you think of something?" I ask, opening one eye, just a bit.

What I see freezes the breath in my lungs. Luthian composes his expression quickly, but it's too late. I saw him. It was as if he looked at me through another faery's face, for in that brief moment, he was unrecognizable to me. Every time he's looked at me before, it's been with a self-assured, almost cocky smirk. As if he delights in owning me, delights in holding me prisoner to our bargain. As if he knows something secret that he won't disclose, and that secret gives him power over me.

But I caught him staring at me the way a lost dreamer looks up to the stars. The way someone gazes longingly at a thing they desperately desire but cannot have.

He clears his throat and turns away to face the fireplace. "We leave for the court tomorrow."

My heart plummets to my stomach.

"So soon?" I squeak out.

He chuckles without humor. "It's been weeks, Cenere. I've taken you as far as I can with your training. You've learned to be adaptable, obedient, and alluring. It's time you try out those skills on a broader audience."

I don't want to.

Of course, I knew this was the end goal, the sole reason I'm with Luthian in the first place. I should be pleased that I'm moving a step closer to my revenge on Thrace. But I'm also a part of Luthian's assassination plot. This feels quite a bit like stepping into a pit of broken glass carefully to avoid cutting my feet.

"I like it here, Guardian," I say softly.

He turns to me with a smile that doesn't reach his eyes. "I'm glad to hear it, honey flower. And I've enjoyed having you. But we can't drag our feet. We have an agreement and a plan."

"Yes, Guardian," I agree in a whisper.

He kneels beside the tub and takes up a sponge, applying more soap to it. He starts at my shoulder and works his way down my arm, pausing now and again to tickle me with sudsy fingers. "Beautiful Cenere. I dare say you're one of my finest creations."

I blush. I thought I was past that now, but his praise lightens my blood, sends it floating upward in joy like dandelion seeds on a breeze. "I hope I live up to your expectations."

He washes me dutifully, the way he usually does, but instead of magically drying me, he uses the towels beside the tub. I support myself with a hand on his shoulder as he bends to dry one foot, one calf, up to my thigh, then the other. For someone who doesn't want to drag his feet, he certainly takes a long time doing something he usually does by magic.

Perhaps, I think, my throat thick with tears, he's saying goodbye.

"Will you be with me at court?" I ask and hope my sadness doesn't show.

He looks up. "Of course, I will be. You're my ticket back into society."

"And will you continue to advise me?" But what I'm asking, desperately, is *will I be alone with you?*

Will this strange bond between Guardian and ward continue?

Will it become something else?

I startle myself with my own thoughts. I didn't know that I wanted something deeper, some attachment to him. I don't. My goal is to destroy Cadwyn Thrace, and I can't do that if I insist on sentimentality.

"It would be fairly fucking difficult to pull off our plan if I didn't." A frown creases his brow. "Why these questions?"

Because of the way you're looking at me. "I'm nervous. That's all."

"Cenere..." He sighs and stands, tossing the towel aside. The water evaporates from my skin and hair with a flick of his hand, and he pushes a few copper strands away from my face. "You are ready for this. You were born for it."

"You were born for it."

Something cold pools in my stomach. He granted my mother's wish. Surely, he doesn't mean...

But that would be absurd. I was born twenty-five springs ago. Mother counted by the crocuses, for they burst into bloom all around Elegwyn Manor while she labored. *"You banished the winter,"* she always said.

"How long have you been away from court?" I ask.

He looks to the ceiling for the answer. "It's difficult to know. Five hundred years, perhaps more." His eyes narrow. "Why do you ask?"

"Fashions may have changed. Customs." I cannot meet his eyes. I want to ask how long he's been plotting against the king. It might be better if I never know.

"That's what I have Sarta for." He smiles kindly at me. "I worry that perhaps you don't trust my judgement in these things."

"Of course, I do, Guardian," I murmur.

"I'll come to you in the morning, though, to reassure you. For your arrival, you should wear something daring, but without putting everything on display. Do you understand what I mean?"

"Now who doesn't trust whose judgment, Guardian?" I bat my lashes at him playfully.

He chuckles and walks toward the door. I almost throw myself at his feet and beg him not to go. Once he leaves this room, everything becomes final.

"You're trembling with nerves." He reaches into his pocket and produces a flat stone the size of his palm, rounded and smoothed and gleaming with a ribbon of light. "This will occupy your time and help you sleep."

My hand buzzes as if I'm holding onto a daisy-wing hive. The stone is in my palm, thrumming deep and steady.

"Make yourself spend. Six times, I think. Without moving the stone from your clit between. That spoils the fun." He opens the door.

"Guardian!" My voice is too sharp. I calm myself. "How will you know that I've done as you asked, if you don't stay?"

"I'll know," he promises darkly. "So don't try to cheat."

I do not doubt that he'll know, but I wish he would stay. He leaves me without a further word, and I climb into my big bed alone.

The stone doesn't know that I'm sad, that I'm frightened of what will come tomorrow. It vibrates cheerfully in my hand. With a deep breath, I spread my thighs and reach down to part my labia.

At the first touch of the stone against my piercing, I gasp. The sensation relays through the hoop, buzzing the delicate stamen beneath my hood. It takes almost nothing for the strange sensation to bring me to climax. But then, it doesn't feel quite so good; I want to pull the stone away from my oversensitive flesh. My Guardian warned me not to, though.

How would he know? my mind pleads.

He must be watching me. I don't know how. I cast my gaze around the room and kick the covers back, exposing myself without moving the stone away. I bend my knees and plant my feet against the mattress. The painful sensitivity passes and throbs into another climb. This one is sweeter, slower, and I rock my hips with it as it flows through my body in a gentle wave.

I reach my other hand down and plunge two fingers inside.

If Luthian is watching, let him watch. Let him see how I would respond to his touch if he were here with me. Although we haven't spoken of that night, of how achingly close he came to giving in, that doesn't mean I haven't thought of it. I have a million times over. And I know he has. He must have. The passion between us haunted every lesson after.

I pump my fingers, press deep on that marvelous spot near my opening. It's not enough. I sob in frustration.

Something cold touches my thigh and my eyes fly open. An object has appeared on the bed beside me, a glass phallus, as thick and heavy as Luthian's own cock, gently curving upward. I recognize it at once.

He is watching. He is longing for me, as I long for him.

I bring the glass cock to my dripping core and plunge it inside, crying out in relief as another climax takes me. I thrust the instrument harder, deeper, faster, using my legs to lift me up in rhythm, meeting every stroke.

"Oh, yes, Guardian," I whisper, and hope that he hears me. "Fuck me. Fuck me."

My mind fills with a fantasy of the door slamming open, Luthian striding in and replacing the glass cock with its living counterpart. I want it so badly that tears fill my eyes. I pound the phallus into me, my arm aching, the stone buzzing.

"Fuck me, Guardian! Make me yours!" I urge.

But I am still alone when a fourth, a fifth wrack my trembling limbs.

"Please!" I cry out, my ass lifting off the bed as I fuck myself relentlessly. "Please!"

My juices coat my fist; it's difficult to keep hold of the glass. *Come to me. Come inside of me. We both want it.*

But when my final climax is wrenched from my exhausted, sweating body, he still does not appear. A burst of wetness bathes my wrist and I scream out his name. Not "Guardian," but "Luthian!"

The flames in the fireplace leap, and the hearth cannot contain them. They burn silvery blue, scorching the ceiling, and extinguish on an icy wind.

Once again, he leaves me alone and weeping for him.

Chapter Sixteen

I wake early to pack my things, only to find almost everything has been packed away during the night. My comb and pretty hair ornaments remain out, as well as my wardrobe book. I open it eagerly to decide on a dress for my court debut.

I've settled on a few options when the memory of last night intrudes. Will my Guardian be cross with me? I used his name when he's told me not to, and names are powerful to the fae. I can't even use the excuse that I was insensate with pleasure—although I was—because he's trained me better than that. Even in my most passionate throes, I would not forget myself that way, and he knows it.

If he is angry, there isn't anything I can do now. I hum to myself as I turn the pages and settle on a dress that fits his instructions, exactly. The night-blue velvet appears on my body like ink the moment I press the pin through the parchment. Its long sleeves nearly sweep the ground, and wide panniers give the skirt a shape that no one could consider revealing, but the low scoop of the neck and the under-bust corset beneath expose the tops of my breasts and a hint of rosy nipple.

Winking diamonds and glittering gold set a field of stars across the night sky of fabric. I look myself over in the mirror, quite pleased with my selection, and with Sarta's handiwork.

"Stunning."

I turn at Luthian's voice. If he is angry with me, he doesn't show it. He beams with pride.

Suddenly, ridiculously bashful, I flush and look down at the dress. "I wasn't certain of the coloring, but—"

"Nonsense. You'd look beautiful in any color." He tilts his head. "Your hair... I think..."

With a wave of his hand, my copper ringlets are braided in a crown about my head, with a few tendrils loose to brush my shoulders.

"We don't wish to reveal too much," he reminds me. "Come to him like this, and the king will be driven wild. He'll want to see all this magnificence undone."

"Thank you, Guardian." The name is strange on my tongue, after last night.

There is a shift in his eyes, the fastest flash of silver, gone almost before it began.

He *was* watching. He heard.

I glance to the fireplace, the scorch marks that stain the white stone and the ceiling. Was that his anger, or...

The thought of him watching me, stroking himself, tormented by my pleas sends a shiver through me.

Frowning, he puts his hands on my shoulders. "There is no need for nerves. You're ready."

"Yes, Guardian." Thank all of my mother's old gods that he interpreted it as a shiver of fear. Perhaps we'll talk about last night, and the night Firo left, but today I must keep my wits about me. This is the future. I can't linger in the past.

Luthian tilts my chin up with the side of a crooked finger. "There. Hold your head like this. Don't deign to make eye contact with them. Enter the court as if you are fae royalty because you will soon be. Don't slouch. Don't let your face give away your fear. And do whatever is asked of you."

"Yes, Guardian." And so, it's time to embark on the next step, the one that will ultimately lead to Thrace's undoing. "I'm ready."

He steps back, and I note that we've selected similar colors for our arrival. The embroidery on his dark blue brocade coat is silver where mine is gold, however. His midnight hair is bound at his nape, and rings of silver and sapphire adorn every finger.

He catches me staring at them. "You're right. You need…"

Rings appear on my own fingers, and something at my throat. I check the mirror to see a slender silver cord, tight but not uncomfortable, banding my neck.

It's a chain. It drapes down my back and coils around Luthian's fist.

"There." Finally satisfied, Luthian offers his hand. I place mine delicately upon it.

I merely blink, and my bedroom has vanished. We're surrounded by faeries, in a room with opulent gold columns and gleaming white marble on the floor. Overhead, a sky-painted ceiling is adorned with real clouds that move on a breeze, stirring the loose curls at my temples.

But as beautiful as the architecture is, it doesn't compare to the gorgeous sea of fae around us. There is skin of pale milk, like mine, as well as russet and black as deep as Luthian's hair. A rainbow of varying intensity colors others, deep ruby, pale violet petal, leaf green and vibrant orange. Their wings are bat-like, dragonfly, daisywing, collections of flowers, delicate spiderwebs sparkling with dew. I spy lace, like Sarta's wings, but also a set of huge buttons, a pair of book pages, a sideways hourglass with silver sand constantly flowing. Every pair flutters with excitement; antennae twitch and spark.

And though I am dizzy with the sights before me, I do not allow my wonder to show. I keep my chin lifted, gaze straight ahead, face as still as that of a haughty corpse.

There is no disguising the beat of my pulse in the hollow of my throat, or the jerk of my bodice with the rhythm of my heart. The place is a wonder of glitter and gowns and finery.

And nudity. I notice several faeries wearing nothing at all, and I know my cheeks blush.

I walk beside Luthian as if we own the room, but it is beneath us. I sense as we pass that not all are pleased to see him. Fierce whispers mingle with the curious murmurs as the crowd parts.

"Luthian of Mithrax!" a voice roars, and the assembly splits into a loose formation of rows on either side of a long, grassy carpet.

At the end of it is a dais, and upon that dais is a throne, and upon that throne is an enraged faery.

Luthian stops. So do I. He bows from the waist, straightens, and nudges my hand. I find my wits and sink into a curtsey.

"Your Majesty," Luthian begins. "It's so good to—"

Spears of curling smoke ring us at the height of Luthian's neck, their barbed points aimed straight and true.

"You were banished five hundred winters ago,"

the king shouts.

He is a handsome king. Perhaps due to my mortality, I imagined he would look like a very old human. He's broad-shouldered, well-muscled, and when he rises to approach us, I note the defined strength of his thighs beneath his leather breeches. I imagined he would have a crown upon his head, being a king, but he simply has a mop of amber-tinged brown curls pushed back carelessly from his square-jawed face.

He stops before us, not sparing me a glance. But his eyes never leave Luthian's. "How dare you disobey me."

"I've come to make amends, my most gracious king." Luthian nudges me forward, but I have no desire to step directly into a barbed spear that will split my forehead. My gaze cuts sharply to him.

"Do you believe I've forgotten, in so short a time, the havoc you visited upon this court?" the king seethes.

So short a time? And then, my mind sticks on five hundred years. Was that the truth?

"You were born for it."

I'll pass out. I'll faint and fall on the spears and that will be the end of both of us.

"I've reflected on my actions," Luthian says. "I owe you an apology, Arcus."

The king's sun-kissed skin goes pale with fury at the sound of his own name.

I trust Luthian. He would not have led me into a trap he could not devise a way out of.

If he dies here, do I still get my wishes?

"I'm deeply sorry," Luthian goes on. "Not just for my betrayal of you, but my betrayal of the late queen. My actions were vile. Disgusting. Not in the way this court usually celebrates."

There's a titter of laughter through the otherwise

sepulcher-silent crowd.

The king notices me then. First, a glance from the corner of his eye. Then he doubles back for a longer look. "Who is this?"

"My bride," Luthian says.

This is not a part of the ruse that he's discussed with me, but I've promised to play along, and it's the only way I'll survive.

"Your bride." The king sneers. "A human."

"They don't last very long, I'm afraid," Luthian says, feigning disappointment. "But you know what they say about them."

"Everyone in this court knows well what is said about them." But the king takes a deep breath through his nose, as if trying to recover control that he's lost. "It's been a long time since I've had one, though."

"My bride has several sisters—"

I wonder at that. Now that I suspect the motive behind my birth, I suppose he could have fulfilled many such wishes.

The king waves his hand, brushing the smoke spears into nothingness. He holds my gaze for a long moment. There are no stars in his, but they gleam like a fold of mahogany silk as he snatches my wrist and turns away. I stumble after him as he drags me toward the dais. Should I fight him? Should I go obediently? Everything moves so quickly. I cast a look back at Luthian and see his stricken face, a hand reaching out toward me as if to pull me back.

"No. I think I'll amuse myself with this one," the king says, crushing my wrist in his grip until I cry out with pain.

"Your Majesty—" Luthian begins to protest, but King Arcus is striding up the dais, to his throne.

He means to take me before the entire court.

To humiliate Luthian.

I have to suppress a smug smile. My Guardian is devious. He's planned this all along. I'm almost giddy with how quickly the king has fallen for our ruse.

Arcus grabs the back of my head, sinking his hands into my bound hair and jerking hard. His tongue paints a hot swipe up my neck. "You've never had a king before, have you? You are permitted, and commanded, to answer me."

I think quickly. His roughness implies he enjoys inflicting pain. His anger implies he wants me to fear him. I force myself to tremble, my voice to quiver. "N-no, Your Majesty."

"I hope your husband has prepared you for our ways, or this will be a nasty surprise, indeed." Arcus chuckles, and I whimper. Across the room, Luthian stands still, his expression stricken, his eyes holding mine.

I almost believe he's truly despairing. To anyone who doesn't know our plans, he would appear to be.

Arcus laughs cruelly and pulls me to stand with my back pressed to his chest. His grip on my hair tightens, bringing tears to my eyes that will add a nice touch of authenticity to the scene. He uses his other hand to jerk down the front of my dress, exposing my breasts. He sucks in a mockingly appreciative breath as I squeeze my eyes shut.

"I see how you were tempted away from your kind, Luthian." Arcus palms my breast roughly, and there's a murmur of appreciation from the courtiers, who watch my humiliation with rapt attention.

Another tug rends the front of my dress entirely. He could merely wave a hand to undress me, so this violence is intentional. I lean into the role I'm playing and sob, try to cover myself.

He slaps my hands away. "No, no. Your husband will learn a lesson today. Hold her."

He shoves me forward. Pins scatter from my hair

as he tears his hand free. For a moment, it seems I'll plummet from the dais, but something catches me.

Sylphs made of cloud grab my wrists. I struggle against them and find they're surprisingly strong. I note that, should it ever come up again.

The king unlaces his breeches and frees himself. His shaft is long and thick, and I widen my eyes at the sight of it, as if terrified.

Size is a point of pride for creatures who have cocks. Luthian impressed that upon me during one of our etiquette lessons. In the case of King Arcus, I don't have to do much pretending to be impressed. I hope my shiver of anticipation is interpreted as fear. I make my face a mask of horror and struggle once more.

Arcus seats himself on the throne and motions to the sylphs. They push me forward, the toes of my slippers barely skimming the floor, as I try to scrabble away. With every renewed struggle, the desire darkening Arcus's gaze intensifies. He's so consumed with his lust for revenge against Luthian, he can't see through my ruse. All the better for me.

"Strip her." Arcus orders.

The Sylphs tear my gown away, rip the panniers and corset with claws of air like knives. I try to cover myself again, and sob openly.

The king holds his cock at the base. "Bring her."

"No!" I cry frantically. "No, Your Majesty, please!"

I scream, kicking my legs as the sylphs turn me to face the court.

They're enraptured. Every faery watches, some of them languidly touching each other or themselves, unable to tear their eyes away from the spectacle before them.

I remember my first night with Luthian, standing on the stage and touching myself while an audience of fae watched me.

Did Luthian know this would happen? Was he preparing me for it?

More sylphs materialize to hold my legs, to bend them into position as all four lower me onto Arcus's lap. The tip of his cock brushes my center and I renew my futile fight.

"She's wet already," Arcus announces, and the court laughs.

"Please, please!" I chant, false tears streaming down my face.

There is no mercy at the Court of Pleasure and Torment.

That's the word that will seal this moment. The plea that will intoxicate him, make him crave me. "Your Majesty, I beg of you! Mercy!"

He grabs my hips and brings me down upon him, filling me in one brutal thrust.

Chapter Seventeen

Unfortunately for the king, his assault on me does not have the desired effect. For him, it does. I'm sure he believes that I'm truly broken as I sob and fight to cover my nakedness, to hide the sight of his thick cock violating me. But I am not inconvenienced in the least getting roughly fucked in front of a room full of leering strangers. And Arcus is, in my limited experience—which does, to be fair, include Luthian's vines—a good fuck.

My only moral objection to it all is the fact that Arcus believes he's doing this to hurt and humiliate me. It doesn't make a terribly good first impression, but he'll be dead soon, so it doesn't matter.

As much as I try to play the part of the terrified human suffering a faery king's cruelty, my body responds in ways I can't control.

"Luthian, does she get this wet for you?" Arcus calls out, and captures my arms, pinning them behind my back.

Luthian doesn't answer. He pulls off a wonderful performance of locking his jaw, staring straight ahead at me, fists curled impotently at his sides.

"Humans feel incredible," the king goes on, his breath becoming labored. Our position and his size create a tight fit. Coupled with my excitement at being observed, I can't stop the soft moans that escape me with every flex of his hips.

"You're enjoying it, aren't you?" Arcus taunts. "You're going to come, in front of all these strangers. You're going to come on my cock while your pathetic mate watches. And he can do nothing to stop me."

His fingers find my clit and stroke it with uncanny skill. My internal muscles ripple around him and I feel my inevitable climax growing closer.

The courtiers are caught up now, the air filled with groans and gasps.

I feel every eye on me.

I lean back against Arcus, pulling all my muscles tight as his fingers race me toward release. I whimper, trying to hold back because that's what's expected of me. That's what's arousing him so, both his cruelty and his desire. My toes curl and I grind back on him, taking him as deep as our position allows. Then, I let myself tumble over, nudged to the edge with the knowledge that if I am here, in the king's lap, I am closer to my revenge. I imagine thrusting a dagger through his heart and come apart a shaking, shrieking mess, the wetness of my release splashing down my thighs.

Arcus laughs breathlessly, then grips my hips and stiffens as he pours into me without a sound.

The assembly claps politely, though some shouts of climax manage to rise above the applause.

The king pushes me off his lap and I tumble pathetically to the floor.

"That, Luthian of Mithrax, is a proper apology." Arcus stands, tucking himself away. "You may return to court, so long as you bring your wife. I'm not finished with her."

Luthian bows. "Thank you, Your Majesty."

"My statement was a bit vague," the king says. "What I mean is, your presence at court and the use of your wife are mandatory."

"Yes, Your Majesty." Luthian remains in his low bow until Arcus strides from the hall.

Luthian rushes to my side, takes his coat off and sweeps it around us. He gives me his hand to help me up, and by the time the coat swirls around my shoulders, we're back in my bedroom.

"You were magnificent!" Luthian catches me up in his arms and swings me in a circle.

Laughter burbles from my throat. I haven't felt so light since Mother died. I haven't had such hope.

Nor have I been so proud of myself, perhaps ever. *Magnificent.* I was *magnificent.*

Luthian sets me on my feet and looks me over. "He threw you down quite forcefully. Do you need healing?"

"My knee is probably bruised. And my thigh. My wrist, definitely." He raises his hand and I stop him. "Don't you think we should leave the marks? If the king plans on taking me again, I get the impression he'll like seeing them on me."

"You're absolutely right." Luthian's eyes sparkle with happiness. "Oh, my honey flower. I told you; you had nothing to worry about."

He's wrong. There's one thing to worry about. "Did the king give me his living essence?"

Luthian reaches down and presses his fingers into my core. It isn't a sensual touch. When he pulls his hand away, he examines the fluid and curses. "I can't tell. Sometimes, it looks different, but I can't be sure. I'll give you a potion to prevent conception, and you'll need to take it every time he's been with you."

A knock at the door interrupts us. I pull Luthian's coat tight around me and adopt my wretched act.

But it's just Brujon.

"I see we're back at court," the old woman says. She picks up the lovely crystal vase from the pedestal near the door and drops it to the floor. "Fuck you and remove the curse."

"Ask nicely," Luthian says, eyeing the mess on the floor.

She pushes the pedestal over, too.

"Lovely." Luthian's eyebrows raise. "Fine. I should have killed you, you know. Anyone else would have. You're free, per the terms of our bargain. And I return you to your previous state."

The air shimmers around the old woman. Her back straightens, her hair burns fiery red, her wrinkled and weathered skin turns smooth and tan. She stands before us a plump, golden faery with wings like droplets of molten glass. She blinks at us as if she doesn't recognize us.

Then she strides toward Luthian and slaps him full across the face.

"How dare you!" she shouts at him.

"How dare I what?" he seethes, cupping his jaw.

"Whatever it is you've done!" Her gaze cuts to me. "Who is this?"

"It's been five hundred years, Brujon," he tells her. "I cursed you."

"I knew it! I knew I was angry at you for some reason—" She pulls her hand back to slap him again and it freezes mid-air. "Five hundred years?"

"Your service has been appreciated, but I no longer need you." He waggles his fingers at her. "Run along."

"I'll bring charges against you." She shook her

finger at him. "King Arcus will—"

"King Arcus will have your wings pierced by hooks and drag you through the streets until nothing is left of you but paste." He catches the palm that flies his way. "You asked me to hide you."

She gapes at him. "I would never ask you for help."

"When faced with a painful death, you're not as brave as you believe." He sighs. "I knew breaking the curse would return you to your former state, but I didn't realize it would erase your last memories before the curse. I should have been more cautious."

"I'll recover my memories," she threatens. "Whatever you've done to me—"

"You were a housekeeper," I say.

Her eyes literally flame with fury. "I was your housekeeper?"

"You were a human woman. A very, very old human woman," I blurt.

"A very, very old human housekeeper," Brujon repeats, nodding her head and rolling her lips tightly together. "Great. That's great."

"The king has granted me a reprieve, but I have nothing for you. You'll have to seek out his forgiveness on your own," Luthian says.

"And how do I beg forgiveness for a transgression I can't even remember?" she shrieks.

Luthian shrugs. "I suggest you bring something to kneel on."

Brujon backs toward the door. "You'll pay, Luthian."

"I believe you meant to say, 'Thank you, Luthian'."

With a cry of rage, she sets my beautiful bed on fire and sweeps from the room, slamming the door behind her.

That's not fair. I'm not a part of this, I think to myself as Luthian hurries to extinguish the flames and restore the bed with his magic.

"What did you do to Brujon, Guardian?"

"You don't have to call me Guardian, anymore," he says, skirting the question. "We're supposed to be mates. Call me by my name."

I did call you by your name. No. I can't think of last night. That was the past, and we're in the glorious present.

"When do we go back to court?" I ask.

Luthian grins. "Go and look out the window."

I narrow my eyes in suspicion. My curiosity is too great. I drop his jacket to the ground and hurry to the window seat, kneeling upon it to look out at the gardens.

They are positively crowded with faeries, strolling past the fountains and along the paths, lying naked together on the grass in couples and writhing groups. I look back to Luthian, questioning, and open the window latch, swinging one outward. The house and gardens are connected to a much larger building with much larger grounds. The white stone shines in the sunlight, stretching endlessly to my right and to my left.

It's as if the entire manor has been slotted into a giant puzzle.

"We *are* at court," Luthian says with satisfaction. He reaches up to close the window and takes my hands in his, leading me back from the inquisitive stares of the people below. "Now that we are here, the game has become much more dangerous. You must watch every word you say, unless you are in my home. I have wards, but their magic doesn't extend to other parts of the palace. No speaking of our plans on the grounds, either."

"Yes, G—Luthian." My heart sinks a little. I've begun to think of him, at least, the version of him who was my teacher and not my partner in this endeavor, by the name he allowed only me to use. The loss of it stings. "But what of Brujon? She's heard you talk about all of it."

"She has no memory," he explains. "At least, no memory of her time as my housekeeper. She's exactly as she was before I cursed her."

"And you did that to hide her?" If he won't give me the entire story, perhaps I can write the missing lines, if given enough information.

"I had to. She also fell out of favor, but not just with Arcus. Her other enemies are dead now, though." From the sudden sharpness of his tone and the haunted silver in his eyes, there is no doubt that he was responsible for those deaths. His coldness and determination frighten me.

There's another knock. Luthian waves away the mess on the floor and calls, "Enter."

The faerie who comes in is a stranger, in pastel green livery and a powdered wig that looks quite ridiculous upon his head, as he is a frog.

I nearly faint.

"From His Most Glorious Majesty, Arcus the Cruel, King of The Court of Pleasure and Torment, Master of All Which Delights and Offends, Ruler of the House of—" the thing croaks.

"Yes, yes, I know who he is." Luthian waves an impatient hand to dismiss the frog courier and shuts the door behind him, already popping the seal on the letter that's been delivered. As Luthian scans the paper, his excitement lights his face with every line. "It's an invitation, my honey flower. From the king. He wants to see you tonight."

"Tonight?" My mind whirls. "I need my wardrobe. And a bath. And..."

Luthian comes to me and puts his hands on my shoulders. He places a gentle kiss on my forehead.

"This is your destiny, Cenere. Trust in it."

He's right. This is my destiny. It's Cadwyn Thrace's destiny, too.

And King Arcus's, though he doesn't know it yet.

Chapter Eighteen

"It is imperative that you keep Arcus's interest," Luthian tells me, not for the first time. He's almost as nervous as I was before we entered the throne room this morning.

I look myself over in the mirror, check my gown from one side then the other. For my private audience with the king, I've chosen a dress similar in style to the one I wore that morning. This one is bright, screaming red, with a deep V that reaches almost to my waist, and nothing beneath it. My breasts are barely contained by the laces across the bodice. "You don't think this is a bit...seductive? After the throne room, I assumed he wanted innocence to despoil."

"If that were the case, you're already spoiled," Luthian says, fluffing my ringlets over my bare shoulders. "He'll view your beauty tonight as a gesture of good will from me. And besides, he thinks you're my mate. He knows you're not innocent."

"True." I go to the immense jewelry box Luthian gifted me this afternoon. He was so pleased by my performance, he said I deserved a reward.

The only reward I want is for him to fuck me. I'm beginning to feel slighted.

I know it isn't crucial to our scheme. Still, the feeling of his cock pushed against me, so close to giving us both what we desperately want from each other, haunts me.

Luthian stands behind me and holds my gaze in the mirror. "Give him what he wants. I need him to trust you."

"He will." I've worked too long at my lessons to fail now.

"Good girl." He leans down and kisses the curve where my neck meets my shoulder. I shiver.

We walk downstairs, to the great hall, where a new egress appeared upon our return. It's tall, with a pointed arch, and swirling, colored glass fills two windows in the gleaming silver door. Luthian opens it onto a long, deserted gallery with black walls and black-and-white checked marble upon the floor. Two sylphs wait for me, reach out to snatch my wrists as they did that morning.

I jerk my chin up and say haughtily, "You will not put a hand on me. I am a guest of His Most Gracious Majesty."

They float back, but they flank me as I walk the length of the gallery, and they open another set of doors when we reach the end. I want to look back at Luthian. I try not to. He would not want me to.

I can't resist.

What I see stuns me. The same rage, the same pain from the throne room twists his features as he watches them deliver me to his enemy. But there is no one to see him here, no one to act for. And when our eyes meet, he looks away and closes the door.

I've seen something I wasn't supposed to see.

There's no time to wonder about it; the sylphs have delivered me directly to the king's chamber. The walls are black with long panels of ruby satin. Various implements are displayed proudly in the way a trophy hunter hangs his conquests. There are rods and canes, whips and paddles, restraints attached to the walls. Various objects for pleasure are there, too, from phalluses of varying sizes and materials to potions like the ones in Luthian's study. One entire end of the long room is a vast bed, made up with black silk and mounds of pillows. Shackles dangle from every post and from the headboard. A wide arch divides the room in half, and I stand before a long, black dining table set with a mouthwatering feast.

At the head of the table is King Arcus.

"Welcome, my lady," he says, gesturing to the seat at his right. "Do come join me."

"It would be my pleasure," I say, swallowing with exaggerated force so that he can see, even from where he sits, that I am afraid of him.

"You look beautiful," he says as I draw closer. "Did you pick that out for me, or did your mate?"

"I chose it. Luthian did not approve." How strange it is to say his name.

"You dressed this way for me." Arcus smiles, transparently pleased with himself. Of course, a king would have no shame. There is no need for it when one holds all the power.

Power.

That's what drives his lust. That knowledge is the key that will unlock my understanding, and therefore, my control, of him.

"He was so angry with me, but I wanted to impress you," I say as Arcus moves the chair back for me with magic. I sit and the chair slides to the table, where there is a plate set before me. *Sorry, Guardian,* I think. *I must disobey you.*

I wish I would have paid better attention at Brujon's lessons.

Arcus's eyebrows lift. "And he didn't? I would have thought that ridiculous climber would have sent you here to seduce me."

I shake my head. "Oh no, Your Majesty. He was frightfully upset with me at what transpired in the throne room today."

"With you?" Arcus pours some wine into the goblet before me.

"Because I liked it." I toy with a fork and don't look at his face. I simply hope that my words have had the intended effect and continue. "He's a fine lover, of course. But such a display of raw power, the way you dominated him and made him look a fool in front of those courtiers... well. You felt the evidence of my appreciation for your skill."

"I sense I'm being played with," the king says, and I glance up to find him studying me with undisguised suspicion.

"Not at all." My heart begins to pound. I force myself to keep calm. "The only reason he returned to court at all was to please me. He knows how much I enjoy cuckolding him."

"Is that so?" Arcus is intrigued. "The Luthian I knew would not have allowed a mortal to bring him so low."

"Your Majesty, if I may be so bold." I lift my skirts beneath the table and turn slightly, displaying my bare body beneath. "Half of your court would do anything to have this."

The king's hot gaze is fixed on the ring poking out between my labia. He takes a long breath. "You *are* bold. I enjoy that."

I lick my bottom lip.

"I enjoy breaking bold creatures who reach above their station." He sweeps the food and dishes near us onto the floor. Hidden among the crystal goblets and bowls of fruit are another set of shackles, these on thick chains.

The sylphs are upon me before I have a chance to react, but I wouldn't have fought them, anyway. I gasp as they lift me up and toss me onto the table, but I don't struggle, reaching my arms out helpfully so they can lock me into place. I am laid out before the king like a banquet, skirt tossed up, ass on the edge of the table and my cunt on offer to him.

He leans forward and takes a long, appreciative sniff. "You do bring a treasure with you. But be warned, you're not the only human who has ever come here believing that their sexual value will keep them safe. I can do exactly as I wish to you, and your mate cannot protect you."

I moan. "Yes, Your Majesty!"

He flicks my clit hard, and I can't help my gasp of pain. I writhe my hips as the pain fades into hunger for more sensation.

That earns me a sharp slap across my mound. He spreads my labia wide and slaps me again, directly on my burning clit. I whimper, "Oh, yes. Thank you, Your Majesty."

"You're either a talented liar or a true deviant, like your mate." He pushes his chair back. "We'll soon find out. Bring him."

Chained as I am, I can't see what enters the room. I hear scraping and shuffling, then a deep, lowing sound like a groan of approval.

"Welcome, old friend." The king claps one hand on whatever has entered. "Look at what I have for you."

"Arcus, you shouldn't have." The voice is so low, it sounds distorted and far away, though I hear the creature breathing like a bellows. It uses the king's name, so "old friend" wasn't a kindly exaggeration. I tip my head back to try and catch a glimpse of the stranger, but they're already walking around the other end of the table.

"Have you had a human before? They are so small and so tight. She might squeeze your cock right off," the king says, and finally, the two of them walk into view.

My heart freezes. It's a minotaur. He towers over the king, easily twice as tall as myself, and as broad as the table. There is a huge golden ring looping through his bovine septum, and his horns gleam with golden points. At the end of his neck, which is as wide as his head, is a body similar to that of a human, but more densely muscled than any I've ever seen. He wears a long robe open to the waist, and when he sheds it, I see that his legs are the same russet-and-white piebald as his head. Between them…

His head is not the only thing that resembles a bull.

Arcus leans against the minotaur and strokes the creature's chest. "You may have her, and then we may both take her at once."

The minotaur chuckles. "I would rather have her, then take you."

"You may have me any time." Arcus places a kiss on one of the creature's human-like nipples; they're both pierced, like the creature's nose.

And, I see as he lifts his long, heavy cock in his hand, so is the tip of *that*.

Arcus picks up a knife and plays with it as he walks to my head. "Are you afraid?"

I hold his gaze. "Do you want me to be, Your Majesty?"

He brings the blade to my throat.

I do not blink. I do not waver. I gaze into the cruel darkness of his eyes, and I do not back away from it.

He takes the knife away and brings it between my breasts, slicing the cords that hold my dress together.

The minotaur makes a snort of appreciation and reaches out to cup both of my breasts. "I can see why you like her. She's beautiful. And I know what you like to do with beautiful things." The minotaur squeezes my flesh until I can't help but cry out. He grabs my dress and rends the skirt in half, leaving me exposed in the ruin of fabric.

I'm in danger, with someone I don't trust the way I trust Luthian. Why does it excite me so?

Luthian promised me that no harm would come to me. He knows Arcus, likely knew that such a scenario was possible, or worse. Luthian would not have made such a promise if he didn't know he could keep it.

"Do I want you to be scared?" Arcus repeats my question with a happy little sigh. "I think you will be. I think you should be. But if you're not, if you do truly enjoy what we do to you tonight... then I believe you're the perfect mate for Luthian. And the perfect concubine for me."

I smile serenely at him. "Well, then. Let's put me to the test."

Chapter Nineteen

The minotaur takes his huge organ in his hand and strokes himself. What I had thought was the length of him nearly doubles as it emerges from its sheath. Arcus moves to stand beside him, his hand joining the minotaur's in a sensuous glide up and down the pink shaft.

"Remember, she's a mortal," the creature says in his distorted voice. "You'll need to give her some help, if she's going to take all of me."

All of him! Now, I *am* frightened; fully erect, his cock is longer than my leg. My eyes are wide when Arcus looks at me, and he laughs.

"Don't tell me you're backing out, now." He pauses. "Oh, that's right. You can't back out. I'm the king, and your wretched mate owes me."

I hate the king. He's vile and cruel and delights in a type of torment that is artless and cowardly. But he keeps accidentally saying things that only arouse me more.

I have changed in my time with Luthian.

Arcus brushes his hand over my trembling belly, down to my core. "There. She'll be able to accommodate you."

The minotaur's human hands are huge. He lays one on my mound and crooks his middle finger to push it inside me.

"I don't think she's as frightened as you believe," he says with a lowing chuckle.

"Is that true?" Arcus asks.

"I can't help it," I whimper. "I've never been with such a beautiful creature."

The minotaur crooks his thick finger and presses upward, and I moan both at the sensation and the obscene, wet noise my cunt makes while I grasp him.

"Thank you," he says, stroking his fingertip over and over that sensitive spot. "It's rare that I find a human woman so enthusiastic."

Arcus pulls out a chair with a scrape and sits beside me, palming one of my breasts with casual boredom. "This isn't an act then, Cenere? You truly desire this?"

"I desire anything, Your Majesty." I moan again to get my point across. "Do you believe Luthian of Mithrax would take a chaste maiden as his mate?"

"Yes," Arcus answers without hesitation. "I think he would take a chaste maiden and turn her into a harlot. Has he done that to you?"

I grin in response and lift my hips in rhythm with the minotaur's thrusting finger.

"I must taste her," the minotaur says with a desperate groan. He drops to his knees and lowers his head, hooking his horns beneath my legs and raising them high. I clench down on his fingers as he withdraws them, mewling in disappointment, but he replaces them quickly with a fat, rough tongue. It rasps over my clit and sweeps down, burrowing into my cunt with enough length to still press against my aching pearl.

It's incredible.

I tug at my chains, frustrated that I can't grab onto those horns and ride his mouth as his tongue twists back and forth, filling me as deeply as any cock could. It's so different, though, curling and lapping at my inner walls until I strain and sweat and drum my chained heels against the back of his neck. My movement is limited; all I can do is hump my hips and babble pleas to keep going, to never stop, to make me come.

Arcus leans over and takes my nipple into his mouth, drawing upon it while he pinches and rolls the other. My wickedness consumes me, and I meet his eyes, willing him to see the lust in my own. I gave him a satisfying performance in this throne room before. Tonight, I'll give him one he'll never forget.

The minotaur's breath chugs hot against my belly as he feasts on my dripping center, speeding up as my cries of pleasure quicken and ascend. The thrusts of the minotaur's tongue are faster, the rough brush against my clit unbearably sensitive. My body tightens and convulses, and I shout to bring down the ceiling as I come under his mouth.

He slurps and groans, his huge hands holding my hips so that I can't move away to seek relief from the now overwhelming sensation.

"He's not finished with you until he decides he's finished with you," Arcus warns.

And I think to myself, *Oh, no! Anything but that!*

It's all I can do to keep from laughing.

I'm not quite as merry about things when I've suffered through my fourth orgasm beneath the unrelenting onslaught of the creature's tongue. His saliva and my own uncontrollable bursts of wetness run down my ass and pool on the table beneath me. My hair is damp at the roots with sweat by the time the beast finally rises and wipes his shining snout.

"She tastes incredible. Would you like to try?" he asks, out of breath and with what I suspect is a terribly strained tongue.

Arcus shakes his head. "Another time. You deserve to fuck her. I suspect you need to, quite badly."

The minotaur gives a nod. His ridiculously long cock is hard enough to stand up on its own now, and it drips long strands of fluid. He takes the base in his hand, uses another halfway down, and backs up to align us.

Whatever magic Arcus has used, it had better work, or Luthian will have to complete his plan on his own.

The head of the minotaur's cock is tapered, so the tip slides in easily, but it's soon clear that his width is more impressive that it looks. I gasp as he stretches me. He has to take steps forward to feed more of his monstrous organ inside, but to my disbelief, I feel no pain, no trouble at all taking him in.

"Thank you, Your Majesty," I pant as my cunt swallows more and more of the minotaur's shaft. "Thank you!"

He chuckles. "Are you this shameless for your mate?"

"I'm this shameless, always." My breath catches as the minotaur's body finally reaches mine. I've never been stuffed so full, so deeply, and the fact that it's at all possible is a stunning work of magic I would never have imagined.

The minotaur lets out a long groan. "Arcus, you are a friend indeed, to share this with me. She's..."

"The best cunt you've ever had?" Arcus sounds dismayed to admit it. "While I would love to find fault with Luthian's skill in creating these exquisite creatures of lust, he's yet to disappoint me. I forgot how much I enjoyed having him at court."

"But this one is surely the best." The minotaur's voice is tight. "I would stay in her all night, if I could."

"By all means, spend in her," Arcus offers graciously. "I know you'll be able to please me after."

Being spoken of as though I'm simply an object spikes my arousal higher. "Oh, yes, please," I beg, barely exaggerating my breathlessness. "Use me for your pleasure."

Arcus laughs. "Look how hungry she is for you. How willing she is to debase herself for us."

"Any time you wish, Your Majesty. My body is yours to use—" I can't finish because the Minotaur withdraws. Not all the way, but a considerable length that drags slowly over every sensitive furrow. He thrusts forward again, and my eyes roll back in my head.

Because of the minotaur's beastly appearance, I wrongly assumed he would rut into me like an animal. He's a highly skilled lover, though, and fucks me with deliberate slowness that soon overwhelms me with sensation. I succumb to my helplessness, to my powerlessness as he wrings moans and whimpers from me that I cannot stifle. I come again, feel my stretched muscles flutter around him, and he bellows to the ceiling.

"Unchain her," he tells Arcus, and at once the shackles no longer hold me. The minotaur jerks my legs around his thick waist and pulls me up flush against him; impaled on his cock, I barely come up to his chest.

"I need to fuck her properly," he snarls, and staggers a few steps.

I cry out in pain as my back collides with the wall and I find myself trapped between two solid objects.

He rams his hips against mine, and I feel the plaster behind me crack under the force. He spears into me in short thrusts, then makes a sound I assume is the bovine equivalent of a growl. He pulls out of me entirely and slings me like a rag doll over his shoulder to stride to the bed.

I'm dizzy, achy, but my body is desperate to be filled again. When he grips me around my waist and slams me down on the entire of length of him, I scream in relief. He lifts me up and down, leaving me nothing to do but hang limp in his hands while he uses me. He lifts his hips and bounces me down harder, until the spell is no longer enough to keep him from battering me and I yelp with pain every time I take him down to the root. The brutal thrusts rake the length of his cock against my clit and I am powerless to keep from coming once more.

I gasp for breath and close my eyes to stop the room from whipping up and down in my vision, grit my teeth to keep them from knocking together. My hair flies around my face, my tits bounce painfully, and finally he pushes me down, his hands on my shoulders to hold me tightly on his cock. His release is scalding and forceful, and it sprays from the seal of my opening around his wide shaft. I slump forward, my sweat-drenched skin plastered against his, while he crushes me in his grip.

"What did I tell you?" Arcus asks smugly.

The minotaur gives a few short strokes, savoring my pussy while he softens. His cock finally falls from me to slap onto the bed.

"Cenere, mate of Luthian of Mithrax," the king says with a hint of amusement. "You may be my new favorite toy."

Chapter Twenty

Despite his proclamation that I'm his shiny new plaything, Arcus doesn't call on me the next day. It's all for the better, because Luthian informs me that the princes, one of whom is my intended—although he doesn't know it yet—have returned from a trip to The Sorrowlands.

I can only imagine what a son of Arcus gets up to in a land of vampires and other assorted horrors.

"Is he quite so insufferable as his father?" I ask while Luthian inspects me in my bedroom.

"Cassan? No. I actually enjoy his company. We've had many delightful encounters." Luthian tugs at the front of my gown. It's a frothy white confection of soft linen that will be nearly transparent in the sunlight, perfect for our stroll through the gardens. The neckline sweeps below my breasts, fully exposing them, and a long slit up the skirt reveals flashes of the copper curls over my mound with every step. He untucks a ruffle at my shoulder and steps back. "You didn't enjoy your time with the king?"

"The king is impressed with me. That's all that matters." The fact that he doesn't understand the art of torment the way Luthian does is inconsequential. The king will be gone soon enough. I lower my voice, though I know our conversations are safe behind Luthian's wards. "When will you dispatch him?"

"As soon as I get the chance." He offers me his arm. "Now, shall we go intrigue your future mate?"

We exit into the garden that once had been deserted during my afternoon strolls, but which now teems with faeries taking advantage of the soft grass and trickling fountains. The atmosphere here is playful, focused on pleasure rather than torment, at first sight. But then we approach a huge circular fountain and I note the ornamentation has changed since the last time I saw it. Where before it was simply a tall column with an overflowing basin atop it, there are figures now. Faeries in chains, hanging from that basin, their legs spread wide as stone fish in front of each of them spit a steady stream of water over their splayed labia. They send up a cacophony of moans and shouts, all of them twisting and writhing in the throes of orgasm one moment, begging and desperately seeking escape the next.

Luthian pulls me to his side and tweaks one of my nipples. "I see that excites you. Should I mark you down as a volunteer?"

I swat his hand away with a laugh. "I think you know the answer. But perhaps it's something Cassan can arrange once he meets me. If he likes me."

"He's young and eager. He'll likely spend the moment he enters you." Luthian pauses. "But he won't like that pointed out. He's proud. No matter what he does, you must lavish him with compliments. Make him feel as if he's the only faery who has ever adequately pleased you."

"Even his father?" I ask.

"Especially his father."

And yet, that point sticks with me. I can't quite comprehend it. "Do you really think he'll be interested in taking someone his father has already had?"

"Familial complications seem to be a mortal hang-up. It wouldn't matter to him if his father took you on the dinner table during the Yule feast. He'd probably fuck you directly after, without cleaning off His Majesty's seed."

"Then I hope we're not still here for Yule," I say, looking ahead to where a large, colorful tent has been erected over a reflecting basin. A royal standard flutters from the center point of the tent's roof.

"I believe we've found the prince," I murmur with a sly glance to Luthian.

As we approach, I note that the tent is made up of finer fabric than even my most extravagant gowns. The wealth and indulgence of the fae is a marvel to me; I always assumed every faery court was like the Court of Seasons, where there were no walls, no finery, nothing but spirits of nature unconstrained.

This all seems very...human.

But I would never say so.

"Is that... Luthian?" a voice calls out from within the tent. "Luthian of Mithrax?"

"Your Highness," Luthian says as a figure moves through the courtiers crowded into the tent.

The faery that bounds toward us is dripping wet. His white shirt and breeches cling to him, transparent from water. The breeches hang open, and he makes no move to cover himself as he jogs toward us. His boyish smile is in stark contrast to his wide jaw and broad shoulders, and he slicks a hand over his black curls, pushing them back from his face.

"That's a better welcome than we got from your

father," Luthian says, reaching out as if to clasp the prince's forearm, but pulling him into a hearty embrace, instead.

"I have no doubt," Cassan laughs. He steps back and looks at me. "We, you say?"

"My mate." Luthian nudges me into a curtsey. "She's human, and this is her first time at court. Do forgive her manners."

"Your Highness," I say, sinking low and staying in that position, but making sure not to tip my head forward. It would obscure the prince's view of my bare breasts, which I believe is all he's truly seen of me, as his eyes have yet to reach my face.

"Please, get up. Get up," the prince says, and offers his hand. "You're the mate of one of my dearest and oldest friends. Call me Cassan."

Dearest and oldest friend? Luthian never mentioned that the connection was so deep. It's beginning to make sense that he would wish to see Cassan on the throne, rather than the elder brother.

Cassan manages to briefly tear his attention away from my chest to lean in close to Luthian. "The fishermen of Siren's Call sent us mermaids. Have you ever fucked a mermaid?"

Luthian laughs. "I believe I've fucked everything."

"You probably have." Cassan frowns, obviously disappointed. He casts me a wink and says, "Your mate is legendary for his prowess."

I wouldn't know, I want to snap, but I can't reveal that Luthian has all but rejected me. "I'm impressed. Especially after what I've seen here, in my short time."

"She took a minotaur last night," Luthian says, a note of pride in his voice.

Cassan's brows lift. "That must have been a sight."

"I wouldn't know. I didn't see it. He's a friend of

your father's. They shared her last night, but I was not invited." Luthian's jaw clenches.

"That's simply bad manners. You know I would ask you to watch if I ever commanded your mate to lie with a minotaur." Cassan swears this like an oath of friendship, and I can't stifle my giggle.

This causes the prince's eyes to light up with merriment. I see my way in. He's not like his father, who revels in cruelty and fear. Cassan is adventurous and fun, and I know he will respond best if I am, too.

"Your Highness," I begin, then correct myself. "Cassan. I've never fucked a mermaid. Would you tell me what it's like?"

"Wet." He shakes droplets from his sleeves, then looks back to the tent. "Why not experience it for yourself? They're very enthusiastic."

I give Luthian a look as if asking permission, and he replies with a slanted smile. "If the prince commands it..."

I grin, hop up on my toes, and peck his cheek for good measure. The more I display affection for him, the more the court will believe that he's desperately in love with me. And that will only make me more attractive to the bastard king.

Cassan offers me his hand, and I place mine atop his as he walks me toward the tent, two steps ahead of Luthian, who follows dutifully behind.

"I've never had a human," Cassan says, in a low tone meant only for me. "I hear it's an unparalleled experience."

"Well, I am no mermaid, I'm afraid," I demure as we step into the tent.

The large reflecting basin is occupied by two stunning beauties with long tails and enormous fins. I've seen paintings of mermaids before, but I've never seen one in person; few have. They're taller than I expected, or longer, rather, as they're reclining horizontally with their heads just below the surface of the water. One of them has dark gray skin, like that of a shark, and a long mop of lavender hair. It matches the iridescent purple of her tail, and paler, frilled fins languidly flutter through the water. The second has dark brown skin all over, with pale white patches where it seems no pigment has touched her. Her long pink locks are pinned back with shell ornaments, and her pink tail entwines lazily with that of the mermaid beside her.

"Ladies," Cassan calls to them, and they sit up eagerly, their long hair cascading over their breasts. "This is my good friend... what's your name?"

"Cenere," I say, as the prince's friends laugh.

"I told her what fun I had with you, and she's dying of curiosity," Cassan goes on.

The mermaids look at each other. The pink one claps her hands with glee. "A human!"

"It's been so long," the purple one says wistfully.

"Try not to drown her," Cassan says, and helps me step over the ledge and into the pool. It's shallow, but still intimidating; this water is their home, and I am quite literally out of my element.

"Don't be afraid," the pink one says, crooking her finger. "It's been so long since I've had a human."

The purple one pushes my skirt open. "And it's like us!"

They both coo in delight.

Their glee intoxicates me, and I find myself laughing along with them. Their laughter is like music.

"Come lie with us," the purple one croons. I sink to my knees in the water, and they guide me to lie on my side between them. The pink one props her arm beneath my head, so I don't go under.

"I'm not sure how—" I begin, and the purple one catches my hand, guiding it down the pink one's body. I've never given much thought to mermaid anatomy. In my home in Grimm, I didn't have a reason to think of them beyond creatures that lived somewhere far away, that I was unlikely to see. Yet now, I lie in their arms, and my fingertips are skating down soft scales to encounter a rounded protuberance about as long and thick as my thumb, crowning two ruffled fins that flank a soft, sucking opening.

My eyes widen.

"We can guide you," the pink one says as the purple one urges my fingers to close around what I assume is the pink's clit.

Purple leans in and sucks my earlobe between her teeth. "We can make you forget all about your human...men."

They laugh together as if it's the funniest thing they've ever heard. I can't help but laugh, as well. They're truly enchanting. I don't even bother pointing out that I'm here with a faery, that a human man has never touched me.

Will I find them exotic, I wonder, should I ever have cause to lie with one of my own kind?

The pink mermaid dips her head to kiss me, and I open gratefully under her soft lips. Purple's hands cover my breasts, kneading them as her own slide against my back through the thin, sodden fabric of my gown. Their bodies are pressed close to me, skin and scale sliding together. Pink takes my calf and urges it over her hip, bringing her clit against my center. It rubs against mine and she undulates her hips, the fluttering edges of her intimate fins caressing me. The rocking motion sets the surface of the water gently lapping over us, and she sighs, closing her pink eyes.

Behind me, purple positions her own clit in the cleft of my buttocks. To my shock, she penetrates me there, slipping her unusual organ into my ass and flexing her tail. It falls between my legs to twine with her partner's, and soon we're moving in a slow, languorous writhe. Their hands are everywhere, exploring me, exploring each other. Our mouths meet, three tongues dancing together. Pink's clit strains against mine, and purple breathes heavily in my ear as she shallowly fucks my ass. I lose track of everything around me except for their bodies, their hands, their expert tongues on my nipples, my throat, my gasping, panting mouth. One moment, I'm pushing against pink, then pushing back on purple.

A noise begins low in pink's throat, then rises in a high, thin, eerie song. It's ethereal and terrible, and purple soon joins in an unnerving chorus. My body burns for release with every stroke of pink's clit against mine, every thrust of purple's hips.

"Yes," I whimper, clinging to them, and soon my own voice is rising, not in their otherworldly notes but a frantic, desperate cry as I move closer and closer to my release. Their tailfins thrash, showering the assembled courtiers with droplets. Our motion is emptying the basin of its contents, but they continue, striving with me toward a climax that takes us all over at once, their songs cutting silent with guttural stops as their bodies spasm against my own writhing form.

I regain my senses to the sound of wild applause.

"That," Cassan says, clapping more enthusiastically than any of the faeries, "has made my journey home entirely worth it."

Chapter Twenty-One

We bid the mermaids farewell, although they do attempt to drag me back into the pool with them. Several times, I almost give in, my legs still wobbling. I can see why sailors are lured to their doom.

Luthian dries me with magic and suggests a nice, sunny spot for us all to bask in, and the prince and my pretend mate catch up while I doze in the grass. Now and again, I open my eyes to watch faeries and other creatures pass by, but then my lids slide closed, and I let myself drift.

That is, until I spot a faery with autumn leaf wings walking with a piebald minotaur. I push myself up on my hands. There is no doubt the faery is Firo; I would recognize his striking profile and gorgeous brown skin anywhere.

When there is a lull in his conversation, I ask, "Luthian, I think I see someone I know. Would you mind if I greeted him?"

"Not at all." He nods toward Firo. "Tell him I send my fondest regards."

I get to my feet and skip across the grass, toward the hedges that line the crushed stone walkway. "Firo! Ambassador Firo!"

He turns, seeking out the sound. When he sees me, he flashes me his gorgeous smile. "Cenere!"

I run into his open arms and give him a crushing hug, hoping he doesn't mind my still-damp clothes.

"You're here with Luthian?" He nods toward the two faeries who are still occupied with conversation.

"Yes. My mate thought it was time to return to court." I stress the mate part.

Firo's brows lift. "Congratulations on your binding."

"Thank you." I turn to Firo's companion. "Sir."

Firo takes a breath as if suddenly remembering his manners. "Cenere, this is my friend, Utrax."

The minotaur makes an expression I believe to be a smile, though it's difficult to tell on a bovine head. "We've met, Firo."

"But I did not get your name," I point out.

He snorts a bullish laugh. "It wasn't the usual introduction."

Firo's eyes widen. "The two of you?"

"His Majesty is very generous to his friends," I say with a slight purse of my lips that can leave Firo no doubt as to what I'm implying.

"How long have you been here?" the faery asks.

"We arrived yesterday." I laugh at his look of surprise.

"And she's made quite an impression," Utrax says. "There are many who wish to have her. I'm honored to have been among the first."

"After the king, of course." I give Firo a little smirk.

Firo's lips twist in amusement. "I had no doubt

you'd do well here at court. And if ever you're in need of me…"

I blush hot as his gaze travels down, over my exposed breasts and what little of my body is hidden by the thin linen. "Your meaning is perfectly understood."

His eyes pinch at the corners. "Is it?"

"Cenere! Lovely Cenere!"

I turn at the prince's voice.

"Go," Firo says. "I'm sure we'll meet again."

"If you survive me," Utrax says, leaning close to Firo's ear.

I hurry off, but I note that the king's friend isn't just walking with Firo, a faery I know. He's speaking with the ambassador from the Court of Time and Destiny. Firo's position at court is wholly political. To be making friends with someone so close to the king is…interesting.

I'll tell Luthian later.

Cassan puts his arm out and motions for me to sit beside him on the grass. When I do, he pulls me in close. "I was just telling your mate about my birthday wish."

"Is he giving away wishes for free now?" I tease.

"I told him that I want you," Cassan goes on. "Presented to me on a bed of silk, denied for so long that you beg for my cock. In such a frenzy that you come the moment I enter you."

"Because His Royal Highness knows that he'll last only seconds in a cunt as exquisite as yours," Luthian says.

I turn my adoring gaze up to Cassan. "I'm flattered that you think I would make such a pleasing gift for you, but when is your birthday?"

"In two weeks." He sighs deeply at the tragedy.

I shake my head. "I will hardly be a novelty. Surely, you'll take me before then. Two weeks seems like such an agonizing wait."

"I don't know why I can't simply have my celebration now." His cock, still unencumbered by his breeches, begins to stiffen. "We could have the entire scenario arranged by this evening."

"Cassan doesn't understand the concept of patience," Luthian says, and tips his forehead just slightly toward me.

Anticipation. A cornerstone of our lessons. I take the hint and run away with it. "That's too bad. I find the waiting, the longing, is such an aphrodisiac."

"You two are made for each other," Cassan says, as if Luthian and I share the same infuriating flaw.

"Just think of it," I say, trying to picture a scene that will flatter and entice the prince. "Me, laid out before you on a bed of silk, wild with desire."

He groans low in his throat, though my words are but an echo of what he's already imagined.

Emboldened, I reach out and dance my fingertips down his cock. Another groan. I take it as my permission to go further, and wrap my whole fist around him, stroking slowly. "Can you see it, Your Highness? My bare body writhing while I whimper and plead for release? My wet cunt clutching, aching to be filled by you?"

"Fuck..." He puts his hand over mine and guides me to go faster. "I'm going to have you right now."

"You may," Luthian says, sounding bored.

The prince has me pinned before I can take another breath. He forces his knee between my legs to spread them, and he's in position, cock at the very entrance of my body before Luthian adds, "Or you could wait. Tantalize yourself with restraint until your birthday and have her for the first time there, in front of an adoring court."

"Ooh, what a lovely idea," I say, though I have no doubt that Cassan is only a heartbeat away from sheathing himself deep inside me. "I do so like being displayed. You could spend all day being denied, as well. Think of how incredible it would be, both of us reaching our ecstasy together in the same breath."

He pushes forward, just a little. Just enough to feel the slickness at my opening.

With a curse, he rolls off me and lies back panting on the grass. "You both make an excellent point. Which is deeply upsetting. But who am I to refuse such a challenge?"

"I don't think you'll be able to hold out," Luthian says, distracted by examining his fingernails.

"Shall we make a bet?" Cassan challenges.

"Certainly. For no stakes at all, I wager that Prince Cassan of the Court of Pleasure and Torment will not be able to withstand my mate's charms." Luthian chuckles. "In fact, I believe that by dinner tonight, you'll throw her over something and breed her like a mare."

Cassan groans and covers his face, muffling his words. "I need my cock and my face ridden, immediately."

Luthian nods to me, and I get onto my knees, shuffling toward Cassan's head.

"No, no," he says, giving my ass a slap. "Get naked. And face your mate. I want you to watch him."

My jaw drops, and I see Luthian's knowing smirk. I expected quite a lot from our adventure at court, but I didn't think I would see my guardian get fucked.

Luthian waves his hand and all three of us are naked, still in the grass. A jar of unguent appears in his palm, and he uses it to grease Cassan's cock. The prince guides me into position and pulls me down, burying his face in my center. I do as he commands and watch Luthian straddle Cassan's waist. He aligns the prince's huge shaft with one hand and sinks back on it, a sharp exhale escaping him. I feel Cassan's moan, more than hear it.

Luthian rolls his hips in a smooth rhythm, stroking himself with one hand. A few faeries stop to watch us, from a respectful distance, so I toss my head and slick my dripping cunt over Cassan's face from chin to forehead and back.

They should know my worth before I am queen, so I have nothing to prove once I gain the crown.

Luthian's strong thighs flex as he rocks back and forth, and his cock drips a stream of precum that pools on the prince's stomach. I've seen the same with Firo, when Luthian taught me to find the spot inside that would intensify and elevate sensation. I catch his eye, drop my gaze to the growing puddle, then back up, wetting my bottom lip with a deliberately slow tongue. Luthian's soft groan is a warning: he's fighting for control, fighting to maintain his unflappable facade.

He takes such pride in his self-control. If I make him come undone here, if I make him mindless and senseless with lust in front of these courtiers, they'll be even more curious about my skills than they already are. I'll be in high demand. And with that popularity will come power. He has to know that.

I lean forward, grinding my clit against Cassan's tongue, and crawl over his body until I'm face-to-face with Luthian's shaft.

"Cenere," he whispers.

I don't wait for him to tell me not to. I open my mouth and suck the tip of him inside. It's as far as I can reach, but it's enough to make Luthian close his eyes and take a few steadying breaths. But when he opens them again, it's to meet my adoring stare while I lap away the salty fluid.

"Will you come all over my face, Luthian?" I ask, batting my eyes. "Or will you throw me on the ground and spend inside me?"

The noise he makes is pained and pleading. He hastens his speed, and Cassan lifts his hips in rhythm, until a percussive skin-on-skin slap sets the beat for all of our movements. Cassan's tongue burrows beneath the hood of my clit and sets up a side-to-side motion over the sensitive points of that unprotected and ultra-sensitive flesh. His muffled grunts of pleasure heighten my passion, but it's Luthian's unrestrained moaning that's going to take me over the edge. Even in the moment of climax, he's always been quiet and controlled with me.

Except for the fire, I realize. I picture Luthian in his bed, though I've never seen his chambers. I imagine his toes curling and digging into black silk as he pounds his cock through his fist. I imagine his cries as he watches me, as my pleas for him to come fuck me torture him. I see the sweat on his brow and the rapture twisting his face as he erupts, flowing over his hand, shouting my name.

I come, my pussy flooding over Cassan's face, and he groans and grabs my hips, holding me tighter, thrusting his tongue into me and lapping up my juices while I squirm and whimper.

Luthian sinks a hand into my curls and pulls my head up, snarling, "Keep your mouth open."

I obey him. I'll obey his every whim. Even when I am queen, I will still bow to him.

He pumps his cock, his hand flying fast, and shouts as he slashes cum across my tongue. I swallow again and again, but his release seems never-ending. Cassan's thrusts speed up and become harder, wrenching another cry of ecstasy from Luthian. The prince arches his back, almost toppling me off his chest, and pulls his panting mouth from my cunt to give a guttural cry as he empties himself inside of Luthian.

Cassan gently pats my thigh in a signal to climb off him, so I roll onto the grass in in a boneless heap. Luthian collapses beside the prince, as well, and the three of us lie in our bliss while the courtiers murmur their excitement.

A group of four faeries have joined us on our grassy spot, limbs and tongues entangling, and Cassan watches them as he wipes his brow. "It seems you're quite inspiring, Cenere. Luthian, I have a new proposal for our wager."

Luthian doesn't open his eyes, but he arches a brow and hums, "Hmm?"

Cassan rolls onto his side. "If I manage to resist your mate's sweet cunt until the night of my birthday...you will give her to me."

"Give you my mate?" Luthian laughs. "Fine. It's a wager you'll lose. In any case, you'll have to share her with your father."

I marvel at Luthian's plans, how quickly he alters them and lays foundations for more in the future. Allow the king to think he's taking me from him. Lose me in a bet to the man he plans to put on the throne.

My guardian is more adept at trickery than I knew.

Is he also deceiving *me*?

Chapter Twenty-Two

After my impressive performances in the garden, Luthian insists I stay tucked away in his house for the rest of the day. I choose to lounge about the library, reading from things that interest me, while he tends to letters and papers at a small desk by the fire.

"What happens if Cassan loses the wager?" I ask.

Luthian doesn't glance up. "He won't."

"How do you know?" I close my book and sit up on the chaise I've been draped across for an hour.

"I'm an excellent judge of character and action. And now that he knows that his father also desires you, he'll cling to his convictions even harder." He puts an audible flourish on the parchment with his pen, then sets it aside.

I watch as he deftly folds the letter and drips sealing wax upon it. "You have everything planned perfectly, don't you?"

"I try." He applies his seal to the wax. "I have a meeting this evening. You'll be on your own. But you will make an appearance."

"By myself?" I don't know why I'm nervous. I went to the king on my own and survived.

"There's a ritual tonight," he goes on. "I think you'll find it entertaining. There is appropriate attire in your wardrobe. Sarta will have marked it."

"A ritual?" I know of only my mother's rituals, in which she welcomed the seasons and helped them change all around our manor. She never spoke of group rites.

"Once every season, the court worships the gift of Living Essence. I find it tedious, but others enjoy it." He pauses. "Obviously, there is group sex involved."

"Obviously," I say with a laugh. "How will I know the etiquette?"

"Observe. I trust you'll be able to pick it up. As I said, it's tedious. And unimaginative." He makes a disgusted face.

"And you so conveniently are otherwise engaged," I point out. "Where and when should I report for this ritual?"

"Follow the crowd from the main gardens when the moon has appeared." He tucks his letter into his jacket. "Now, I must leave you. Bring me a full report tonight."

As he passes, he stops, as if without thinking, and drops a kiss on my forehead.

* * * *

Walking through the darkness of the gardens, I adjust my mask so that I can see better. The robes Sarta designed for the ritual are long scarves of transparently thin emerald silk, held into the suggestion of a garment by a tightly-cinched belt of ivory around my waist. My mask is a collection of verdant leaves, splayed across my face like a butterfly's wings from the bridge of my nose.

I don't know what I'm meant to be disguising; everyone at court has already heard of the human woman of voracious and adventurous appetite.

The path to the king's gardens is lit with fires on evenly spaced plinths. I see courtiers moving down the tiers and follow them. Unlike Luthian's gardens, which seem to stretch on forever, the king's garden ends abruptly at the tree line of a dark and imposing forest. I'm grateful to have someone to follow, though the sound of drumming might have led me to the right place on its own. As the winding path brings me closer to the drums, firelight flickers through the trees, and the oddest sense of anticipation tingles in my blood. I know magic. I've felt the rise and fall of it, held a ball of it in my hands. I can't direct it, but I recognize it, and I let it draw me along, just as the crowd sweeps me toward the sacred clearing.

An immense bonfire licks at the sky above, dwarfing the standing stones that surround it. Inside the circle, identically dressed priestesses in robes of moving water walk a clockwise circle, their lips murmuring a chant I can't make out. Each of the stones bears a chained and naked faery, all of them with cocks that stand out from their bodies, swollen and jerking. They're blindfolded and gagged with strips of leather.

I glance around the outside of the circle, where the court has assembled in numbers so vast, they spread far into the trees. Some of them hover, wings fluttering, others have climbed into branches. Everyone wears a mask, but I find the king immediately; he's the only one seated, on a throne of quartz that hums with power.

He finds me, too, his eyes settling on mine from

behind his mask of amethyst. I drop my eyes demurely but see him gesture to one of his sylph guards. Still, I feign surprise when they approach and urge me to the king's side.

"Cenere," he says, patting his knee. "Come, sit on my lap."

Cassan stands to Arcus's left, his face covered with a leather mask of a stylized fox. An appropriate animal, given the impression I have of him. I flash him a sly smile and tilt my chin as I pass him, and he doesn't hide his grin.

To the king's left stands a much taller faery, shirtless, his muscular body clad only in a small leather loin cloth. His gleaming amber eyes give the feathered owl mask he wears an uncanny effect, and golden hair cascades down his tanned back. The firelight casts every line of his powerful muscles into deeper contrast. He doesn't look at me, or at the king or prince beside him. He doesn't appear to want to be here, at all.

Arcus notices where my gaze has landed, and he catches my hand to pull me onto his knee. "That's my son, Kathras. Unpleasant bastard. Loathes participation in my court."

"It's a lucky thing for me, then that my king is immortal." Kathras keeps his gaze trained straight ahead.

In the circle, the maidens have stopped before the bound faeries, each of them holding a golden cup. The drumming picks up its pace, and my heartbeat strives to match it. The captive faeries twist and groan, as if tormented by an unseen force. The drumming reaches a crescendo, then abruptly stops. The fire flares brighter, and in unison, the chained faeries come, their seed falling into the goblets.

The drumming begins again, slower, and the chained faeries moan, some in agony, some in pleasure. One of them shouts and strains at his bonds.

"Have you seen such a ritual before?" Arcus brushes my hair back to press his lips to the hollow of my throat. "Your fragile mortal heart is racing."

"No, Your Majesty. Never." I breathe and squeeze my thighs together. I think of Firo, of tormenting him in the library and how powerful I felt. I wonder if he's here, remembering the same thing.

Arcus's hand falls to my lap and pushes through my robes. He delves between my thighs and thrusts two fingers inside me. When he withdraws them, a web of fluid stretches between them. "You're enjoying yourself."

"I've enjoyed everything I've experienced here, Your Majesty." *Even your attempt to terrify me.* "Will you explain it to me?"

"The priestesses are the Gwragedd Annwn," Kathras says before his father can speak, still not looking at me. "They are water. The fire should be obvious, even to a human."

I bristle at that. "And I suppose the seed represents the soil?"

"No." Now, he does look at me, to reach out and touch my mask. "You represent the soil, and all that grows from it. Do you see the others dressed like you?"

I loathe that I was wrong, when he is so haughty and dismissive, but I do see more plant masks.

"And air?" I gesture overhead at a merry dance of winged fae whose masks are adorned with feathers like his.

"All of this talk of ritual bores me," Cassan complains.

"Cenere has a promising future here at court," Arcus says, lazily waving his hand. "Your brother is right to educate her on the customs Luthian never bothered to."

"Luthian?" Kathras's face blanches visibly, even in the warmth of the firelight.

"Father allowed him to return, thanks to this luscious human," Cassan explains.

"Having Luthian at court is a small price to pay for such a wonder." Arcus moves one of my flimsy scarves aside to bare my breast. He cups it and rubs his finger over my nipple, turning it flush and hard.

In the circle, the drums have again reached a peak, and the bound faeries grunt and moan as they empty themselves into the goblets again. When the drumming starts up once more, some of them begin to weep.

"Pleasure and Torment," Arcus whispers. "Wait until I have you next, and you will learn the depths of both."

I have already learned, from a far better tutor. But I shiver, which he seems to enjoy, and I reach up to brush my fingers over his mask. "And you, Your Majesty? What element do you represent?"

"Magic." He flicks his finger against the arm of his crystal throne, and it lights from within with a short pulse of white.

I let out a little gasp to show how impressed I am. For a king, he's shockingly easy to manipulate. Perhaps having such an inflated sense of self-worth makes one blind to how malleable they truly are.

Kathras speaks again, as if his lesson wasn't interrupted. "When the goblets are full, they'll be passed around the courtiers to share, to take in the power that was raised."

"And then, lovely Cenere, we'll celebrate our new power with a game," Arcus says.

"A game, Your Majesty?"

He taps the end of my nose. "I wouldn't want to spoil the surprise. But expect to be taken tonight. And expect me to take you."

"If you find her first," Cassan says casually.

Should I taunt him about the wager? For if he does take me tonight, he'll have already lost. I'll wait until I know if the bet is a secret or not.

"I'll have her, anyway," Arcus growls, his pride unmistakably wounded. He reaches between us to unlace his breeches.

I move obediently into place, sliding from his knee to stand. He lifts me onto his cock, parting my legs around him, and I find myself in a position very like the one from the throne room. His thick shaft opens me, and I moan, leaning my head back on him while he thrusts with the lazy rhythm of the drums.

"She's mine," the king warns his sons. "She may be Luthian's mate, but this cunt belongs to me."

The more Arcus talks, the more I look forward to his death. I keep my gaze fixed on the activity in the circle, though I don't forget to perform appropriately for the king's ego. He speeds up when the drums do, go still when they stop, resumes when they pick up again, and soon I'm no longer feigning my enjoyment. His fingers trip across my clit while his other hand holds me upright, mashing my breast. I move with Arcus, forgetting how personally repugnant he is, and I come again and again with the faeries in the circle.

I glance up now and then to track the movement of the moon across the sky. By the time it reaches its apex, the chained faeries are no longer crying out or resisting. They whimper, their mouths slack, some of them drooling as their heads loll on their necks. The drums stop one last time.

The goblets are full to the brim, and the Gwragedd Annwn move through the gaps between the stone. Courtiers fall into line, awaiting their turn to drink from the vessels.

One by one, I watch as they swallow the living essence, then vanish. A priestess approaches our royal cluster, and Arcus withdraws from my body, depositing me on my feet. I shift my toes through the leaf litter on the forest floor, my sex throbbing; I was so close when the drums stopped.

"You should go first," Arcus says. "I'll be along after. Be sure to give me a good chase."

I don't know what that means, but I step forward and let the Gwragedd Annwn press the rim of the goblet to my lips. I take a swallow, and the clearing is gone.

Chapter Twenty-Three

I have vanished. To where, I don't know.

I'm in near total darkness, the faint blue light of a few scattered will-o'-the-wisps all I have to examine my surroundings. There is no night sky. One of the small blue orbs drifts upward and I see that I am in a tunnel. The ceiling is woven branches. The light dips and weaves. The walls are branches, too, twisted and black.

I walk forward a few steps, my hands in front of me. Eventually, when I've covered enough ground, I encounter another wall impeding my path. I turn and retreat.

Somewhere, something roars. Someone giggles. Both sounds echo through the air, which has grown chill and damp.

A slight breeze turns my head. Arms out to protect me, I seek the source and find an egress into another tunnel.

It's a labyrinth.

A scream shatters the quiet, and the hairs on my neck raise. *"Be sure to give me a good chase,"* the king had told me. Something sighs further down this tunnel. As I come closer, slowly, trying to keep my footfalls silent, I hear the unmistakable grunting and panting of coupling. It's possible I'll trip over whoever it is if I keep going forward, so when I find another turn, I take it.

There are more will-o-the-wisps here, but the light is still too weak for my human eyes to rely upon it, and the darkness terrifies me. For every moan and peal of laughter, there is a scream of sheer terror. Never before has the court's name so frightened me. Will I find pleasure here, or torment?

There's movement behind me. I sense it, hear it over the pounding of my pulse, the ragged breaths tearing from my chest.

Is it worse to see the thing that's pursuing you? Is it better to know why you should be running? I cannot say, but I look over my shoulder, trembling.

The wisps glide about in their looping dance, and I see the outline of broad shoulders, a bare chest.

The mask of an owl.

I take a few steps back as he advances. "I-I'm meant to be caught by your father."

Kathras says nothing.

I keep backing up. "He'll be angry with me," I try again.

Kathras never slows his determined steps.

Two wisps circle each other at the end of the tunnel, enough to show me in their dim blue light that there's a juncture there. I don't need Kathras for my plan. I need to be caught by either Cassan or Arcus.

I break into a run, arms pumping, feet pounding the hard-packed dirt. I'm nearly at the junction when I make a foolish mistake.

I look back.

Kathras is running after me, he's nearly upon me, and my momentary curiosity is my undoing. My foot catches a root and I tumble to the ground. A hand closes around my ankle and jerks me back. I claw forward, sinking my fingers into the dirt and pulling with all my futile might. But he's impossibly strong. My flimsy excuse for robes tear. He grabs me by the hips and hauls me up to meet his, ramming his cock deep into me.

I shriek in surprise; he's shockingly large and long, and he has no plan to be gentle. His grip is crushing, his thrusts punishing. I try to push myself up and he shoves me down again, one hand holding my cheek in the dirt.

He says nothing. Makes no sound at all while I gasp for breath under the onslaught of this debasement. I knew I would be called upon to perform all manner of depravity at court, but the darkness, the violence of it, the inability to escape all wind together into a brutal nightmare.

A voice faraway howls in outrage. Someone else pleads. Another cries out in the throes of ecstasy.

Yet, Kathras is unnervingly silent. The slap of his hips against my ass, the wet squelch as he fucks my already used cunt, and the moans I try to keep silent are the only sound. Soon, I don't bother to keep them silent; I wriggle my hand beneath me and find my clit, rubbing frantically.

He plows into me so hard, my knees come off the ground and the dirt scrapes my face. It's not as painful as things I've done before, certainly not as frightening as Luthian's pet abomination, but there is an element of danger in his stoney silence and I break, clutching all around him on a cry of release.

The only way I know that he has finished is when he plunges deep and stills, erupting hot and strong inside of me. His cock twitches once, twice, and then he pulls out.

I roll onto my back. "Your Highness—"

He's gone, and I am still lost in the darkness.

* * * *

I wander for hours, hearing the occasional rustle or moan, but I don't encounter anyone else. Arcus never finds me. Cassan never finds me. When the tunnels are lit by the gray light of dawn peeking through the gaps in the branches, I finally give into my aching body and curl up on the damp ground. Something like sleep comes over me, though I'm not entirely unconscious. I hear a bird's song, the scurry of a fieldmouse through the hedge walls.

I wonder if anyone is looking for me. Surely, I'll be missed.

Luthian will not let me be forgotten here.

But in the meantime, I'm thirsty and achy, and the scrapes on my cheek, knees, and palms sting. My silk robe is in tatters, and my skin is streaked with dirt. I long for my bed, for a full day of sleep.

And for a reason. Kathras knew his father wanted me. Was that why he took me? He seemed so disaffected, so disinterested, so...

Disgusted.

He was disgusted, standing beside me as I rode Arcus's cock. Prince Kathras must have thought me a common human trollop, something so foul and beneath him that he wished to debase me in such an aggressive manner.

I hope he felt the pleasure I took in it. I hope my cry of passion shamed him.

"Cenere!" A familiar voice calls from somewhere far away. "Cenere, are you out here?"

"I'm here!" I croak from my parched throat. "I'm

here!”

Footsteps approach and Luthian appears. He stops, his blue-gray skin going nearly white as he looks at me.

I try to push myself up, and that snaps him back.

“Don’t,” he says, hurrying to my side. He lifts me as if I am a feather and tucks my head against his shoulder. Cradled to the warmth of his chest, I feel how cold I truly am, and my teeth begin to chatter.

“I’ll kill him,” Luthian seethes, and I want to warn him of what he told me before: that we must always watch our words, that his wards cannot protect us on the grounds. But I’m too tired, my throat too sore.

I reach up and stroke his cheek. “I know.”

We’re not in the labyrinth anymore. His strides take us across a room I’ve never seen before. The walls are black, the candelabras on the walls silver. There’s a fireplace burning with blue flame, and a huge, black-covered bed exactly like the one I imagined when I thought of Luthian that last night before we came to court.

“Where am I?” I ask, though I’m sure I know the answer.

“My chambers,” he confirms, and conjures a bathtub of steaming water from the air. He lowers me into it, and my ruined clothes melt away at the touch of the water. “What did he do to you?”

“It was a game,” I explain. “Surely, you must know—”

“It isn’t a game to strand a vulnerable human in the cold all night.” Soap appears in his hand—sorrow lily, without even having to ask—and a sponge. “You could have frozen to death.”

“It was not freezing weather,” I say softly.

“Look at you. He didn’t even bother to heal you,” Luthian goes on.

“Perhaps he did not know that I needed healing.”

I'm beginning to worry that Luthian's rage will get the better of him, that he'll do something foolish to avenge this slight against me. "It was dark and chaotic. We didn't even speak."

"There's no excuse!" Luthian paces, daubing some of the soap onto the sponge. "Arcus knows you belong to me. He's punishing you to make me suffer. But this is beyond even the boundaries of the court!"

"It wasn't Arcus," I quickly correct him.

Luthian's rage is momentarily paused. "He bragged this morning about having you."

"He did. During the ritual," I explain. "Not after. Not in the maze."

This reignites Luthian's fury. "There is still no excuse. I'll find who did this to you, Cenere, I swear it. You will not be treated this way again."

"No, you won't," I say gently. I wait for him to argue, but I think I've stunned him to silence. I seize the opportunity and go on. "I was doing exactly as everyone else was in that maze. Hunting, being pursued. It was rough and frightening, but it was exciting. You taught me that fear can be arousing. I used that lesson. I took the pain and the degradation, and I turned it into pleasure. Just like you taught me."

"Whoever it was... they should have healed you," Luthian protests. "I should have been there."

"You were there. Just now. You came to my rescue, just like I knew you would. But please, don't do something foolish. Don't try to defend my honor at the expense of everything we've worked toward." I search his face and see the hatred in his eyes soften and fade. "I knew you would save me. I knew you would heal me. So, I was never truly afraid."

The soap and sponge clatter to the floor, and he's upon me, leaning over the tub to kiss me breathless. He wraps his arms around my wet body, crushes me to his fine brocade coat, muddy streaks and all. His hands roam up my back, into my hair, and he holds me tight, his tongue taking my mouth as roughly as Kathras took me in the maze, and that's when I recognize what drove both of them.

Possession.

Luthian kisses me to claim me, just as Kathras, I'm now certain, meant to fuck the memory of his father's cock from me.

Tears sting the corners of my eyes. Luthian wants me. Not just my body, not just the prize between my legs that everyone at court covets. He wants to protect me, to care for me.

He *wants* me.

I whimper against his mouth.

The spell is broken.

He pulls back, gasping. "I'm sorry."

"Don't be sorry, I—"

"We should get you healed and cleaned up." He straightens his soaked, ruined coat, then summons another, stiffer and more starched than the last. It's as if he's donning armor against the very idea of wanting me. He finds the soap and sponge and kneels beside the tub. "Give me your hand."

Slowly and methodically, he washes the dirt from my skin and makes my scrapes disappear. He picks twigs from my hair and washes my curls thoroughly, and when I am clean and whole again, he lifts me from the tub and magics me dry before putting me to sleep in his huge, empty bed.

I reach for him. "You don't have to go."

"I have business to attend," he says. "Sleep for as long as you need to."

"Please," I say, my eyes filling with tears. "Please, stop pretending that you don't—"

"Sleep," he says, waving his hand, and I cannot resist his command.

Chapter Twenty-Four

Luthian's spell wears off at dawn. I feel drugged and drowsy from too much slumber and confused and disappointed to find myself in my own bed. I cannot help but imagine what it would be like to sleep in his arms and wake with our legs wound together.

I console myself by thinking that I would get tangled in his hair, anyway, and so it's all for the better that I woke alone.

Since we no longer have Brujon, breakfast is served in the great hall, where Luthian conjures our food. He's waiting at the head of a table laden with fruit and pastries, and the strong beanstalk tea that he prefers. I wrinkle my nose at the smell as I take my chair.

"Feeling better?" he asks.

Better than when you rejected and ensorcelled me? I smile and nod, reaching for a decanter of juice as if nothing is amiss.

"Good. The king wishes to take you riding this afternoon." Luthian passes me a plate of flaky, moon-shaped biscuits.

I frown and select one of the rolls. "Is that a euphemism?"

"Probably. I advise you to prepare for that eventuality. But I have it from a trusted source that Arcus is quite smitten with you. He may actually wish to talk."

A cold sweat pops out on my brow. "We've never practiced that."

Luthian barks a laugh. "And yet you're so prolific."

I nudge his ankle threateningly with the toe of my slipper. "You know that isn't what I mean. What do I tell him? Should I have a history? What if he asks how we met?"

"Tell him you met me at the tree beside your mother's grave. That your sobs were so piteous, it moved my heart." Luthian shrugs.

"Will he believe that?" I am incredulous.

"It doesn't matter if he believes it, when it's the truth." He emphasizes the last word. "As for your background, I've put it about that you're a changeling. Your mother asked me for a child, and I gave her one. You needn't tell them more than that."

"Why not?"

His words taunt me. *"You were born for it."*

"Arcus finds you exotic because of your humanity." Luthian's mouth hovers at the rim of his cup. "Don't sully that with a mention of magic."

I choose to believe that's the real reason. Whether or not he granted my mother's wish to plot his revenge, making Arcus in any way suspicious will sink my own goal.

"Good morning!"

I jolt at the chipper voice. "Firo!"

He strides into the great hall shirtless, smiling at both of us. But before he sits across from me, he drops a casual kiss on Luthian's forehead.

My bite of pastry tries to claw its way up my throat.

"You were asleep for quite a while," Firo says, oblivious to the dagger he's thrust through my heart.

Luthian won't look up from his plate. "She had quite an ordeal in the maze."

"So you said." Firo looks me up and down. "You're all right now, though?"

I nod with enthusiasm I don't feel. "The king is going to take me riding later today."

"From what I understand, he's quite—"

"Smitten?" I reach for my glass. "So I've heard."

Firo laughs. "You've truly taken the court by storm. If I was a betting man, I would wager you'll have a crown on your head by the end of the summer."

"That long?" I press a hand to my chest in mock offense, proud of myself for not dissolving into tears. Firo is my friend. My acquaintance, at least. I don't want him to be my romantic rival.

You flatter yourself. My own mind sneers at me. *You really believed that Luthian could be, what? Growing to love you? He's giving you away to the prince. He only cares about what he'll gain.*

I've been so stupid.

My chair makes a terrible scrape when I stand, startling both Luthian and Firo. I pretend not to notice. "I can't eat. I need to decide what I'll wear. What time do you think I'll be summoned?"

"I'm sure you have time—" Luthian begins.

My laugh is somewhat hysterical. "Better to be prepared. I never know when those sylphs will appear."

"This is why she's a much better student than I," Firo says, giving Luthian a slow smile that sears my heart like a flaming blade.

I cannot bear to watch more. I run from the room, feigning eagerness until I'm safely behind my bedroom door.

Only then do I let myself cry.

* * * *

The dragon is easily the height of a house, and as wide. I gape up at it, unable to speak when confronted with such breathtaking size and beauty. Its scales are red, flashing with a gold and green iridescence as the light plays off them. The fearsome beast's talons are black and deadly sharp, each one as tall as I am. The dragon kneads the ground like a cat and rubs its face into the grass with a distinctly feline purr that shakes and trembles the soil beneath my feet.

"I thought you meant horses, Your Majesty." I mean it to be teasing and coy, but I can't help the wonder in my voice.

Arcus grins, pleased with his own largesse.

"If it helps," a deep, lazy voice booms overhead, "I did eat several horses for lunch."

It isn't shocking to me that a dragon can speak, but knowing a fact and experiencing the truth of it are two vastly different concepts. My mouth falls open, and Arcus closes it playfully with a finger beneath my chin. "A ride on horseback is too simple for you and requires too many guards for adequate privacy. I long to have you alone, Cenere. Away from the palace, where too many can overhear."

"Your Majesty flatters me," I demure.

Instead of a saddle, a large wicker basket is strapped firmly to the beast, anchored by thick iron rings that pierce two of the horned protrusions dividing its back in a serrated line. I look about for a ladder, then realize my foolishness. Of course there is no ladder. The king can fly.

"Shall we?" Arcus asks me, and without waiting for an answer, scoops me into his arms and takes to the sky. I am no stranger to flying; my mother took me up above the trees to survey the whole of our manor when I was a child. I loved flying, then. When I came of age and it became apparent to me that I wouldn't sprout wings of my own, it became torture, and I refused to fly again.

My heart aches at those refusals. What I wouldn't give to be in my mother's arms, experiencing the exhilaration of not only flight, but her unconditional and all-consuming love for me.

No one will ever love me in that way again.

Arcus lands us in the basket, the walls of which are tall enough that we won't be swept out. They're lined with black velvet, and mounds of cushions surround a picnic laid out on fine red brocade.

I'm more concerned with those rings pierced through the dragon's flesh. "Oh, dragon. Doesn't that hurt you?"

The beast turns its head back on its long neck, bringing me disturbingly close to one giant, yellow eye, and its mouth full of impossibly long teeth. "Such tender care. I didn't believe I would meet a human today. You're much kinder than our stories would suggest."

I feel its voice through my feet.

The dragon goes on. "No. The rings don't hurt me. There is no feeling in these plates."

"Like fingernails." I hold up my hand to show it.

"I suppose." The dragon squints with great interest. "I've never seen a human this close before. Well, unless I was eating them. But to be truthful, I haven't bothered to take stock of their anatomy, as they're usually cooked by then."

"You're scaring her," Arcus scolds the beast, though nothing in my manner suggests fear. In truth, I feel much safer with the man-eating dragon than the sadistic king behind me. He arranges some cushions to lounge upon and pats the spot beside him. "Come. Sit with me."

I fix my most pleasing smile upon my face and go to him, sinking down on the cushions. He pulls me to his side and sighs with contentment. He calls out, "We're ready."

The whole of the basket lurches with the movement of the dragon as it stretches its back and, with a mighty, deafening woosh of its wings, takes to the sky. The wind passes over our heads, broken by the shelter of the tightly woven walls around us. I consider my reaction and decide to throw myself fearfully across Arcus's chest, clinging to him and trembling.

He chuckles at my feigned fright. "Cenere, my sweet. I would never allow harm to come to you." He pauses. "At least, nothing I couldn't undo."

"Your Majesty is so thoughtful." I sit up as if suddenly realizing my behavior and begin to apologize profusely. "Oh, Your Majesty! I am so sorry. I should never have put my hands—"

He takes one of the named parts and guides it to his cock. "You may touch me however you like, Cenere."

I blush and dip my head. "I've never spent so much time in the company of royalty."

"I have never spent so much time in the company of a contradiction. One moment, you're shy and respectful. The next, seductive, and hungry to be used." His voice is full of wonder. "You are a delightful puzzle to me."

He leans forward and finds a crystal bowl of

succulent red syrup berries, selects one, and says, "Open your mouth."

I obey, and he squeezes the berry. Its skin splits and the center, like liquid ruby, falls onto my tongue.

He groans. "I would fill your mouth in other ways, Cenere."

I swallow and whimper, "Oh, yes, please."

"When we've reached our destination," he says, and pops the berry into my mouth. It's delicious, and tastes of violet petals. "Right now, I'd like to talk."

Between bites of fruit and cheese that he feeds me, he questions me. Where am I from? How did I meet Luthian? What about the Court of Pleasure and Torment draws me, and how do I enjoy it so fully, when humans are known to be reserved and proper?

The first two, I answer exactly as I practiced with Luthian. The third, however, is not one I've thought of, and it takes me longer to answer.

"I suppose," I begin hesitantly, "my interest was simply due to my husband's desire to return. In truth, I dreaded it, a bit. He took time to teach me what to expect, though, and his talent as a lover and a guide drew out something in me that I didn't know was there."

My answer, it seems, is not the correct one. Arcus's expression goes dark. He looks away from me and responds petulantly, "Oh, yes. I have heard rumors of Luthian's prowess."

"All exaggerated," I quickly assure him. "Once I arrived here at court and sampled the delights to be had with you, Your Majesty, I gained more...perspective."

There is a strange, mean thrill that comes with denying Luthian's talents. It's all a lie, but one that I hope would hurt him if he overheard, the way he has hurt me with his callous behavior and betrayal.

But was it truly a betrayal? I ask myself. Luthian

never promised to fall in love with me. Never promised to not fall in love with someone else. And I don't know if he loves Firo.

But Luthian left me, when I begged him to stay, and spent the night with Firo, instead.

My stomach pitches as the dragon suddenly dives. This time, when I cling to Arcus, my fear is genuine.

He seems to love it. "We've arrived, my treasure."

Treasure. A thing to be owned and prized. Another clue he's given away that will help me further manipulate him, for treasure is sought out and won. He won't be satisfied if I merely give myself to him. He wants to pursue me, but he needs to be assured that he will win me in the end.

I can use that.

The dragon lands in a forest clearing. When Arcus takes us to the ground, I say, "Your Majesty, I hope this does not end with me in another labyrinth, waiting for you to hunt me down."

"I did not mean to disappoint you," he says. "Consider this an apology for the pleasure you missed."

He turns me to face the mouth of a cavern, lit from within by shimmering shadows of water.

"Shall we go inside?" he asks, as if I have a choice.

I do not. He is a king. A dangerous one, who has already removed the head of his queen.

I'd like to keep mine, so I give him my hand and let him lead me inside.

Chapter Twenty-Five

Faery baths are naturally occurring magical springs that appear all over Fablemere. They aren't confined to the places where faeries live, though it's said that once, eons ago, faeries ruled all of Fablemere. Legends about the fae who created the baths abound, but those stories were never my favorite among the tales mother told. Who cares, after all, about magic springs and legendary caverns, when one can hear stories about the far-off Smuggler's Sea and the pirates who brave it?

Arcus stops me steps beneath the rocky outcrop that shelters the mouth of the tunnel. He waves a hand to completely disrobe us both. "This is a pure place and must be kept so. This is the last faery bath to be used only by faeries."

He steps away, holding my hand, but I stick fast to my place. "Your Majesty may have forgotten that I am no faery."

"It doesn't matter," he says with a dismissive wave. "This place falls under my dominion. The presence of your beauty honors these enchanted waters."

I follow reluctantly. Though I am human in body, my spirit is fae. My presence feels profane here.

A warm breeze, flecked with shimmering motes, wraps around me as if in invitation. Perhaps because I was born of a wish, born of faery magic, I'm not truly trespassing. I let Arcus guide me deeper into the cave.

The ring of darkness at the mouth of the tunnel passes, and we enter a vast, high-ceilinged cavern. The sand-colored walls are brightly lit with the luminance of the opaque blue water. Steam rises from numerous, naturally occurring cauldrons of varying height; some spill over into each other, but never empty. The glittering motes fill the air, echoing the swirls of iridescence winding through the waters.

"Do all the faery baths look this way?" I ask, and add a hasty, "Your Majesty?"

He stops me, places his hands on my shoulders. "In this place, I am not a king. I am a faery, on the same footing as you. You may use my name."

It's a nice sentiment, but I don't trust it. I'm sure he believes it, but I'm reluctant to test it.

"Please." He dives a hand into my loose curls, his thumb stroking over my cheek. "I want to hear you say my name."

I sway into him, and it's not entirely an act; the atmosphere lulls my body into dreamlike languidness, and I melt against him, my chin tilted up to his. "Arcus."

His mouth descends upon mine with such ferocity that it brings to mind the kisses that Luthian and I have shared. But where I can feel Arcus's passion, I feel none of it myself. I let him ravage my mouth desperately, make the appropriate whimpers, clasp my arms around his neck, but while my body responds eagerly to his touch, inside, I am hollow.

Under Luthian's mouth, I am whole.

If I keep thinking of Luthian, keep lamenting what I've lost but never had, I won't be able to give the king what he needs to be convinced of my desire for him. I concentrate on his touch, the warm, solid strength of his muscled body pressed to mine. The smoothness of his skin, the skill of his tongue. I swoon, and he supports me with a hand around my back, a satisfied noise rumbling deep in his chest before he lifts his head.

"I would hear you say my name a thousand times today, Cenere. I want you to scream it in your passion."

"Then make me scream," I breathe, my gaze holding his fast.

This is a dangerous request. I know he can hurt me. But from his manner, his openness, it doesn't seem that he's brought me here to demonstrate his cruelty. And when he kisses me again, I know I've judged correctly.

He's brought me here to show me that he can be tender.

Breathing fast, his cock hard against my stomach, he motions to the pools. "Let's get in."

Once again, he lifts me in his arms to fly with me, taking us down into the central basin. It's surrounded by tall columns bearing other pools, which spill down all around us in a curtain of enchanted water. Slowly, he lowers us to the surface. For a moment, bathed in the curls of steam, I am afraid I might be scalded, but my toes break the water, and I find it's the perfect temperature and deliciously hot. It's deep enough that we submerge to my shoulders. Arcus, much taller, must crouch to my level.

The water is pure, heated silk, slipping over my

skin like a caress, and I sigh as all my muscles relax. I didn't realize how tense they were; perhaps I am more afraid of Arcus than I cared to admit. But even fear can't touch me, now; I'm melting into a sensuous abyss of relaxation.

Arcus still holds me. He grins down at me with pride, as if he is responsible for this place and its effect on me. The king's ego knows no bounds.

"You see now, why this place is sacred," he tells me. Like he can read my simple, human thoughts. If he could, he would see eyes rolling in my mind. "I brought my queens here, before we were mated."

My brow crinkles. "Queens?"

"Theeda and Parphia," he replies, bemused. "Luthian taught you court manners, but no court history?"

I blush and look down.

"Theeda was my first queen. She was a good mate and bore my heirs." He speaks with true fondness in his words. "I was disappointed when she died."

"How did it happen?" I ask softly, touching his cheek as if to comfort him.

"She was at Palat Scylas, in the Sorrowlands, when they were infected." He says no more, and I don't press him. I have little knowledge of the Sorrowlands apart from what everyone in Fablemere knows: nothing grows, nothing lives. I don't know how it got that way.

"I'm so sorry." I take his hand and bring it to my lips, pressing a kiss in the center of his palm.

He smooths my hair back. "You are a tender-hearted thing."

"I can't help it. I'm human," I say apologetically. "What about your other queen?"

He dismisses her with a wave of his hand. "Parphia? She isn't worth discussing. Especially not in this sacred place."

"Well, I thank you for bringing me to such an important site, Your—" I pretend to slip up. "Arcus."

He lifts my chin and studies my face. "You are a wonder, Cenere. In all my thousands of years, I have yet to encounter someone so human, and yet so fae. I think it would be a mistake to let you slip from my grasp."

I summon tears to my eyes and blink to ensure that one falls. "I am mated to Luthian."

"Do you take me for an ogre? A pixie?" He laughs. "You made a promise to Luthian, not the old gods. It's never been our way to yolk ourselves to each other inseparably. With a word, I can cleave the bond between you and your mate and have you for myself."

Is it a threat or an offer? I can't tell.

He lowers himself more, pulls me down with him. My copper curls turn to wavy, dark tentacles on the surface of the water. He urges one of my legs around his waist and the tip of his cock touches me. "Is that something you would desire, Cenere? Would you wish to be my queen?"

I desire Luthian. I would take a binding oath before the old gods if he asked me. But that is not why I've come to court.

With a gentle push, I free myself from Arcus's arms and float just out of his reach. "It's impossible."

"Why should it be?" Arcus demands, shockingly gentle.

"Because..." I stop. I came to this court specifically to become Cassan's queen. To claim the throne at *his* side. To exert my power and punish Cadwyn Thrace. To claim my justice. Does it matter now if I achieve it according to Luthian's plan? What I want is in the palm of my hand, outstretched to me for the taking.

Luthian would take it.

If I break my bargain with him, I will lose my wishes. Will I even need them if I am Arcus's queen?

But Luthian still plans to kill Arcus. I wouldn't be queen for long. Perhaps, not even long enough to end Cadwyn Thrace. And while I could simply inform the king of Luthian's scheming...

I love Luthian. Standing on this precipice of betrayal, I know I can't step off it. I want to hurt Luthian because I am hurt. But I can't end his life over something as trivial as unreturned affection.

My mind whirls. Arcus trusts me enough to be alone with him. No guards, no dragons, naked and vulnerable in my arms. He would have me as his queen. Luthian and I didn't plan it that way, but it could still help us, without betraying him.

"Because," I gasp on a sob that Arcus will believe because he wants to. "I am a lowly human. I'm fortunate that Luthian can overlook such a thing."

"There is nothing to overlook, Cenere," Arcus vows. "You are more perfect than any faery."

"But could your courtiers overlook such a thing?" I shake my head. "I know I've impressed them with my displays. The mermaids, for example—"

"Mermaids?" Arcus laughs. "I would have liked to see that."

I fake a tremulous smile. "I want to belong at court. If I am queen, will they resent me?"

"They will see you as I do." He pushes my hair behind my ear. "Because I will command it."

He knows nothing of ruling, I realize. To him, the title is power, the power absolute.

It will come as a shock when he's assassinated.

"There is...more." This is where I alter our plans. Luthian will simply have to trust my judgment.

"Tell me," Arcus urges.

"My stepfather. He's a faery, like my mother was. I believe he murdered her. When Luthian found me weeping on my mother's grave, he promised me I would have my revenge." I force another burst of tears to my eyes. "That was months ago, and yet Cadwyn Thrace lives."

"And that is what binds you to Luthian?" Understanding flashes across Arcus's face.

I nod fervently. "I want Thrace to answer for his crimes. I want to have my revenge upon him, and Luthian promised that I could. Yet, he's made no move. His motivation ever since we were mated has been gaining entry to your court. It worked, but... I fear he will never make good on his promise."

Arcus can. Even without a crown upon my head, I know Arcus will deliver Thrace to me in chains. And I've seen his lust for violence, for cruelty. He'll revel in my vengeance.

"This isn't the first time I've heard of Luthian's faithlessness," Arcus growls. "As queen, you will have all the power you need to set your retribution in motion. You owe Luthian nothing. I'll see him banished from court—"

"No!" I cry. "Not before I am your queen."

He smiles down at me. "You wish to be my queen?"

"Do I wish to spend my days and nights with you? Enjoying all the pleasures of your court?" At this, I take his shaft in my hand. The water aids me in a silken glide as I pump him. "Do I wish to fall asleep with our bodies joined? Wake to be ravished every sunup? Are these the things you're promising me?"

His kiss is a punishment and a vow, all at once. He lifts me up to penetrate me, sliding me slowly down his length. I shudder and moan accordingly.

"I promise you the world, Cenere," he groans against my throat, lifting me to thrust in again. "I would give you all of Fablemere, if you asked. Simply say the word, and you will rule at my side."

"Yes," I whimper, and clutch around him. "Yes. I will be your queen."

Chapter Twenty-Six

We return to the palace at nightfall, and I am escorted to Luthian's house by the sylph guards. I asked Arcus to keep silent about our engagement until it's publicly announced, for fear that Luthian might spirit me away. Arcus agreed but warned that the announcement will come soon.

Back in the house, free of the sylphs, I lean against the door and take a few deep breaths. Then, I rush to Luthian's study. When I don't find him there, I try the library. Finally, I venture to his bedroom.

I'm about to knock when I remember that he may not be without company. I brace myself to find him with Firo, and rap my knuckles against the wood.

"Enter."

I step inside and find Luthian thankfully alone. He's in his dressing gown, lounging in a chair before the fire, reading. He looks up, his expression lighting with interest. "How did it go?"

"Better than we could possibly have expected," I tell him, and hurry to kneel in front of him. "Arcus is going to make me his queen."

I expected… I don't know what I expected. A whoop of joy? A congratulations on a job well-done? But Luthian's face turns to stone.

"I-I thought you'd be happy." I don't understand. "He trusts me. I'll be close enough to him to—"

"To lose your head, like the last queen," Luthian snaps. He stands so quickly I must lean back to avoid being knocked over. "You didn't agree, did you?"

"I did. I thought it was the best thing for us," I say, still utterly blindsided by his anger.

He scoffs and paces to the fireplace, leaning with both hands on the mantle. "Whenever did you get the impression that you were to decide what was best?"

"I—"

He whirls to face me, cold eyes filled with silver rage. "You forget our bargain, Cenere! You were never to defy me—"

"I was never to say no!" I protest, climbing to my feet, for I will not grovel. "There was nothing in our bargain about me saying yes!"

"What will happen, do you think, once you are queen?" he demands. "Do you think I'll be allowed to stay?"

"No, he plans to banish you," I spit back. "He never intended to let you stay at court."

"That's the point of the plan!" Luthian shouts. "To remove him. To remove Kathras. To install Cassan so that I will be allowed to stay."

"Shouldn't it be easier now that I've gained Arcus's trust?" I counter. "We were alone together today, Luthian. No guards. In the forest, at a faery bath. He went somewhere alone with me because he trusts me. We can use that to our advantage. And when I am queen—" *I can make you my king.*

I have no idea the thought was simmering in my mind until I nearly, disastrously, speak it.

"When you are queen, and you are discovered to have killed Arcus, you will be executed," Luthian points out. "When you are the only person alone with him, his blood will be on your hands."

He's right. But I won't admit it. "I was in a precarious position. How was I to say no to a king?"

Luthian's shoulders slump. He presses a hand to his forehead. "Forgive me, Cenere. I did not think."

"You didn't think beyond using me as bait," I finish for him.

His shame is visible in his defeated posture, in his silence. My own heart is heavy with it; I considered breaking our agreement, letting Luthian fail for my own ends.

I am a wicked woman. Faithless. As faithless as Arcus believes Luthian to be.

Finally, Luthian speaks. "This complicates things, but it doesn't sink us. I need to think about next steps."

"You don't have much time," I admit. "The king plans to announce our engagement. After that, he'll banish you from court."

Luthian shakes his head. "He won't. You're going to ask him to keep me here until the wedding. So that I will be properly humiliated."

His mind works so quickly. Perhaps that's why I've fallen in love with him. I admire him, and I've confused that admiration with romantic inclination.

"You're more than capable of convincing him, I'm sure," Luthian says, and steps toward me. He touches my cheek. "I shouldn't have shouted at you. You've only done exactly what I wished you to. You simply did it too well."

"I had a skillful teacher," I say.

He smiles. "I'm sorry we fought. I sometimes forget that you have a stake in this, too. I become too focused on my own revenge."

"Because you've been planning it for so long?" Long enough that he could grant a faery's wish and wait for that wish to bloom into a sufficient tool. But I don't ask. As much as I want to, I still can't convince myself that particular truth won't hurt me.

"Once your engagement is announced, we will have to work fast," he says, dropping his hand and turning away to pace. "The date has already been set for his death. Now, it will have to change."

Was that why he was with Firo, then? Did Luthian seduce the ambassador to the Court of Time and Destiny for that favor?

"When it does," he goes on, "I might need you to carry out the deed, yourself."

My stomach drops. I'd thought myself willing to do it, but when faced with it as a fated certainty it carried a much heavier weight. "Kill the king?"

"I vow to you; it will not be your head on the block. That, I've already assured."

I believe him. Though I don't think he loves me, I do trust the bargain we made. He promised I will be safe.

"In the meantime, I want you to turn your attention only to the king. You will not lie with anyone else unless he requests it. He must believe you are taken with him and him alone." Luthian puts his hands on my shoulders. "I cannot stress how important this is."

"I think I know how to manipulate Arcus." I giggle a little. "In fact, that is what I call him. He loves to hear me say his name."

There is a flash of jealousy that Luthian is not quick enough to repress. I revel in it.

"Good," he says stiffly. "Even his last queen was

not afforded that privilege. He must be truly infatuated with you."

At least, I think, *someone is.*

* * * *

I go to Arcus the next morning, as promised. The sylphs allow me to enter his chambers freely, and I wonder if Luthian's plan won't simply be for me to stroll in with a knife. No one would stop me.

What does stop me is the sight of Kathras at his father's dining table. His boots are propped on the tabletop, and he gives me a look of contempt when I enter.

"Your Highness," I say, sinking into a curtsey.

He makes a disgusted noise. "No need to be so formal, *mother.*"

So, Arcus has informed his sons. I wonder how Cassan took the news, considering his bet with Luthian. In stride, I assume.

"Please, don't call me that," I say, lifting my chin. "Especially since—"

"Especially since I fucked you?" He sneers at me. "Don't worry, it won't happen again."

"I know it won't. I'll be queen. And your father's mate."

Kathras sniffs. "Interesting order in that sentence, Your Majesty."

The title is a mockery.

I refuse to endure it. "You shouldn't address me so. It's disrespectful to the crown."

"And what does a human know of the crown?" he demands. "What do you know of a faery court? You've only just arrived. Oh, I've heard all about your prowess, your exhibitionism. It's the talk of every salon and card game. But do you know, really, what it will mean for you to be my father's queen?"

"King Arcus is a wise man. I trust that he will teach me everything I must know."

Kathras laughs. "Good luck with your trust."

I'm about to retort when a door beyond the archway opens and Arcus emerges. "My sweet! You're earlier than I expected."

I go to him with a skip in my step. "I apologize, Your Majesty. I simply couldn't wait any longer to see you."

Kathras scoffs.

Arcus's attention shifts to his son, then back to me. "This will take but a moment, Cenere, my love. Why don't you sit on the bed and wait for me."

I do as he asks and wonder if I should disrobe. I'm certain he means to have me.

Kathras rises and bows to his father. "You summoned me?"

"Yes," Arcus says. "After you left last night, I thought of the things you said. Your attempts to dissuade me from making Cenere my queen."

I narrow my eyes at Kathras. He is in an interference I will be glad to remove.

Arcus continues. "I couldn't put my finger on what bothered you so about my lovely new mate. Then, the solution came to me."

The king looks between me and his son.

"You want her," Arcus says finally.

"That's absurd," Kathras replies.

"Why wouldn't you want her?" Arcus goes on, dismissing Kathras's denial. "She is intoxicatingly beautiful. A mortal, born of a faery wish. She's like a story. You see it in her. How enticing she is."

Kathras's jaw is tight. "I'm happy you're pleased with her, but I have no interest."

No interest! After the labyrinth? After he pinned me down like a rutting animal?

"Come now. I know you better than that. You are

my own flesh and blood. And my flesh and my blood are..." The king sighs helplessly as he looks me up and down. "Very interested."

"Then I'll leave so that you may indulge your interests." Kathras heads toward the door.

"Don't be petulant, boy. I'm offering you the chance to have her before she is queen and it's forbidden." Arcus waves toward me. "Take her now. Slake your lust, and this whole temper tantrum of yours can be over."

Kathras's spine straightens. "I do not object to the human on the grounds that I want her for myself, Your Majesty. I object because I do not trust her mate. I do not trust her."

"He objects," I insert myself, seething, "because he has had me before."

Arcus goes deathly still.

"The reason you could not find me in the maze," I say, locking eyes with Kathras, "is because your son was using me as if I were a stray dog in an alley."

Arcus turns to him. "Is this true?"

"It is." Kathras swallows, and I see real fear pinch the corners of his mouth. "It was dark. I had no idea I was coupling with a human. If I had, it wouldn't have happened."

"You had no idea?" Arcus strides to me and pulls back my skirt. I yelp at his fury, scramble back on my hands instinctively, but he plunges his fingers deep into my unprepared cunt. "You felt this, and had no idea?"

I shudder at his withdrawal and hurry to cover myself.

Arcus strides to Kathras and waves his fingers beneath his son's nose. "You smelled this, and had no idea?"

Kathras, to his credit, keeps his eyes forward, looking past his father into nothing. But his nostrils do flare, slightly.

When Arcus drops his hand, Kathras says, "I've spent the past seven months fucking humans, father. The difference never crossed my mind."

"It wouldn't have happened," Arcus says, repeating his son's earlier words. "But you've been fucking humans for seven months?"

Kathras settles his cold gaze upon me. "Desperation sometimes overcomes disgust."

"You will not speak to my future queen in such a manner!" Arcus gestures wildly to the door. "Out, before I banish you from this court!"

Kathras bows stiffly to his father before he leaves. I wait silently as Arcus watches him go. When the king turns back to me, his expression is still twisted and angry, but he covers it in a flash.

Now, I know what his insincere smile looks like. That will be useful in the future.

"This was not what I summoned you for," Arcus says, leaning over me until I must lay back. The bed dips as he braces a knee on the edge. His mouth finds my ear, my jaw, my collar bones as he speaks. "You will never experience such indignity at my son's hands again."

No, I think. *Only at yours.*

I need to endure Arcus's narcissistic, violent behavior until his death. I *can* endure it until then. And in the meantime, I can take my pleasure while pretending he's in control.

There is something delicious about knowing a repugnant person's death is close at hand.

I lift one leg to draw him closer, and he groans. "No, no, fair Cenere. I wouldn't spoil you for the surprise."

I mewl with feigned disappointment. "You would deny me your magnificent cock?"

He laughs, the sound of a well-stroked ego. "I

have something you'll find... not better, but more interesting, I think."

Before I can sit up, I find myself standing, clinging to Arcus in a dank, windowless room. The walls are coated in damp, with algae dripping down from the cracks between the slime-blackened stones. In the center, only steps from us, is a pool of blue, illuminated like the water from the faery bath. It casts rippling shadows on the ceiling and walls, and across Arcus's suddenly stern face.

"You made quite a spectacle of yourself in front of my court." His voice is laced with venom. "Wantonly cavorting with mermaids."

My brow crumples with confusion. There was no understanding between us then, and even if there were, isn't wanton cavorting what this court is about? "I apologize, Your Majesty. I never thought—"

"You participated while my son rutted with your mate in the gardens," Arcus goes on. "Do you think it appropriate to make yourself a whore to everyone in my court?"

I shake my head, open my mouth to protest. "Your Majesty—"

"It won't happen again." He grips my chin roughly and forces me to meet his furious glare. "And you will call me by my name. I don't wish for you to fear a king. I wish for you to fear me."

I do. I don't have to pretend for him. In this moment, alone, in this dungeon-like room, I can do nothing but quake with fear. "I'm so sorry, Arcus."

His touch turns gentle, petting my hair and smoothing a tear from my cheek that I didn't know had fallen. "It's all right. I know that it will never happen again."

I exhale in relief.

"Because you'll learn your lesson," he adds, and I see the immense satisfaction he takes in my renewed fright.

Something brushes my ankle, then squeezes hard. I look down to see a thick, dark red tentacle snaking from the pool to wind around my leg. Instinctively, I try to shake it off, then wish I had not, for my terror will please the king greatly.

"Since you so enjoyed your time with the mermaids," he says with a dark chuckle, "this seems a fitting punishment."

"Arcus—" I begin to plead, but the tentacle jerks and pulls me into the water.

Chapter Twenty-Seven

I am drowning.

My lungs burn as I try to stop myself from breathing, but all the air escaped me on a startled shout when my feet were ripped from beneath me. I try to shake loose from the tentacle's grip, but it holds me firm. I can't swim to the surface, anyway; my gown is too heavy now that it's wet.

Through a haze of bubbles stirred up by my own futile thrashing, I see the creature that holds me. I cannot put a name to her, for I've never seen anything like her. Translucent white skin on a human-like upper body fades into a flush, throbbing purple-red that unspools into a jumble of the fearsome tentacles. She has no hair, but her head ends in a hanging sack of the same visceral crimson, and her face...

She would be beautiful, if her eyes did not glow like coals, if her smile was not a gaping maw of needle teeth. I cannot scream at the sight of her, and it is the worst kind of torment.

The tentacle she grips me with releases, and I flail to the surface, gasping. Arcus stands over me, no emotion on his handsome face. I open my mouth to plead with him, but I'm pulled down again.

This time, the creature reels me in to her, face to face, and scrapes my cheek with her terrible teeth in a crude imitation of a kiss. My blood fills the bright blue water in a muddy violet cloud, and she runs a forked tongue through it. Her human hands grip the front of my gown and she pulls with remarkable force and speed, considering the fact that we're underwater. I am no match for her strength. I am in her element, totally at her mercy.

Surely, Arcus won't let her kill me. He said I'm to learn a lesson. That what I did before won't happen again.

Those words sound less like a guarantee of safety now that I reflect on them.

My body begs for air, and, as if the creature can sense my need, she pushes me back to the surface. The cold stings the cut on my cheek. And still, Arcus merely watches. He doesn't seem pleased or aroused or even interested. He's simply...watching.

I have never overestimated my importance to him. But I have deeply underestimated how dangerous he is.

The horrible creature strokes my face with the tip of one tentacle. Small, muscular rings line the underside, and they stick and pop against my skin as they roll across it.

Perhaps I should beg for mercy. Perhaps that's what Arcus wants. Not to feed me to this creature, but to know that I'm afraid, that I respect his power.

"Please," I whimper. "I'm so sorry. I would never have done it if I had known—"

The tentacle slaps across my face.

"You will not speak to your king that way!" the creature hisses. Her voice is strangely melodic. As quickly as she slapped me, she moves to soothe me. She uses her hand to caress my cheek and runs her thumb across my bottom lip. "You will not speak at all."

I don't know if she's forbidding me or if she's done something to silence my voice. My fear is too great to test it.

I am so distracted by her hand on my face, I don't see the other tentacles beneath me until one brushes against my sex.

There is no mistaking what she plans to do.

I shake my head, open my mouth to scream, and nothing comes out. Still, I cannot tell if it's magic silencing me or my own horror. The tip of the appendage touches me, finds my opening, and thrusts inside.

There is no enchantment upon me, making me silent. My wail rings off the dirty walls of the room. The small, sucking cups on the tentacle pull and release against my inner walls, a sensation too strange and disgusting to comprehend. She stuffs more and more of it inside, curling, twisting, while I sob in revulsion.

She lifts me so that I am impaled on her, and her penetration of my body is fully exposed to Arcus. Another tentacle prods my ass, slips between my cheeks. I fight, but she is stronger, and I scream as she forces her way inside.

My eyes roll toward the ceiling and find it is a tarnished mirror. I see myself, spread and violated, and my memory jolts.

Luthian's pet.

The image stirs my blood. It's easy enough for me to ignore the sight of the horrible creature holding me, easy for me to imagine that I'm being held by Luthian's vines, ravaged by them. I relax in her hold.

I'm supposed to be scared. I will not give Arcus that victory.

"The slut enjoys it," the creature hisses. "She grows wetter even now."

"You will not speak of your future queen in that manner," Arcus warns her. "Get on with it."

Get on with what? I think. Will the beast rend me limb from limb? Drown me? Devour me?

It is the last one, I realize, when she drops her mouth to the space between my neck and shoulder and sinks her teeth deeply in.

My head swims. She laps greedily at my blood, draws on the wound, her tentacles working in and out of my ass and cunt while I writhe in her arms. Another tentacle lashes across my breast, those sucking rings finding my nipples. I cry out at the shock of sensation, feel another tentacle girdle my hips. The tip pushes between my labia, attaching to my clit with impossible force. I kick my legs, not certain if I'm trying to escape or if I'm simply overcome by the feeling.

Luthian said that pain, that fear made things more pleasurable. His lesson serves me now; if I did not know this about myself, I would be ashamed, mortified by my body's enthusiastic response to this attack.

Instead, I'm angry. If this were not intended as a punishment, I might have truly enjoyed it. I suspect, though, that the creature delights in my fear and pain, and would have caused them, anyway.

The creature's mouth on my neck is its own kind of pleasure, warm and obscene as she revels in the taste of my blood. The tentacles inside me alternate their movements, and I rock my hips with them. It takes barely seven breaths before the suction on my clit is too much to bear, and I come, screaming, back bowing, hips pumping.

"Enough!" Arcus shouts, and the beast drops me into the water, withdrawing from my body and gliding off on a cloud of blood-red ink.

I cannot swim, but some instinct pulls me through the water, to the ledge where Arcus stands.

"This was but a taste of what will happen should you disobey me again," he warns, his boot crushing my fingers where I clutch the stone lip of the pool. "Next time, you will not enjoy it."

That's why he's angry? Because I climaxed when I was supposed to be suffering? Because I ruined the horror he meant to punish me with?

I wince as he grinds his foot down harder, and finally cry out with the pain.

"Next time, I will let her drink as much as she pleases. To have you any way she chooses," he goes on. "I will allow that because I will it. I choose your partners, Cenere. And if I tell you that you will not cavort with other members of my court, with my sons, you will not."

He crushes my other hand, and I sob.

"Be ready for this evening. I'm announcing our engagement to the court." He turns away. "I'm finished with you."

"Don't leave me here!" I scream. There is a flash of white.

"Cenere!" Luthian is beside me in a moment. "Don't leave you where? What's happened? What did he do to you?"

"He... He..." I'm in the great hall of Luthian's house, naked and crouched in a puddle of water. I blink in confusion. "I was in a... I was..."

Firo appears over Luthian's shoulder. "She's bleeding."

"I see that she's bleeding," Luthian snaps, and conjures a wide strip of bandage from the air. He presses it to my neck. "This isn't her only injury. She's covered in bruises."

I look down at my arms and legs. The marks aren't bruises, but rings left behind from the creature's tentacles.

"Heal her," Firo says, and conjures a blanket to wrap around me.

"What has he done to you?" Luthian demands.

"There was a... some kind of monster. I don't know where we were." The pain in my neck is gone when Luthian takes the bandage away, and the blood upon it pulls from the surface, suspended as droplets that disappear into the air.

"I know this monster," Firo says grimly. "I've heard it spoken of at court."

"I know it, too." Luthian's eyes are hard and far away.

"A Cephalopire," Firo says quietly. "He uses it to punish his enemies."

"Not just his enemies." Luthian drifts in some horrible thought that I cannot discern but snaps quickly back to the present. "Did he tell you why he did this?"

My limbs are cold, and I tremble. "I'm to be his queen. And he doesn't want his queen to...display herself. He was angry about the mermaids, about his sons..."

Luthian curses under his breath and takes me into his arms, almost crushing me with his fierce protectiveness.

It's only then that I can feel truly afraid. "I only did what you told me I should do. I thought—"

"I know." He kisses my forehead. "I'm so sorry. I should never have brought you here."

But that was our bargain. I knew this would be dangerous. Perhaps, not this dangerous, but I did not enter this arrangement thoughtlessly.

Who could have imagined such a horrible possibility?

"Do you see now, ambassador?" Luthian asks, his voice sharp with recrimination. "Do you agree now that something must be done?"

I lift my eyes. Firo stands helplessly beside us, his face awash in regret.

"I see now," he says. "Arcus must die."

Chapter Twenty-Eight

A sylph messenger arrives with a formal, sealed letter only moments later. It's for Luthian.

He snatches it and orders the being away from his door.

I sit beside the fire, wrapped in a blanket, unwilling to do anything more. Though Luthian has healed me, there are wounds that cannot be tended to with magic. My body can be made whole, but my spirit is exhausted.

Firo stays by my side, and I'm glad for his presence. I hate that he's captured Luthian's heart, but I'm glad for his friendship, nevertheless. I have a strong feeling that I'll need to rely on him more than ever in the coming days.

"What is it?" Firo asks as we watch Luthian scan the page.

"A royal summons. I'm to meet with Arcus to discuss my payment for my crimes against the court, and the terms of my permanent return." He folds the letter and pushes it into his jacket pocket.

"Payment for your crimes?" A hysterical sob rises in my throat at the thought of Luthian in the grips of that terrible creature. I must force it back to ask, "He doesn't mean that you'll... that thing..."

Luthian shakes his head. "No. I don't think so. But I've survived that once before."

My stomach turns. Luthian endured the same humiliation and torture as I did? No wonder he looked so haunted when I told him what Arcus had done. My heart aches for my guardian and I long to embrace him, but I can't find the strength of will to make my limbs move.

"He's going to tell Luthian that he's separating the two of you. So that Arcus can take you as his queen," Firo says, glancing up at Luthian. "There has been talk of little else, today."

Luthian grimaces. "So soon?"

I nod. "He's going to announce the engagement tonight."

"Which means that this is the last time the three of us will all be together," Firo points out. "He'll remove you from Luthian's quarters immediately upon the announcement. And I don't expect him to allow the two of you to have contact."

"Which is why you must help us," Luthian says, his hands curling to fists. "Firo, I cannot risk her falling into that creature's clutches again."

Separated from Luthian? I can't breathe. "No!"

My outburst startles the faeries.

"Cenere," Luthian begins, his voice thick with emotion.

"No, it cannot be. I can't... I can't..." Whatever small spark of strength and dignity that was left in me after the horrors of the morning is doused. I throw myself at Luthian's feet. "Don't make me go!"

"This isn't something either of us can stop," Firo says gently, laying a comforting hand on my back. "You will be safe, as long as you do whatever Arcus asks of you."

"I did what he asked," I sobbed. "I did everything that he asked, and he punished me for something that I did before we were betrothed!"

"Arcus is an unreasonable, unpredictable tyrant," Luthian says, and reaches down to lift me to my feet. "You are better than him. Better at playing the game. Better at hiding the truth of your feelings. Better in every other way. I know that you can do this."

I shake my head, ready to deny him again.

"You can do it."

Please, don't say that I was born for this, I think, for I could not stop myself from asking the truth behind his words if he utters them.

Instead, he leans his forehead against mine. "I know what you endured today. Even knowing that, I would have taken your place. But what's done is done, and we have reached the point of no return. You will leave me tonight and go to Arcus. You will simper and praise him and please him and do nothing to evoke his wrath. I promise you; this will be over soon."

A point of no return. We can't simply disappear from court now; Arcus would look for me, I am certain of it. The only choice before me now is to live to see the king assassinated or die myself. Because I refuse to ever again experience what I suffered today.

I wipe my own tears away and step back from him. "We came here to do a job. You thought I was capable enough when you chose me for it. I would hate to let you down, now. Go to your meeting."

He looks to Firo, as if pleading for another solution.

"Go," Firo says softly. "I'll take care of her."

Still, Luthian hesitates.

I place a hand on his chest, feel the warmth of his body beneath his clothes. We are on a treacherous path now. We have always been, though I did not appreciate the danger before. He covers my hand with his, and I close my eyes. "Go, Luthian."

"If this is the last time we see each other," he begins.

I shake my head. "It won't be. Go."

He lifts my hand to his lips and brushes a kiss across my knuckles before he disappears.

My shoulders sag and I double over, hugging myself but unable to cry.

"Come on," Firo says, putting a steadying arm around me. "You need to be beautiful for the announcement tonight."

My eyes are puffy, my face likely red around the nose from my weeping. I laugh and hear the thickness of water lingering in my lungs.

"We can fix all this," Firo promises as he leads me toward the stairs. "We'll make you so beautiful and so strong, Arcus will fear you."

* * * *

The royal throne room is even more crowded the second time I enter it. Luthian is at my side, but his presence is not a comfort now. He is to deliver me to the king, to be humbled before the entire court.

The splendor of the room, which overwhelmed me the first time I saw it, is even more dazzling now. Everyone is dressed in their finest, heaped with jewels, skin shimmering, wings aflutter.

Every eye is on me as I walk beside Luthian. He's dressed all in black, as if in mourning. I managed to write a cheerful note to the king, asking what color he'd decided on for the night's festivities, and I've dressed to match him. The satin of my gown is the same wine hue as his velvet doublet, and the jeweled choker around my neck—more like a collar, considering the event—winks with garnets to match those in his golden crown. He sees me from the dais and rises, extending a hand.

An image flashes through my mind, so vivid I'm afraid it's truly happening. I see myself clinging to Luthian, begging to break our agreement, asking him to take me away from this place.

It's too late. It was too late this morning. It's certainly too late, now, with every eye in the court upon me.

Pretending to be cold to Luthian is easy; it means I don't have to give him one last look or trust myself not to weep as we part. I don't spare him even a glance as I drift from him toward the dais, my expression joyously serene.

"I have the pleasure to announce to you all tonight that you shall have a new queen." Arcus takes my hand as I climb the shallow steps, the murmurs and polite audible interest of the court rising behind me. The announcement stirs them to applause, which Arcus quiets with a gesture so that he can continue. "Cenere has agreed to leave her faithless mate and join herself to me. From this moment on, she is not a simple human courtesan or a court plaything. She is your queen, even before the coronation ceremony. Any who touch her without my permission will face severe consequences."

I would think that a threat like that would dampen a party, but the courtiers seem to find it amusing. Someone calls out, "Huzzah!" and the rest follow suit.

Arcus wraps an arm around my waist and pulls me close to his side. His breath stirs a tendril of hair near my ear. "They love you, Cenere. They will worship you as you deserve to be worshipped."

I've never thought, even once, that I deserve worship. What a ridiculous expectation for anyone to have. But I flutter my lashes at him and smile sweetly.

He doesn't need words in response. I'm sure he's already decided what I feel.

Addressing the court once more, Arcus announces, "A celebratory feast has been prepared, with entertainments from the farthest reaches of Fablemere. Go, be merry. Celebrate my good fortune and the justice that has been dealt to my enemy."

Luthian lowers his head as if defeated.

"Luthian of Mithrax is now reinstated to the Court of Pleasure and Torment, with full privileges and honors. What little of the latter he has displayed," Arcus continues.

Bowing low, Luthian says, "I thank Your Majesty profoundly."

"I thank you." Arcus's fingers skate over the tops of my breasts above the low neckline of my gown. "For your understanding. Not every faery could withstand the humiliation of his mate preferring another."

Ah, so that's the line. My mouth twists with distaste. Arcus would have the court believe that I chose to leave my mate. The king's ego will never be satisfied.

"Go forth!" Arcus calls out. "Feast!"

Doors on both sides of the hall open in unison. Light, colors, delicious smells and enticing music swirl beyond each one. The party seems to spread through the entire palace.

"Oh, Arcus," I breathe, tilting my chin up to gaze at him adoringly. "This is far too much. I am not worthy of such—"

"Nonsense." His lips find my throat. "You deserve

to live in splendor for the rest of your mortal days."

My mortal days. I'm lucky, at least, that I will age and die and escape him, should the assassination plot not work out.

It will work, I promise myself. I am queen of the Court of Pleasure and Torment. Or, will be. And once I am able, I will use that power to punish Cadwyn Thrace.

What then?

It's a question I haven't asked myself until this moment. Once I kill Thrace, will I return to Elegwyn Manor, with its rotting walls and leaking roof? Will I be content to tend it and live quietly, now that I've seen and experienced all that I have?

Will I be able to live without Luthian at my side? For once we achieve our mutual end and Cassan is on the throne, he will be gone from my life, probably forever.

I search the crowd for him and see that he's already gone. Vanished, I assume, back to the house I have come to think of as home.

"Come," Arcus says, shocking me out of my grim revelation. "I would show you your new chambers."

"But the party, Your Majesty," I say, already hearing moans of ecstasy from the open doorways.

Not that I will be allowed to partake in any of that particular type of entertainment. Arcus has made that gruelingly clear.

"We'll come back," he promises. "I wouldn't abandon my own celebration. But I have a gift for you, as well."

A bejeweled chastity belt? I think to myself with a mean little giggle that Arcus interprets as a laugh meant for him. He beams down at me and waves a hand.

We are no longer on the dais, but in a blindingly white room that makes me shield my eyes from the light. Pure white flame flickers in sconces on the walls, between mirrors that stretch from the white granite floors to the swirling ornamentations on the ceiling overhead. In the center of the room is an enormous, round bed, made up all in white, beneath a skylight shaped like a many-pointed star. The dark sky overhead is the only color, aside from that of our reflections, reproduced hundreds of times in endless tunnels as the mirrors look into each other.

I turn to Arcus in exaggerated wonder. "This is my room?"

"Your own private sanctuary." He nods beyond the bed; a large, empty basin in the shape of a crescent moon curves around it, with steps to descend inside. "That will be filled with water from the very faery bath where I fell in love with you."

It would be grand and romantic if I did not loathe him so.

There is a knock, and Arcus calls, "Enter," rubbing his hands together. "And now, the gift."

A sylph enters, carrying a mirrored box tied with an enormous white bow, and stops before me.

Arcus gives me a sly look and nods.

I pull the ribbon with a giddy laugh, preparing to *ooh!* and *aah!* over the jewels inside. But when the ribbon releases, the sides of the box fall open to reveal something that kills the smile on my face.

Cadwyn Thrace's head.

"I hope you like it," Arcus says, self-congratulatory pride dripping from each word like a rancid syrup.

I am numb. I am faint. I am furious and grief-stricken all at once. My beautiful revenge has been snatched from me. The only thing I sought when I entered into my bargain with Luthian has been stolen by this disgusting worm of a faery who watches proudly while my dreams are shattered.

The effort it takes to force down my disappointed

tears exhausts me. How I manage to pretend that I'm grateful, I cannot fathom. I turn to Arcus and fall to my knees before him, bowing my head. "I do not deserve you, Arcus. You are more to me than I could ever possibly dream. There is no way I can repay you for the honors you've bestowed upon me."

"You needn't repay me." He places a hand on the back of my head, chuckling, and one hand works the laces of his breeches. "But if you wished to thank me…"

I smile up at him, feeling nothing but cold emptiness beneath my skin. "Of course, my beloved king."

This time, when he takes me, I cannot escape into my fantasy of vengeance, because he has destroyed it.

And he has destroyed me with it.

Chapter Twenty-Nine

The celebrations show no sign of slowing when we return to them. The only difference between when we left and when we return is my sorrow and anger.

As I am not allowed to engage in any of the sexual entertainment, I lay at Arcus's side on a mound of pillows while he is fellated and ridden by a dozen courtiers, at least. I ply him with faery wine and bites of desserts, compliment his prowess and press his face to my cleavage.

All without the comfort of my promised prize.

It's harder now to pretend to love him, to desire him, to admire him. The effort should be an impossible task, but I somehow find it in myself to smile and kiss him and stroke his cock between partners.

Luthian passes through the crowd, and without thinking, I turn desperate eyes to him. He pays no attention to us and snags the hand of a pretty young male faery with pale, silky hair, to lead him out the open doors into the garden.

The faery atop Arcus now cries out in crudely feigned passion, her breasts bouncing as the king pounds into her from below. He gives her a push, saying, "Off! I'm about to spend. I would do it in my queen."

Lifting my skirts, I crouch over him, feel the slick wet that the faery left behind. I slide down Arcus's cock and breathe, "Oh yes, my king. Yes, like that!" as I clutch on him.

He reaches up with both hands to grab my breasts while I ride him, and it takes only a few slow glides of my hips to make him curl up, groaning as if mortally wounded. His cock twitches and leaps inside me as he comes, and it takes all of my will power to pretend I enjoy it.

That will is quickly wearing down.

To my relief, Arcus's eyelids grow heavy from the wine and the fucking, and soon he wavers between consciousness and sleep even as he softens and falls from my cunt on a wet slide.

"I grow tired, my love." He rubs a hand up and down my arm. "Go. Enjoy the party. The music, the dancing, the food... but do not give yourself to anyone else."

"I have no need to," I promise him.

"Guard her," he tells the sylphs who flank our nest of cushions.

I don't want to be guarded. I want to find a quiet place to cry and curse his name. I can't stand to keep up this act a moment longer.

"Arcus, no," I say softly. "No one would dare lay a finger upon me. I would rather they watch over you. I won't be able to enjoy myself if I worry for your safety."

He gives me an indulgent smile. "All right. I suppose you know the penalty for disobedience and won't be tempted to test me."

I nod solemnly. This is something I don't have to fake. I never wish to encounter the cephalopire again, although I don't doubt that he'll subject me to her on a whim, should he decide to.

I stroll through the party, nodding serenely to courtiers as I pass, but never stopping to talk. I must reserve that, Firo instructed me in preparation for tonight, for when bestowing my favor with a conversation will be useful. If I need to gain the goodwill of one house, a simple compliment on a gown or a particularly masterful game of cards will be the only currency necessary to buy loyalty.

I feel every set of eyes upon me as I walk through the halls and salons, past faeries being flogged and whipped, bound and gagged. I stop to admire the performance of two male faeries at a gaming table. A clockwork contraption with oiled sleeves pumps both of their cocks while courtiers place their bets on each participant's endurance. The moans and pinched expressions of both participants indicate that the contest is close; when one erupts immediately before the other, a cheer goes up from half the spectators around the table. The other faery bucks his hips and grunts as he finishes, his cum splashing across the pile of wagered gold.

The winner is released from the machine. The loser is not. He curses and whines as the clockwork stroking continues, and more bets are placed on how long he'll last before he comes again, and how many times he'll come before he begs for them to stop.

I'm hot and slick between my legs at the spectacle, and not just because of my copulation with Arcus. The sight of the tormented faery, his pink body flush with sweat, his iridescent wings buzzing and setting up a wind around the table, the way his fists clench and release as if grasping for something to help him escape, it's all too arousing. I want to do as I see others around the table doing and relieve my lust under my own hand.

The debauchery all around is an incredible torture. I need privacy, quiet, and to escape the tantalizing moans and pained screams of those enjoying what I cannot. I know that after my time with Luthian, no one else will satisfy me. Certainly not Arcus; I cannot give myself over to pleasure with someone who has so deeply wronged me.

It's this thought that drives me outside, into the gardens and, accidentally, to where Luthian and the faery he'd left with are locked in writhing, moaning passion. I halt and watch them lying in a carpet of night-violets together. They are naked and entwined, Luthian curled around his partner's back, entering him from behind.

Another faery wanders over to them, bare breasts displayed above a tight corset, the only garment she wears. She lies down in front of Luthian's nameless lover and takes him into her cunt, leaning forward to capture Luthian's mouth over their shared partner's shoulder.

Luthian's eyes meet mine, and I watch the hunger and sadness fill those silver depths.

I turn away, tears burning in my eyes. I hold myself together as I walk further from the palace. The groups of copulating faeries thin, until I am alone, beyond the torchlight, at the mouth of the forest.

That's when I allow myself to cry. A sob wells in my throat and I don't stop it from bursting out. I run without a destination in mind, down the path to the sacred circle. I plunge through the trees, the branches whipping my face and snagging my hair. I may be lost. I hope I am lost. I pray that some creature will snatch me and devour me, so that I no longer have to endure the pain and finality of justice slipping through my fingers.

Perhaps if I'd married Thrace, I would have been able to kill him myself. I would have no doubt been caught, but I would rather face the consequence of execution than the threat of the cephalopire, the depravity of Arcus's desires that are cruel for cruelty's sake.

I know he will die. Luthian will succeed. Perhaps Cassan will take me as his mate, even though I was his father's queen; he doesn't seem the type to be troubled by that prior relationship. But even if he does, even if I am someday queen of the Court of Pleasure and Torment and free of Arcus forever, what's the point now? Thrace is dead. I don't need the crown.

I haven't just lost my revenge. I've lost my purpose.

My lungs give out and I must slow, but I don't want to stop walking. Perhaps no one will come to look for me. I could walk until my feet bleed, until I am so completely lost that I'm no longer myself. Until every vestige of my previous life is erased and I am forgotten to time.

Eventually, the trees thin and I find myself in a familiar clearing. I blink in confusion. There's the mouth of the cavern. The entrance to the faery bath.

Arcus had taken a dragon ride to a place close enough for me to walk in a ball gown and satin slippers. A dismayed laugh burbles up my throat. The pathetic, self-aggrandizing fool sought to impress me with a flight that seemed to take hours. We likely circled the clearing again and again, just so I would believe he spirited me away to some far-off sanctuary.

And I'm to be his mate, and his queen, and I'm to live out my days among pleasures that are empty because Luthian will not be mine, even after Arcus is dead.

Because I was born for this.

I have no doubt now that Luthian will dispose of me once he reaches his aim. Though he has not confirmed it, though I have not been able to ask, the answer seems so clear to me now beneath the uncaring stars.

He granted his own wish when he granted my mother's.

I have never existed for my own sake.

The mouth of the tunnel shines with the warm, spectral illumination within. I remember how heavy my gown became when the cephalopire pulled me into the water.

Wiping tears from my eyes, I walk toward the mouth of the cavern.

If I have never existed for myself, it's better that I don't exist at all.

Chapter Thirty

A sense of calm comes over me as I walk into the faery baths. Arcus is wrong. I don't belong here. I don't belong anywhere, for I do not exist. I am a means to an end, a tool to be used. An advantage.

I have never been a person, with a fate of my own, and the only destiny I could claim has been taken.

I stand on the ledge that overlooks the pools, and eye the carved steps that lead to the ones in towers above. I don't wish to jump. But I don't know which to choose.

I'm mulling it over when footsteps echo in the cave entrance, and someone says, "Cenere."

Of course, it would be Kathras. If anyone were to find me, it would be Arcus's equally repugnant son. I turn to him and give a faint smile. "Which, do you think, would be deepest?"

His brows draw together. "Deepest?"

"I wouldn't want to sit in something up to my

waist and try to drown," I explain with a hysterical laugh. "I need something deep. So, I can be dragged down."

Kathras takes a step toward me. "You've been drinking."

"I have." That didn't cross my mind when I was running. Or when I made this choice. It was the only way I could endure the party.

"Come back to the palace," he urges me. "We can talk there."

I laugh again. "No, we can't! Do you know what he subjected me to when you left?"

His eyes darken. "I do."

My breath leaves me.

"He did it once to someone I loved very much." He holds out his hand. "Please. Come with me to the palace."

I shake my head. "I can't go back. I can't. He…"

"I know." Kathras's eyes plead with me. "I believe you. I'll listen to you."

I crumple to my knees, covering my eyes. I thought I calmed after my race through the forest. I thought I cried all my tears out there. But now, the painful sobs return, shaking my entire body.

Kathras kneels beside me, leans over my back as if shielding me from some battering force. But the pain is in my chest, bursting through my ribs, ripping me apart from inside, and even the screams that echo through the cavern don't release enough of my sorrow to heal me.

Kathras pulls me into his lap and cradles my head against his chest. "Tell me."

Lying in his arms, I tell him about my mother. About Cadwyn Thrace's treachery. About the revenge I wanted to take against him. I tell him how Luthian trained me, brought me to the palace in the hopes that I could climb my way through the court and ex-act my revenge. I don't reveal Luthian's plan to kill him and his father. While the penalty for treason doesn't matter to me now, I would die before I endangered Luthian.

The whole time I talk, Kathras holds me and listens. He doesn't ask questions or pass judgment. He listens, sympathetically stroking my hair or brushing away my tears.

"It was terrible," I tell him, my limbs shaking at the memory of those tentacles restraining me, entering me. "I didn't want to like it. I think he enjoys that, the most. The humiliation. I understand that pleasure and torment can entwine, and I did find pleasure in what the cephalopire subjected me to. But then... he crushed my hands. That wasn't about dark pleasures. It was about hurting me, for no reason other than to exert his control. And now, I'm going to be mated to him."

For the first time as I told my story, Kathras speaks. He tucks his fingers beneath my chin and lifts my gaze to his. "Cenere, I vow that you will never face that punishment again."

"You can't promise that," I whisper. "No one can."

"I can. He will never punish you with that creature again."

I want to believe him, to feel relief at his promise. But I don't have the strength to believe promises, anymore, and Arcus will almost certainly find worse torments. I take a breath, look away, and continue. "But the worst of it was tonight. The worst by far. He told me he had a present. It was Thrace's head."

Kathras stiffens. "He stole your revenge."

His words are a lightning bolt striking my heart. He understands. Without a single word of explanation or justification, he knows exactly why this hurts me, far more than being fed to a monster.

"Oh, Cenere. I'm so sorry," he whispers against

the top of my head, tightening his arms around me.

Fresh tears spring to my eyes, but I'm beyond sobbing now. I cling to him, taking comfort in the most unlikely source. He understands.

Something changes as he holds me. His pulse quickens beneath my ear. I lift my tear-stained face and search his stricken expression. He doesn't just understand. He grieves the loss beside me. I'm drawn into the sympathetic depths of his crystalline green eyes and reach up to touch the sharp plane of his jaw.

There is no question in his eyes, but I answer him in a whisper. "Yes."

His mouth descends on mine and when I yield to him, he groans as if he's lost some battle with himself. There is no fight for me. I don't grapple with my conscience or consider the consequences. I don't care if Arcus finds out.

There is a restrained strength in Kathras's body that makes me want to force him to unleash it, as he did in the maze. I whimper at the memory of the hot, thick slide of him in my cunt, the euphoric fear of being chased.

But it's different now, and somehow more frightening. He kisses me deeply, again and again, leaves me panting for air when he moves on to my throat, and then I pant for another reason. His hand slides up and down the tight silk bodice of my gown, over the tops of my breasts, to the necklace I wear.

"Who gave this to you?" he murmurs against my neck.

I swallow. "Your father."

With a jerk of his fist, the necklace breaks and falls to the ground. I gasp, and he kisses me again, fiercely, and brings me to my feet.

He doesn't vanish my clothes, but asks, "May I see you?"

My blood burns at the request. I reach for the laces at the front of my gown, but he passes a hand over the silk and only then does it disappear, leaving me exposed to him. He gazes at me for a long time, as if memorizing every part of me. The hand he extends toward me trembles.

"I knew," he whispers. "In the labyrinth, I knew who you were."

He brushes my aching nipple with the back of his fingers. "I saw you when you arrived. I wanted you then. But I knew my father would have you. I couldn't bear to see you exploited as a show of his power. When he did it at the ritual, when he took you in front of me, I knew that it wouldn't stop."

"You can have me," I say. "Not to spite your father. You can have me because I want you."

And to spite his father, a more honest voice in my mind says. I don't want him to take me out of spite, but I do offer myself up for the satisfaction of defying Arcus.

When I return to the palace, I'll fuck him with his son's cum still inside me.

I take Kathras's hand and move it down my body, the curls that cover my sex. "Please. Take me. Erase the feeling of him in me."

In an instant, Kathras's clothes are gone, and he stands beautiful and naked before me. I've seen the lean, muscular lines of his body in the firelight at the ritual, as he'd been barely clothed then. I'd felt but never seen his cock, however, and in the light, I'm stunned at the size of it. It's long enough that it brushes his navel, as thick as the vampire member that Luthian used on me. My cunt aches with emptiness at the sight of it.

He takes me in his arms and flies to one of the nearby pools, but I tell him, "No. That one."

I want him to fuck me in the same pool where his

father had me. I want nothing about me to belong to Arcus alone. Not even my memories.

We slip into the pool and Kathras stands me beneath one of the rushing waterfalls. It makes me laugh, but his teeth on my nipple cuts off that laughter with a sigh. The hot water cascading over me eases a tension I didn't feel before, while Kathras's mouth on me raises another kind. His knee parts my leg, and he brings his thigh up to fit tight against my mound.

"Make yourself come," he murmurs against my ear. "Grind your pussy on me until you come."

The silky water makes it easy to glide back and forth over him, as do my own juices. He sucks and teases my nipples while I ride his thigh, using my hands on his shoulders for leverage. The ring through my hood flips back and forth on each slide of my hips, and every pull of his mouth on my breasts sends sensation straight to that most sensitive part.

But it's his voice that pushes me close to the precipice every time he lifts his head to look me in the eye and encourage me along. "That's it. Use me for your pleasure. You deserve to come."

I gasp and tip my head back.

"I'm going to fuck you, Cenere," he says, a hand closing gently around my throat. "So deep and so hard that whenever you're with anyone else, all you can think of is me. All you can feel is me. Every time you fuck my father, you'll be fucking me in your mind. Remembering how I feel inside your tight little cunt."

I cry out, my legs shaking with the force of the climax that takes me. This is exactly what I want. An escape from what's to be, from the inevitable. A fantasy to replace the one that I lost when Arcus presented me with Thrace's head.

This will do, I think, as my body bucks in his arms. *This will do.*

He slides me smoothly from his thigh to lift my leg around his waist. I follow with the other, feel his cock against my opening.

"Hang onto me," he orders, and I cross my ankles behind his back, wrap my arms around his shoulders.

He unfurls his wings and we rise into the air, up and up, until the top of his head brushes the ceiling of the cavern. My stomach drops and the bottoms of my feet tingle. I shudder in fear and grip him tighter.

"Do you remember what I said?" he whispers in my ear. "How I'm going to fuck you?"

"Deep," I moan, my body parting around the slow advance of his cock. "And hard."

"Why?"

"So I never feel anyone but you." I wriggle, desperate to be filled despite my precarious position. "So that I am yours."

"You are mine," he says, releasing my waist to grip my chin and hold his gaze to mine. "And I want to look into your eyes when you feel this."

Kathras drops us suddenly, and I shriek in terror, until he pulls up short and uses the force of the stop to thrust the whole, enormous length of him into me. The thickness of his shaft stretches my cunt and I wail in relief. He lifts me up, so that just the tip of him rests inside me and does it again. Another short drop, another deep thrust. He grips the hair at the nape of my neck, never takes his eyes from mine as we fall together over and over, until his toes touch the surface of the pool.

We rise again, up and up, all the way to the ceiling once more, and I brace myself for another exhilarating drop.

Instead, he pries my arms from around his neck

and lifts me over his head, pressing my shoulders to the rough stone. His wings beat steadily, lifting him closer, and he tilts us back until I am splayed atop him, the ceiling at my back, his knees against the stone, his body the only thing stopping me from plummeting to my death.

A death which only moments before wouldn't have frightened me quite so much. And that fear, just as Luthian promised, makes the pleasure so much better as Kathras strokes into me, hard and fast, his wide shaft tugging at my clit. It's terrifying. It's ecstatic. The fear and pleasure spike higher and higher, and I wonder if, when I come, I will fall, spasm out of Kathras's grasp and plunge down, a scream of release my last words. I'm so close, I don't care. I chase my climax, meeting his thrusts, moaning with his own strained shouts. I come screaming, wetness bursting over us both, raining down to the cavern floor.

He grabs me in his arms and we spiral back down to the pool, splashing into the water before the final waves of my orgasm have a chance to subside, while I'm still moaning and gasping.

"I hope you don't think we're finished," he groans against my ear.

Chapter Thirty-One

Kathras takes me, over and over. On a smooth, stone ledge. Against a wall that scrapes my back in the most delicious way. Once, with water falling between us, cascading over where we join and thundering against my clit until I can take no more and faint from the unrelenting pleasure.

There is roughness in his passion, but not cruelty. When we are both spent, he holds me, and we laze in the warmth of the pools. He heals me, not just from the abrasions of the stone in the cavern, but the slashes left by branches on my face and thorns on my ankles. He holds me, cradles my head in the hollow of his shoulder, and asks nothing of me.

But I have questions for him. One, in particular. "Why?"

His chest rises beneath my back, holds, then slowly falls. "I don't know. I suppose because you looked so lost. I felt your misery call out to me, so I followed."

"You followed me all the way from the palace?" I sit up slightly in alarm. "What if you had been seen?"

"I wasn't seen." He states it so assuredly, it's difficult to doubt him. "It's one of my abilities, inherited from my father."

"Arcus can move around the palace unseen?" My heart beats frantically against my ribs like an animal trying to escape a snare. How often have I had conversations that he's overheard? Could he have gotten past Luthian's wards?

"That isn't what I meant." He pulls me back to him, to sit on his knees and face him. "I was able to feel your sorrow, and it drew me to you."

It seems too empathetic a power for someone like Arcus.

"I don't usually find that kind of sadness here at court," Kathras goes on. "Envy. Rage. Jealousy. Hatred. Those emotions run high, but rarely true sadness. The courtiers are deliriously happy, most of the time."

"I can see why they would be." It would be easy to lose oneself in a life dedicated solely to sensation. Even pain, I've learned, can be euphoric. "But why bother to follow me? When you know the risk of the king catching us?"

"The king will be unconscious for days, judging by how much of that enchanted wine he drank." Kathras's voice drips with contempt. "I came to you because I know what it's like to live under my father's tyrannical rule. Not just as a courtier, but as someone he views as a possession. I've seen him break even the strongest fairies. You're human. You can't withstand the torment he would inflict upon you."

"I can withstand far more than you'd think," I argue, but if he doesn't believe my words, I can't blame him. I don't believe them, myself.

"I'm sure you can," he placates me. "I felt your pain, and your loneliness. I don't know what kind of a life you had with…"

His voice dies away, and he swallows as if he would be sick to say the name.

"With Luthian?" I ask.

He nods sharply. "As I said, I don't know what kind of life you had. But the emptiness within you was too much to bear. And this was the only way I could show you kindness."

Of course, it was. If he's lived his whole life at court—with the exception of his time in the Sorrowlands, which I ache with curiosity about—then how could he have learned anything of gentleness or tenderness that didn't involve sexual pleasure?

Still, it rankles to hear him admit that he's just fucked me senseless out of pity. "I thought it was because you desired me."

"If you think I could have managed this without desire, then you have a very high opinion of me." He smiles slightly, and it transforms his serious, brooding face into something more boyish. I see the resemblance to Cassan that I didn't notice was missing, before.

There is such a difference between the two brothers. I wonder how that came to be.

"I do desire you, Cenre," he says, his eyes roving over my face, my neck, my breasts. "If a single faery at court says they don't, they're lying. You can't possibly see yourself the way we do. There's a light around you, an energy of youth and newness that we rarely see."

"Yes, I've noticed there are no children at the palace." *Obviously, that's for the best,* I think.

His brow crumples. "There are no faery children at all, Cenere."

This isn't something my mother ever told me. "I'm not sure of what you mean."

"We're the mingled essences of our parents, born of wisps of light." He seems truly astonished to have to explain this to me. "We come into being in the nursery hives, grow through the seasons, and are delivered back to our parents fully formed."

"Through the seasons?" I shake my head. "You mean, one cycle of the seasons and you're... like this?"

"We're immortal creatures, Cenere. We're born with all of the knowledge that we need to survive. From there, it's matter of refinement to fit into your court. If that's how you choose to live." He pauses. "You didn't know any of this?"

"I assumed there were children..." My mind wanders to my mother's wish. Why, if faeries didn't have children, would my mother have wished for one? "My mother never told me. And I don't understand. Why did she want a baby, if that was never to be a part of her life, anyway?"

Kathras's brows rise as he considers the answer. "Perhaps she simply saw the way humans are with their young, and wanted it for herself?"

I wish I could ask her. I wish I could demand an explanation for my birth, for Luthian, for her expulsion from the Court of Seasons. She died and left me nothing but unanswered questions I never knew to ask.

"We should return to the palace," Kathras says, pressing a kiss to my forehead. "I think we both know that this can never happen again."

My heart sinks, but he's right. It's too dangerous. Even being here with him now is a mortal gamble. I think of the cephalopire's teeth and shudder.

As if he can read my thoughts, he lifts my chin. "I promised you that you would never suffer that terror at my father's hands again. I do not break my promises, Cenere."

He steps from the pool, and I look about for my gown. "I can't return to the palace naked—"

My words are no sooner uttered than I am blinking in the harsh white of my new chambers, reclined in the crescent pool, now filled with water from the faery bath.

* * * *

The next morning, the court is called to assembly by a rage of bells in the corridors.

It takes me some time to find my way out of my mirror-paneled room. The door isn't readily apparent. I begin to panic that perhaps there is no door, and that I am here at Arcus's whim, to be released as he deems necessary. But finally, I find the handle and push out, directly into the hall leading to the throne room.

I think of how the door to Luthian's house opened onto the hall to the king's chambers when I needed to go there. Perhaps all the rooms in the palace function in that way, anticipating where one needs to be.

I'm not certain it's something I can get used to, but I suppose I will have to, once I become Arcus's queen. And then Cassan's.

Because Kathras will be dead, too. I swallow down the panic that rises in my chest. I still feel his hands on my body, his strong arms holding me suspended in the air. There must be a way to dissuade Luthian. Some way for him to install Cassan on the throne without harming Kathras.

Perhaps if I tell Luthian that I owe Kathras my life...

The crowd of courtiers moving along the hall sweep me into the throne room, but once inside, they part to let me move toward the dais. I am, after all, their future queen.

Arcus stands before his throne, fury scrawled over his expression with a heavy hand. He looks coldly over the assembled courtiers. Though he sees me in the crowd, he doesn't motion me forward.

"A great wrong has been committed against me." As he speaks, his voice rises in anger. "One of you has stolen from me and returned the item in deeply damaged condition."

The sylphs appear from behind the dais, bearing dripping, severed tentacles and the pallid head of the cephalopire. Its jaw gapes. All of its teeth have been pulled.

Relief mixes with fear at the sight of it. The smell of blood and rot and the foul dampness of the monster's cell which still clings to its mutilated corpse, causes the courtiers around me to cover their noses. I cannot. I'm frozen in fear at the sight of the monster. The chatter and alarm that surround me fade to a high, ringing noise in my ears.

Only Arcus's voice cuts through. He is red-faced with his rage. "I will find who destroyed my property, and you will suffer exactly as it suffered before it died!"

As he stalks from the throne room, I spot Kathras in the crowd. His eyes meet mine before he turns and leaves, too.

"I promised you that you would never suffer that terror at my father's hands again. I do not break my promises, Cenere."

Chapter Thirty-Two

I don't know why I seek out Kathras. It feels as though I'm bringing danger to him, as if every eye in the palace is upon me. For the first time, though, I am not the object of fascination. Everyone is on edge, picturing their own heads with gaping, toothless mouths.

What do I mean to say to Kathras? What *can* I say? That he's angered his father? He knows that already, even if his father hasn't yet deduced who is responsible for the cephalopire's death. Am I going to shame him for killing the creature? I wanted it dead.

And yet, by killing it, Kathras has only increased the danger I'm in. Arcus is unpredictable at the best of times. Now, I can become a convenient outlet for his rage. It's a thing I could have endured before, when it felt like I was working toward a purpose. Now, the king's cruelty can break me.

I find a door and go through it, trusting that the

palace will bring me to the place I intend to go. The place where I will find Kathras.

The Court of Pleasure and Torment boasts an impressive library. The subjects of the books, I am told, are mostly prurient tales and instructions on interesting things to get up to with one or more partners. And that knowledge has filled a hall so long and so tall, I cannot see to the end of it, nor can I see all the way to the top of the shelves. The ceiling vanishes into darkness high above the towering windows, which light only the first few floors.

Marble statues of faeries and other creatures in erotic repose are arranged in a single line down the center of the library. As I pass two human women engaged in frozen congress, one stone hand lazily reaches for me. I gasp and jump back, and the statue, looking disappointed, returns to its original position.

"You can join them," Kathras says from somewhere nearby. "Any of them at all. There's a centaur further down who particularly enjoys—"

"No, thank you, Your Highness," I say, turning around to find him.

He's reclined on a chaise that's floating near the second level, a book in his hand.

"Are we alone?" I ask, wondering if that's the meaning for his cold reception and demeanor. The Kathras I was with in the faery baths would not have spoken so crudely to me. It must be a facade.

The chaise slowly lowers, and he puts his book down with a sigh of annoyance. "We are never alone. But no, there is no one in this room."

I assume he's cautioning me about how I use my words now. I need just one. "Why?"

"I told you. I keep my promises," he says with a shrug. "Is that all?"

It is, but I'm wounded at this change in him.

While I know we can't be as open with each other as we were in the privacy of the baths, and while I know what passed between us can never be again, his quick dismissal wounds me.

"How can you be so callous?" I ask, forgetting to mind my tongue. "After last night? And now this? How can you treat me as if I'm a nuisance?"

He rises and advances on me, backing me into the stone arms of a statue, which hold me fast. I cannot fight stone, so I don't try. I also don't wish to give Kathras the satisfaction of my fear. He should have had his fill of it in the maze.

"You forget yourself, human. You're speaking to a prince." He stands too close, looms his incredible height over me to stare into my eyes. "I will forgive this slight once."

"And then what, Your Highness?" I ask and curse my temper. I'm trying to seduce his father and his brother to steal the throne that rightfully belongs to Kathras. I know that his death is a part of Luthian's plan, and yet I didn't say a word of it to him. I could now, and still I do not, bound to my agreement and what I am beginning to view as my only true purpose.

My only true purpose involves Kathras's death.

And I have the gall to demand, what? Affection?

"I have more than proven my loyalty to you," he snarls. "And my feelings."

"Feelings that you now deny." It isn't as if he can declare love for me openly. He might not even feel it. Kindness in a time of sorrow doesn't require romantic passion.

Slaying a monster does.

"You know I must deny them," he says, but he leans closer to me, his gaze falling to my mouth. "A word of advice, Cenere. It's easier to not have those feelings if they can't be acted upon."

I laugh in bitter derision. "It must be nice to have such control over yourself. Such mastery of your feelings that you can so easily let your guard down for a vulnerable woman in a precarious moment!"

"Are you accusing me of taking advantage of you?" I note the way Kathras's demeanor changes from dismissal to rising anger. "If you hate it here so much, why not leave? You said yourself that your only purpose was your revenge, and now it's been taken from you. There's nothing left for you here. So, go."

"I..."

He wants me to leave. But I remember the look on his face when he found me in the cave. Though he may claim to have purged his feelings, what I had with him in the faery baths is not something so easily put out of mind. Not even for a faery. Not even for a son of Arcus.

"I made a bargain," I admit.

"Any bargain you've made with my father will only be to his benefit. Break it now and flee." He flicks his gaze toward the library doors nervously, then back to me. "I can have you far from here by nightfall."

"It isn't a bargain with your father," I say softly. "It was a bargain with Luthian."

In the cavern, I described Luthian as a kindly guardian who agreed to train me, with no mention of the deal I struck. I can't reveal it now, either; how can I tell Kathras that I'm a willing participant in a plan that will lead to his death?

A death which I cannot allow. Not anymore. But if I leave court, as Kathras suggests, I won't be here to stop Luthian.

"A bargain. With Luthian." Kathras repeats, his tone cold enough to frost the windows if he willed it.

"My mother raised me well and taught me the faery ways. Nothing without a price. I agreed to Luthian's price." The moment the words leave me, I realize I may have made a mistake. Kathras killed the cephalopire to keep his promise to me. Would he take Luthian's life to free me from my bargain?

He considers my words, his expression unreadable. "You made a bargain to become my father's queen."

"I didn't!" *I made a bargain to become your younger brother's queen.*

Kathras's mouth becomes a hard, humorless line. "You weren't just here to find a powerful benefactor to help in your revenge. Luthian brought you here for a crown."

"When I entered into the bargain, I did not flatter myself to think that I, a lowly human, could ever become the favorite of a faery king." *I thought I would become the favorite of a faery prince. In truth, I wish it would have happened that way. Cassan is less likely to feed me to something for his own amusement.*

Kathras's eyes narrow. "I see through you. I see through Luthian. If I were you, if I were him, I would find a nice cottage in The Baneful Wood and never set foot in this palace again. Let the court forget about you and your pathetic scheming."

"I will not break my promise to Luthian." I hope Kathras feels my deliberate use of his words. "I was here for revenge. Now, I cannot have it. But Luthian still wishes to be among his own kind—"

"His own kind." Kathras makes a noise of disgust. "Then he is in the wrong place. I'm sure there's a Court of Treachery and Murder somewhere. If not in Fablemere, then Faeryland."

"And me? You'd have me live in that cottage in The Baneful Wood all alone?" I scoff, though I'm not sure it's impossible. Humans have hewn a rough existence there, and I am human. Perhaps he's right.

"No. I want you to be safe, somewhere far away from my father, from Luthian, from anyone who would use you for their own gain," Kathras growls. A few strands of his blonde hair fall over his forehead. His anger has made him a wild, disheveled thing. "I want you to keep your head! They have a tendency to come off when Luthian is involved."

Something swims vaguely up through my memory. Luthian said something, the night we made our bargain. Something about the queen losing her head for an indiscretion similar to his.

I assumed at the time that the incidents were unrelated. Did Luthian mean that his banishment had something to do with the queen's death?

When Kathras's expression softens, I know my confusion is clear on my face. He takes a step back. "You don't know."

"I've only been here a few days. I've hardly had time to take in a history class." I sniff derisively, but I don't think it's enough to fool Kathras. One slip of my face, and I've exposed how little I truly know Luthian.

Kathras nods to the statue and it releases me. I step away from it, just in case, but try not to appear too unnerved.

"It will work, you know," he says, his tone far calmer now.

"What will?" My heart pounds. Can he read my thoughts? See Luthian's plan written across my mind as easily as the words across the pages of his book?

"Luthian's desperate grab for power. He brought you here to whore you to my father and brother to secure his place." Kathras grimaces in disgust. "Before your engagement to my father, Luthian made a wager with my brother. If Luthian lost, he would hand you over to Cassan as a prize."

"I know." I lift my chin, defiant. "I didn't object."

Kathras utters a laugh of pure disdain. "You're a more fitting mate for Luthian than for my father."

The words seek out and mock my tender feelings for Luthian, the love he doesn't return. Kathras can't possibly know how he's stung me, but I want to slap him, anyway. I know better than to strike a prince. I glower at him, instead. Kathras is intelligent. Too intelligent. I fear that if he thinks hard enough about my actions, he'll see through to the whole plan. He'll know that Luthian intends to kill him, and Arcus.

The easiest way to stop anyone from thinking is to make them angry. Kathras didn't kill the cephalopire because I fucked him. He didn't fuck me because I was convenient. He wants me, and I can use that to wound him.

"I see," I say with a cruel laugh. "You're jealous. You're furious that I haven't pursued you, that I've settled for your brother and your father. You don't care about my safety. You're trying to get me to leave court altogether, so you don't have to face daily something that you can never have. And here, I thought your brother was the vain, oblivious one."

I bite my own tongue to stop myself speaking. What will happen if he repeats those words to Cassan?

Kathras advances on me again. This time, the statue remains, wisely, uninvolved, but I do back painfully into it.

"Something I can never have? I've had you." He takes a step. "You gave yourself to me." Another step. He towers over me, but he does not touch me. It's almost worst than being grabbed and roughly handled. "You know, as well as I, that you will never again lie with someone without remembering me inside you."

My throat sticks shut, and I desperately need to swallow, but I don't want to show him that his words have had an effect on me. I hold his gaze calmly. "But will *you* be able to lie with someone without remembering *me*?"

All of his anger drains from his face, leaving nothing behind but a blank, cold mask. He steps back. "Enjoy your time at court. For however long it lasts."

His head turns sharply, toward something I don't sense. Perhaps the whisper of clothing, the click of a footfall too soft for my own ears. But something has alerted him to danger. I glance in the direction of his furrowed gaze.

Utrax, the same piebald minotaur who fucked me in the king's chambers stands only a few feet away from us. How much has he overheard? Does it matter, when Kathras and I stand so close? Our very proximity indicates guilt.

Kathras's eyes meet mine. He waves a hand over my face.

I blink, and suddenly I'm somewhere very familiar.

I'm in my bedroom in Luthian's house, and I'm holding a book. The book that Kathras was reading when I interrupted him.

I open it, expecting to find an erotic novel or a manual of devious pleasures. To my surprise, it's a journal, the slanting cursive written with a quick hand. I scan the page, intrigued. Descriptions of a ball. I flip to another page and find a list of ladies to invite to a tea party. Why would Kathras have this or wish to read it?

I slam the book shut. Gilt embossing on the leather cover catches my eye. The room spins about me, the floor almost comes out from beneath my feet as I stare at the simple name stamped there:

H.R.M. Queen Parphia.

Chapter Thirty-Three

It's dangerous for me to be in Luthian's house. I know that. But after a single night in my new chambers, I am homesick for it. I feel I've been away for centuries.

Kathras sent me here for a reason, gave me the diary for a reason. I know instinctively that Arcus does not want me to see inside the pages of this journal, so I cannot take it back to my royal chambers. Neither would I have Luthian know what I possess. I climb into the bed and duck beneath the blankets, leaving only a small gap for light to show through.

At the start, the queen's journal is a bore. Tea, gowns, who's sleeping with who and other court gossip. There's shockingly little dedicated to the depravity of court.

But about halfway in, a name scrawled on the page stops me.

I grow weary of Arcus's gilded cage. Everyone else

at court is allowed pleasure freely. Why should I not have with Luthian what my mate has with the entire court?

My guardian spoke so casually about the former queen's death, I never suspected he could have been involved in it. But here he is, mentioned in the pages of her journal. It can't be a coincidence.

I read on.

My heart will never long for Arcus the way it longs for Luthian. He is my true mate, no matter how destiny might separate us. I need him as flowers need sunlight, as crops need water. Every moment we're apart is a torment crueler than anyone at this wretched court could devise.

There is nothing in the entry about Luthian returning her love. I'm surprised she wrote even this much. It would have incriminated her if anyone found it.

Was that how she'd been caught?

I turn the page.

He was at the ritual tonight. I couldn't take my eyes off him. I found myself jealous of the spell that milked him of his essence. I want to make him come, with my hands and mouth. Seeing his seed shared among so many made me wild with rage. There is no fidelity at this court, but I would keep him all to myself, as Arcus keeps me.

I vividly imagine Luthian bound to the stone, his chest heaving in the firelight, his body spent and yet forced again and again to spill into one of those golden goblets. The picture in my mind would have made it easy to understand the queen's infatuation if I did not already share it.

The next few pages are short entries. Arcus's trip to Lua is discussed, and how she is left behind despite desperately wishing to see the city. I grow to loathe him more as I read his late wife's words.

Then, I find an entry that is pages long. My throat sticks closed as I read it.

My heart is so full that I almost dare not write this down in case I've imagined all this happiness. Arcus hasn't been gone a day, and Luthian has already come to me, at my invitation. He bade me burn the letters I sent him, for he said he had not the strength to destroy evidence of our love himself.

Our love! I'm overflowing with joy I thought I would never experience in my immortal life. Before Luthian, I saw only endless tedium with Arcus, nights of frustration as he pleased himself with others and denied that freedom to me.

But Luthian is right; we cannot write down our declarations, lest someone find them. Even these words are a risk. But if I'm to be content only with memory, I will not let a single one fade. I will write it all down, so that I will never forget his hands on my body. The way he filled me. The desperation in his voice as he breathed my name while we lay, still joined in the aftermath of our hours of pleasure.

Why should the words of a dead woman pierce my heart so? The sympathy I had for her is difficult to summon as envy darkens my heart. And why? Because Luthian loved her? Because they shared these intimate moments in a romance that was destined for tragedy?

And though I know how it ends, I can't help myself. I turn to the last pages. The final entry is smudged with tears.

How to explain to such a wonderful being that I am leaving this world? If I had stopped for a moment and considered that death might be the outcome, of course I wouldn't have done what I did. I would never have chosen Luthian over my life. I never did. Who could foresee that so great a love could turn to darkness?

My stomach churns. Luthian loved her. She died

because of it.

This was never about gaining power at court and punishing Arcus for the insult of exile. He seeks vengeance for someone he loved, just as I did. How did I not see it? He warned me about my anger at Thrace, how it would extinguish my spirit. He could warn me because he already knew. We walked separate paths to the same destination, but now my path has ended.

Yet, when I was ready to simply wish my revenge, he talked me out of it.

I missed my chance at vengeance because he was too busy seeking his.

"Cenere?"

I stuff the diary under my pillow and throw back the covers, standing and turning my back to him. My guilt is no doubt written across my face.

Luthian hurries to my side. "I know things are difficult, but you can't be here. If Arcus finds out—"

Tears glaze my eyes. I hate crying when I'm angry. I know I look foolish and childish. How can I expect an immortal being to take me seriously if I crumple to bits in my fury?

Luthian stops himself. "What's happened? Has someone done something to you?"

"Yes. You did."

I turn to find him, mouth open, unable to utter words.

"You didn't tell me why you're really here."

I can see it the very moment that he knows. His silver gaze goes mirror-like, then dark. "Who have you been speaking with?"

"It doesn't matter who I've been speaking with." I can hardly admit that I've encountered revelations from the dead. "You said you wanted Cassan to be king. I never questioned why. I took you at your word when you told me you simply wanted to regain favor at court."

"Taking a faery at his word was your first mistake." He paces, unable to face me. "Your mother should have—"

The mention of my mother opens another wound, which has been festering ever since, *"You were born for it."*

"My mother was desperate for a child! She would have agreed to anything for those wishes. Did she know what you were going to use them for?" I demand. "Did you know you were going to use me?"

"Cenere—"

"No! Your first word should have been a denial!" Tears flow freely down my face. "Anything you say now is some excuse you've constructed. The only thing that will stop me from leaving this place forever is the truth! You were in love with the queen. Did she die because of you?"

My words hang in the air like a noose awaiting his neck. I watch a lifetime of sorrow play out on his face in the heartbeats before he speaks, and though I expect him to break, he does not. "I loved her. I love her still."

"She is dead!" I pound my fist against my chest. "I live. And I want you. I've made no secret of it. Yet, you choose Firo. You choose a dead queen over me. I will never be the one you choose!"

"Because I cannot have you!" Luthian roars. I've never seen him so angry. "I cannot have you and my revenge, and I choose my revenge!"

If he thinks I can't match that anger, he is woefully mistaken. "And what of my revenge? What do you have to offer me in this bargain now that it's been stolen from me?"

"I didn't take your precious revenge." He throws a hand out as if pointing at Arcus, though he is, I hope, far from here. "Arcus did that. I'm sorry for you, I truly am. But I have waited centuries. I have planned for centuries. The things I've done—"

"Like giving a faery a human child you would later exploit?" I shout. "Creating me as a weapon with singular purpose? What is my existence for once you achieve this grand revenge?"

"What you do with your existence after I visit my vengeance upon Luthian is not my concern." It's a lie. Not even a master manipulator can hide it.

He cares for me. He simply cares for his revenge more.

"I cannot uphold my end of the bargain," he says simply. "If you wish to be released from it, that is all you need to say."

"I wish to be released from my bargain with you." The moment the words leave my mouth, I know I have been tricked.

"Then you are released," he snarls. "You have one wish left."

My eyes brim with tears. "How can you be so cruel?"

"I have always been cruel to you." There is nothing in his voice now but contempt. "It's not my fault that you interpreted it as love. Now, leave my house, for I am finished with you."

"No, please!" I cry, but he vanishes. The fire in the hearth goes out. The furnishings disappear, one by one, until all that is left is an empty room, and Parphia's journal lying on the floor.

I collect it up, wipe the tears from my face, hold my chin high, and walk down the stairs. The great hall, too, is absent of its table and chairs. The curtains are drawn against the daylight.

The place that I thought of as home is gone now.

Clutching the queen's journal, I step out of Luthian's house for the last time, the door opening directly into my new, mirrored cell.

* * * *

I stroll through the gardens aimlessly, until my legs are as numb and aching as my heart.

It's nearly nightfall when a scream of pure terror rings out over the burbling of fountains and the chirping of songbirds.

I follow other alarmed courtiers through an archway sculpted in a hedge; the faeries can locate the sound far better than I can. Some of them fly rather than use the paths the rest of us take.

We exit into a part of the gardens I've never seen before, decorated by statues quite like the ones in the library. The courtiers all recoiled though, from a central figure.

An alabaster minotaur, draped in a familiar piebald hide, still dripping blood.

Chapter Thirty-Four

The entire court goes into mourning.

The minotaur, whom I merely assumed was a good friend of Arcus, was one of the architects of the palace. He was responsible for the enchantment that has delivered me precisely where I need to go.

This makes me glad that he's dead. Who knows if he was keeping tabs on me, spying through that same enchantment. Wasn't he strolling through the garden with Firo, while Firo was spending so much time with Luthian? Did the architect tell Arcus about the mermaids? About my dalliance with Cassan?

One thing that I do know is that he didn't get a chance to tell anyone about Kathras and I in the library. And I know exactly who doled out that silence.

Does any of it really matter, though? Now that my revenge has been lost to me, now that Luthian has severed our ties? Kathras's suggestion that I flee the palace haunts me, especially as Arcus has closed me up in my hall of mirrors.

I lose myself in the words of his late queen and find myself greatly sympathizing with her. She endured centuries of captivity under his control. It's only been a day and already I'm going mad.

But I'm more fortunate than she was; her diary details incident after incident of abuse and humiliation at Arcus's foul hands. So far, he has not thought to alleviate his anger by attacking me, an indignity that she suffered throughout their union. I have no doubt that such a time will come, if Luthian doesn't succeed in his assassination attempt.

My heart aches at the mere thought of him. I flip past endless pages about his great love with Parphia, the tender words he whispered to her in candlelit hallways, the danger of discovery heightening their passions.

No romance that begins in the perilous secrecy of the weight of a crown can meet any other end.

I tell myself that over and over when my thoughts stray to Kathras.

Twice now, he has protected me. I want to deny it, to reason that the minotaur posed as much a threat to him as to me. That Kathras killed the architect to hide his own secrets.

That doesn't explain the cephalopire.

A knock at the door startles me. I've been staring at the same page of Parphia's journal for so long that I don't remember what I was reading. The sylphs don't knock, and Arcus would have simply appeared. I approach with caution.

"Your Majesty." Firo bows at the waist when I open the door.

I almost catch him up in a hug, I'm so relieved to see a friendly face.

The room beyond my door is small, decorated all in frothy pinks, with satin wall coverings and delicate furniture. Gilded ornamentation sparkles from the legs of the chairs to the medallions at the corners of the ceiling. Even the hearth is gold.

"What is this place?" I ask, stepping out of my bedroom.

"The queen's formal salon, Your Majesty," Firo says looking around. "You haven't yet been introduced to it?"

"I haven't been crowned yet." If Arcus finds out what Kathras has done and why, I may not have a head to wear a crown. "And you are aware that I am in a delicate position."

"Indeed, I am." He rolls his wrist, and a glass pot of amber liquid appears atop his palm. "This might bring you some cheer."

"What is it?" I take the jar and turn it over in my hands. A bejeweled serpent coils on the lid. The substance inside is thick, like—

"Honey," he says. "The king's favorite. Rumor has it that he is in a foul mood. Perhaps this will sweeten his disposition."

"How thoughtful." Though, I have no doubt that the only thing the king will enjoy is torturing me. I wonder what it will be this time. An ogre in chains? A tree beast? One of the statues from the library?

I think Arcus would allow a troll to rip me apart for his own amusement if the notion took him.

"Perhaps permanently," Firo adds in a near whisper.

My gaze whips to his and he holds it, silently willing me to understand.

I do. And rage fills me from my stomach outward, sending a dizzying rush to my head. "You mistake me. I am no longer a part of that plan."

"That isn't why I offer it." He searches my face. "You need this, Cenere. You won't last long here with his temper."

I turn the jar over in my hands. "I thank you for the gift. Whom shall I say it is from?"

"You won't be called upon to divulge that," he promises. "Just a small taste, and you'll both be at ease."

"I'm so careful about what I eat here," I say, my tone heavy with double meaning. "I don't wish to consume anything that would disagree with me."

Firo clucks his tongue and shakes his head. "Don't worry, Your Majesty. It won't harm you at all."

It won't harm me, but it will harm Arcus.

I fold my hands over the jar, which has become my savior. "I am grateful to you. For such a kind, thoughtful gift in my beloved king's time of sorrow."

"I thought you would be." Firo again bows to me. "I will leave you to your mourning."

He vanishes, and I head back into my room, gripping the jar tightly. I need to hide it. If I'm caught in position of a poison that will only work against faeries, it will all but seal my guilt in the deaths of both the architect and the cephalopire.

The sooner it is out of my hands, the better.

Which means that I must act immediately.

* * * *

I do not await Arcus's invitation. Judging by Parphia's journal, it may be weeks or months before his bad mood passes and I am called to him. I can't hold onto such an incriminating object for that long. So, I bathe and perfume myself, bedeck myself in gold jewelry with amber stones to match my weapon, and go to him otherwise nude. My door helpfully opens directly into his bedchamber.

I spy him sitting in a chair before the hearth, staring into the flames. His back is to me. I see only his chestnut curls, lined with gold from the firelight, and his hand draped morosely over the arm of the chair.

"I wish to be alone, Cenere," he says, without sparing me a glance.

"As I expected. But your sorrow is so heavy. I felt your very spirit crying out to me, urging me to come to you. To comfort you." I move slowly to stand beside him, placing the honey carefully on the table. "To distract you."

With a long, slow exhale, he leans his head against my chest, that limp arm rising to rest across the small of my back as he pulls me closer. "You are a dear human, my love, and well-meaning, but naive. I am your king, and I will have your obedience."

I swallow my fear and say, "I am to be your queen. And I will not have you suffer so great a loss alone."

Only now does he look up, a wonder written across his features that does not match the gravity of his words. "You would defy me?"

"I defy anyone to keep me from comforting my beloved." I fall to my knees beside him. "But I know of only one thing I can provide to alleviate your burden."

He turns away again.

I glance back to the honey on the table. If I try to persuade him to eat it and he refuses, he will suspect me if I bring it up a second time. I must be sure, but it also has to be now.

"It is past midday, and the plate set out for you is bare and untouched. Have you not eaten?" I ask.

"I have no desire for food at present," he says boredly. "As I said, I wish to be alone. I will come to you if I need your aid."

"Of that, I have no doubt. But to put my mind at ease..." I go to the table and pretend to look over the food that is laid out there and grown cold. I pick up the jar as if I'm noticing it for the first time, acting out my part even though he cannot see me, and go to his side again. He's annoyed with me, and I know I've pushed him too far already. "Ah, this will do."

I lift the lid from the jar, and the ruby eyes of the golden serpent seem to wink at me. I sweep my finger inside. *"Just a taste,"* Firo instructed. The shining glob on my finger is all it will take to free me.

And, I realize, to get another, less satisfying revenge. Arcus's death will pay for the one he robbed from me. It will not be as satisfying as killing Cadwyn Thrace, but it will wash away some of my bitterness, knowing that the faery who stole my justice has died at my hands.

"Just a taste," I murmur, echoing Firo's words. "Then, I can go back to my chambers and know that you've had something to eat, no matter how meager."

I offer him my finger and the honey that has begun to run down to my hand. His eyes lock with mine and my breath halts painfully. Can he tell? Am I too conspicuous in my urging? Does my intent show on my face? He opens his mouth, and I'm sure his next words will be, "Seize her!"

Instead, his gaze grows hot, and he grabs my wrist, drawing my hand to his mouth. He sucks my finger in and swirls his tongue around it.

My knees buckle with arousal. Though I find him detestable, the relief I feel at watching him slurp his death from my hand is almost strong enough to make me climax where I stand.

When he's licked my finger clean, he says, "I would rather taste your honey, Cenere."

I grin down at him, something truly wicked unfurling through me like Luthian's vines. Arcus has sealed his doom. I do not know how long his death will take, but the thought of it cutting him down while he ruts inside of me is as erotic as my fantasies of tearing Thrace's wings off.

I want to ride Arcus while he suffers his death throes. I want to whisper that it was me who killed him while he gasps for breath and tries to call for help.

The honey is still on the table. I go to retrieve it, and his hand lingers on mine as I walk away.

I return to him, that jar of his doom glowing beautifully in the fire light. "You are king. You may have both."

Chapter Thirty-Five

Arcus watches, a slow smile curling his lips as I pour a stream of honey onto my breast. A drop falls from my nipple onto my stomach, and he cranes his neck up to catch the next. He pulls me into his lap with a growl.

I gasp, intoxicated by the knowledge that my suffering is finally at an end, and that his is just beginning. His mouth closes over my nipple and I cry out with true pleasure, rolling my hips. His cock rises in his breeches and presses against my thigh.

He takes the honey from me and pours it onto both breasts, devouring it hungrily while I grip his hair and hold him to me. I cry out things like, "Oh yes, my love!" and beg, "more!" He obliges, until the jar is half-emptied, then stands swiftly, lifting me with one arm to take me to the bed.

"The mess!" I cry as he drops my still-sticky body onto the coverlet.

"That's none of your concern," he says, pouring a line of the honey down my stomach. "You came here to feed me, remember?"

I squirm beneath him as he laps a path closer and closer to my center. It occurs to me that he might die before he arrives at his destination, and then I feel like I might die, should that happen.

I am impossibly aroused, attuned to Arcus in a way I would never have cared to be before. But I want to know the moment the poison begins its work.

He pushes my legs apart and lies between them, his face close to my cunt. Slowly, he peels open my petals to reveal the bud inside. He pours the honey over my clit and swipes his tongue over it, poking his tongue through the loop of my piercing to get every last possible drop. I curl up from the bed.

Two of his fingers enter me. He swirls them about, withdraws, and meets my eyes while he sucks them clean. "I don't know which is sweeter."

"Oh, please, Arcus," I beg him, mindless with my desire.

He dips his fingers into the honey, scooping out a huge, messy dollop, and stuffs it into my cunt. The moment his tongue enters me, I lift my hips, humping against his face as he licks me clean from the inside. He thrusts his tongue like a cock, and I take more of the honey on my fingertips to rub it into my clit. He groans against me; I cannot tell if it's pleasure or pain from his impending death. My back arches and I lock my thighs around his head. Perhaps the poison won't have time to work on him; I might suffocate him.

That thought drives me higher than his tongue ever could, and I let go with a shout of pure ecstasy, bathing his face in my juices.

He lifts his head, smeared with honey and my

wetness.

"Oh please," I whimper, palming my breast and pulling the nipple between my fingers. "Let me have your cock."

He slides from the bed and stands. Is he a bit unsteady, or am I imagining it? I bite my lip and watch as he removes his shirt, his breeches, and I moan in anticipation at the sight of his cock.

"Let me ride you," I plead. "It's been so long since you last took me, and I am so empty."

He chuckles. "It's only been two days."

"Two days is an eternity when one craves something as I crave you." I bat my eyes at him.

He sits on the bed and slides back, toward the pillows. "I cannot deny you anything, my love."

Except for my freedom. A feeling of safety. A life without fear.

It is when I first sink down on his length that I notice a faint gray cast at the edge of his hairline. He holds my hips and pulls me into an easy rhythm, but I note a tremor in one of his hands. I close my eyes and tip my head back, reveling in the tug of him deep inside me as I stroke him with my grasping cunt. He gasps, and it is, finally, not a pleasurable sound.

"Cenere," he whispers. "I don't feel well."

I open my eyes.

Though I anticipated his death, I did not expect him to look so like a corpse before it happened. His face has bloated and gone grey. His veins are thick and black and bulging in his neck. They make an oily spiderweb across his chest and down his arms. The hands at my hips can no longer hold me. He tries to lift his head and cannot.

Pure panic flares in his eyes, the delicious sign that he has never, until this very moment, experienced fear of the magnitude he's imposed upon others.

"You're dying, Arcus," I say simply, never stopping the easy rock of my hips.

He opens his mouth, and I see that the word formed on his swelling lips is, "guards!", but no sound comes out.

"No one will hear you cry for help," I tell him, and let myself smile genuinely at him for the first time. "I want you to know that this didn't start off as a personal revenge. I came to court to kill you—well, Luthian came to court to kill you, but I knew I would help."

My cunt drips, gushes with renewed arousal. Despite being on the brink of death, Arcus's cock never flags for a moment. It's funny, and fitting, somehow, that the king of the Court of Pleasure and Torment should meet such a tormented end while I take my pleasure in it. I reach down to rub myself, pausing a moment to moan and squeeze on him before I continue.

"You made it a personal revenge, Arcus." My breath speeds up. I lift myself on my knees to thrust him harder and faster inside of me. "When you tortured me. When you humiliated me for the sake of power instead of pleasure. When you stole my vengeance against Cadwyn Thrace."

Arcus is choking now, tarry black leaking from the corners of his mouth. I grasp my breast and plant one hand against his chest for balance as I fuck myself on his throbbing, swollen cock. He can still hear every word; I see the rage in his eyes. I lean down, my mouth beside his ear. "You feel so good. You're going to make me come one last time. It's a pity that you won't."

He gurgles in response.

"Your son is so much more talented than you," I say breathlessly, leaning back and rubbing myself shamelessly. "He killed your friend the minotaur. He killed your pet horror. And he did it for me. Luthian was right. When we planned all of this together, he told me that you and your sons were too weak to resist a sweet, human pussy. I didn't believe him, but look at you now, poor Arcus. You lapped your death straight from that source."

His body convulses. He grimaces in agony. The skin of his chest pulls tight over his ribs as he struggles futilely for breath.

It's beautiful.

It's vengeance.

And I have escaped him.

I come so hard, I see stars in a sudden blackness behind my eyes, a blackness the color of Arcus's air-deprived face. I cry out, riding the last waves of my pleasure.

When I open my eyes again, the king is dead.

And I am free.

The door bursts open and my hope plummets. I am caught. They will put me in chains. They will do worse to me than feed me to a cephalopire. I imagine hot tongs searing my flesh, consider screaming and pretending that I don't know what's happened.

But it isn't the guards.

It's Kathras.

He walks slowly to the bed, looks down with disinterest upon the face of the now dead king and me, still astride his twitching cock.

"Get up," he says, and offers me his hand.

My entire body shakes. I'm drunk on the pleasure of my climax, but drunker still on the knowledge that I have killed. A laugh burbles from my throat. "March me to my execution. I don't care. I'm glad he's dead."

Kathras shrugs. "I'm glad he's dead, too. As I am king now, you have no fear of execution."

I look down at the mess of his deceased father, who is rapidly melting into a disgusting puddle of black goo.

"Was it iron, then?" he asks. "It looks like it was iron."

"I don't know," I admit. "But perhaps you shouldn't touch me. Or the honey pot."

He spies the spilled jar and nods. "We'll leave it there. I'll sprinkle some fruit around him, maybe smash a plate. You won't be implicated."

"You're not angry with me?" I ask.

"It was him or me," he says flatly. "It was always him or me. I believe that's true of any faery king and his heir."

"Your father saw his death reflected in you," I muse.

"When he should have seen it in you." Kathras narrows his eyes. "I am not so deluded by my own grandiosity that I will be an equally easy target."

He knows, then, that he is part of Luthian's plan. Kathras could kill me on the spot—it would be the intelligent thing to do—but while his thinking isn't clouded by ego, he is certainly not clear-headed in his feelings for me.

"I do not wish to kill you," I tell him, and I mean it sincerely. "My quarrel was with your father."

"Wasn't everyone's?" he chuckles darkly. "This is your kill, Cenere. But it is Luthian's revenge."

I say nothing.

"Go. Bathe and dress and stay in your chambers. Speak to no one. When you hear of my father's death, it will come as a shock to you. You'll be overcome with grief," he instructs. "If the inquisitors wish to speak with you, I'll warn you in advance."

"Thank you," I whisper, and leave him to stand over the faintly burbling mess of the former king.

* * * *

By nightfall, Kathras has been jailed by the inquisitors.

Chapter Thirty-Six

"Luthian!" I storm into the dark, cold great hall of his house, screaming the walls down. "Luthian! Don't ignore me!"

There is no answer.

"I've done exactly what you asked of me!" I shout, tears raining down my face. "I did exactly what you trained me to do, despite our broken agreement. You owe me!"

"I owe you nothing!"

The room swirls back to life all around me. The chairs, tables, the fireplace burning and the candles glowing. Luthian stands before me in his dressing gown, hair unbound around his shoulders. His eyes are blank silver with anger. "You didn't kill Arcus for me. You killed him to save yourself!"

"From the predicament you put me in!" I shout back. "Now, an innocent faery will be put on trial for the death of the king you assassinated."

"The king I assassinated?" He laughs venomously. "I don't remember assassinating anyone. You, however, have just admitted it to me. Perhaps you should inform the inquisitors of their mistake and free Kathras yourself. Or would you prefer that I did?"

My entire body is seized with the trembling that has come and gone in fits since I left what remained of Arcus. The excitement has exhausted me, the fear has made me restless. And now, to hear Luthian threaten me... Luthian, who I thought I loved...

"You wouldn't," I whisper, my vision wavering behind my tears.

"You have far more faith in me than you ever should," he warns.

"And you underestimate me," I spit back. "I would name you before my head ever touched the block."

"You have a wish remaining. You could waste it on Kathras's freedom." Luthian shrugs coldly. "Unless you were saving it for something else."

I was. In the back of my mind, even from the moment that Luthian and I ended our agreement, I've held that wish apart. I didn't want to admit it then, but there is no denying it now. "You know what I was saving it for."

"Was?" He arches a brow.

"Was," I repeat. "Why would I waste it on you, now? When I see you for what you really are?"

Something flashes across his face, too quickly for me to read it. I think it could be sorrow. I hope that it is.

"You want to me to believe that you've fallen out of love with me?" His dismissive laugh stings my heart, for we both know the truth. I love him still, even in this moment.

"Believe what you will. It's no concern of mine!"

He steps close to me, reaches out with those elegant fingers to trace the curve of my jaw. "One wish,

Cenere. Two desires. Which do you choose? Kathras's life, or my love?"

I swat Luthian's hand away. My chest aches. I feel I may faint. But I hold his mirrored gaze, lift my chin in defiance. "Why would I ever want love that I must wish for?"

"Then say it," he whispers. "Wish for his freedom. Deny my love."

My stomach turns sour, and I barely manage the words. Everything in me fights against saying them. But it isn't right to let Kathras die for what Luthian and I have done.

"I wish for Kathras's freedom and safety."

Luthian's face falls. The silver in his eyes goes dull, then black. He grabs my shoulders, pulls me against his chest, and covers my mouth with his in a crushing, painful kiss.

I go weak. I don't want to. I want to shove him away. I want to beg him to take back my wish. But I spoke the truth when I told him that I wouldn't want to be loved because I wished for it. I sag against him, let him ravish my mouth with his tongue, thread his fingers into my hair to hold my lips to his. I work my hands between us to jerk the tie of his robe free, and my hands smooth up his chest to push the fabric from his shoulders. I feel his naked skin against mine; my clothing has vanished like it did so many times before. He pulls me with him to the table and sweeps place settings and candles to the floor, extinguishing the flames before they can catch the rug beneath our feet on fire.

Luthian has never been gentle with me. That was a part of our training and expected. But he's never been as wild and hungry as he is now. I cry out in shock and pain when he slams me bodily onto the table, my head and elbows drumming the wood with cracking thumps. I plant my feet flat, arch up to rub my aching sex against him. I've wanted this. How I have wanted this. We've been so close, much closer than this, but I know he cannot stop. He will fuck me like it's a punishment. He will fuck me like it's revenge.

I know enough of both now that I do not fear them. I welcome his deep, battering thrust as he enters me and shout with relief at finally, finally taking him into my body.

He slaps his palm on the table beside my head, cursing. "How dare you! I never offered you my love, I offered you a kingdom!"

"I know," I sob into his shoulder, locking my ankles behind his back, just under the space where his wings meet his body. I want to fall into him, and him into me, to remain in this moment of pain and anger and passion unrestrained forever.

"I don't want you!" His cock plunges into me hard again, and the slick wood at my back pulls my skin. "I never wanted you!"

"I don't care." I kiss his neck, hold onto his hair.

He pounds into me, digs the fingers of one hand into my thigh as he braces himself over me. "I was better off before I found you." But his hurtful words are less forceful now, and the sorrow in his voice is unmistakable. "I don't want you."

He does. He can't deny it now, when he's buried so deep inside me, helpless to make himself stop. I put my hands on his face, lift his gaze to mine.

His eyes are lit with stars in the night sky and lined with tears of quicksilver.

"I don't want you," he whispers again, and kisses me.

The table is no longer hard at my back; we're in Luthian's bed, lying between the sheets. When he lifts his mouth from mine, he says, "This wasn't supposed to happen, Cenere."

"I know." I arch up, grinding against him. "But I wanted it to."

He gives me exactly what both of us need. The two of us, no tricks, no toys, no games. Just the slow, deep stroke of his cock, my hips rocking with his rhythm. His hand between us, thumb circling over my clit with such skill that it seems unfair. I wish he didn't know my body so well. I wish he couldn't make me feel such pleasure. I wish I didn't love him so much.

And I am out of wishes.

I give myself over to the frantic sway of our bodies as we strive for completion, to Luthian's lips on my neck, his tongue in my mouth. I tremble and cry out with every climax, and he lasts as long as he can, wringing as many from me as my body will allow. Only when I'm so worn out that I can no longer meet his rhythm does he let himself go.

He isn't controlled and silent, the way he has been in the past. He moans a little more with every slow, deliberate thrust, growing louder as he picks up speed until, with a roar, he rams deep, and I feel the hot surge of his cum filling me with every jerk of his cock. I hold his face to my breast, stroke his hair, soothing him as he convulses with the last of his pleasure, and my heart shatters.

This is the only time. I knew it when we started, but I haven't truly believed it until now, when he's breathing hard, sweat dripping onto my chest, slowly coming back to his senses. When the lust has passed and reason returns, he will be finished with me. Forever.

He slips from my body on a groan of finality that pierces my heart. Falling back on the pillows, he stares up at the canopy over the bed. A mirror shows us there, tangled in the black sheets, my pale body flushed where he's been pressed against me, his blue-gray skin slick with sweat.

Our eyes meet in that reflection, and he looks away.

"This won't happen again," he says, his voice flat and removed from the act we just shared.

"I know." But I don't move. If I stay here, in this bed, the memory of his body still imprinted on mine, it isn't over.

With no wishes left, there isn't a reason for us to see each other again. Luthian loves me. I felt it in every touch. But something stands in the way of that love.

Parphia.

"You love her still," I whisper.

"I do." The admission is emotionless. "And until I no longer love her, I cannot love another."

I reach for him, but he rolls away and rises from the bed. He conjures his dressing gown from the air and puts it on, meticulously arranging it with his back still turned to me. "I've handed you over to Cassan. I told him I don't want you anymore, that he's won the bet by default. You will be queen, after all."

I sit up and pull my knees to my chest. "And you?"

"You won't see me again." Still, he does not look at me. "Thank you, Cenere, for your help."

"I was helping myself."

His shoulders move with a grim laugh. "I've taught you too well. Good-bye, my honey flower."

He lifts his hand, and I call out, "No, wait!"

But I'm back in my mirrored room, and I am alone.

Chapter Thirty-Seven

The funeral for King Arcus, five-thousand-year ruler of the Court of Pleasure and Torment, draws faeries from all over the kingdom.

The only people missing are Luthian and Kathras.

I sit beside Cassan on a matching throne outside the ritual circle. In the center, a bier has been constructed over the cold remains of the bonfire, and atop it is a small bundle, wrapped in white.

All that was left of Arcus when the poison did its work was a tarry stain on his coverlet. That's what will be burned today.

I suppose it's preferable to the smell of a burning corpse.

Through the black veil drawn over my face, I note that Cassan looks...bored. As if his father's funeral is an inconvenience. Indeed, he hasn't said a word about his brother's escape, and seems mostly troubled with the fact that court mourning will interfere with his birthday celebrations.

Which, he has assured me more than once, he looks forward to with great anticipation.

"It is too soon to sleep with my father's fiancé after his death," Cassan explained over the breakfast he summoned me to this morning. "And while Luthian was glad to hand you over to me, we had such grand plans for my birthday celebration. Now, I fear they've all been ruined."

"Not ruined," I promised him. "Delayed."

I have no ill feelings toward him over his ambivalence to Arcus's death. If I had lived my entire, immortal life under the thumb of that tyrant, I wouldn't care if he died, either.

While the priestesses circle the bier with censers of burning herbs and low, droning chants, Cassan leans over to me. "I never expected to be king. This is very strange."

I place a comforting hand on his arm. "You'll be a good king. Perhaps even a better one than my beloved Arcus."

Cassan blows out a breath. "It won't be difficult. And you can drop the 'beloved' act. At least, with me. In public, you should still grieve appropriately, but I know you didn't love him."

"Your Majesty—"

"If you did love him, you would be foolish. And I know you are not foolish, Cenere. Luthian praised you as the best student he's ever had, and he's taught many to adapt to life here at court." He pauses. "Did you know that he was once the official court tutor?"

"I did not." The mention of my guardian turns my blood to ice in my veins.

"I might order him to come back," Cassan muses.

No, I want to say. *I will not survive if I must see him and not touch him. I will die if I have to watch him love another.*

A slow, steady drumbeat begins, and a priestess lights a torch with flame conjured from the air. One by one, the others set their torches alight in a chain that begins from that first flame, standing in a circle around the bier.

"All right. I did not love him," I admit in a whisper. "He wanted me to love him, and I took pity on him for that."

Cassan nods. "He needed everyone to love him. It was a sickness. So many consorts over the centuries did not survive his possessiveness."

So, there were others after Parphia, before me. I wonder how many of them were tutored by Luthian and handed over to that monster. How many innocents were sacrificed for Luthian's revenge?

"A fitting end, I think, to a cruel man." Cassan flicks a fallen leaf from the arm of his throne.

"How did he die?" I ask, images of Arcus's bulging eyes and blackened mouth flooding me with giddy warmth. I hope I didn't smile when I asked that.

"Honey, as it turns out." Cassan chuckles and hides it as a cough. "Melted him to his bed."

"Can faeries not have honey?" I worry I may be playing too ignorant, too innocent, but I need to express curiosity, so Cassan doesn't become suspicious.

Although, I'm not certain he cares enough to suspect anyone, especially when Kathras has been deemed guilty in the eyes of the courtiers.

"The inquisitors say it was tainted with iron. Probably stored in an iron container for long enough to poison the honey." He shrugs. "My brother must have been planning this for a long time."

"Do you really believe it was Kathras who poisoned your father?" Do I go too far in defending him? I don't know Cassan well enough to read him. I can't tell if his carefree act is a mask for a more devious mind. After meeting his father and seeing how easily Kathras kills, I cannot imagine how Cassan has turned out differently.

"It was him, no doubt." Cassan murmurs, watching as the priestesses put flame to the bier. "They found a lid to the jar. It was emblazoned with Kathras's seal."

My stomach lurches. I nearly vomit my breakfast onto my mourning gown.

"Stupid of him, really. I think he believed that inheriting the throne would protect him from prosecution, but the rules of fae succession simply don't work that way. Otherwise, we'd all be murdering each other, all the time." He gestures a limp dismissal with his hand. "Well, some of us."

Another point he'd brought up at breakfast. Cassan doesn't want to be king; if anything, he resents the time it will take from his carousing and debauchery.

"That's why it's so important that you have a strong queen at your side," I whisper, and give his hand a comforting squeeze.

The bier catches fully, and flames rise into the air. Heat crumples and consumes the last remains of a foul king, dispatched in a foul way, with foul treachery behind it.

Luthian gave me that honey with Kathras's seal upon it so that Kathras would be suspected. Was that always a part of the plan? Or was it revenge for the labyrinth?

Or perhaps Luthian didn't care that Kathras's seal might implicate me, if I hadn't wished for his escape. Kathras could have simply blamed the entire assassination on me and accused me of framing him.

But the escape has set the court's opinion. Why did he run if there was nothing to run from?

Because sometimes, running is the only option. There is no reason that I should run from Cassan, yet I wish to. I study his handsome, boyish profile. He looks exactly like someone whose affections I would have been eager to win in my human life. Though he is serious now, I know his smile is breathtaking. Though the crown somewhat flattens his messy black curls to the sides of his head, I have seen that without it, he appears rakish and wild, like a forest spirit disguised as a faery. I should want him.

I came to this court to be his queen, and now I am, though I will not be crowned before a respectful amount of time has passed in the wake of Arcus's death. But without the prize of my revenge, my victory is hollow.

We lead the procession back to the palace, my arm through Cassan's. The sky is uncharacteristically gray, and the strangest, most irrational rush of anger comes over me. How dare the sky mourn a tyrant king. How dare it mock the degradation I experienced simply because he willed it.

* * * *

After dinner, I find my way to the new royal chambers. Cassan has no wish to occupy the room his father died in, which I understand. When I am queen, I'll request a change to my living quarters, as well.

Cassan's room is both nothing that I expect and everything I would have guessed. The walls of the circular room are painted in shades of green ranging from sedate to garish. There is no fireplace or candles, but floating orbs of golden light drift about in the air to illuminate the space. Fire would be inadvisable, owing to the enormous tree that reaches almost to the top of the high, glass-domed ceiling. All the furnishings are of polished wood that matches the tree's broad, sturdy trunk. I find that a bit ghoulish; the tree must stand among the mutilated corpse parts of its brethren.

My mood is perhaps too grim for the task ahead of me.

Cassan made it clear that after dinner, I was to meet him in his chambers. I assume he's changed his mind about waiting to have me. Knowing what I know of him, he will expect a seductress, ready to please him in every way. And while I appreciate that his tastes don't seem to run toward the painful, I don't feel the enthusiasm for erotic congress that I once did.

How do these faeries stay interested for centuries and millennia? How do they enjoy themselves, night after night, in empty pleasures and shocking pain? I grow weary of it already.

At least, I was smart enough not to wish for immortality.

A staircase rises in a spiral around the tree, disappearing into the long chains of leaves that fall from its gnarled branches. The leaves part for me as I ascend, revealing a round bed nestled in the space where the branches converge. Without the benefit of magic, I must remove my own clothes. I drape my gown over the railing and set my slippers carefully aside, where they won't trip Cassan when he comes to bed. Nude, I arrange myself on the green velvet coverlet, spreading my hair out like an aura of copper around my head and tilting my legs just so, to hide the most tantalizing part of my anatomy. I pluck at my nipples to harden them, then languidly pose my arms above my head.

This will be the first time Cassan fucks me, and I want it to be perfect for him. So perfect that he won't have any thoughts of ridding himself of a human queen who will not last long. I want him too drunk on lust to ever suspect me of his father's death at all.

"Cenere?" he calls from below. I say nothing, so as not to spoil the effect. His boots thunk on the stairs as he approaches. He reaches the top, and his eyes go wide as he beholds me.

"I've been waiting, Your Majesty," I purr, and shift my legs slightly, offering just a flash of the curls at my center.

He groans and smiles. "You are too tempting."

"Am I tempting, or are you simply eager to give in?" I ask, arching my back. I lay a hand between my legs and gasp at my own touch. "I'm eager for you."

But he doesn't make a move toward me. "I didn't ask you here to fuck you."

I don't mean to drop my seductress act so easily, but I blurt, "What?" so forcefully, there is no reasonable way to return to my simpering. "I thought you changed your mind."

"I want to," he quickly assures me. "Believe me. I've been endlessly counting down the days."

"The wager is over," I remind him. "Luthian said—"

"Luthian said that it would be more satisfying to wait. He taught me well and he's never given me bad advice, so I plan to wait." Cassan's gaze rakes over my body. "For perhaps the first time ever, I am declining a truly delectable offer."

He snaps his fingers and I'm fully clothed. I sit up, examining the sleeves of my black mourning gown.

"Please, don't take it personally," he goes on. "If it makes my rejection sting less, know that I nearly came in my breeches the moment I saw you lying here."

I laugh in disbelief and sit up. "Luthian made you

out to be some kind of—"

"Deranged sex monster?" Cassan chuckles, moves to sit on the bed, then thinks better of it. "Please, come downstairs before I prove him right."

Cassan leads me to a small table nestled in an alcove. One of the globes of light follows us and hovers above our heads. He motions over the table and a teapot with two cups appears before us.

I reach to pour for him, but he waves my hand aside. "You are my guest. Allow me to serve you."

"I am your queen, Your Majesty," I say softly. "I live only to serve you."

"Nonsense. You live to enjoy all the pleasures of my court. Including tea." He fills my cup, then pushes it toward me. "And call me Cassan. You'll find me a much less formal ruler than my father was. And less vindictive."

I try to form a response, but his words are too kind, when I haven't heard much kindness.

That's not true. You had Kathras. For a whole night, you had Kathras.

I shake my head and force a smile as I stare down into my teacup. "Your father was—"

"I know what he did to you," Cassan says. "I helped my brother cut up the cephalopire."

"I—"

"When he told me what our father was doing to you… It wasn't right. And maybe it wasn't right to kill that creature when it was only feeding. When he was probably starving it. But Kathras *was* right when he said that as long as my father had access to it, he would use it to hurt you." He reaches over and touches my hand. "I'm not going to hurt you, Cenere. I didn't call you here tonight to fuck you or punish you. I called you here to tell you, in private, that you are safe now."

The tension that has been steadily winding in me

since the moment Luthian appeared in the graveyard bursts apart like a spring in an over-wound clock. There is no fighting the flood of emotions that burst from me, beginning with hysterical laughter and ending with chest-crushing sobs.

Cassan comes to my side and lifts me up, taking my chair and settling me in his lap. He soothes me, kisses my forehead, and rubs my back while I cry.

"You will never have cause to fear me, Cenere," he promises. "Never."

And yet, after all I've endured, his kindness might be the most frightening thing to face.

Chapter Thirty-Eight

The day of King Cassan's birthday celebration arrives, and it is as splendid and lecherous as he meticulously plans it to be. After an indulgent breakfast of sweets and pastries, he takes us to my salon, which has been cleared of all its furnishings to make room for two large, gilt tables. Soft straps and fur-lined cuffs dangle from each corner, and a row of beautiful, bare-breasted faeries stand behind an assortment of instruments. Brushes, feathers, phalluses, vibrating stones like the one Luthian gifted to me, spread out like a carnal buffet.

"No matter how we beg," Cassan instructs them, "do not let us come."

"There is a spell that will prevent it," I suggest to him. "Luthian must have used it on you before."

"Alas, I don't have Luthian's powers. This will make endurance all the more important." Cassan winks at me and unfastens the cuffs of his sleeves.

To the faeries, he says, "You may begin."

Four of the beauties step forward, smiling coquettishly. They are rainbow hued, two of them pink and purple like the mermaids I lay with before. The other two are green, with pointed ears and wings that mimic tattered leaves. Their eyes are pupilless, just two orbs of shining gold that unnerve me. One of them stands to the left of me, the other to the right, but they both lean in to claim my mouth with frilled tongues.

The faeries that have gone to Cassan giggle as they undress him. He holds his hands out wide while they tear playfully at his clothes.

The pink and purple faeries are much gentler with my garments. They work the buttons down the back of my gown and slowly peel down my bodice. They loosen the laces of my corset while the green faeries eagerly free my breasts, pressing their own against my exposed skin. They feel like silk, and their mouths taste of morning dew. My body responds eagerly, unaware of how long it will be denied release.

"Your Majesty," the purple one says, touching my foot. I raise it so she can remove my slipper. One of the green faeries leans down and takes my nipple into her mouth while I step out of the other slipper.

Cassan's faeries cover his neck and chest in sucking kisses. His cock strains at the front of his breeches, but they make no move to release him.

I, however, am quickly naked, and led to one of the tables. The faeries secure my wrists and ankles, spreading my legs apart wide.

"Would His Majesty like to see?" One of his faeries giggles. They surround him and urge him to stand at my feet, their hands stroking over all his bare skin that they can touch.

"Think of how easy it would be," my pink faerie coos to him. "You need only climb up onto this table, and you could be inside of her.”

“You won’t break me so quickly,” he says with a laugh. “Perhaps in a few hours, it will be more of a struggle to deny myself.”

“You are too smart for us, Your Majesty,” a blue faerie says, leaning her head on his shoulder and allowing her hand to drift down his ridged stomach. Her fingers touch the top of his breeches and pull away swiftly.

“And you have such restraint,” a pale one with long, white hair says, running her tongue around the shell of his ear. “If given the opportunity, I would be upon her in an instant. I would delve my tongue into her sweet pussy and lap up every bit of her nectar.”

As they talk about me, my faeries produce a bottle of shimmering oil. They pour it on their hands and massage it into my skin, one at each arm and one at each leg. The green faeries have taken my arms; they work their fingers almost painfully into my muscles, leaving relief in their wake. But when they reach my breasts, they retreat on a long, slow path back to my wrists.

Cassan is similarly strapped down. “Wait,” he says, once the final restraint is placed. “This is wrong. Let me correct it.”

I gasp as my table tilts up, but the pink and purple faeries simply drop to their knees to continue massaging my legs. Cassan and I are both upright now, facing each other.

“This way, I can better see you,” he says, his eyes trained on my breasts.

The faeries tending to him apply oil, as well, rubbing his arms and feet while he groans in rapture. I am similarly transported as the knots in my muscles release under skilled hands.

But as time passes, I become more and more aware of how close fingers come to touching places on my body that are beginning to wake up. Once, twice, the pink and purple faeries' hands accidentally brush the hoop protruding between my labia, but they never touch me there. They avoid the entire area, their fingertips dipping into the crease between my thighs and my mound, but never straying further. My breasts ache for the green faeries to return their mouths to my nipples, but they focus on my shoulders and chest, never touching my breasts directly.

Cassan still has his breeches on, but a faery with skin the velvet dark of a night sky and luminous, starry eyes works the laces and frees him. His cock looks already painfully hard, the tip swollen and nearly purple.

He catches me staring and grins. "They may be touching me, Cenere, but this is all for you."

"I can't wait," I breathe, and it surprises me to realize that I'm not acting. When I first arrived at court, it seemed not even an hour could pass without sex, but Cassan has not called upon me even to take him into my mouth. Days have passed without the touch of another's hand, and I feel as though I'm starving.

"I haven't fucked anyone else," he says, grimacing as the faery traces an arc of oil on his stomach, avoiding his straining cock.

"I haven't even made myself come. Not since Luthian told me he was surrendering."

"That's quite a long time," I say, gasping a little as my piercing is nudged again.

One of the fairies cups his balls through the breeches. "You're full to bursting, Your Majesty. Imagine releasing all of that into her tight, sweet pussy."

He hisses as she walks her fingers alongside his shaft.

"Think of it," one of the green faeries murmurs in

my ear. "So much thick, hot cum filling you."

"You're so lucky, Your Majesty," the pink one says, gliding her oiled hand down my inner thigh.

I lock eyes with Cassan and smirk. "If he lasts a minute, I'll let him sentence me to another full day of this torture."

"I'll hold you to that," he says with a breathless laugh.

The purple faery collects four of the paintbrushes and distributes them to her partners. The bristles are long and thin, pointed in a tip no wider than a single hair. They barely touch me with them as they skim the outlines of my fingers and each toe. It's as if they're painting my portrait on me with teasing, tickling touches. They dip the brushes in the oil, spread it over my skin with delicate strokes that make me squirm.

"Look how she enjoys their attention," the dark faerie tells Cassan. "I think I would like that type of attention paid to me."

His fourth faery, a lovely sea foam thing with frothy white curls kneels before the dark one. "I'll pay attention to you, if they pay attention to us."

My core gushes as I imagine exactly what the faery's tongue feels like slicking up between her partner's labia. The dark faery cups her own breast and toys with the nipple, giving a long moan. "That feels so good."

My clit aches for contact, but my faeries touch me everywhere but where I need it, bathing every inch of me in the oil, one tiny paintbrush stroke at a time.

"Oh, fuck," Cassan groans, and I note a shining, clear drop drooling from the head of his cock.

"What's the matter, Your Majesty?" A golden faery taunts him. "You don't like watching her get her pussy eaten?"

"I fucking love it," he says through his locked jaw.

The green faeries give up their painting and lean in to suck on my neck; it tickles, but since they flank me, I can't avoid their mouths. And still, the other two work their brushes over me. I feel my body striving for release without contact. My legs shake. I'm about to warn them that my climax is inevitable, but they seem to sense it and stop on their own.

All of the faeries stop touching us, leaving us to hang helpless in our straps as we watch the two lovers between us. The dark faerie hooks her knee over the sea-colored faerie's shoulder, opening herself for better access. They moan and gasp in their performance, the blue-black faery urging, "Yes! Don't stop! Don't stop!" while her hips rock frantically against her lover's face.

"Oh fuck, do not stop," Cassan orders, his head lolling against the table. "By order of your king, do not fucking stop."

Precum flows from his cock now, and the golden faery falls to her knees and leans far back, mouth open wide but never touching him. She runs her tongue through the stream and reaches between her legs to stroke herself.

The dark faerie squeals and shrieks, grinding against her companion's face as she comes. I envy her, even after such a short time. And there is so much more denial left for Cassan and me.

"She is ready again," one of the green faeries says, and reaches down to part my labia with her v-spread fingers. Simply being touched here, when the rest of my skin is alight with sensation, is enough to bring me to the very edge. The air of the room cooling my intimate flesh is like tongues against my clit.

"Careful," the purple faerie warns. "Humans are so much weaker."

"I am not weak," I say, but my fingers curl around the straps.

The sea foam faery rises, her face shining, and approaches Cassan. "Do you want us to touch it, Your Majesty?"

He nods, his head thumping the table behind him. "Yes. Yes, I do."

She laughs like wave hitting the shore. "Clean my face, first."

"Fucking gladly." He cranes his neck to reach her, his tongue extended, and laps at her face.

"She's ready," the green faery says again, and this time, the pink faery's brush doesn't stop at the top of my thigh. She runs it along the edge of one of my inner petals, up and down, barely making contact. My clit leaps every time the bristles approach, but they don't touch it. Up one side and down, up the other, then down, working between my folds and circling my opening, dipping into my juices, until I finally beg, "Please, make me come!"

"His Majesty said no," a green faery teases.

I look helplessly to Cassan, but he is locked in torment of his own, as the dark faerie circles the tip of a feather around the head of his cock.

Yet again, I'm at the brink and the green faery stops me.

"How are you doing that?" I pant. "How do you know?"

"I feel it," she says and unstraps one of my hands. She guides my fingers down her body, to her dripping sex. "I feel everything you feel. But you… you can't feel this, can you?"

She pushes my fingers inside her. She is wet and tight and hot and while I've never wished to have a cock before, I want one for the mere chance to bury it inside her.

"When I make myself come on your fingers, you won't feel my release." She pumps my hand in and out, rubs my fingers over her clit. "You're so close," she gasps, her voice rising in pitch. "You're so close, so I'm so close, and I'm, I'm…"

I wail with frustration as her cunt spasms around my fingers, but no relief comes to me.

"Cenere, you can't be so despondent already." Cassan laughs, but it's weak and breathy. "We have hours yet to endure."

The tips of two brushes trace up, up, finally coming into contact with my clit for a delicious second before they pull away again.

I fear it will be the longest day of my life.

Chapter Thirty-Nine

The prince's party is held beneath a pavilion in the garden, erected especially for the occasion. The black court attire of mourning has been banished, and everyone is required to attend dressed in golds and reds, by royal decree.

Even I am dressed so, by the faeries who have tormented me all day. They worked their magic upon my appearance as they worked their magic upon my body, and I arrive at the party on a canopied palanquin with sheer golden curtains and red velvet cushions. I am bare, flushed, and desperate, my wrists restrained by golden manacles.

There hasn't been a single moment of the day that I haven't been on the very brink of climax. I loathe the faeries who carry me, loathe more the one that rides the palanquin, kneeling between my legs and working a slender phallus in and out of my dripping, aching cunt. I feel myself reaching the peak and no longer hope that this time will be different. I can only sob weakly when the instrument is withdrawn and the treacherous green faery waits until I'm ready again.

I've watched her and her matching counterpart come again and again, robbing me of pleasure that should have been mine. I've watched Cassan struggle and beg, too, and it's the only reason I don't resent him for this foolish plan.

I haven't seen Cassan since sundown. The faeries thought it good fun to position the two of us face to face, still restrained, so close that we could feel the warmth of each others' straining, sweating bodies. The faeries took turns stroking the head of Cassan's cock back and forth over my clit until we both begged to be loosed from our bonds. Any other thought that might have been in my mind tonight has been drowned out by the relentless need of my body, my hunger for Cassan, and my desperation for release.

They bring my palanquin beneath the red-and-gold striped roof of the pavilion, which is brightly lit with luminous globes. There are no chairs or tables, but piles and piles of cushions, all occupied by writhing masses of fae bodies. There is a round dais placed directly in the middle of the pavilion, and that is where the faeries lower my palanquin.

They've brushed my curls into copper waves, painted my lips crimson, and draped a thin, golden chain around my waist. The ring through my hood has been replaced by a curved bar topped with a ruby, the small gold ball on the other end tucked directly against my clit. Every jostle threatens to tip me over the edge, but the wicked green faeries know when I am too close, and exactly how to keep me from coming.

A mixture of applause and appreciation rises above the wet smacking and feral grunting of the copulating courtiers.

I look about for Cassan, relieved that our ordeal has nearly ended. I spy him at the end of the pavilion, bound to a gilded post with his hands behind his back, bucking and shouting under the ministrations of a faery in a gold mask. The faery rubs his own cock against the prince's with two oiled hands, stopping whenever it is evident that Cassan is close. The prince's eyes meet mine and his chest heaves with a sigh of obvious relief.

"She is here," he calls out. "Take me to her."

The green faery hops down from the palanquin to stand beside it. She grasps my foot and plants it flat, bending my knee up slightly. The purple faery pulls my knee back, and the other two faeries mirror their position, holding me open as Cassan is brough forward, arms still bound behind him. The four faeries who carry him are all fully nude, with impressive, thick cocks and bodies that look chiseled from stone. I'm not certain that one of them isn't truly made of alabaster, like the statues in the library, for there seems to be no pigment to any part of him. Two of them look as Cassan does, golden tan, but with shining blonde hair, and the fourth is the same sea foam green of the faery from earlier. They lift Cassan up as they mount the dais to lower him over me.

The faeries holding me are strong. Though I want to reach out for Cassan with my legs, pull him into my body, I cannot. Neither can he control his own motion; one of his blond attendants grasps the prince's raw, sensitive cock and moves it into position.

A drumbeat begins. Slow, at first, but gaining speed as the blond faery slicks Cassan's tip back and forth over my clit, then moves it down to rest at my opening.

"Please," I chant, my eyes squeezed shut tight.

"Please, please."

"Look at him," the purple faery whispers. "You'll want to see his face the moment he enters you."

She's right. It's something of a triumph, that a prince has waited so long to have me. That he's allowed himself to be tortured relentlessly in preparation.

"Look at me, Cenere," Cassan gasps. "I can feel you clutching at me already."

I am; my opening flutters desperately, making wet, sucking kisses against the head of his cock. My body trembles. The drum speeds up. The pink faery reaches between us and takes Cassan in her hand, pumping the length of his shaft while the tip rests against me, every motion stimulating me a little more. She strokes him to the beat of the drum, growing faster and faster while he squirms in the hold of his captor. My pulse speeds to match the drum, too, and I'm getting closer, closer than I've been all day.

Courtiers have moved forward to watch. Some are bold enough to touch us. Hands pet Cassan's back, my arms, my breasts. The moans and cries of the faeries lost to their own pleasures crescendo with the ever-increasing throb of the drum.

"Let me fuck her," Cassan growls, struggling against the faeries who hold him. He's a wild thing, truly broken by the torment, as I am.

Torment. This is exactly what Luthian prepared me for. Not the pain and humiliation Arcus inflicted upon me. This is the type of torment the court's name implies. I understand it. Cassan understands it.

We are the perfect rulers for this court.

The faeries holding Cassan rock him against my opening, not penetrating me but simply dipping the very crown of his cock past the rim of my cunt. I try with all my might to bring him inside, but I am mortal, and no match for the strength of the fae. I'm so close, so close... I feel all the denied pleasure, every orgasm that's been withheld from me, building from my toes up, from the top of my head down. My muscles tense. The drum beats faster, louder. Cassan roars and bucks and begs. It's going to happen this time. I'm going to come. They're going to let me. Finally, finally, I'm going to...

The drumbeat stops. The faeries shove Cassan's hips forward. He thrusts deep.

My vision blurs, stains with a wash of red as I freeze, not breathing, in the grips of the strongest, most agonizing climax I've ever felt. Vaguely, I feel Cassan erupt inside of me, feel his hips battering my inner thighs as he moans like he's dying.

The courtiers clap and hoot their approval as I spiral back to my body, too sensitive to bear another moment. But the faeries still hold us. Cassan gasps, "Wait!" but they ignore him, ignore both of our pleas as they continue to mash us together like obscene dolls. Cassan whimpers and cries actual tears as his sensitive member is thrust into me again and again, each stroke hitting my clit. His cum drips out of me, and courtiers reach between and beneath us to scoop it up and taste it or smear it playfully on each other. Some of those fingers enter me alongside Cassan's cock, making the fit tighter.

Cassan thrashes and kicks, but he is powerless in the grasp of his attendants, and they fuck me with his cock ruthlessly, ignoring his ascending cries until he stiffens again, a guttural noise of raw despair tearing from his throat. He fills me again to overflowing, sobbing as his hips pound the last few thrusts of his own volition. I arch my back and cry out with another climax, and the cuffs release me. So, too, do the bonds holding Cassan. He sags forward and collapses over me, his cock still twitching as our sweat-

and-cum-slick bodies entwine.

He kisses my forehead, skims the tip of my nose with his own, and holds me as if we are not sur-rounded by a room full of leering fae.

Weakly, I lift my face and smile. "Happy birthday, Your Majesty."

He laughs, stirs to life inside me again, and moves against me slowly. "I could not have wished for a better present, my queen."

Chapter Forty

Life with Cassan is so much better than I imagined it would be. When Luthian and I embarked on this plan, I had visions of strict propriety and ceremony, and a selfish, cruel prince I would need to simper for and lavish praise upon. But Cassan is respectful. He doesn't order me about—unless we're playing a naughty game—or desire my fear. He simply enjoys me, my body and company, and we often stay awake long into the night talking. He likes stories of my human life and expresses envy at times when I describe my home and the long days of innocent play I had as a child.

"It's difficult," he tells me one night, lazily stroking my hair as I snuggle at his side. "Faeries are never children. I wouldn't even know how to begin to let go of all my knowledge and simply experience wonder."

And so, it becomes my mission, in the days before

our official coronation, to teach him wonder.

"Look closer," I urge him when he picks a flower from the grass and I part its petals to reveal the daisywing asleep inside. "Listen," I tell him on one of our walks through the forest, silencing him so he can hear the songbirds calling out to each other. And Cassan marvels at every small, inconsequential thing I show him, for he has never been taught to appreciate them.

But at night, when he's well-fucked and happily asleep, I often can't make my mind rest. I can be happy with Cassan, but I will never love him.

For I love Luthian.

And I love Kathras.

I don't understand how it is that I can love them both, but the mere thought of either of them brings tears to my eyes and raises a gnawing disappointment that threatens to consume me. I hold all of this inside, though I do consider the possibility of a diary, until I remember Parphia's journal sitting in my trunk. I am not immortal, destined to live out my days until some misfortune befalls me from which I cannot recover. I am mortal, and no matter how safe I am kept, I die more every day. When that time comes, will I want the next queen to read my innermost thoughts? Will I want her to read about my great, unrequited loves when they might be perfectly happy with my king?

There is no point in dwelling over Kathras or Luthian in a journal. It won't bring them back. It might prolong my sadness. If I simply stop thinking about them, eventually, I will not remember how it felt to have their hands on me, their bodies joined to mine.

But Kathras had warned me. *"I'm going to fuck you, Cenere. So deep and so hard that whenever you're with anyone else, all you can think of is me. All you can feel is me."* I simply had no idea that such a thing was possible.

When I am beneath Cassan, I feel Kathras pounding into me, hear his heavy breaths beside my ear. I feel Luthian's arms around me, his cock stretching me. Cassan is a skilled lover, but what is all the skill in the world when I long for two others?

It's not fair to him, I know. It would be easier if he were vapid and vain. But he is kind and sensitive and sweet, and with every day that passes, I feel more like a betrayer. It is already too late for me to change my mind; after all, where am I to go now that my life's purpose has been fulfilled? But coronation day will make things even more final, and it's fast approaching.

We take a walk in the garden the night before the ceremony, arm in arm.

"You seem sad, Cenere," Cassan says, breaking me from a long, thoughtful silence I didn't realize I fell into.

I put my other hand on his arm and give a brief squeeze. "Not sad. Anxious."

"There's nothing to worry about," he assures me, then pauses. "Well, I don't think there's anything to worry about. There hasn't been a coronation in five thousand years, and I didn't attend the last one because I hadn't been born yet."

"But you're not nervous?" We've practiced the entire ceremony, from our entrance in the throne room and the initial crowning, to the procession to the sacred circle and the sharing of enchanted wine, the ritual mating. The courtiers who've meticulously arranged the event are as anxious and serious as the dread inquisitors, and they did not appreciate the merriment with which Cassan and I approached our rehearsals.

He shrugs and sighs. "What will happen if I don't get the words just right? Will they behead me? No.

I will still be their king. If I can't pour my seed onto the sacred stone, will the crops wither and die? What crops? We conjure all the subsistence we need."

I feign umbrage. "What do you mean if you can't spill your seed? Has that been a problem any of the times we've practiced?"

He laughs. "I have no doubt you could make me come even if I were half dead."

A memory of Arcus's face as he died unsatisfied flits through my memory, and I snort. Cassan interprets it as a laugh over his remark.

"You have nothing to worry about, Cenere. I want you to be my queen, so my queen you shall be. And if anyone takes issue with anything you might do tomorrow... well, fuck them." He frowns. "Well, don't *actually* fuck them. They don't deserve you."

I rest my head on his shoulder. "I'm pleased that you think so highly of me, my king."

"No, call me your prince. This is the last night that you can," he murmurs, and stops walking to tilt my chin up with his fingers. "Let me hear it."

"My prince," I whisper, smiling against his mouth as he kisses me.

His heart is too good. Too pure. I hate that I cannot open mine to it. Will I always feel this guilty, pretending?

"I won't claim to know what my father put you through," Cassan says, searching my face. "But I hope that someday, I won't see that sadness in your eyes."

I force a smile and nod down the path. "Let's go inside. I've grown hungry."

When we enter the palace, the doors admitting us directly into the royal dining room, we are besieged by a slender faery with a face that reminds me of a marketplace puppet show. Dour lines pull down his mouth and his head is oddly tall. He is one of Cassan's chamberlains, and his arms are full of scrolls. Ink stains his white hair where he's tucked a quill behind his ear.

"More news on the invitations, Your Majesty," he says, before even asking for permission to speak.

That is something that Casssan must work on, I think. He can't simply allow his courtiers to flout the protocol they followed with his father.

"Tell me." Cassan walks us past him, straight to our seats behind the table on the dais.

"Baron Scylas sends his regrets. He hints at troublesome visitors," the chamberlain says, lowering his voice.

"Ah. So, we know where my brother is." Cassan chuckles at that.

"Should we send a detachment of inquisitors to arrest him?" the chamberlain asks.

This makes Cassan laugh harder. "Why would I want to bring him back? To execute him? I should be thanking him. He's the reason I'm even inheriting the crown."

"And if he changes his mind about that and moves against you?" The chamberlain looks to me uncomfortably, as if pleading with me to make Cassan see reason.

In terms of royal succession, the chamberlain is right. Kathras did flee, but there's nothing stopping him from later regretting the decision to give up the throne and returning to claim it. But Cassan already knows this, and I will not urge him to kill someone I love. Someone who protected me.

"Should that time come, and I don't believe it will, Cassan is strong enough to deal with it, then," I say, reaching for the wine a servant pours for me.

"My mate speaks the truth," Cassan agrees. "And I will not kill my brother, anyway."

The chamberlain opens another scroll, clearing

his throat. "Luthian of Mithrax sends his regrets, as well."

My heart plummets. There was a chance I could have seen Luthian again? Though I did not know it until now, it disappoints me so keenly that tears spring to my eyes. I take a sip of wine to cover my reaction.

"He sends a gift, though." The chamberlain gestures across the room to another servant, who comes forward with a large, stone pot bearing a flowering shrub.

My stomach lurches and I nearly vomit the small amount of wine I've consumed.

The blooms are unmistakable.

"A honey flower bush?" Cassan's brow wrinkles. "What an odd present."

"It could be a ghoulish reference, Your Majesty," the chamberlain suggests. "Perhaps another matter for the inquisitors."

Cassan shakes his head. "I am not my father. I don't take murderous offense to simple jokes. In fact, I'd like to have it planted on the spot where his ashes were buried. Luthian will find that terribly funny when he visits again. What say you, Cenere?"

I beam at him, trying to hide the effort of holding my broken heart together. Luthian will never come here again. Kathras is in exile. And I am about to become queen to a king that I can never love.

"Of all the things he could have sent." Cassan half-smiles in amusement. "Honey flower."

Chapter Forty-One

I cannot sleep, and my restlessness leads me to the horrible, mirrored bedroom once more. There is nothing for me there but horrid memories. Thrace's head presented to me, stealing my dreams. Bathing the poisoned honey and the king's blood from my body in the water from the faery baths. Even that water reminds me of Kathras.

There is nothing at court, however, to remind me of Luthian. At least, there wasn't, before he sent the honey flower bush.

Was that his purpose? To hurt me? To remind me of him, every time I see it?

He knows I love him. He loves me. And yet, I stand on the precipice of an event that will forever change my life, and he does nothing. Worse than nothing. He mocks me for it with his cruel gift.

I don't know what intent brought me to the queen's chambers, but I do remember where Parphia's journal is hidden. That is a link to Luthian, I realize. I can feel his love through the dead queen's words. A love that I wished to have, but which he refused to give me.

He can't stop me from loving him. And he can't stop me from reading what it would be like to be loved by him.

I sit on the bed and pull the journal from its hiding place inside a pillow cover. I worried for a time that it would be found in my possession, but I couldn't let it go. Now that I know Cassan better, I'm certain he will not punish me for having the journal, but I'll still keep it a secret. Something of my own, my private connection to Luthian.

I open to a page at random and read.

Never have I experienced such a perfect day. We made love in the grove of sweet trees, while their petals fell all around us. Luthian never rushes our pleasure. Today, he took his time touching every part of me, leaving the most delicious places until the last, and then he explored those with his lips and tongue. I have never experienced rapture with Arcus the way I experience it with Luthian.

Perhaps, she should have tried killing him. That certainly brought me pleasure.

The entry goes on. *I told Luthian how I begged Arcus for a child. His sons are all he needs to secure his line. How I envy their mother, for she knew the joy of bearing their creation light. Luthian won't give me a child, either; he says it's too cruel to bring another faery into the court while Arcus rules it. But when I imagine who that faery might be, I see her so clearly. Skin of snow, hair of fire, beauty that will bring the court to its knees.*

The queen wanted a child, and Luthian refused her? I know nothing of faery conception, beyond the need for living essence, or what it might mean for him to make that refusal, but he granted my mother's wish, didn't he?

But then, my mother was not a part of Arcus's court, and he was never any danger to me.

"You were born for it."

The words taunt me. No, Arcus was inevitable. Luthian had been patient, far beyond the boundaries of time, and carefully planned to bring me to this place, simply to kill the king he loathed.

But for all the love he bore Parphia, he did not give her a child, for the next entry reads, *Luthian will not budge in his stance against my child. It isn't fair that Arcus should have two and I should have none at all. If he will not help me, there are hundreds of courtiers who will. I will order one to my bed and take his light. I will have my daughter. I will have my princess. All I need do is convince Arcus that it happened while he was too drunk to control himself and he spilled living essence. That I begged him not to, and that my pleas drove him into a lustful frenzy. He will not disbelieve that. It's too like him.*

I devour the next entries. Parphia's selection of a young faery with the attributes she desired in her child. Copper hair, pale skin, a wry smile and laughing eyes. She took him in the labyrinth, during the monthly ritual, and commanded him to give her his living essence.

Her plan was successful.

There are entries about her pregnancy, her labor, the wisp of light she birthed and took to the nursery to be nurtured. She has such hopes for that wisp of light, a daughter she named...

After the Cenere tree I labored beneath, tended by a midwife of the Court of Seasons.

I throw the book aside as if burned, lurch from the bed and double over, vomiting up my dinner onto the pristine marble floor. My head swims. I am dizzy with the truth. Not the truth. The coincidence. It must be a coincidence.

I was born of a wish. Luthian gave me to my mother to fulfill her wish. She named me after the tree I was born beneath. She raised me, a human child...

A human child that she taught the ways of magic. Of flying. Raising plants from the ground. Listening to the birds. Noticing the flowers.

A human child of no consequence, raised by a faery woman who desperately wished for her.

But it is my name on the pages of this book. My appearance. My birth that is described. My mother named as midwife.

This cannot be.

It cannot be.

I have no wings. I have no magic. I am human, in all respects. I age. I bleed with the moon and burn beneath the sun.

I am human.

I am human.

The diary lies like a viper, waiting to strike me once more. My hands tremble as I lift it and trace the loops of my name, written in my mother's hand.

My *real* mother's hand.

Then, I turn to the next entry and read on. *Luthian is furious. He thinks me too foolish to understand the consequences of my actions if I am found out. But how will Arcus find out? He believes the child in the faery nursery belongs to him. He celebrated her with a banquet and beamed with pride. He already has suitors lined up for her when she comes of age and returns.*

I laugh with hysterical, giddy relief. Of course, it's all a coincidence. Luthian was banished from court for five-hundred years, after Parphia's death. I am not five hundred years old.

The cenere tree must have held special signifi-
cance to Luthian because of Parphia. That's why he
granted my mother's wish there. It probably wasn't
even the same tree, just the same, common type.
There are cenere trees all over Fablemere. It is a coincidence.

That is what my heart wants to believe. My mind,
however, accepts the grim likelihood that that diary I
am reading belonged to my mother.

I'm drawn back to her final entry.

There is one person I can seek out to learn the
truth of it. Not Luthian, for he will merely pile more
lies upon the lies he already led me to believe.

I need Firo, and our meeting cannot wait until
morning.

"Take me to Firo," I order the palace walls, and
stride to the door.

It opens onto a room full of clocks. Hourglass-
es, great tall, ticking things, smaller ones that rest
on mantles and tables. All around me is the chaotic
clicking of gears, faces without numbers, or with the
numbers in the wrong order. Pocket watches dangle
in the air; some of them have no numbers upon them
at all. The ceiling appears to be missing, replaced,
instead, with a swirling purple mist and a void somehow illuminated by darkness.

And in the center of it all stands Firo.

I wipe my eyes hastily on the sleeve of my robe.
I'm a queen or will be in a few hours. I must occupy
the role.

He doesn't ask why I'm there. He simply says,
"You could not know until the correct time."

I open my mouth to protest, to demand how he
knows and why he did not tell me. But he is from the
Court of Time and Destiny. The only answer he will
give me is the one he already offered.

Instead, I ask, "What does it mean?"

He gestures to a table, a huge clockface under glass. I do not recognize the hundreds of symbols around its edge and spiraling into the center, and I don't know how to read the multitude of hands, some of them moving slowly, some quickly. Firo pulls out a chair and directs me to sit, then takes his place across from me.

"It means that you are the daughter of the late Queen Parphia." He frowns. "You did read that diary, didn't you?"

"Of course, I did! Why would I be here if I hadn't?" I snap.

"I worried that I revealed the secret too soon." He sits and conjures a fire in the hearth. The warm light lines the angles of his face. He looks more tired than I've ever seen him.

"I woke you," I say, ashamed of my rudeness. That I am a queen is no excuse.

"No. I knew when to expect you." He points to a symbol beneath the glass. A thin arm draws the eye toward it. "This is you, now. And this..." he strokes his fingers backward on the spiral, "is where Kathras left you the diary."

I suspected he might have done so on purpose. "You told him to?"

"No. I don't interfere with destinies. I merely watch them. I can no more influence the future than I can prevent it." He meets my gaze with serious intent. "And I cannot, and will not, tell you what happens next."

"Because it will alter destiny?" I ask.

"Because it hasn't been written." He touches the glass again, above another of the clock arms, and traces its quick, steady circle around the spiral. "This is possibility."

"For me, or for everyone?" It seems unlikely that such a clock exists for everyone in Fablemere.

"For this court, and its history. For Arcus and Luthian and Kathras and Cassan. For Queen Theeda, for Queen Parphia. And for you."

I shake my head, tears flowing down my face. "No. This can't be. Luthian granted my mother's wish."

"No, he didn't," Firo says, and offers me his handkerchief. "He gave you to the faery who raised you and paid her in wishes to raise the queen's child."

"A child," I remind him. "There are no faery children."

"That's true. Which was why it was so important to hide your faery nature. It was your mother, your true mother, Queen Parphia, who placed the enchantment upon you that stunted your growth and made you appear human." He looks down at the symbols again. "It was her last act before the inquisitors took her."

"That was five hundred years ago," I protest. "Certainly I have not lived for five hundred—"

My mother. Not Parphia, but the mother who raised me, changed the seasons on our lands. A year could have lasted as long as she wished it to.

"You're beginning to see the truth," Firo says softly. "You understand now, yes?"

I touch my chest. "I'm a faery."

"Under Parphia's spell, you're a human," Firo corrects me. "When the spell is lifted, you'll be a faery."

"Then lift the spell," I say without hesitation. I've spent my entire life not knowing quite what I am. Born of a wish, a human with a faery mother, there was never anyone like me. Now that I know what I am, I want to fully embody my faeness.

Firo shakes his head. "It's not that simple. I can't break another faery's spell."

"Parphia is dead," I protest. "Surely, there's some loophole—"

"You would need to speak to someone who knew

the spell that was used. Unfortunately, Parphia cannot be questioned. Your mother might have known. The only other involved was—"

"Luthian." He doesn't want to speak to me again. Now, he doesn't have that choice. He put a similar spell on Brujon once. He knows how they work.

"Cassan might be moved to help you," Firo says. "He's quite besotted with you."

"He's besotted with human pussy," I snap, then offer Firo an apologetic glance. "I'm sorry. I'm tired."

"You're not in a position that I envy. But the power that you gain from this revelation..." He's studying the clock face. "I can't tell you what you will do next. But I can tell you that you're smarter than you give yourself credit for, and stronger. You braved all of Luthian's games. You survived Arcus's torments. You can handle whatever comes next."

I don't feel smart, or brave, or strong. I'm confused, frightened, and angry.

"Why did Luthian bring me here?" I ask, for I know now that Firo has more knowledge of the plot than I ever had. "For revenge against Arcus, or to win the kingdom for Parphia by installing me on the throne?"

"Both," Firo says. "But I don't think he intended to fall in love with you along the way."

A tearful laugh catches in my throat. "Would that he hadn't. Would that I hadn't."

"You could wish for it," Firo suggests.

I have no wishes left. Luthian tricked me into giving the first away. I used the second to free Kathras.

But perhaps there is hope. Perhaps I could get another wish, somehow. "Do you think that if I wish for Parphia's enchantment to be broken, I could be restored? I could be a faery, as I was born to be?"

"Wishes are the strongest magic there is," Firo says. "I doubt even Parphia could have created a spell strong enough to withstand it."

A wish is an important thing. They don't come along every day.

One must be careful what they wish for.

One must be mindful of the consequences.

"What I truly wish for," I begin, knowing that my wish is not guaranteed, "is to see Luthian again."

And then he is there, standing before me.

Chapter Forty-Two

The Luthian who appears before me is not the faery I met in the graveyard, and he is a shadow of the faery who left me here at court. He's always been blue-gray, but now he is paler, like the snowy side of an ash. His dressing gown is askew, his expression tired, and I know that isn't because I've woken him. He has the look of someone who lost a fight with wakefulness days ago.

He blinks at me, and at Firo. "What's happened?"

"Cenere used one of her wishes to bring you back," Firo says calmly.

"I-I had no wishes left," I whisper to myself.

They don't seem to hear me.

Firo tells him, "She knows everything."

Luthian's eyes widen.

"Everything," I repeat. "I know the truth behind every one of your lies. I know about Parphia's child, and that I am that child."

"Then you have all the answers, and my presence isn't necessary." He tilts his head, daring me to go further.

I will not be cowed by him any longer. "The favor you have done for me is finished. Our agreement was voided, remember? Because I *wished* it? In a few hours, I will be queen of this court. I owe you nothing."

"Did you prepare that speech before you summoned me?" Luthian laughs, but I see through it. He is frightened of me, now that I know the truth.

"No. I wished for your presence because there is still something I do not understand." I turn to Firo. "Thank you for your counsel. I will see you at the coronation."

"You will?" Firo's eyes dart to the clock table in surprise.

He may not be able to tell me the future, but he's horrible at hiding it.

"Luthian of Mithrax," I say, walking toward the door without sparing him another glance. "If you try to leave court, I will have you hunted for sport. Follow me."

"Yes, Your Majesty," he says, and my heart thrills at his forced obedience.

It thrills just to see him. I don't know how I stopped myself from lunging at him, throwing my arms around his neck, begging him to forgive me and to stay with me, but I'm proud of my restraint. I want to tell him that I've missed him, that I can't stand the thought of a life behind these palace walls without him. But above all of that is a profound anger, a fury I have every right to express.

And a deep confusion that I've managed to bring him here, at all. I had no wishes left.

I open the door and we enter my royal bedchamber. I study his expression as he takes it in, recognizes where he stands.

"You've been here before," I say. It is not a question. He knows what I've learned.

"I have." He looks past me, through me, stiff and grim.

"You had a chance to tell me everything. When we spoke about what I found in the diary. You had the opportunity then to tell me the truth, and you didn't." I clasp my hands together to stop them shaking.

"That is true."

"Then why didn't you?"

I want the answer to this question more than I want my faery nature.

"Tell me!" I command him.

"You had the diary," he says with a disinterested shrug. "I assumed you'd be smart enough to figure it out yourself."

"I did figure it out myself," I snap. "I'm asking why I had to learn it from a dead queen and not from you."

He doesn't even attempt a lie. "Because I had no intention of telling you."

"Why?" I demand.

"Because whether or not you knew had no bearing on how the situation benefited me." He says it with maddening neutrality, as if it makes no difference that he hid such important information from me.

My nails dig into my fingers as I clutch my hands harder. "It didn't *benefit* you to tell me of my true parentage."

"If anything, you knowing could have ruined the entire enterprise." He speaks as though his betrayal is a simple matter, not another rift opening between us. "If you knew your true parentage, you might have told someone. Cassan, Kathras. Arcus, though

I don't think you're that foolish. If you did not know, however, you couldn't even mistakenly tell."

"So, what? Not telling me was... protecting me?" I scoff.

"Partially. I was protecting myself, as well." He paces to one of the walls, rubs a smudge on one of the mirrors with his sleeve. "I did consider telling you, at the beginning. I thought perhaps I could entice you to help me if you knew that Arcus had killed Parphia. But you were already so filled with rage and violence that I didn't need to. You had your own revenge planned. Telling you the truth might have changed the way you felt about your mother, and you might not have been so eager to accept my proposal."

How is it possible that I've fallen in love with such a monster? How foolish of me.

"You would have let me live my entire life here, never knowing?" My voice trembles.

"I think so, yes." He considers. "If I thought you wouldn't remove my head, I might have told you."

"Don't be so sure that I won't, now!"

He laughs at me. At the soon-to-be queen who could very much order his head removed. "You won't."

"Why?" I glare at him as he wanders about the room. "Why do you believe I'll have more mercy for you than I had for Arcus."

Luthian is before me in a flash, towering over me. "Because we both know that you would die in the same instant I did."

I open my mouth to deny it.

"You love me." He says it like an accusation. "You let me become more important to you than your revenge, than a crown. You complicated everything."

"I suppose it's my weak, human nature," I spit back at him. "By all means, remove it from me!"

"I will not!" He shouts in my face, and I shrink back from him. The silvery rage in his eyes fades, leaving only remorse behind.

It is in that flare of anger that I see my own pain reflected. I wanted to have my revenge on Thrace because he took my mother away, but when he died... it was as if she died all over again. Luthian has his revenge. Arcus is dead. And now that it's over...

"The spell is all that remains of Parphia," I whisper.

He closes his eyes. "Cenere..."

"You didn't tell me, and you didn't remove the spell, because once you do, Parphia is gone. Truly gone." I take a step back and look down at myself. The human body I thought I inhabited. The human feelings I so often cursed myself for having. These are all that remain of a long-dead faery queen.

"No. I didn't tell you the truth because when you found out... you would be gone."

I meet his eyes. "That isn't true. I'll be a faery, the way I was meant to be before all of this secrecy and treachery and betrayal."

"But you won't be the human Cenere that I fell in love with."

I feel as though I'm sinking, though my feet remain on the floor.

"I have never pretended to be selfless. Or honest." He chuckles ruefully. "Yes, Cenere. I love you. And the love of a faery is selfish and consuming and possessive. I would never have let you change if I stayed. That's why I left you."

"You love me," I whisper. I knew it, to the depths of my being. I should be furious with him, but I can't be. I'm just relieved that it wasn't something I imagined.

"Kathras knew," he goes on. "I gave him the diary and asked him to give it to you."

"That's not an excuse."

"It wasn't meant to be."

We stare at each other for a long, silent moment.

"You framed Kathras for his father's murder," I say.

Luthian nods. "Yes."

"Why?"

"Because it was a part of the plan." Luthian tilts his head down. "And because I suspected that you loved him. Do you deny it?"

"I do not." My feelings for Kathras are complicated, but beneath them all is a foundation of love. Much like what I feel for Luthian.

"I couldn't stand the thought of you being with him." Luthian smiles sadly. "A faery's love."

Selfish. Consuming. Possessive.

"I should have known." I shake my head and twist my nightgown in my hands. "I should have known."

"Should have known what?" he asks.

I lift my chin and stare into his eyes. "I should have known that I was a faery."

"You could not have known." He turns away.

I don't allow him to escape me. I rush to him, throw myself into his path, and grasp his arms, holding him fast. There is a battle waging behind the silvery depths of his eyes. He lifts his hands and holds my forearms, as if deciding whether to push me away.

"I should have known, for I want to possess you! I want to consume you!" My admission is a plea. "Possess me. Consume me. Because, selfishly, I love you, too."

With a wretched sob, he pulls me into his arms and claims my mouth with his.

Chapter Forty-Three

I fall into Luthian as if from a great height. Dizzy the moment my feet leave the cliff's edge, exhilarated by the danger, knowing that what awaits me at the end can only be pain.

Luthian has taught me plenty about pain. But nothing could have prepared me for the ache of losing him. Now that I know what it feels like, it makes me hungry to avoid feeling it again. I cling to him, almost climb him in my desperation to physically hold him here with me.

I expect him to leave. That this is a final, passionate kiss goodbye to mark the ending of everything we could have had together.

He lifts his head and whispers, "Cenere. My love. My honey flower."

"Don't leave me again," I beg him. "If you love me, you won't leave me."

"You're about to be the queen of this court," he

reminds me. "It's what you set out to achieve."

"I set out for revenge," I remind him. "The crown is an empty bauble now. My purpose...is you."

His mouth is on mine again, for long, gasping moments that leave us both breathless and staggering. He backs me toward the bed, until I can go no further and we tumble down. Our previously dressed bodies are bare, our skin pressed together everywhere we can touch.

I wonder what he thinks, as his kisses trail down my body. Is he here with me, or revisiting past memories of this bed, with another queen, in another lifetime?

Then, his mouth drags down my stomach, he finds his way to my center, and I don't think anymore. He knows my body too well, his tongue is far too skilled, even when he is frantic with need. He seeks out my clit, sucks at it and toys with my piercing, two fingers working their way inside me to find the sweet, aching place that intensifies the sensation. I bury my hand in his silky black hair and hold him with my thighs, grinding against his mouth as the pressure builds, builds, then bursts. I come, wailing, my juices slicking down his face as he continues to pump his fingers mercilessly and flicks his tongue over my too-sensitive pearl. I cry out and arch my back, shouting my pleasure again. I am boneless in the wake of my climax, but I somehow push him off me, onto his back, and sit astride his face, leaning forward to grasp his cock and worship the head of it with my tongue.

His moans vibrate through my core as he feasts on me. I take him into my mouth, to the back of my throat, still swirling and sucking. He tenses, strains, and his breath bursts in little puffs against my opening while I slide my cunt back and forth over his face. He grips my hips to stop my squirming, delving his tongue into my sex and drinking from me as if dying of thirst. He lifts up rhythmically, thrusting into my mouth. I'm stunned to realize that I know his body, his responses just as well as he knows mine. He's so close to coming, salty drops already leaking out to coat my tongue. I maintain the same tempo, the same motion with my tongue, and he pulls his mouth free long enough to cry, "Wait!"

It's too late. Cum hits the back of my throat, spurt after spurt, as he shouts and groans. I choke on it, cough some from the corners of my mouth, and he pulls out so I can swallow the rest down.

He pushes me off, pins me to the mattress on my stomach, and drives his still hard, still erupting cock into my aching, clenching cunt. He whimpers and curses as he strokes in and out, though he's the architect of his own torment. He grasps my hips and pulls me back, driving deeper, plunging over and over until I'm shivering from the shocks of pain.

"Harder!" I beg him, and he complies, pummeling me with his thrusts. I slip a hand beneath myself and find my swollen, slippery clit with my fingertips. It takes me but a few heartbeats to bring myself to climax again, just in time for Luthian to give over to another, brutal peak. He grabs a fistful of my hair with one hand, pushes my shoulder to the bed with the other, and stays buried inside me while his cock jerks and bathes my pussy with his cum.

I lay gasping beneath him. It was not the most artful coupling, but it is by far the best I've ever had.

"Don't leave me again," I beg him. "Never leave me again."

He kisses my ear. "Never again in our immortal lives."

I jolt. My life is not immortal, not while Parphia's curse is still upon me. It may have been an enchantment in her eyes, but to me, it is a cruel sentence.

Tears flood my voice so that I cannot respond.

But Luthian senses it and rolls off me. He strokes my back and murmurs, "Cenere. What's wrong?"

I sniff and shake my head. "I'm not fae. Not yet. And I may never be. The spell can only be removed by Parphia. Firo thought perhaps you could help me, but it feels hopeless. I could have wished for it, but..."

"But what?" he asks. "You could still wish for it."

"I'm out of wishes. You know that." I roll onto my back and count them off on my fingers. "I wished for an end to our agreement, and I wished that Kathras would escape."

"You aren't out of wishes," Luthian admits quietly.

I sit up. "What?"

"I never took any of your wishes." He sits up, too, but he can't face me. "I helped Kathras escape, and I only said I took the first because I was angry with you. You had three wishes that I paid your mother. She did not wish for a child. She saw taking you into her care as an honor and a blessing, but it did not cost her a wish. You inherited three, Cenere."

Perhaps, I would have been angry with him for lying if it didn't mean a solution to removing the spell.

"I have three wishes?" I whisper.

"You have two. You used one to bring me here." He nods to me. "Wish."

I rise from the bed and stand before the mirrored wall. I see a thousand Ceneres in the tunnels of the reflections all around me, all of them human. I take them in for the last time.

She is who I have always been, despite the faery beneath the enchantment. She is the human child who ran too fast and fell, cried over a scraped knee. The human child who watched the bumble bees tumbling from flower to flower and chased them, giggling with wonder at the world. These are experiences that no other faery has had. A life no other faery could live.

On the precipice of returning to my true form, which is unfamiliar to me, I regret. Will I lose those human memories? Will the human Cenere die so that the fae Cenere can live?

I run my hands down my naked body. Will I feel different? Will all this voluptuous flesh become lean, the skin less pale? The freckles that dot my nose and shoulders and arms, will they vanish, another part of my mortal self to be forgotten?

Luthian comes to stand beside me. "You are beautiful, Cenere. And you will still be beautiful when you change."

"It isn't my beauty," I say, but words to explain my inexplicable sadness fail me. Of course, I will become fae. Of course, I will accept my true nature. But I must mourn for the human life that is ending. It's not something Luthian, who has always known himself, could understand.

"I'm worried that when I change, I will no longer be me," I confess. "And I like me. I've learned who I am over these past weeks. Even the darkest parts of me that I would never have admitted to before."

"Such as?" he prompts.

"I enjoy pain. Torture. When it's inflicted for fun, not for cruelty's sake. But I do embrace cruelty. I've killed, Luthian. I watched Arcus die while he was still inside of me and the feeling was... transformative. I enjoy killing." Saying it out loud, it makes me sound dangerous. I am not. "I won't kill for the sake of killing, that isn't what I'm saying."

"I know you wouldn't." He runs his hands up and down my arms, meeting my eyes in the mirror. "But I love you for reveling in it."

"There are other things, too," I admit to him. "I've

learned that I can hold more love inside of me than I would ever have dreamed possible. As I love you with all of my heart, so do I share that heart with Kathras. It doesn't make sense; how can I give all of me to you, and all of me to him?"

"It's possible," Luthian says gently. "I've learned that about myself, too."

I face him slowly. "You still love Parphia."

"I will always love her, fool that she was. And I love her as fiercely as I love you." He kisses my forehead.

"You weren't banished because of your love for her," I say softly. "You were banished because you hid me."

"I have spent the past five hundred years protecting you." He searches my gaze. "Why would I let harm befall you now?"

I nod. I know he's right. It's time now.

He turns me to face the mirror once more. "Make your wish, Cenere."

I take one last, long look at my mortal body. "I wish to end Parphia's enchantment upon me."

For a moment, there is nothing. I feel no difference in my body or the air around me. There is no sense of magic at work, the way I felt it when my mother would raise the flowers or change the leaves. I stare at myself, will myself to change, suddenly panicked that it hasn't worked.

And then, a shimmer in the air. a rain of diamond dust, suspended around me. Magic glides like silk over my flesh, teasing my nipples to hard peaks, stroking shivers down my spine. My forehead tingles, and two slender antennae sprout there, tangled in my hair, which has grown wilder, thicker, my curls askew and tumbling like whirling rivulets of molten copper spiraling over my shoulders. The flesh on my back puckers and rises; behind me, two huge, bat-like wings take pale shape, pink-white and the same pearlescent sheen with which my skin now glows. My eyes go milky, the irises and pupils vanishing, though my sight becomes sharper. The glittering air surrounds my wings and settles there, studding me with blinding flashes of crystal.

The rest of me, though, stays the same. My soft belly, my round hips, the generous flesh on my thighs all remain. My freckles are gone, sadly. Perhaps I'll draw them on with cosmetics and start a trend at court.

The thought makes me laugh, and my laugh has changed; it's the sound of tinkling chimes on a breeze. I clap my hand over my mouth, unable to stop the hysterical tide rising.

Luthian's eyes rake over my body. He reaches out to touch my wings, and the moment he skims them, they flutter protectively.

"They're sensitive," I say through my laughter. "Is it because they're new?"

He shakes his head and smiles. "No. They'll always feel that way. Wait until you fly with them."

I try out my new muscles, flexing my wings to feel their motion. My feet lift off the ground. "I thought it would take time to get used to them."

"No. You've always been a faery, Cenere. It was merely suppressed." He strokes my glowing skin, gazing up at me in wonder. "She was right. It would have been impossible to hide you."

I drift back down to stand before him, a sudden thought occurring. "Being human was what made me so irresistible to everyone here at court. Will you be disappointed to lose the human pussy you love so much?"

He laughs and kisses me, sweeping me into his arms, and my wings fold in tight. *He was right,* I think. *They do move out of the way.*

"I'm sure I'll get over it," he whispers, rubbing his nose against mine. "Though, it might require practice."

And so, we do practice, again and again, all night.

But it doesn't take us nearly that long to perfect it.

Chapter Forty-Four

"Luthian of Mithrax!"

I startle awake, clutching the sheet to my chest, and see Cassan at the foot of my bed, staring down at Luthian and I entwined.

Lost in wonder over my new body and the intoxication of Luthian's love, I managed to forget perhaps the most important detail in my life: I am supposed to be crowned queen today. Now, my mate towers over me and my lover, taken without his permission. I sit up, ready to throw myself across Luthian's body to shield him from Cassan's royal anger.

But there is nothing of Arcus's jealousy in Cassan's expression. He seems overjoyed at his discovery.

"Luthian! You've come to fuck me and my queen!" Cassan jumps onto the bed, launching himself between us. "This is a much better gift than that silly bush."

"Your Majesty," Luthian begins.

"You're not going to start calling me that, too, are you?" Cassan groans. "There's already too much talking and not enough fucking. You're ruining my coronation present."

"Cassan," I begin gently, laying a hand on his shoulder. My wings are heavy against my back, so I adjust my position, leaning slightly forward. He looks up at me, narrows his eyes.

"Oh. You're..." He reaches up and touches the two sensitive antennae at my hairline. "You're a faery now. When did this happen? Luthian, did you see this? Cenere is a faery."

"I did see it, Y—" He stops himself before using the title. "We have much to discuss. Most of it about your mate. But it isn't a conversation that can be had in bed."

"Unfortunately, I have a coronation to attend." Cassan pushes himself up and offers me his hand. "And your dress will need altering, I think. Your wings are huge. I mean that in the most complimentary way."

They buzz happily at the mention of them, and I force them to still.

"Cassan, we have to talk about all of this before the coronation," I say gently. "It's not something that can wait. After you hear it, you might not want me to be your queen."

"If you say the coronation can wait, then it can wait," he says. "But can we speak somewhere less reflective? This room makes me dizzy."

He snaps his fingers and the three of us sit, fully dressed, at a small, round table in the pink salon.

"The last time I was in here," he tells Luthian happily, "I was tied down and being edged mercilessly by some of the most talented faeries at court. Cenere can attest to that, can't you?"

"Indeed, they were very talented," I agree as Cassan conjures a tea pot and cups. "There's something I must confess—"

"No. I must confess it. Cenere is innocent in this. I will face the consequences, but you must swear that Cenere will bear no recrimination," Luthian says.

"I could never hold anything against Cenere. She's my favorite," the prince says happily.

Though I fear I won't be when he's heard the truth, Cassan is shockingly accepting of everything Luthian tells him. Queen Parphia's infidelity, her secret child, Luthian's part in all of it. The assassination of Arcus, the framing of Kathras, my involvement in everything, including the manner of his death. The entire time he listens, Cassan sips tea and conjures cookies, offering them silently to us while the tale unfolds.

"Cenere used her last wish to break the spell and return to faery form, and... that's all." Luthian bows his head. "I await your judgment."

Cassan looks to me, then back to Luthian. "What judgment?"

"I killed your father," I say, pressing a hand to my chest in a bid to calm my heart. "I killed the king."

"I killed the king," Luthian argues. "You were merely the weapon. She has no responsibility here—"

"I don't care who killed him." Cassan's expression is half-confused, half-relieved. "I'm just happy that he's dead. I'm a bit disappointed that it wasn't Kathras; thinking he killed father made me like him so much more. But what am I supposed to do? Punish you for getting rid of my terrible father and handing me the throne?"

"You're not angry with me?" I can only dare to whisper.

"No. I'm not angry at either of you. Luthian,

you're one of my oldest friends. You only just returned to court, and you ran off again. I'm just happy that you've returned." Cassan sighs happily and takes a bite out of a cookie, chewing as he says, "Now, everything is just right."

"But I love Luthian," I remind him. That part hadn't been left out of the story. "I'm in love with him, and not with you."

Cassan shrugs. "Of course, you love him. Who doesn't? To tell you the truth, I've been in love with him at times, myself. Be in love with him. What does it matter to me?"

"You wanted me to be your queen," I protest.

"You can still be my queen." Cassan laughs, as if Luthian and I are histrionically exaggerating the situation. "Clearly, someone can be the queen of this court and be in love with Luthian. It's what got Parphia killed."

The breath Luthian takes draws him up straighter.

Cassan takes a sip of his tea, oblivious. "You'll be my queen, Cenere. I've chosen you for it. But I won't stand between you and true love. I'm not a monster."

A laugh of disbelief bursts from me.

"You'll stay at court," Cassan orders, pointing playfully at Luthian. "I won't have my queen's heart filled with sorrow, pining for you. And you'll make her happy, or there will be consequences."

"What about Kathras?" I ask.

"He's the heir to the throne I'm about to take so..." Cassan makes a ticking noise with his cheek. "I know I'm supposed to kill him, but I'm so bored with mourning black. We're immortal. We're not meant to think of death so much and for such extended periods."

"Can he return?" I dread the answer, for while Cassan has said he won't deny me Luthian, he's correct in thinking that Kathras's life is a threat to his rule. "To be with me? I love him, as I love Luthian."

Cassan considers. "He would need to renounce the throne, first."

"I don't know if he's willing to," Luthian says carefully.

"I could convince him!" I blurt, though I'm not sure that I can. While I did fall in love with Kathras's tenderness in the faery baths, and though he did go to the dungeons without implicating me in Arcus's assassination, I don't know how he feels about me.

But I want to try.

"Do we know where he is?" Cassan asks Luthian. "Have you heard from him?"

"No. Kathras and I aren't friendly," he replies.

"You did frame him for murder," I point out. "I don't think your friendship will blossom as a result."

"Baron Scylas hinted that he may have returned to the Sorrowlands." Cassan rubs his chin in thought. "I could send you as an ambassador, Luthian."

"Kathras won't speak to him," I protest.

"An ambassador in the queen's retinue," Cassan says, and gives me a wink. "Give me a week to recover from the party we're about to have tonight, and it will be arranged. The two of you will travel to the Sorrowlands, forge important diplomatic relations with that disgusting old vampire Scylas, and bring my brother home."

I leap from my chair and throw my arms around Cassan's neck. "Thank you!"

"Thank me by preparing for the coronation," he says, gently disentangling himself. "And Luthian?"

Luthian rises and bows. "Your Majesty?"

"Limber up. Now that she has wings, I have loads of ideas for us to try out with her tonight."

I stand before the doors of the throne room, my hand atop Cassan's. Beyond, the entire court has assembled to see their faery king and human queen begin the day of ceremony and spectacle that will cement our standing in the Court of Pleasure and Torment.

"I expect you'll come as a shock to them," Cassan whispers, slightly inclining his head toward mine. "If anyone asks, it's a gift from me. No need to dredge up the past."

"Of course." Perhaps one day, the truth will come out, and I will be known as the daughter of Queen Parphia, but Cassan has given me more than any mortal king would have allowed. More than Arcus would have, certainly. I can keep a secret in payment.

Chimes begin to ring beyond the doors, rising in a storm of music I taste on my tongue. My heightened fae senses continue to astonish and delight me. The light through the windows dances in waves my mortal eyes would never have noticed. It writhes to the song of the bells in celebration. The palace itself seems to throb with excitement.

The doors open, and Cassan and I step inside.

The looks of anticipation and admiration turn to wonder and disbelief as I pass them, my crystal-flecked wings shimmering behind me. I see delight and envy written across the faces of the courtiers, and I relish their admiration. They have witnessed me humiliated, degraded by Arcus. Now, I walk beside Cassan not only as a queen, but as a faery. I am not an oddity or a toy. I am their ruler and their equal.

I glance ahead to the dais and the two thrones there. Beside mine is a chair, and in front of that chair is Luthian.

Gaping, I turn to Cassan, and he offers me his sly wink.

The priestesses stand in a semicircle around the dais, and they part to allow us through. I feel Luthian's gaze on me with every step that I take. I stand before my throne and face the court, but my awareness is centered entirely on him.

Two priestesses step forward, holding ceremonial wreaths of blossoms. When they bring them closer, I see which kind.

Honey flowers.

I look to Luthian. The pride on his face is not about his triumph in this moment, the power that he has gained. All I see is the love he has finally acknowledged and accepted. The love that we have been granted by the friend at my side, and the destiny that awaits us.

I sink down to accept my wreath and straighten as Cassan does the same. The courtiers clap and cheer.

"Your King, Cassan The Kind," the chamberlain announces. "Your Queen, Cenere the Fae."

A tear of joy slides down my cheek. Cenere the Fae. Not Cenere the orphan, Cenere the pawn, Cenere the helpless. I am now what I was always meant to be.

And I will be so, so much more.

The World Of Fablemere

FABLEMERE

The Ogre's Fairytale Bride
(Available in ebook, paperback, on Kindle Vella and Ream)

The Vampire's Willing Captive
(Coming soon to ebook and paperback; currently available
on Kindle Vella and Ream)

The Mage's Reluctant Assistant
(In progress on Kindle Vella and Ream)

FABLEMERE FAE

A Kingdom of Pleasure and Torment
(Available in ebook, paperback, and Radish fiction app)

A Kingdom of Wonder and Sorrow
(Coming in 2025)

ALSO BY ABIGAIL BARNETTE

THE SOPHIE SCAIFE SERIES

The Boss
The Girlfriend
The Bride
The Ex
The Baby
The Sister
The Boyfriend
Sophie

BY THE NUMBERS

First Time
Second Chance
Baby Makes Three

HARDBALL DUOLOGY

Long Relief
Double Header

CANIS CLAN

Bride Of The Wolf
Wolf's Honor

TAKEN BY THE ALPHA KING SERIES

Taken By The Alpha King
Rise of the Alpha God

STAND ALONE NOVELS AND NOVELLAS

Bad Boy, Good Man
Surrender
Awakening Delilah
Choosing You
Where We Land

WRITING AS JENNY TROUT

Nightmare Born
Such Sweet Sorrow
Say Goodbye To Hollywood

Abigail Barnette is a pen name of blogger and USA Today Bestselling Author Jenny Trout. As Abigail, Jenny writes award-winning erotic romance, including the internationally bestselling *The Boss* series, as well as new adult novels.

As a blogger, Jenny's work has appeared on *The Huffington Post*, and has been featured on television and radio, including *HuffPost Live, Good Morning America, The Steve Harvey Show,* and National Public Radio's *Here & Now.*

They are a proud Michigander, passionate advocate of accessible and diverse community theater, mother of two, and spouse to the only person alive capable of spending extended periods of time with them without wanting to kill them.